# PRAISE FOR TRACY CLARK

## *Hide*

"A Chicago cop still mourning her late partner transfers to a new precinct just in time to catch a truly creepy case. Solid . . . work from a writer who knows the dark side of the Windy City."

—*Kirkus Reviews*

"[Detective Harriet] Foster's dogged approach to catching killers will resonate with Michael Connelly fans. May the wait for the second Harriet Foster police procedural be brief."

—*Publishers Weekly*

"*Hide* is an astonishing crime novel that broke my heart and then sewed it back together again, stronger than before. It hits all the right notes—a captivating protagonist up against a nightmarish serial killer, their hunt played out across a Chicago so immersive, so flawlessly rendered, that you can hear your own footsteps slapping the streets—while managing to create something completely unique. One of the best books I've read in years."

—Jess Lourey, Amazon Charts bestselling author

"Tracy Clark's not-so-hidden talent is for conjuring characters who are engaging and achingly real. Detective Harri Foster is a stellar recruit to her new team and to our crime fiction shelves. *Hide* is a page-turner with heart."

—Lori Rader-Day, Agatha Award–winning author of *Death at Greenway*

## Runner

"You know those books that are wonderful, but that envy, the worm in the bud, makes you shy away from praising because you wish you'd created that prose or those insights? *Runner* by Tracy Clark. She understands the streets, kids, the way a PI and a cop really work. Kudos."

—Sara Paretsky, *New York Times* bestselling author of the V.I. Warshawski series and cofounder of Sisters in Crime

"Clark writes with purpose, her sense of social justice never venturing into dogma but remaining fully rooted in Raines's actions and personality. She saves, but is no savior, because she operates in a world where survival is the benchmark, and pain remains in the aftermath."

—*The New York Times*

"Clark has a unique voice in the PI genre, one that is articulate, daring, and ultimately hopeful."

—S.A. Cosby, Anthony and ITW award winner, *The Washington Post*

## Broken Places

"Engrossing and superbly written—I can't say enough good things about *Broken Places*!"

—Lisa Black, *New York Times* bestselling author of *That Darkness* and *Unpunished*

"Unforgettable . . . Distinctive, vividly written characters lift this promising debut. Readers will be eager for the sequel."

—*Publishers Weekly* (starred review)

# FALL

# ALSO BY TRACY CLARK

# FALL

**A DETECTIVE HARRIET FOSTER THRILLER**

## TRACY CLARK

THOMAS & MERCER

Text copyright © 2023 by Tracy Clark
All rights reserved.

Published by Thomas & Mercer, Seattle

www.apub.com

Amazon, the Amazon logo, and Thomas & Mercer are trademarks of Amazon.com, Inc., or its affiliates.

ISBN-13: 9781662512551 (paperback)
ISBN-13: 9781662509520 (digital)

Cover design by Damon Freeman
Cover image: © Yaroslav Humeniuk / Shutterstock; © MrIncredible / Shutterstock; © Ravindra37 / Shutterstock; © DEEPOL by plainpicture

Printed in the United States of America

# FALL

# CHAPTER 1

Detective Harriet Foster stared at her son's killer. She told herself that she needed to see if he'd changed in the four years since she'd seen him last, but that wasn't it. The test was for herself. Could she look at him and despise him less? Could she be in the same room again with Terrell Willem and not feel rage and contempt and an ungodly impulse to forfeit everything she was to end him?

Willem was here for a resentencing hearing. She was here to give another impact statement. Willem couldn't have appeared more disinterested as he sat sullenly in his tan prison two-piece, his paunchy body—fueled by cheap prison carbs—squeezed into the county-issued uniform, its washed-out V-neck top revealing a dingy white T-shirt beneath. Foster stood at the front of courtroom 211 at the Cook County Courthouse, her hands resting on the lectern, but Willem wouldn't look at her. Slumped at the hearing table, dull eyes focused on his feet, he was here in body only.

His lawyer, a young public defender, outwardly nervous, sat beside him fiddling with file papers, her bright-green eyes, pixie cut, and rosy cheeks strangely jarring in a place like this. Willem, now twenty-two, had spent the last five years in prison for murdering her son, Reg. But the look on the young man's dark face, the sneer, the vacantness of expression, told her that five years could have been fifty for all the difference they had made. No change. Terrell Willem was the same. Prison, free, here, there, he would always be this and only this. She might have been able to bring herself to lament the loss of his potential were it not for the fact that this waste had cost her the life of her fourteen-year-old son, her only child. But she was angry at more than Willem.

Willem didn't amount to nothing on his own. Cognitively disadvantaged, slow, he'd been failed by a lumbering, inefficient school system and by a mother who bore him at age fifteen and hadn't a clue how to parent. Willem could barely read, had never held a job. He robbed and sold drugs and whatever else he needed to do to feed himself. His arms and neck were covered in violent tattoos that glorified death and killing and the gang to which he'd sold his soul. Detached from civility, devoid of remorse, Willem was a hard and nasty chaos machine with no conscience.

Harri had memorized his arrest record; she had learned all she could about Willem. *Know thy enemy, keep him close.* She knew him by the sour twist of his thick, dry lips, saw him in the false bravado that had him leaning back in his chair, his long legs spread wide under the table, as though nothing worried him, as if he had no stake in what was being said or by whom. He was a child in a man's body. A child who hadn't been taught, who'd been allowed to grow as a destructive weed might and live like a feral dog that lurched undeterred from impulse to impulse. Willem had wanted Reg's bike, his sneakers, so he took them, but that hadn't been enough. He had to take Reg too.

*Waddnt no big thang. People die all the time, dawg, so what? Gave me the bike quick, but he too slow givin' up them good shoes.* It's what he had said at trial. Then he'd chuckled, revealing two gold teeth. Foster still heard that chuckle in her nightmares. There'd been sneers at the trial, too, and eye rolls, more blank looks. At one point during the proceedings, Willem had appeared to fall asleep and had to be nudged awake by his court-appointed lawyer. A bike or a life, shoes or a wallet, all the same to him.

Harri stood with her back straight, her eyes on the killer at the table. She'd worn a black suit, her badge clipped to the belt at her waist, but hidden. Her gun too. Both were tools of her trade, tools that defined her, marked her, steadied her hand.

Resentencing. That's what they were here for. Because Willem had been just seventeen at the time of her son's murder, a lawyer, not Pixie Cut, had successfully argued that he deserved a break on his sentence of ninety-nine years and a day, no parole. Willem's side was trying to whittle his punishment down to seventy-five years with parole on the table. Foster was here to stand for Reg. Willem was damaged goods, lost half a lifetime ago to abuse, neglect, and depravity. And she wanted him to serve every minute of those ninety-nine years, even the day tacked on behind it. She wanted Willem to die in prison. On bad days, and there were many, she dreamed of being there when he did.

She glanced around the old courtroom, its dark wood and brass fixtures hearkening back to a foregone era when Al Capone or one of his associates might have strutted along the marble floors on their way to the witness stand. The room felt close and hot as heat hissed out of the heavy vents, the old school building's answer to the February chill outside the heavy leaded windows. Harriet had been here a million times or more testifying in cases, doing her job locking up killers like Terrell Willem. But what happened next in rooms like this wasn't up to her. There were always lawyers and judges. Always Willems.

Harri scanned the room, glancing over the handful of observers that included her ex-husband, Ron Jamison, in the first row and Willem's mother and two sisters across the aisle in the back, as if they'd chosen the farthest point to sit for fear of recrimination. Willem's family looked just as hard, just as broken as he was, she thought, the meanness, the misplaced defiance, the confusion on their faces an explanation for Terrell, but not an excuse. The room smelled of sweat and furnace and oiled leather from her holster and Ron's and the guards' who'd brought Terrell in.

She wasn't naive. She knew abuse was generational. She knew poverty and race played a part, and lack of opportunity made up the rest of it. That crime and gangs became the reality when there was nothing to counterbalance them, and that boys like Willem almost never made it past thirty. Harriet knew all this because she was charged with fixing it, or at least arresting it.

She turned back to Willem, having memorized every line on his face from before. His was the last face her son had seen, and knowing that made it difficult for her to sleep. Willem could have taken the bike, the shoes; he didn't have to take Reg, but he did. He did because Reg meant nothing, because life held no great value, because imprisoned or free, ninety-nine years or seventy-five, it was all the same.

"When you're ready, Ms. Foster," Judge Ceresti said gently. He didn't have to identify her as a cop. Everyone knew it. But she wasn't here in that capacity. She was here as the mother of a murdered son.

Harriet pulled her eyes away from Willem and stared at the statement she'd written, the edges of the single sheet of paper curled and damp with her sweat. These were her reasons for wanting Willem to stay where he was. Ninety-nine years felt like justice. Seventy-five felt like compromise.

When she looked again at Willem, she was met by his oily golden smile. Then his devil eyes slid from hers, and his chin dropped to his chest. She watched as he picked at his cuticles, like he couldn't be bothered, like they were keeping him from something more important. She heard RJ shift in his seat and clear his throat. She could hear the heat hissing. Harriet turned to look at RJ in his shirt and tie, his trench coat slung over the back of the wooden bench, his service weapon duly secured at his side. He'd always been an attractive man, tall, dark, steady. Not hers, someone else's now. They both served and protected their city and the people in it, but that hadn't been enough to save Reg from Terrell Willem.

"Reginald Stewart Jamison," she began, her voice strong, unwavering. The breath she took afterward was not because she was afraid to face the monster, but rather because it was taking everything in her not to do the other thing, to forget who she was and forfeit all. Even reciting her son's name, saying it out loud, having it burn her throat, and having to listen to its echo as it bounced off the wood and the brass, made her want to scream. She flicked a look at Willem's mother, who glared at her as though Harriet had been responsible for putting them all here. It was a cycle, she knew this. And she saw no end to it. There were millions of Terrell Willems. Millions of mothers who shouldn't be mothers. Millions of failures, missteps, lost chances, acts of violence, deaths, bikes, shoes.

What good would a statement do? What impact would it have? She plunged a hand into her blazer pocket and felt around for the half dozen or so paper clips she'd secreted there. It had become her habit to mark tiny triumphs in getting through the day by slipping a clip into a pocket. The clips were a tangible reminder that this too would pass. She turned to the judge, who waited for her, but she folded up the paper. She didn't want to say those things anymore.

She let a moment go. "My son would have been nineteen years old now. Off to college. On his way. He loved music and astronomy, and dogs. He was loved, and we miss him." She turned to address Ceresti. "Terrell Willem didn't kill to defend himself. He didn't kill because he was hungry and needed to survive. He killed for a bike and a pair of shoes. He made a choice. He could easily have made another. Given the same chance, he'd do the same again, and we all know it."

Willem's eyes fired. He glared at her like he wanted to gut her. "I ain't scared of you." His muttered words echoed in the quiet room. "No woman." His lawyer leaned over to quiet him, but he snatched his arm away from hers. "Naw. She ain't nothin'."

Harriet's eyes held his. He was afraid. She could see it, smell it. He'd likely been afraid his whole life, yet she could muster up no forgiveness for him. She held tight to her hatred of Terrell Willem. But he was wrong, she thought. She wasn't nothing. She was Terrell Willem's boogeyman. She was the ghost who was going to haunt every step he took until the day he died.

Judge Ceresti took only a couple of hours to deny Willem's request for an amended sentence. The ninety-nine years and a day would stand. Harriet's relief seeped out into the world in the form of a weary sigh, and she watched as Willem was escorted out of the proceedings in handcuffs, headed back to prison, back to a cell, back to nothing. Reg was still dead. The earth still turned. Life went on outside the courthouse. There would soon be another Willem sitting in the chair this Willem had just vacated. She felt for the clips again as Willem's mother and sisters filed out too. They shot her murderous looks and muttered *bitch* under their breaths as though it was Harriet who had failed to raise Terrell right and then put the gun in his hands. She grabbed her bag from her seat, then exchanged a look with RJ as they both strode out into the hallway last. He was grayer, leaner since the last time she'd seen him, more than three years ago, she noticed. He'd remarried and had stepkids and a new baby daughter, whose name she couldn't recall. RJ had built a new life, and she had to admit to a certain amount of resentment, not for him so much, but for herself. She felt like a butterfly pinned to a display board, stuck, inert.

They'd discussed the bike for Reg's birthday, and she had preferred to go with a new computer he could use for school. RJ went out and bought the bike anyway, the fanciest one they could afford. But guilt and blame were useless things.

"He's something, huh?" RJ said.

He walked alongside her on the way to the courthouse's slow elevators, confusion in the wide hall as courtrooms emptied out and people rushed for the exits, the sound of footsteps in dress shoes, clicking and clacking along the marble floors, the hush of low voices occasionally broken by one or two riled into belligerence and defiance they were forced by circumstance to swallow.

She turned to take a closer look at him. They were intimate strangers, family once, but that was a long time ago when she was different. "Hi, RJ."

"Headed back to work?"

She kept walking, checked her watch. She'd put in for a few hours of personal time, but that was up. She was due back in the office. "Yes. You?"

"Same."

Her eyes swept over him. "It's good seeing you. Say hello to—"

"You never pick up my calls. I heard you got banged up on a case a few months ago. I wanted to make sure you were okay. Had to get the whole thing from Felix."

Felix, her older brother, and RJ had been friends first before she and he had gotten together. The friendship survived, the marriage hadn't, and Felix now served as the link between them, at least for RJ. She eyed the elevator. It was close, not five feet from her. "I'm fine."

"Yeah, that's what Felix told me. Had a feeling there was more to it, though."

Foster held her hand up so he could see it, revealing the scar left by more than thirty stitches needed to knit together the gash made by a madwoman's knife. There were also scars on her right forearm and along her left side across her rib cage. Her new partner, Detective Vera Li, had come away with a concussion, a dislocated knee, and a broken ankle. They both could have died. "Not much more. All healed."

They stood there, awkwardly silent. He looked so much like Reg. Even as a baby, Reg favored RJ more than he did her. Looking at him now, she could see a glimpse of what her son would have looked like had Terrell Willem passed him by. It hurt her soul to stand this close to RJ, to hear his voice, to see her son the way he never would be.

"I should get going," she said, turning to leave.

He gently cupped her elbow; she stiffened at his touch. "Harri, wait?" He drew his hand away. "What're we doing?" She looked a question. "Reggie's gone, babe. That kid? That kid's behind bars till he dies.

7

We got our justice. We buried Terrell Willem in a hole he's never getting out of. We can let it go now."

People moved around them, chatter ebbed and flowed, the air hung heavy. We? From where she stood, RJ seemed to be doing all right. Hadn't missed a beat, in fact. New wife, kids. The flash of anger surprised her—then it didn't. They were different people. She had drawn in, locked herself away, frozen in place, waiting for . . . what? Death to change? For God to change his mind? Death was final. Gone was gone. She couldn't police death, she couldn't lock it in a cell and toss the key away, but she could be Terrell Willem's worst nightmare. That's what she could do.

"It's done, and I'll make sure it stays done. But you're right. You want to move on."

"Harri, it's not about that . . . you obsessed with Willem . . . it's just not healthy."

She hitched the strap of her bag higher on her stiffened shoulder. Defense. The elevator arrived with only two people on it. Unusual for the busy courthouse at 11:00 a.m. on a Tuesday. Four people got on. She stepped on, too, angling her gun side away from the strangers sharing the car with her, waiting for the inevitable shift as they smelled the cop on her and backed away, giving her a wide berth. Her eyes met RJ's as the doors began to close. Nice eyes. Her son's eyes. RJ was another life, another time, another her.

"Nice seeing you, RJ."

Guilt and blame were useless things, but that didn't stop either from eating a person alive. But today, a victory. Terrell Willem was headed back for his ninety-nine years and a day.

# CHAPTER 2

Marin Shaw would never forget the sound of prison doors locking behind her—the whoosh and heavy thud, the dungeon scrape, the almost medieval clunk of the metal workings, or the slow slide of the impenetrable barrier, its opening preceded by a warning blare, a Klaxon cry, when a prisoner was on the move. She knew those sounds, as desolate as a catacomb, as devoid of life as death itself, would wake her in the night in a cold, hard sweat for as long as she lived. The sound of the cell door had already nested in her gut like a watchful raven with twitchy eyes, taunting her, not letting her forget for even a second how she'd thrown her life away for $5,000, a two-martini lunch, and a lie.

"Sign here," the incurious clerk at the prison-release window said, her blank expression proof that she had become inured to the routine of the turnout process. Prisoners came and went like trains on a track, like loaves of bread down a conveyor belt. The only things that changed were the day and the time and the signature on the form. The clerk pushed a large plastic bag toward Marin. "Check what's there against the list. Make sure everything's accounted for."

Marin pulled the bag toward her, breaking the seal. These were her things. The clothes she'd been wearing that last day in court, when the jury found her guilty of corruption and the judge ordered her taken into custody then and there. Probation had been the hope. Home confinement. But things hadn't gone her way. Marin hadn't even gotten a chance to kiss her daughter goodbye or explain where and why she was going. Judge Norman F. Reitman. Three years. Logan Correctional. And three years she'd served, almost to the day.

She'd been Alderman Marin Shaw then. A progressive Democrat, a respected member of the city council. She had also been a lawyer, a wife, a mother, and none of it had been enough. That's what the alcohol was supposed to help with. It hadn't.

Marin opened the bag and stared inside to find the remnants of her old self, a woman who now felt as foreign to her as a stranger's kiss. A navy suit, a silk shirt, pumps, nylons, expensive underthings. Every item well chosen to transmit confidence, assurance, competency. She'd worn the suit many times to city council meetings, knowing that it fit her well and made her look like a boss. There were fifty aldermen on the council, representing fifty wards. That meant fifty bosses, fifty potential felons. Fifty opportunities to cut a deal, bestow a favor, sever a lifeline, or take the dirty cash offered with a nod and a sly wink and have it all end in a pair of handcuffs, a perp walk, a trial, a verdict, and then a humiliating stint. And shame. She couldn't leave out the shame.

It was all a far cry from her present situation. She glanced down at the baggy jeans, the no-name gym shoes, and the oversize gray hoodie she was going home in. She could literally feel the grit and dead skin cells on her washed-out face. No makeup. Not in three years. She'd pulled her auburn hair back in a bun, the expensive cut and highlight job long gone. This was the Marin Shaw about to meet the world again.

The clerk nodded to the male guard, the signal that Marin was done. Free. Signed out and no longer an inmate. *Vaya con Dios.* Kick bricks. "Good luck, Ms. Shaw."

Marin nodded a thanks, then eyed the door as the guard unlocked it and beckoned her forward. No smile. No words of encouragement. No advice for the road. Just an open door. The state was done with her. She was on her own. The time she'd spent inside was all she owed; the rest of what came next was up to her.

The guard led her out. Instantly, the cold hit her like a sledgehammer and nearly took her breath away. It took a moment to adjust, to remember what a Midwest winter was.

"They got cameras at the gate." He gave her a critical look, head to toe and back. "Everybody wants a look at ya, I guess." He exhibited not a shred of real interest or concern. He was just noting the media's presence, like he might alert her to an impending rainstorm. *Rain's a-comin'. Might want to get that umbrella out.*

But Marin wasn't the first alderman to pass this way, nor would she be the last. Corruption and those who fed on it and kept it going were baked into the bricks in Chicago. It was the fuel the city ran on; without it, very little moved. That's what had made it so easy to succumb to temptation, to play along to get along—at least that's what she told herself in quiet moments. In quiet moments, she could almost convince herself that there had been cause, reason, justification for her actions. That a souring marriage, a husband who cheated, alcohol dependence, well hidden but there, had made her vulnerable and not completely responsible.

But that was wrong. All this was on her.

Marin looked over the lawn of Logan Correctional toward the high fence a distance away to the hub of reporters, news cameras, and curious onlookers clustered around the gate. She was famous, or infamous. Yet another Chicago politician sent down for taking what didn't belong to them. A greedy lawmaker who'd sold her soul for less than the cost of a midsize car, betraying the trust of her constituents, dishonoring her family and herself. That's how they'd played it, then. That's how they likely saw her now. But there'd been more to it. There was always more.

Marin clocked the black SUV parked in the intake slot. Her ride to freedom. The back passenger door opened, and Charlotte Moore, her lawyer and friend since law school, emerged dressed like Marin had once, back when she was the other Marin, the one who thought she had the world on a string, only to find out at the bang of the judge's gavel that she had been the puppet, not the puppet master.

Charlotte sported designer sunglasses, though the day was gunmetal gray. She held a heavy coat in her hands, smiling. "You're going to need this."

Marin ran for the coat, trading her bag of old things for it, wasting no time putting it on and zipping it up.

"Welcome back to the land of the living," Charlotte said as she held the back door open for her. "Let's get out of here, huh? This place reminds me of my failures."

Marin slid her a look as she jumped inside. "Mine too. Sunglasses?"

Char grinned. "Late night."

"He have a name?"

"I beg your pardon. It was quite respectable. John. James. Something with a *J*. Drinks at the Marq, and then his place. All very classy."

Marin hadn't expected her husband or daughter to pick her up. They'd discussed it, and neither she nor Will wanted to expose Zoe to any more of the circus than they had to. Thirteen-year-olds had enough to deal with without having to share the shame of a convict mother. Besides, Will hadn't insisted on being here, anyway. They hadn't spoken more than a handful of times in three years, and there'd been no visits. He cited concerns for Zoe's well-being, of course, but Marin knew that wasn't it. Her husband was a selfish man. His reputation and image meant everything to him. He would never stoop so low as to walk through prison gates, for her or anyone else. The few times they'd spoken on the phone, she'd heard anger in his voice, resentment, coldness, and worse, an air of righteousness. He blamed her for the taint she'd placed on him and his business interests. He was guilty by association, he'd told her, seething, and had lost clients as a result. She'd heard the same anger in Zoe's voice after she'd been inside about a year. It was likely the result of Will's influence. Marin had let them both down, that was clear. She'd left Zoe without a mother at a time when she needed one most. There was a lot to rebuild—trust, forgiveness, love—and the work was all Marin's to do.

"Breathe," Charlotte said when she slid into the back seat next to her.

"I am."

Charlotte flicked her a skeptical look. "Breathe better." She put a comforting hand on Marin's. "It's done. You got this."

Marin settled back against the leather seat when the car started moving. She inhaled, held it, then exhaled, watching through the window as the prison complex got smaller and the car got closer to the gate.

"I appreciate the tinted windows."

"I knew you'd look like someone who just got out of prison. Thinner, though. What diet were you on?" Charlotte grinned.

"I was on the I-just-fucked-up-my-life plan."

Charlotte angled her head, considered it. "Nah, I'll pass."

Marin studied Charlotte, who looked as she did once, powerful, gym fit, pulled together in all the right places. Before this, they could have passed for sisters; both were world beaters. Now, Marin had a record, no profession, and a mess to clean up at home.

"Hopefully, they're not camped out in front of the house," Marin said as she ducked her head in shame as she passed the reporters, their cameras zoomed in hoping to catch a glimpse of her silhouette through the glass. "Maybe they at least have the decency to give me that much."

"They've been there for days," Charlotte said flatly. "Ever since news of your release leaked."

"Leaked how?"

"Doesn't matter. We're not going there."

"What?"

"I'll explain later. Let's get out of here first."

"Stop the car," Marin called to the driver, tapping the back of his seat. "Now."

"What the hell are you doing?" Charlotte watched the reporters race toward them, frenzied looks on their faces. "Marin, they'll eat you alive."

The car eased to a stop. Marin could hear the running feet as reporters stampeded toward the car for a chance at a juicy sound bite. "Tell me."

"I don't want to do this here, Marin. These vultures have been waiting three years to get to you."

The reporters weren't her concern. What could they do to her at this point? What was left of her dignity to protect? "All of it, Char. *Now.*"

Charlotte placed a hand on the back of the driver's seat. "Tom, could you step out for a sec?"

Tom flicked a nervous look at the horde of reporters surrounding the car. "Are you serious?"

"Just for a minute. You'll be fine. It's her they want. Tell them nothing, not even your name."

Tom shut the car off and stepped out into the cold, closing the door behind him. Charlotte shifted in her seat, resigned, then reached over to make sure the car doors were locked before her eyes met Marin's. "Fine. You want all of it here and now, here it is." Outside, reporter voices shouted rapid-fire questions through the glass, video cameras and cell phones trained on the back and side windows. None of them paid Tom any attention.

"You're an entitled crook. A cross between Ma Barker and Leona Helmsley. That's how they're playing it. You masterminded the entire scheme, you ran it, and were out to get whatever you could get. Shady businesses paid you, and you greased the city council wheels to turn in their favor. I know you weren't in it alone, but because you refused to flip, cutting me off at the knees, I'll remind you, you got sent up for the full weight." Charlotte held up her hands to stop Marin from interjecting. "I know. Whatever. Water under the bridge. But you know me, I hate to lose. It burned my ass then, and it's still burning. Those bastards threw you under the bus, double-crossed you, and then slid right back into their ratholes unscathed. You tied my hands, Mar, and you denied the feds the bigger fish, and that's why you ended up here." She pointed an angry finger at the window. "But now, those assholes out there smell a hell of a good story, and they want it. And the rats are shitting bricks about what you might say. You're the 'get' of the century, Marin Shaw, and they're not going anywhere." She resettled in the seat. "As for home . . ."

"It's Will," Marin said, reading the truth of it on Charlotte's face.

Charlotte checked on the reporters again. "God, I wouldn't take their job on a bet. Look at them. They're practically salivating."

"*Char.*"

"All right. He feels that with all this attention, things might be better for Zoe if there was a bit of a transition period. An easing back in? He'd like you to hang out in the condo downtown for a week or so just until things *maybe* die down. Then he'll reassess."

"*He'll* reassess? He told you this?"

"He sent a letter to my office . . . certified mail. He's not one for a face-to-face confrontation, is he?"

Marin stared out the front window at the driver on his cell phone, the reporters ignoring him. "And Zoe?"

Charlotte let out a sigh. "Quiet. Confused. Noncommunicative since I told her you were getting out. She's afraid of what comes next."

"You were there for her, for me. Thanks, Char. You made things easier." She reached over and gripped her hand. "You're a good friend. Always have been."

Char smiled. "I love Zoe, and it's good practice for when I finally get it all, I figured. Lunch, shopping, plays, the zoo. I never forgot her birthday or Christmas. Then there were all those girl questions. Remember having those at her age? Everything so dire, so mysterious. I kept you in the loop. But the kids at school, you not being there. She's angry . . . and, again, thirteen. I was an okay substitute, Mar, but I was still a sub. You have a lot to clean up." The look she gave Marin was one of compassion. "You had to know things would be different?"

A reporter beat on the door, pressed his face to the glass. Marin turned her back and burrowed into the warm coat. A record, no job, and now no home to go back to.

"Not to pour salt," Charlotte said, "but I told you not to marry him. Will looks good on the arm, but he's no Albert Schweitzer. He'd sell his own mother for a cover on *Fortune* magazine." She snickered. "But I probably would too. You've met my mother. Difficult woman." She slid Marin a sideways look. "I can never please her. Doesn't stop her from cashing my checks, though, does it?"

"I want to see my daughter," Marin said. "He can't keep me from seeing her. And that house? The one he doesn't want me to come back to? My family's money paid for it. There's someone else, there always is. But not in my house, around my kid. That's the line."

Charlotte tugged at her buttons, checked the reporters again. "I hear you. You're too good for him, always were, but love's tricky."

Marin stared out the window. "Was it love? I'm not sure. I think we just photographed well together. It's surprising even to me what I overlooked, what I settled for." She sat up, squared her shoulders. "Not anymore. I need to close some doors and open new ones. Settle some things."

"What things?"

Marin didn't answer.

*"Marin?"*

Marin eased back into the seat, warmed in the coat. "Nothing to worry about."

"You know when a lawyer starts to worry? When her client tells her there's nothing to worry about." Charlotte leaned over and tapped on the window for the driver, who rushed in and started the car up again. "Let's go." She settled back as the car drove away. "To the condo, my friend."

Marin offered a single nod. "For now."

16

# CHAPTER 3

Alderman John "Cubby" Meehan commanded the back booth in his favorite steak house in the West Loop, far away from city hall and the investigative reporters who prowled its corridors gunning for him. Dino's was his place, the spot he came to when he wanted to hold a special meeting or do real business. He was partial to the tomahawk steak and garlic smashed potatoes and had already placed his order with his regular waitress, Lil.

Meehan had planted his prodigious frame into the rich burgundy banquette and now scanned the empty private dining room, the one Dino's always had ready for him at a moment's notice. He was a VIP in the city council, one of the highest-ranking members, a wheeler-dealer, a suspected crook who'd never had a charge stick. Meehan was power itself, a man who could make things happen, or not happen, and everyone, including Meehan, knew it.

He ran his hand along the white cloth on the table, crisp, clean. Up front, there would be other diners having lunch unaware that the room in back was occupied by him, and that big things happened back here at the powerful man's table. He eyed the back entrance that led out through the kitchen, the one he used so that prying eyes wouldn't clock him, or whoever he was meeting with. There were quiet, out-of-the-way spots like this all over town where CEOs and politicians, mayors and cops met to discuss things of great import, yet not for public ears. No spot was better than Meehan's spot, though, as far as he was concerned. He'd been cutting deals in Dino's for more than thirty years.

Meehan stared around the table at his fellow aldermen, Deanna Leonard, George Valdez, Sylissa Franklin, then checked the doors again just to confirm that private was private. The whiskey in front of him begged for that steak, but first things first. "She's been out a couple weeks now. Somebody's gotta make contact and see what she's up to. I wanna know where her head's at."

"She's been quiet," Leonard said. "Hasn't made a statement to anybody. Leave it at that."

Alderman Valdez took a sip of his highball, the ice tinkling in the glass as his hands shook. He was new to this side of Chicago politics. Greed and ambition had gotten him a seat at Meehan's table, but now that he was here, he didn't feel at all comfortable being included, though he was in too deep to walk away. He'd accepted the money in the white envelope. The hook was in. "If it was me, I'd be concentrating on getting my house back in order, not on us. I agree with Deanna. We leave her. We've covered ourselves, haven't we? Nothing sticks, right?" He looked around the table. "So, we're good."

There were shamed looks on Leonard's and Franklin's faces. They all knew what they'd done and at least had the decency to feel bad about it. Meehan? Not so much. Meehan had been born dirty. He'd started stealing a moment after he'd taken his oath of office. What made it worse was that everybody in the city knew he was doing it; they just couldn't catch him. He was that good at being bad.

Franklin adjusted her glasses, then ran a nervous hand through her dark cropped hair. "I'm with them. Haven't we done enough damage?"

"I feel guilty for bringing her in." Leonard turned to Meehan.

"Yeah, you didn't notice she had a little problem with the drink? That she might be a little iffy on account? You nearly ruined all of us here. If I hadn't a pulled some strings, well . . . we might all be in her shoes right now."

Leonard bristled. "We needed someone on the finance committee, and I had the connection. I promised her it would be a win-win for all of us." She lowered her head, then picked up her glass of bourbon from the table and gulped what was left in it like it was the last she'd ever get, like it had been years since the last one. "I don't know who screwed up, what we missed, but the feds went right for the weakest link, didn't they?" She glared at Meehan. "And we closed ranks and left her to them. For *what*?"

Meehan sneered, leaned forward, his belly hitting the table and rocking it, the fat straining against his custom-made silk shirt with his initials engraved on the cuffs. The gold cuff links were twenty-four karats from Cartier. His navy-blue suit cost more than a mortgage payment. "For *what*? Well, let's see, Deanna. You drove up here in a nice Mercedes, didn't you? And wasn't that you who just plopped down a mint on that summer place in Grand Beach? The papers would love to get the details on that, I bet. I'm sure they'd really like to know how an alderman bringing in a hundred forty K a year springs for beachfront property costing five times that?"

Valdez scoffed. "No honor among thieves, that it, Meehan?"

Meehan turned to him. "None. And make no mistake, *Jorge*, we are all of us thieves here." Valdez's eyes narrowed at Meehan's use of his Latino name because he knew he meant it as a put-down. "You all ate at the table, so you're all a part of this. Neck deep. Marin Shaw was sloppy. She got drunk, and she got careless." His eyes narrowed. He stared at Leonard. "Poor choice on your part. A poor choice that could have sunk us. Now we need her to stay the fuck quiet."

Franklin shifted in her seat, uncomfortable with the conversation. "Hasn't enough damage been done? I agree with George and Deanna. We leave her alone. We move on, more careful from here on out. Maybe we slow things down for a while, let things sit and cool. Then we reassess."

"I don't like loose ends," Meehan said. "I don't like not knowing where she's at." He leaned back again. "This will come as no shock to you, but I'm making a run for the fifth floor next election."

"You can't be serious," Valdez said. "You really think you can run for mayor with the dirt you've got under your fingernails?"

Meehan's predatory eyes met his. "I've got backing, quietly, the unions are behind me, and I have no intention of letting Marin Shaw screw things up. I called in a lot of markers skirting that Operation Takedown business, to make it look like it was just her and not us. Markers I now have to make good on. So, I'm not letting anything go."

"And you're just fine with that, aren't you?" Deanna Leonard asked, shocked, but not really surprised by Meehan's pragmatism. "I knew you were greedy. I knew you cut corners and skimmed off the top, but you have no actual sense of right or wrong, do you? The woman spent three years in prison. Three years away from her daughter, her home. *We* put her there. Enough is enough now."

Meehan's beady eyes fired. "I say when it's enough." His ruddy face bloomed red, the color spreading right up to his receding hairline and the thinning hair dyed an unnatural shade of black, the facade of youthfulness belied by the deep crevices in his jowly cheeks and the ropy sag of his hands and neck.

"No. This is as far as I go. I'm stepping away from this time bomb." Leonard stood, gathered her things.

Valdez stood too. "Same for me. I'm out." He buttoned his suit jacket, glanced down at Franklin. "If you've got any self-respect left, Sylissa, now might be the time to use it." Franklin didn't move a muscle. Valdez scoffed. "Right. The money's a strong pull. Once you've fed at Meehan's trough, it's hard to go back to scratching at the ground for scraps. That's what he's counting on."

Franklin's eyes blazed. "You don't know me, Valdez."

He smirked. "Yeah, I do. Last time it was Marin. Who's next? Deanna? Me? You?" His eyes met those of Meehan, who appeared to be having a whale of a good time, his calculating grin wide. Like the devil's. "I'll have no part in doing anything with Marin Shaw." He picked up his glass and finished his drink. "And if you even think of sewing me up like you did her, forget it. I know where the bodies are buried, and I won't go down quiet."

"Meaning?" Meehan asked, the playfulness gone.

Valdez took the fat man in, a distasteful sneer on his lips. "Meaning, I know who I got in bed with. I go down, *everybody* goes. No more Grand Beach. No mayor's office." He eyed Franklin. "And all that skimmed cash hidden in all those shell companies you set up, Sylissa, that goes too. I'm not Marin, remember that."

"And you'd do well to remember that your extramarital . . . proclivities . . . with Marin, and others, are not as secretive as you believe them to be." The two held a look. Franklin raised her glass, smiled. "The more you know."

Meehan shook his head, grinned. "And just so's I'm sure. You both do know you're talking to your future mayor? And that I have a memory like an elephant?" His eyes hardened. "That no one walks away?" His eyes cut to Valdez. "I know where the bodies are buried, too, fella. And if I can stitch up Shaw, I can stitch you two up just as easy. How's your mother doing in that swanky nursing home your greed pays for, huh, *Jorge*? And you, Deanna, with your special-needs grandkid getting all that extra therapy your city pay don't cover? C'mon, guys. We all know what's going on. What we're in it for, and we all know there's no out. So, relax. There's no call for anybody to get all showy and start making dying declarations."

Valdez and Leonard paled slightly as Meehan's threat sank in. Deanna hoisted her bag on her shoulder, her lips twisted in disgust. "This conversation is turning my stomach." She grabbed her coat from the back of her chair. "Nothing happens to Marin. Nothing happens to George or to me either. I also have protections, John. I may have turned for the easy money, that's on me, but I'm not a fool. You ever want to see your name on the door of the mayor's office, you'll think twice."

Meehan's face grew even redder. He wasn't used to being challenged, and he didn't like it. "Now *that* sounds like a threat, Deanna."

Leonard smiled, drew toward him. "Then here's another. Every reporter in this city is dying to know exactly how the sausage is made." She looked around the dining room. "In rooms like this, by snakes like you. All it'd take is one phone call. Do not push me."

"Death by circular firing squad, Meehan," Valdez said. "It's a terrible way to go."

Alderman Franklin sat with her head lowered, eyes on her Manhattan. "There are worse ways."

Valdez turned to her. "Firmly in his pocket, where you've always been. He must have something really good on you. Have you ever been clean, Sylissa?"

She looked up. "Honestly? I can't remember."

As Valdez and Leonard left the table and walked out through the back, Franklin looked over at an angry Meehan, knowing the man far better than they did. Meehan hadn't survived this long being this bad without going too far more than once.

"Shaw's an unknown factor," Meehan muttered. His eyes narrowed and plastered to the door Valdez and Leonard had just walked through. "Looks like I'll have to take the bull by the horns and have a little talk with her. What do you think, Sylissa? You all right with me and Shaw having a little talk?"

Franklin took another slow sip before answering. "Nothing wrong with a little talk."

"I can always count on you, huh?"

"I've made my bed, John. It's nothing to do with you."

# CHAPTER 4

Marin sat quietly at the table, knowing her husband and daughter didn't trust her. She'd done damage, and she could see it in their faces. But there had to be first steps. Will had insisted on today. Tuesday. A school night. His way of ensuring the visit would be short. She'd dressed simply in slacks and a sweater, and she had made an effort with makeup and jewelry; her hair, too, had been cut and styled. No more prison drab. There were more gray hairs mixed in with the auburn now, but she'd decided to leave them as a reminder of the time she'd lost and had to make good on. Besides, Marin had earned every one of them and saw them as proof of her resilience. It didn't look like Will had gone through any great travails in the past three years. Still getting his weekly facials, she could tell, still hitting the gym. He was a real estate developer obsessed with looking powerful in his power suit, and he was definitely having an affair. He always let his hair grow longer and had his nails manicured when he was seeing someone. He had no idea she'd noticed the pattern years ago. At this point, it didn't matter who. She was a different Marin, grayer, wiser. Even the house, this damned table she was sitting at, no longer meant anything to her. She'd outgrown Will, this house, and the life she had unhappily lived inside it. All she wanted was Zoe, the waifish thirteen-year-old with freckled cheeks, who could barely look at her.

There'd been no grand embrace at the door, no kisses. Marin could have been a stranger off the street for all the affection shown. Hurt.

Pain. Marin had done the unthinkable. She'd committed a crime and hadn't thought through the fallout, what she was putting in jeopardy— Zoe, Will, this family. Marin had forgotten what was important. It wasn't until the trap had been sprung that she had realized what a dangerous game she'd been playing. Marin found out quickly that she had no friends and that every door she needed opened had been locked shut against her.

Zoe's ash-blonde hair was so long and beautiful. She'd grown so much. She was no longer the ten-year-old lovebug Marin remembered, who obsessed over rainbows, unicorns, and glittery art projects, who would crawl in bed beside her and braid her hair and share her little-girl secrets and include her in her nightly prayers. Will she had already let go. She would file for divorce. They would end things officially. Will would make things complicated. But Zoe, Zoe she wanted; Zoe she had to get back.

Three years might have felt like a lifetime, but they were not. She had time to make things right, to explain things, to apologize. That's why she was here at the table in the house she no longer wanted, being stared at, judged by a man she no longer cared two beans about.

"You look well, Marin," Will said as he cut into his salmon. Always Alaskan. Always fillet.

Will liked the finer things, even back when he couldn't finance them himself, she thought. She had been the one to bring the money into the marriage. Her father had been in textiles. Will was an up-and-coming developer who'd benefited from the boost of capital, not to mention the boost in social status, network access. She ignored him. She wished he'd just get up from the table and go away, but she knew he wouldn't.

"Zoe." She watched her daughter as she picked her fork through her vegetable medley, never taking a bite, never lifting her eyes. "I'm sorry."

Zoe dropped her fork, tearful eyes meeting hers. "Why'd you do it, Mom?" The words came out pleading; it was a wounded cry.

Marin's breath caught in her throat. "Honestly, I don't know. It was a stupid mistake. I . . . didn't think. I have no excuse. At least, I won't make one. You can ask me anything, honey, and I'll try to answer. But, please, talk to me?"

Zoe began to cry and bolted from the table, running out of the room, up the stairs. Marin squeezed her eyes shut, waiting for the slam of Zoe's bedroom door. She didn't have to wait long for it. The enormity of the suffering she had caused, the heavy lifting she would need to do, the repairs she would need to make, it all plunged her into an instant depression. But she couldn't stay there. She had to move forward. She had to make the change.

She stood, tossed her napkin on the table, prepared to leave. There was no good that could come of forcing a conversation with Zoe tonight. She'd try again another time. She'd keep trying.

Will stood too. "Marin, we need to talk."

"No, we don't." She headed for the front door. "I came to see my daughter."

"There's the matter of—"

She cut him off. "Zoe. *That's* why I came."

His face turned to stone. "Have you any idea how your little stunt has affected me, my business prospects, my reputation, for God's sake? It's no picnic being the husband of an ex-con, Marin."

Looking at him now, the pomposity, she could barely recall what had attracted her to him in the first place. She supposed she'd misconstrued his misplaced arrogance for confidence, his prep-boy boastfulness for self-awareness.

She opened the door and stepped outside into the cold. Instinctively, she checked for reporters, but there hadn't been any when she arrived, and the street was clear of them now. She was old news, she hoped, and that was a relief.

"Do you realize the shame you've caused." Will whispered it, as if the night had ears and might overhear. "We're ruined socially, do you know that?"

25

The overhead light on the portico shone down on the two of them as though they were actors on a stage in some Tennessee Williams play. He hadn't come once to visit her in three years. He hadn't allowed her to speak to Zoe on the phone for more than five minutes at a time on a number of calls she could count on one hand. In three years. Lord knew what he'd done to poison her against Marin, what he'd said about her. What *she'd* done to ruin his reputation? The shame *she'd* caused. Marin slid a look at his manicured nails, the telltale sign of his infidelity. "Goodbye, Will."

Marin stood at the car, listening to the night, letting the cold cool her down, the cold a relief after the hot recrimination she'd just endured inside. It was not possible for her to feel any lower than she did. She felt for her keys, then looked up, startled to see Zoe standing at her bedroom window, her small face pressed close, staring down at her. Marin smiled, offered a tentative wave, holding her breath. Zoe just stood there, watching, finally returning a slight wave before stepping back and closing the drapes. Marin let out the breath she'd been holding. Her daughter didn't hate her. She was angry, hurt. She felt betrayed, but she didn't hate her. There was hope.

From the car, she made a call, one she'd planned and rehearsed in prison. Marin had been free for three weeks now but hadn't had the courage to begin. Tonight, though, was the night. She was done hiding, done licking her wounds. She'd just shed a husband, and now there were other things she needed to get behind her. She'd made a list.

"It's Marin," she said when the person picked up. She knew there'd be silence, followed by an attempt to explain. She listened to the stuttered starts, the quiver in the voice, but they didn't soften her resolve. Three years in prison made that impossible. "We need to meet."

# CHAPTER 5

Deanna Leonard parked her Mercedes on level six in the public garage they'd agreed upon and waited, the engine idling. Maybe this wasn't the smartest thing to do? She felt a little nervous about it. But there were cameras everywhere and security in the lobby if things got heated. She wasn't expecting trouble. They were just going to talk. They were both rational people. Friends once.

Sitting listening to Luther Vandross on the radio, the car's engine purring like a kitten, she had to admit she loved the car with its heated leather seats and its wood dash. It was a power car. It made a statement. Meehan had some nerve mentioning it, like her Mercedes was any worse than the luxury boat he parked out in Burnham Harbor every summer.

It was business. Politics was dirty. Sometimes you had to make a bad deal to get a good one. She did good for her ward, for her community by bringing in resources and opportunities. Her ward on the far South Side was a food desert. Wasn't it she who brought a major grocery store chain to the neighborhood? And that small business incubator didn't just pop up out of the sidewalk cracks. That deal had taken two years to cobble together. Deals. Negotiations. You had to cut corners to get things done. At least that's what she told herself as she ran her hands along the smooth steering wheel. She felt bad about Marin, she really did, but there were always risks. Marin couldn't have expected the rest of them to fall on their swords to help her. There was just too much at stake, especially for Meehan. Still, the least Leonard could do was apologize for her part in it. It was the right thing to do, and she was big enough to do at least that.

She jumped at the rap on the passenger window, then recognized the long coat and hat. The clock on the dash read 10:00 p.m. Right on time. This wouldn't take long. A little talk to clear the air, and then they would go their separate ways. Deanna unlocked the door. It opened. And death eased in. A short intake of startled breath was all Leonard had time for. Even the handgun in her lap, the one she'd placed there for added security, was of no use to her when there was another pointed at her head.

A hand reached out for Leonard's gun. "It's not personal."

"What is it then?" Leonard asked, her voice heavy with fear and resignation. She had no way out. There was no one around to hear her scream.

A shrug. "A means to an end."

Leonard grabbed for the door, until her own gun was pressed to the side of her head.

"The sooner we start, the quicker we finish."

"You don't have to kill me, okay? Please . . . I'll . . . I'll call the papers tomorrow and tell them what we all did." The words came out in a rush, ending in a desperate plea. "I have a family."

"Every betrayal has a cost."

Leonard squeezed her eyes closed, knowing all was lost "God help me."

———

Philo Benson rode up in the elevator to level six of the garage at six o'clock Wednesday morning, tired of his life and his lot in it. He was thirty-eight, still rudderless, working at a garage changing lightbulbs, sweeping up trash, mopping the floors, killing his soul. He watched as the numbers changed, level three, four . . . the car rising, lumbering up on tired cables and groaning gears. Six a.m. was an ungodly hour as far as he was concerned, but what did it matter? He had nothing else going. He had to make a change. If he didn't do it now, when would he? He couldn't let another day go by working here, or else he'd slit his own throat.

The doors opened, and Philo grabbed the stepladder he'd brought up with him, then the long fluorescent bulb he'd propped against the car's wall. Easy job. Shouldn't take long. As he stepped out, the blinking bulb overhead pointed the way. He sneered up at the sputtering light, then sighed, ready to get on with it. That's when he noticed a car parked thirty feet away. A red Mercedes. But it wasn't the make that was the oddity—it was the time. It was too early for the usual office crowd, he thought, even for those nutcase lawyers and high-finance freaks who worked nonstop, fueled by adrenaline and caffeine, thinking sweat equity would win the boss's attention and favor, only to drop dead of coronaries at forty.

Had the car been here overnight? He peered through the glass that separated the bays from the garage proper. Philo could see exhaust blowing out of the tailpipe. "That shit's running. Fucking idiots." He debated going out, giving the freak an earful. But the bulb was his business, not the car. They didn't pay him enough to get caught up in other people's drama. Then Philo thought medical emergency. He heard about those all the time. Some old guy had a heart attack flying a plane, or the driver on a CTA bus suddenly slumped over at the wheel.

Philo grabbed his walkie and called down to the lobby office. "Yeah, Tate, we got a car up here on six, engine running. Somebody might want to get up here and check it out."

Static roared back, and then, "Aren't you up there?"

Philo's eyes narrowed into angry slits. Tate was a lazy son of a bitch. He was just fine being manager, with all the perks that came with it, as long as he didn't have to work too hard. "Aren't *you* the manager, Tate?" God, Philo hated his life.

"Check the car out, Philo. Probably some drunk sleeping off one of them office holiday parties."

"It's *February*, Tate."

"Whatever. If it's anything serious, call back." Tate broke the connection. He likely had a cruller he needed to get back to, Philo thought.

Philo left the ladder and the bulb and pushed through the glass doors, his eyes on the idling car. He could smell the gas already. Halfway there, Philo could see there was someone inside slumped back in the driver's seat.

"Yep. Heart attack."

At the car, he saw the streaks of red on the driver's side glass and knew instantly what it was. Peering inside, he saw a woman slumped in the seat, a bullet hole in her head, her right arm flung out beside her with a gun nestled in it. He sighed, stepped back, then calmly scanned the empty parking spots. It was just him and the Mercedes.

Philo wasn't afraid of death. He'd seen too much of it in Afghanistan for it ever to shock him. He didn't even have enough left to feel sympathy for the dead woman. All that emotion, that feeling, had been burned away years ago. It's why he worked here in the garage where it was quiet, usually. Where the only challenge to that quiet was the boneheaded Tate.

He pushed the button on the walkie. "Tate, put the cruller down and call the police. We got a dead woman up here."

# CHAPTER 6

Foster walked around the Mercedes again, coming to a stop at the driver's door, peering in at what was left of Alderman Deanna Leonard. "She's been here a while it looks like." The detective stared down at the body, at the vacant eyes of one of the city's leaders, now laid to waste. Mascara was smudged below the eyes and streaked around the sockets, as though Leonard had sweat or cried the makeup away. She was dressed casually in slacks and a sweater, wearing a wool car coat, not the full-length mink she was known to glide into city hall wearing. A casual dinner? The theater was just around the corner. There had been a performance of *Jersey Boys* the night before. Or maybe Leonard had worked late at city hall or come in early. Either scenario seemed uncharacteristic, but Foster supposed it could happen.

One round had left an angry star-shaped hole at Leonard's right temple where gun barrel had met skin and let loose its deadly projectile. A streak of dark blood trailed from the entry wound down Leonard's cheek and chin. Her head, tilted back against the headrest, was angled toward the driver's window, her eyes open. Foster's eyes slid down to the gun in Leonard's right hand. Her index finger was positioned outside the trigger guard. The hand was slightly open, not clenched shut around the grip. Too early for conclusions. There was nothing in the back seat, no sign of struggle, no indication anyone else had been in the car with her, or if they had, they hadn't left anything of themselves behind that she could see. Maybe the techs would get a print or two, she hoped.

"The blood doesn't look completely dry," Li said. "Dry in spots, entry point still looks a little gummy."

Foster didn't have to look at her partner to know that she was staring at her, assessing her with those dark, intelligent eyes. Li needed to know that she was solid, good, that this death, tragic as it was, wasn't dredging up the death of Foster's ex-partner, Detective Glynnis Thompson, who'd driven her car into the police lot one morning, put it in park, and then shot herself in the head. The why was an unanswered question. The damage done to Glynnis and her family, the guilt Foster struggled with, was the thing she worked on. She finally looked over at Li, so that her new partner could see that she was fully there and dialed in. That she was seeing Leonard and not Glynnis in the front seat of the Mercedes with a round in her head.

"Nobody around to see anything. Empty level, except for her car, but was it empty when she got into it?" she asked. "Did she come late or early?"

Seemingly satisfied, Li pulled her eyes away and bent down to scan the inside of the car again, noting a transponder to the garage entry system clipped to the visor on the driver's side. "Transponder ought to give us the time."

They'd cordoned off the area for the squad cars and tech vans. Foster took a quick look at the uniformed cops standing along the perimeter.

"Kimber Micro 9," she said, taking in Leonard's hand again, the manicured nails, the bold nail polish. She'd seen Leonard on the news many times giving rousing stump speeches, cutting ribbons at community centers. She was a character, a straight talker, a real pull-yourself-up-by-your-bootstraps success story. Right out of Englewood, as she recalled, a real champion of the community, with a fondness for minks, cars, and expensive handbags. "Decent firearm for concealed carry."

Li eased open the glove compartment, her gloved fingers lightly picking through street maps, city guides, a tin of breath mints, a tiny compact. "Her being an alderman, she'd have gone for that. Her bag's on the floor this side. Vuitton. Nice." Li closed the compartment, then reached down and gently picked at the contents of the open purse. "Wallet's accounted for. ID, cards, eighty, no, a hundred in cash."

"Phone?" Foster asked, opening the driver's door to its widest point and then squatting down to check the floorboard on her side. "Wait. It's here. Between her legs." She wanted to remove it, check it, but left the phone where it was for now. She'd wait for the techs. "Might tell us something."

Li stood, backed away from the car. "There are going to be so many eyes on this. The alderman thing, for sure, but Leonard's got some baggage. Remember that big corruption thing a couple years ago? Her name was whispered. Nothing much came of it, but you know politicians."

"Maybe something about that weighed heavy on her is what you're thinking?" Foster asked.

Li shrugged. "Possible. Or maybe something else was coming down she didn't want to face. Or family troubles. Health reasons? Could be a million things." Li brushed her hair back from her face, tucking the sides behind her ears. "I don't want to jump to conclusions." She grinned at Foster, having just parroted back her partner's grounding investigative principle.

Foster shot Li a wry smile. "Cute."

They both turned when they heard the crime scene van roar up to the cordon and saw the tech crew tumble out, grab their gear, duck under the tape, and head their way, like a band of jaded Ghostbusters carrying light stands, cameras, and evidence-gathering equipment.

Foster stepped back from the car. "Well, TOD will start us off."

Rosales spotted them and frowned, his hooded eyes narrowing. "You two. Step away from my body. Why is it you cops, especially you two, insist on swarming all over my crime scene like ants on a picnic basket? Back up. Give me room." He bustled forward, his battered bag of tech paraphernalia gripped tightly in his hand.

"We know the drill, Rosales," Li said. "We had to ID her, didn't we?"

Foster looked over at Leonard. "And check for signs of life on the off chance . . ."

"I even memorized the steps I took," Li added, "so there."

Rosales turned to Foster. "You memorize yours too?"

"Minimal steps." Foster flipped back a page in her notepad and showed it to Rosales. "Even mapped them here. Gloves on the entire time. The car was idling. I reached in once to turn it off, so we wouldn't all get asphyxiated. There's a cell phone wedged between her legs. Can we get that quickly, please?"

Rosales squinted into the car and spotted the phone right where Foster had said it was. "Gotcha. Now back." He glanced around. "Man, this is a shit-ass place to die, isn't it?"

Foster and Li moved farther back out of Rosales's way, watching as the photographer documented Deanna Leonard from every angle, capturing every inch of the car inside and out. If this was indeed a suicide, this might be all that Foster and Li would have to do for her.

Foster walked over to the patrol officers first on scene as they stood near their car several feet away. Li came with her for the next phase of things. Her eyes swept over the male officer's name patch on his bulletproof vest and then did the same with his female partner. The barrel-chested white guy with the formidable moustache was Fetterman. His partner, Jones, was African American, barely five foot five or six, and lean as a greyhound. An odd pairing, but no odder, Foster thought, than her and Li.

She was Black; Li was Asian. Li was married with a young kid; she was divorced with no child living. She was quiet; Li could talk the ears off a monk. Standing together they looked like two andirons with badges, lean, straight. Li usually wore her black chin-length hair in a neat bun, all business. Foster's tight twists served the same purpose. Li was light; she was less so. Li moved fast, like someone was timing her; Foster was more deliberate. Yet they were the same where it counted. She would bet good money the last held true also for Fetterman and Jones.

"Which one of you wants to take it?" Foster asked as she flipped to a clean page in her notepad. "911 call came in when?"

Jones spoke first. "0617. We pulled up five minutes later. The only car here was hers. We got out, looked inside, and found her like that."

"We moved the maintenance guy back," Fetterman added. "Then *we* moved back and blocked the area off. When we ran the plates, they came back as the alderman's. The guy, the janitor, swears he didn't touch anything, but we got no way of knowing."

Foster stared at him. "The *guy* have a name?"

"Philo Benson."

"You have reason to believe Mr. Benson lied about not touching anything?"

Fetterman stiffened. "People tell you all kinds of things out here, I guess you know that. We can't prove he didn't go in there, look around. Take something. I'd get his prints."

Foster watched as Fetterman hooked his thumbs behind his duty belt and stood tall, seemingly proud of his contribution to the investigation. "Thank you. Anything else you'd suggest we do, Officer Fetterman?" He had the good sense to blanch. She then looked over at Jones, who didn't look like she wanted to step in and help her partner pull his foot out of his mouth. "Officer Jones?" Jones only shook her head, her lips pressed tight.

Li grinned and addressed Jones. "Did he say how he found her?"

"He came up to fix a light," Jones said. "He saw the car and came over to check it out. He called it down to his boss, the boss called it in."

Foster jotted the information in her notepad, her eyes on the page. "Anything else?"

"All there was," Fetterman said.

"And *you*, of course, didn't touch anything, did you, Fetterman?" Li asked.

Foster looked up, eyed Fetterman. She'd been told often that her stare was as cold as a vampire's grave. Fetterman met her look, then averted his eyes, clearing his throat nervously.

"*Me?* No."

Jones piped up. "Neither of us did."

Foster flipped her notepad closed, the faux-leather cover emitting a dull snap. "Thanks. Let's start walking this level. See if there's anything that might belong to her or that might relate to this. Slow and thorough. Appreciate it." The POs walked away to get started on the search, other officers joining in outside the red tape.

"Ah, I remember those days," Li said, watching their retreat. "Walking a grid, climbing into dumpsters to pick through rancid garbage. POs are the backbone of this whole freaking operation. Saved my hash more than once."

"Mine too," Foster said.

Li cocked her head. "Fetterman's not soup yet, though. Odd pair too. Big and little, Black and white, moustache, no moustache. Fetterman looks like he could fell a tree, while even Jones's knit cap looks too big for her."

Foster thought for a moment. "Yeah, but it's the little ones who'll knock you out."

They rejoined Rosales and the techs, watching as the ballet of evidence collection played out in front of them. Foster watched as Rosales gently lifted the Kimber out of Leonard's hand and slid it into an evidence bag, then proceeded to swab her palm and her fingers, slowly, paying an equal amount of attention to every digit, especially under the nails. It was meticulous work. Vital, necessary, but by no means quick.

Rosales stood after a time. Found them standing there. "I've dusted the phone. You want a look?"

Foster moved before he finished speaking, her hand out to take the evidence bag with Leonard's cell phone inside. "Thanks."

Li moved around to the driver's side to take a closer look at Leonard's body. "Why here, though?" She looked around at all the concrete, the cop cars, the empty parking slots where morning commuters would have been parked were it not for this. "Like you said, Ro, this is a shit-ass place to die. The last place I'd want to see before . . ." She didn't finish. Foster knew why.

Switching into a fresh pair of nitrile gloves, Foster eyed Li. "How long are we going to do this? You can stop walking on eggshells and tap-dancing around, okay?"

Li nodded, her steady eyes on Foster's. "I'd like to talk about that once this is done. Unpack it." For a moment neither of them said anything, and then finally Li did. "Right. On with it."

Foster slid Leonard's phone out of the bag, a little unnerved by Li's call for an unpacking. Partners needed complete trust in one another, and Li was telling her in just that brief exchange that she wasn't quite there. Foster had to respect that. It was something Glynnis would have said.

She watched Li as she moved around the car, observing her as she kept out of Rosales's way; then she went back to the phone. They still had to notify Leonard's family before her death leaked to the press. Getting their numbers from Leonard's phone would be quicker than tracking them down back at the office.

Rosales looked grim. "We've swept the car. I'm going to take one final pass, then move her. I don't want her sitting here any longer than she needs to. This is what I know so far. The gun's been fired. There's one round missing. There's a wound that would indicate she died by bullet, though I cannot confirm that as cause of death. There do not appear to be any additional wounds on the body, but I cannot confirm that, either, until Grant gets her on the table. What I can say after dusting the gun and her hands is this . . . there is only a small amount of GSR on her right palm, which you might expect to see given the gun's sitting in it, and it's been *recently* fired. But there is no GSR on her right index finger and none under her nails. There's also no bloody grip impression on the hand or any spatter. Strange, but not unprecedented. Clothing? We won't be able to tell you that with any level of certainty until we get everything back and looked at."

"Are you trying to say somebody else might have shot her?" Li asked.

"All I can tell you is what I found and didn't find. I can't even confirm that's the gun that was used without testing." He looked down at the dead woman. "I'd put time of death at maybe eight, nine hours ago? Body temp's tricky, right? It's friggin' February. This is Chicago. The garage is unheated, cold, but the car was on, which means the heat was on."

Li drew her coat collar up against the chill. "The car idled for eight or nine hours without running out of gas?"

Rosales flicked her a look. "Cars can idle that long, longer, depending on how much gas is in the tank. What's this, a Mercedes CLA coupe?"

Li looked blankly at him. "*Is* it?"

Foster was listening to the exchange and had already googled the make and model, including the tank size. "The gas tank holds thirteen and a half gallons. Eight or nine hours. Let's say eight, at a gallon used every hour, according to this source, that's eight gallons gone, leaving five and a half to empty, that's assuming the tank was full. What's the gauge on?"

Li tucked her head inside the car as Rosales's eyes narrowed again. "About a quarter tank left." She looked over at Foster.

Foster made the note in her pad. The car could have idled for eight hours. Moving on. "Can you see any way she could have fired that gun and there not be a lot of GSR left behind?" Foster asked, though she already had an idea of Rosales's answer. This wasn't her first death scene, his either. She just needed to hear him say the words, so that she could be sure.

"Gloves?" Rosales said. "But then where are they? She couldn't shoot herself in the head, slip out of a pair of gloves, chuck them somewhere, then lie back and die with the gun sitting in her hand like that. Although, I had a case where death wasn't instantaneous and—"

"No." Li shot him a warning look, shook her head. "Thanks, Ro."

"And gloves wouldn't account for the little bit of GSR you *did* find."

Foster concentrated on Leonard's phone. "This isn't password protected. I've got her emergency contacts. Call log." She could feel Rosales move away and Li draw closer. "Her last incoming was at six fifty-two last night. Call duration thirty-three seconds. From an unknown caller. Too long for a wrong number."

"Too short for a real conversation," Li said.

"Long enough to arrange to meet somebody you knew. You wouldn't sit on a random call for that long."

"So, a meeting with a friend or an acquaintance." Li checked her watch. "Ten hours ago. That would put it at ten p.m."

Foster dialed the number, waiting for Leonard's last caller to pick up. Li leaned in to hear. Someone picked up on the fourth ring. A woman.

"I meant every word, Deanna." The voice was angry, hard. "You owe me. You all do."

Foster let the silence sit for a second before breaking it, hoping the woman on the other end would say more. When it became clear she wasn't going to, she identified herself. "This is Detective Harriet Foster, Chicago Police Department. Who am I speaking with, please?"

There was a shocked intake of breath before the line went dead.

"What the hell?" Li said, taking a step back.

Foster jotted down the number and dialed it again, but got no answer. "Not picking up." She scrolled through the outgoing call log, flicked a look at Li. "You mentioned the trouble Leonard might have skirted a while back?"

Li shrugged. "Politics. Some questionable deal. Leonard wasn't the primary player, and hers wasn't the only name that got floated around, as I recall. Alderman Marin Shaw did go down, though. I think she got like two years? Some zoning scheme."

Foster heard Li, followed along, but it was all about the phone. "Marin Shaw. Right. I remember that. Do you remember the names of the other aldermen? I think John Meehan was one, but he's a perennial favorite."

Li chortled. "Alderman Cubby Meehan, the dirtiest clean guy on the city council. He's like a nonstick skillet, isn't he? Yeah, I think he might have been mentioned. Not sure about the others now. I'd have to look it up."

Foster's eyes met hers. "Could they have been George Valdez and Sylissa Franklin?"

"Could. My memory's good, but not *that* good. Why?"

Foster held Leonard's phone up so Li could see the screen. "The last three outgoing calls Leonard made were to aldermen John Meehan, George Valdez, and Sylissa Franklin. Duration: four minutes and change for Meehan, half that for the other two. A lot to talk about, apparently. Hours later, Leonard's dead of an apparent suicide . . . without significant traces of GSR found." She glanced over at the Mercedes as the techs gently lifted Deanna Leonard's corpse into a body bag.

"Marin Shaw just got out of prison a few weeks ago," Li said. "It made the news."

Foster watched as the body bag got zipped up. "Uh-huh. I saw that." She turned back to Li. "The woman on the phone said, 'You owe me. You all do.'"

"Shaw?"

"Let's find out."

# CHAPTER 7

"So, it's not straightforward is what you're saying?" Sergeant Griffin fixed ice-blue eyes on Foster and Li as they gave their report on the Leonard scene. Sipping from a ceramic Starbucks cup with holiday snowflakes all over it, Griffin waited for the details, her chair slid away from her cluttered desk and legs crossed.

Foster was getting used to Griffin's cracker-box office, festooned with Irish shamrocks and green fedoras from past Saint Paddy's Day parades, but still it felt strangely to her like business in the front, party in the back. The setting was a little light for homicide, especially on this gloomy February morning with one of the city's leading politicians lying on the ME's table. Foster glanced warily at the knobby shillelagh propped against the wall, streamers of metallic kelly green tied around the knob.

"You'd expect more GSR," Li said.

"But it's too early for Rosales to say," Foster added.

Griffin took Foster in, then swallowed another sip of good coffee, not the cop swill from the office pot in the break room. The boss was dressed as she always was—no-nonsense flats, blazer, pants, and shirt, all neatly pressed and sharp, her blonde hair pulled back, her badge clipped to her belt. She was always cocked and ready, in case the extraordinary thing happened and the city ran out of beat cops and she, Sharon Griffin, had to chase a perp down in the streets. "Right," she said. "What else?"

"Transponder on Leonard's car clocks her into the garage at nine forty-six Tuesday night," Li said. "It's a twenty-four-hour lot, skeleton staff overnight. One guy, in fact. Tuesday night, that was the manager, Kenny Tate."

Foster consulted her notepad. "Tate said it wasn't unusual for anyone to come in that late. The garage is a block from city hall. It's also surrounded by offices—lawyers, bankers, CEOs—they keep crazy hours. So, Leonard rolls in, the transponder kicks, but Tate's unaware."

"No monitors in the office?" Griffin asked.

Foster nodded. "There are. Sounded like Tate wasn't watching them too closely. We've asked for a printout of entrances and exits for that entire day. Any video too. We're waiting on that. There are security cameras on every level."

Griffin's brows lifted. "Good. Let's hope we get a face we can move on."

Foster consulted her notes. "Fingers crossed. That garage was dimly lit. At night? Let's hope something came through."

Griffin sat her cup on top of a pile of papers on her desk. "And the hang-up. Anything new on that?"

"Unknown number," Foster said. "I've dialed it a few times more. No pickup. We're trying to track the number now."

"A woman, you said."

"The voice sounded female."

Griffin's eyes narrowed.

Foster shrugged. "All I can say."

Griffin rolled her eyes. "A politician sitting in her car in an empty parking garage late at night. Nothing suspicious there. Sad that the first thing I think of is payoff, not suicide. Well, first moves?"

"Already made them," Foster said. "Death notification's done. We'll double back in a bit to talk to the family in depth. Meanwhile, we're trying to track down the unknown number of the hang-up. While we wait for the ME's report, we dig on Leonard to see if she was in some trouble and might have had reason to want to kill herself."

"*If* suicide's what we're looking at," Li added.

Griffin thought for a moment, her brows creased in concentration. Foster's eyes wandered around the office again before landing on Griffin's jumbled desk and the framed photo of her pale-faced, freckled kids sitting on it. That photo sat next to one of Griffin captured upright and stern of face in her CPD dress blues. That was the face, Foster noted, that could make grown cops cry.

"Get to it, then." Griffin leaned forward in her squeaky chair and picked up a pen. "A fricking alderman, no less. This is going to get press." She smoothed a hand through her hair, careful not to upset a single strand. "All right. Thorough and deep. Keep me posted." They'd been dismissed and had turned to go. *"And."* They stopped, turned back to find Griffin glaring at them with those freaky eyes. *"Fast."* The eyes seemed to turn even icier. "And if either of you even *thinks* about going rogue on this, like you did with Davies?" She looked at Foster, then Li. "I don't think I have to finish that, do I?"

With a quick look exchanged between them, the two detectives silently agreed that Griffin did not and took their leave of her. They padded back to their desks, ready to move out. Until the autopsy results came in, they needed to talk to Leonard's family and see what they could turn up about her last movements, hopefully before reporters and news cameras went crazy and plastered news of Leonard's death all over the place.

"I don't think she's completely human," Li said. "That Irish stuff could be a smoke screen. I've *never* seen her kids. They could be plants. Which reminds me, I'm going to call and check on mine. Give me five." Li walked away, her cell phone to her ear.

Foster got her bag out of her bottom drawer, readied her notepad, tossing pens into the outside pocket of the bag, then plucked a paper clip from the desk and slipped it into her pocket. The clip was a token of resilience, tangible evidence that she'd bested another hour, a new day. The clip today or the thumbtack tomorrow were little prizes for big victories. Willem flashed in her mind, and she wondered what he was doing at that moment. His life was forfeit, and she felt no joy in that, only resignation. She was solemn but ready and waiting when Li came back.

"Everything okay?" she asked, taking one look at Li's face.

"My baby might be a psychopath. My mother just said he tried to drown the cat in her foot tub. Literally drown him. Should I be worried?" Li's face paled. "Sorry. I . . . I'm doing it again."

"You can talk about your kid, Vera. I won't break." She let a moment go. "You're right. After this is done, before the next thing pops up, we need to talk things through. Over coffee or lunch."

"Dinner," Li said, grinning. "I can't remember the last time I actually sat down in a restaurant and had dinner with an adult."

Foster smiled. "Dinner. Ready to head out?"

Li grabbed her coat. "After you, partner."

"As to your son being a psychopath? He's barely two. I'd give it a couple years before you worry."

Detective Bigelow, a linebacker of a Black man in his early fifties, walked up, his overcoat slung over his arm and his black teardrop fedora in hand. "Yeah, you're heading out to talk to the family on the Leonard case. Mind if I tag along?" Foster and Li shared a look. "I used to work security for the alderman," he added. "I might be able to add some background on the way."

"I thought you and Kelley were on that drive-by?" Li asked.

"I can juggle more than one ball at a time." He glanced around the room, took a step closer to them, lowered his booming voice. "You're going to want my insight on this. I know the family. I knew Leonard."

Foster stood for a moment staring at Bigelow, listening to what he said, but also to what he wasn't saying. "Intimately," she finally said.

"We spent some time. Long hours. Stress. You know how it is. Nothing untoward. We were grown. Unattached, both of us . . . nice lady." Bigelow's glum expression was her only clue that the connection was likely more than what he was making it out to be, but stoicism and discretion in a cop were expected, and they both knew it. He searched their faces. "Look, we don't have to get into it. The point is, I have some inside knowledge that's going to be useful. You want it, or don't you?"

"When's the last time you saw Leonard?" Li asked.

"It's been a minute. At least three years. I quit her detail and her at the same time. Clean break. Neither one of us cried over any spilled milk."

"Her family know?" Foster asked.

"We kept it on the QT. It was brief. Just a month, little less. So, we good?"

"That's it?" Foster asked. "Nothing else?"

"Nope." Bigelow put his hat on, adjusted it, ready to get going. "All there was to it. Look, I'm no lovesick Romeo here, if that's what you're worried about."

"We'll take the information," Foster said. "The insight. But only that."

Bigelow nodded. "Like I said, your case, you're the leads on it." He buttoned his coat and stood there for a moment. "And not that I was listening in while you two weren't looking, but I'm with Foster on your kid being a psychopath, Li. It's way too early to label him. Now if he'd tried to set that cat on fire, or—"

"Shut it, Bigs," Li said, pushing past him.

# CHAPTER 8

Deanna Leonard had lived south in Bronzeville, so Foster slipped off the Drive at Thirty-First Street and headed the unmarked car west. She could instantly feel the pull of the neighborhood as she drove vibrant block by vibrant block, as even the air appeared to change and take on flavor.

Bronzeville had been the destination for many African Americans fleeing the South and Jim Crow during the Great Migration that began in 1910. They stopped here, rooted here, prospered here because this was where they were allowed to be, as redlining, bigotry, and racial hate barred them from going farther west or south or north where whites lived. Bronzeville was where they staked their claim, where creativity took wing, where family after family made a way out of no way.

Foster lived here and knew firsthand the neighborhood had a rhythm, a jazz, a heartbeat. Businesses thrived. Art, music, and culture, too, as did struggle and dysfunction handed down through generations. All of it echoed off the bricks. All of it made up a potent brew that filled the air and filled the lungs of the people who walk Bronzeville's streets and called it home.

It was winter, cold, but Foster cracked the window to let the aroma of barbecue slip in on a smoky wave. She breathed in deeply. The sweet smell of familiarity was as good as a paper clip or a thumbtack in her pocket.

"Now I'm hungry," Bigelow said from the back seat. "That's Uncle Honey's smoke."

Li inhaled deeply, grinned in appreciation. "How could you not be. That smells delicious." She checked her watch. "Kinda early for barbecue, isn't it? It's not even noon."

Bigelow glared at her. "Early? They started smoking that meat before the sun came up. Plus, there's no bad time for barbecue, Li."

"Hmm. Guess not. And that's not a bad smell to wake up to."

"Damn straight."

———

When they pulled up in front of Leonard's brownstone, Foster could clearly see that her place was crowded with people. Mourners. Those who had likely come with flowers and food and sympathy the moment they'd heard of Leonard's passing. They were there to give solace to those left behind, to ease their burden and dispel the darkness of grief, at least for a time.

There were also three news trucks on the street with three reporters and three cameramen standing on the sidewalk, cameras facing the house. A dead alderman was big news. The manner of death, a bullet to the head, a suspected suicide, explained its lurid appeal. "And there are the jackals right on time," Bigelow groused. "God forbid they let somebody die in peace."

"If it bleeds it leads," Foster muttered sourly, resigned. "But they're just doing their jobs, like we have to do ours."

Bigelow sneered at the cameras. "Jackals."

Li glanced past the cameras toward the house. "Full house, it looks like. Emotions will be high."

They got out and stood on the walk, watching the front windows as people passed by them inside. "We get as much as we can, as delicately as we can," Foster said. In the car, Bigelow had given them a rundown of his brief affair with Leonard. From Foster's perspective, it didn't appear damning. They were both adults, both divorced, no harm, no foul. Leonard, though, had had a complicated relationship with her son, Aaron Parker, a screwup, by Bigelow's account, who ran to his mother for fixes when he got into jams. She'd had an easier time with her daughter, Jeniece Eccles, a lawyer, married with kids of her own.

"One last thing," Bigelow said. "Aaron's an angry guy."

Foster slid him a look. "Angry at what?"

Bigelow sighed. "Life. He likes to play things big, but he can't get anybody to sign on to it, if you know what I mean. He's small change, a hustler. This whole thing? He'll find a way to turn it around on us, the city, the mayor even, if it gives him a chance to perform. Believe me, he's all hot air."

"Seems you know him pretty well," Li said.

"His case? It didn't take much."

Foster squared her shoulders. "Well, we get what we need to get, and we get out . . . no drama." She looked over at Bigelow. "Bigs?"

His eyes widened at the mild rebuke. "Me? Look, I told you I got no dog in this fight."

Inside, there was barely room to walk, the place nearly wall-to-wall people, standing, sitting, chattering, murmuring, many crowded into the entryway, spilling out from the living room and dining room. Foster could see the kitchen at the end of a long hall, filled with women in aprons preparing food, bringing it out to the table, keeping busy, helping, softening the blow of death. The aromas of Bronzeville—fried chicken, collard greens, pound cake, buttered biscuits, and macaroni and cheese—mingling with the cloying perfume and strong after-shave of the mourners lined up like fence posts around the house as Mahalia Jackson's "Take My Hand, Precious Lord" played low in the background.

"There he is," Bigelow whispered, his head cocked toward a slightly built Black man holding court in the center of the crowd.

Foster scanned the room, her eyes landing on Parker, his brows furrowed, jaw clenched, his face set in a disagreeable scowl. He seemed nervous as he shifted his weight from one foot to the other, his shoulders hunched, his eyes not on the people around him, but on the tops of his shoes.

Bigelow scanned the room again. "And there's Jeniece." Foster took her eyes off Parker to take in the woman clad in a conservative black dress, two sorrowful preteen boys beside her. Jeniece was the spitting image of her mother, she thought—heart-shaped face, big doe eyes, slender features. But Foster recognized, too, the hollow look, the forced smile, the shock of sudden loss that stole your breath and left you changed.

"Okay, let's—" Before she could finish, Aaron Parker spotted them and stormed over, weaving through the huddle of mourners that slowly parted like the Red Sea to let him pass. "Heads up."

"What are you all doing back here? This is a time of *bereavement.*" Parker looked around himself, checking to see that he had everyone's attention. "The city just can't wait to pick over her bones, can it?"

The sea of people moved back and away, leaving the four of them space in the middle of the living room. Suddenly, all conversation stopped. They were the main event.

Foster said, "Mr. Parker, again, we're sorry for your loss. We'd—"

"And with *him?*" Parker's black marble-like eyes narrowed at Bigelow. Then he capped the frosty look with an equally distasteful sneer. "Who's got nerve showing *his* face." He took a step forward. "This city's a cesspool. Nobody's safe in it. Not even a prominent leader in the community, like my mother. What are taxpayers paying for, huh?" He looked the three of them up and down. "What are we getting for our money? It sure isn't protection."

Foster pushed forward. "We realize this is a difficult time, but we'd like to ask you a few questions about your mother."

Parker scoffed, turned to the crowd. "Now they got *questions.*"

Jeniece eased in and stood next to her brother. "What's this?"

"If we could speak to you both," Foster said. "Privately?"

Jeniece placed a gentle hand on her brother's shoulder. It was a subtle restraint, one Harri was sure she'd employed many times before. "Of course. Let's talk in Mama's office." She turned to those gathered around the room. "Please, everybody, go on back and get yourselves something to eat. The church ladies have been cooking all morning, and it sure smells good back there."

The murmuring crowd slowly moved toward the dining room as Jeniece led Foster, Li, and Bigelow into the next room. "I'm sorry, I've forgotten your names," she said, closing the door behind them. "It's been . . . a day." She turned to Bigelow. "Him I know."

Foster handed over her business card; Li did the same. The small room they were standing in might have been a den before it was converted to an office. There were built-in shelves recessed into the wall and a nook for an entertainment center and television that Leonard had filled instead with files. There was a city flag hung on the wall behind an executive desk, and the city's crest beside it, like the mayor might have at city hall. The piles of municipal books, the ward maps, and the stacks of paper on the desk suggested that Leonard had done a fair amount of work from home.

"Yeah, we know him." Parker glowered at Bigelow. "I can't believe you had the nerve to show your face back here. Did he tell you two he used to work for us? That when things got real, he up and quit and left us high and dry? We had reporters climbing all over this place trying to get to Mama when that bogus fed case broke, and he just bolts." He looked Bigelow up and down like the man was garbage. "Some security."

Bigelow bristled. *"Us?"*

Aaron's eyes fired. "Did he tell you he was sleeping with her?"

The room got quiet, stuffy, awkward. "No drama" was suddenly off the table.

"Aaron, stop it," Jeniece said. "That's got nothing to do with anything now. I want to know what they have." She turned to the detectives. "What do you know?"

"Things are still preliminary," Foster said. "We're waiting for the ME's report, and we haven't yet gotten everything processed from the scene this morning. But your mother sustained a gunshot to the head at approximately ten last night. She was found in her car in a garage a block from city hall. She was discovered by maintenance at approximately six this morning. Her car was still idling."

"Was it a robbery?"

"It doesn't appear to be," Li said. "Her bag was in the car, wallet intact, as far as we could tell. There were no other outward signs of physical violence."

Jeniece frowned. "You think she killed herself. That this was suicide. That's what it looks like, doesn't it?"

"Suicide?" Parker said. "No way in hell. The city's just trying to cover up something here. Crime's off the charts—"

Foster cut him off with a look that invited no debate. "At the moment, this is a death investigation. The autopsy and the tests will tell us more." She turned back to Jeniece. "We'll update you as more information comes in. Meanwhile, anything you could tell us about your mother would help. Was she under any unusual stress or pressure lately? Did you notice any changes in her behavior?"

"Of course not," Parker barked. "She was fine."

Jeniece's eyes welled up with tears. "She was a little preoccupied." She slid her brother a look. "You wouldn't have noticed, but I did. Something was on her mind."

"She didn't say what?" Li asked.

"I asked, she said it was just work." Jeniece glanced at her mother's full desk. "You can see she never stopped. There was always something she had to do, somebody she had to talk to, a meeting she had to set up. I called her yesterday about grabbing lunch, to catch up, but she said her schedule was packed. She sounded rushed but okay. She made a joke about burning the candle at both ends. But that was Mama. She thrived on pressure. That's why I don't understand how she . . ."

Foster scanned Leonard's desk, her eyes landing on a leather-bound calendar the size of a schoolkid's notebook. "Would you mind if we looked at your mother's calendar? It might tell us something."

"You need a warrant for that," Parker said.

Foster turned to look at him. "Not if you volunteer to show us. Any reason why you wouldn't want to?"

Jeniece scowled at her brother, then moved toward the desk. "Of course not. Here." She opened the calendar, then stepped back so Foster could take a closer look. "We've nothing to hide."

She was interested in the night Leonard died and flipped pages until she got to the date, only to find the page empty. Nothing scheduled. "Mind if I check a few more pages?"

Jeniece shook her head. "Do whatever you need to."

Foster quickly went through the pages, which wasn't a great task since it was just two months into the new year. Then she had an idea and flipped to the date of Marin Shaw's release from prison to find that Leonard had circled the date without a notation. She checked the other pages. None of them were circled.

"This date's circled," she said. "You have any idea why it would be?"

"She sometimes circled things in her calendar she wanted to remember. She also has a calendar on her computer. Do you want to see that too?"

"Please." Foster stepped back and let Jeniece boot up the laptop on the desk.

Again, there was nothing scheduled for the day Leonard died. "No notation for the date she's got circled in the book." Foster scanned through Leonard's schedule, reading through council meetings, community forums, school events, church visits, and constituent office hours. There was nothing pertaining to a late-night garage sit and nothing to do with Marin Shaw. She stepped back. "Thank you."

"What time yesterday did you speak to your mother?" Li asked.

"About one o'clock. I was just out of court. I called on my way back to the office. And I called her again around six, I think? Just to talk. I usually talk to her a couple times a day." Jeniece dabbed at her eyes. "Talked. We saw each other all the time. I'm in and out of city hall regularly. I'd pop my head into her office, we'd go to lunch."

Foster jotted down the time in her notepad. "Was she at home when you spoke to her last?" Jeniece nodded. "And you, Mr. Parker? The last time you spoke to your mother?"

He'd crossed his arms against his chest stubbornly, like a petulant child. "It had been a few days," he snapped. "She was all right when I talked to her."

"Can you think of any reason why she might have gone to that garage that late?" Li asked. Both Jeniece and Parker shook their heads. "Could she have gone there to meet up with somebody?"

Parker huffed, dropped his arms. "What are you trying to say?"

Li stood her ground. "It was a question, not an accusation."

"No," Jeniece answered. "I don't think Mama would have gone there on her own like that. She was very security conscious."

"Is that why she carried a gun?" Foster said.

Jeniece looked up. "Yeah. There are a lot of crazies out there. Everything was legal. FOID card. Registration. She took classes on how to shoot."

Parker glared at them. "Look, all this is a waste of time. You all ought to be out there busting the streets up looking for who did this, not standing around in here badgering us."

Jeniece dropped her head in her hands. "Aaron, stop."

"No, no. If we let them drag their feet like this, we'll never find out what happened."

"Aaron!"

At the angry snap of Jeniece's voice, Parker stopped talking, but continued to fume in silence, his lips pressed into an angry, thin line, his eyes blazing with disdain. Foster found the family dynamic interesting. "Any family tensions?"

Jeniece smiled, sliding a look at her brother. "The usual. We had our moments. Our mother was the boss, and she ran everything, even us, like she knew it. Sometimes that caused some problems, but nothing serious."

"Any enemies?" Foster asked.

Jeniece managed a wan smile. "Just political ones. There were always battles and alliances and disagreements. Sometimes constituents could get combative, but she was used to that."

"Either of you familiar with any of your mom's colleagues?"

"We met a few of them, sure, but . . ." Jeniece shook her head.

"Did she have any recent contact with Marin Shaw?" Li asked.

The room plunged into silence.

"Marin Shaw?" Parker said, anger rising again. "Oh, so *that's* what this is? You're trying to bring up all that old shit? You think maybe the feds were after Mama, too, and so . . ." He paced the room, furious. "She was never charged with a *damn* thing, okay? Despite *Marin Shaw* doing everything she could to drag Mama down with her. And I'm not going to stand here and let you three try and do the same thing, so that's it. Get out."

Jeniece studied her brother for a moment and then turned her back to him. A clear dismissal. "Mama never mentioned Marin Shaw, but she could have been the reason she was so distracted. They were friends before Marin's trial, not so much after. Mama never wanted to talk about any of that."

"One last question, for now." Foster readied her pen. "Where were each of you around ten last night?"

"I was in bed asleep . . . with my husband," Jeniece said. "School night. Work night."

Foster turned to Parker. "Mr. Parker?"

His beady eyes were cold and hard. "Now we're *suspects*. In what?" Foster stood silently, her question hanging. Parker's anger and combativeness were worrisome, and she wondered what they could be masking. It took a moment, but with all eyes on him, he finally answered. "Home watching the game. Alone."

"The Bulls game?" Li asked.

Parker frowned. "They played the Pistons and lost 114 to 108."

Foster stuck her pen in her notepad and closed the cover. "Thank you both for your time. We won't infringe on your grief any longer. We'll be in touch."

Aaron Parker jabbed an angry thumb at Bigelow. "What about this guy? He gets to just sail off?"

Bigelow took a step toward Parker, but then drew it back, likely remembering his job, his pension, and his badge just in the nick of time. Foster noticed that Parker flinched at the step. All heat and little steel, she decided as she stood waiting on Bigelow to make up his mind which way he'd go.

A slow, dangerous grin formed on Bigelow's face. "You have a nice day, Mr. Parker. Again, sorry for your loss."

Foster and Li followed Bigelow out of the room, out of the house, and onto the sidewalk, where they were passed by more people heading inside. The reporters looked like they were about to approach, mics up, but the warning glares from the three detectives stopped them cold. The newshounds heeded the warning and stayed put. In the car, watching as another news van pulled up, no one said a word for a time.

Then Li turned in the passenger seat to Bigelow in the back. "Well, so much for the family not knowing you were sexing Leonard up."

Bigelow groaned. "Man, it took all I had not to pound that little bastard like a nail."

Foster glanced at Bigelow through the rearview. "He hates you."

Li snorted. "That's an understatement."

Bigelow waved Li's remark away. "Man, Parker's a punk. He made this whole thing sound sleazy, and it wasn't. I worked for her, we had a brief thing, it was over. Period. And just so you all know, Parker's nothing but a user, okay? A leech. If he'd been as smart as Jeniece, he might have made something of himself, but he isn't. Deanna managed to get him a city job, which he wasn't satisfied with or qualified for. Still, he thinks *he's* the guy."

Li sat back in her seat. "I could have taken him."

Bigelow chuckled. "Big Bird could whip his ass. What'd you get from the calendar?"

"Leonard had nothing scheduled for the day she died. But she had the date of Shaw's prison release circled. Could be coincidence. She could have circled the date for something else."

"I don't believe in coincidences," Bigelow said. "Shaw and her were friends. The two would do lunch and brunch and drinks all the time. Plus, calls going back and forth. Seemed genuine. I think she circled that day for her release."

"So, it's not strange that they might arrange to meet?" Li said.

Bigelow shook his head. "Nah. It'd be stranger if they didn't."

Li buckled her seat belt and eyed the house and the people streaming in. "Parker, though. I could literally feel the heat radiating off him. How does a person live with so much rage in their body?"

Foster started the car. "You'd be surprised by what people can live with." She gave Leonard's crowded house a last look. She was thinking about voices, the one on the phone, Jeniece's. Similar tone, different inflection, but she was no expert. "Parker was the problem child. Anything on Jeniece?"

Bigelow thought for a moment. "Nothing. Seemed like she was Deanna's pride and joy. The family success story. And don't think Aaron doesn't resent the hell out of that. Her shutting him down in there just now? Guaranteed he didn't like it. But why're you asking about Jeniece?"

"Just thinking."

Li's hand shot up. "I call BS. Foster's always got a reason for everything."

Bigelow sighed. "True dat."

Li flicked her partner a look. "Isn't it good to be seen?"

Foster shook her head. "Not always. No."

# CHAPTER 9

The next morning Li sat at her desk watching the latest news report on Deanna Leonard's death on her phone. "Every newscast," she said. "Top story. They're really whipping this thing up." She looked over at Foster sitting across from her. "Apparent suicide. Wonder where they got that? This department leaks like a sieve."

Foster pushed away from her computer, frustrated already, and it wasn't even 10:00 a.m. "How hard is it to trace a phone number? We need to know who called Leonard." She scanned the office, looking to see what everybody else was doing. The place was busy—smelly cops, overworked, amped up on cheap caffeine and jadedness going about their business.

"I know you don't like to *assume*, but I'm thinking the trace might just be confirmation. My money's on that voice belonging to Marin Shaw." Her thumbs danced around her phone's keypad. "Listen to this, and tell me I'm wrong." Li held her phone up, an old news conference on the screen, the sound on speaker. "This is Shaw."

Foster watched Marin Shaw face news crews at city hall, talking about some controversial ordinance, but the words weren't as important as the voice. That she concentrated on, closing her eyes to focus on its tone, its timbre. It was a short clip. Over in less than twenty seconds.

"Could be," Foster said. "It's similar."

Li nodded. "You have to factor in the prison time. That changes everything." She slid her phone back into her pocket. "And right after she called Leonard, Leonard called Meehan, Franklin, and Valdez. That, partner, is an unmistakable chain. I know you see it too. You're just cautious. I get it. But sometimes, Harri, things are that simple."

"I don't trust simple."

Li leaned back in her chair, shook her head. "I'm aware. I'm also aware that you've got Shaw's name circled in your notepad, waiting on autopsy results. In prep, I've pulled her home address and put together a background profile. I figure we head her way once we know for sure how Leonard died. Until then, we're stuck in a holding pattern."

Foster stared at Li with a newfound respect for her thoroughness and Zen-like approach. She made a noncommittal *hmm*, then turned back to her monitor, not sure what to do. Li was right. Until they knew how Leonard died, they had no idea what tree to shake or if they even needed to shake one. She didn't like the feeling, so when the phone on her desk rang, she lunged for it. "Foster."

"This is Grant. I've taken a preliminary look at Deanna Leonard, because, of course, *alderman*, and why shouldn't they jump the line." She said it facetiously in her usual booming voice. "I found something you're going to want to see."

"What is it?"

"Can you see through the phone, Foster?"

She blinked at the sharp comeback but pressed her lips tight and let a second go. Grant was not one to get on the wrong side of. "On our way." She hung up. "Grant's got something for us to see."

"What is it?" Li asked.

Foster glanced over at her to see the smile on Li's face. She'd obviously heard the conversation that just ended. "Detective Vera Li, ace investigator *and* comedian."

Li flicked her eyebrows, smiled. "Lucky for you I'm playing here all week."

Foster glanced around the autopsy room, with all its steel and scales, hoses, and biohazard bins. Not her favorite place, not anyone's she'd venture to guess, except maybe Grant's. The ME seemed well suited to this dead place. It was nearly 2:00 p.m. by the bold-numbered wall clock. Grant's music of choice today was something new age that sounded like a babbling brook backed up by wind chimes and birds. Foster's eyes landed on the metal autopsy table with Deanna Leonard's body covered in plastic sheeting lying on it. Dr. Olivia Grant stood at the metal pedestal table in green scrubs, her generous lips twisted in irritation, dark eyes peeking over a pair of bifocals. A Black woman in her early sixties, Grant was a formidable ME, one who ran the office like a drill sergeant after several of her predecessors had plunged it into controversy by mismanaging cases, losing bodies, and stacking others like kindling in cold rooms instead of with the respect they deserved. Not on Grant's watch. She had come in like a bulldozer and had kept the motor running.

The room was chilly, but it always was. Foster gripped her notepad. "Dr. Grant. You have something for us?"

"Something we needed to *see*," Li added.

"We'll get to that." She stood up straighter, her gloved hands resting on the table almost like she was protecting Leonard from any final indignities. Foster knew that Grant had an order of how she wanted this encounter to go and was not going to deviate from it. Li knew it, too, so they waited like a couple of soldiers preparing for marching orders. Grant's autopsy room was no place for a power play.

"Suicide's highly unlikely." Grant stepped away from the table to lean against the metal sink that adjoined one of the puke-colored walls. The autopsy room, no matter when she stepped into it, Foster thought, put her in mind of what hell's basement might feel like—echoey, windowless, subterranean, the ultimate point of no return.

"Don't bother taking your coats off. This is going to be short and sweet."

"I wouldn't *think* of taking my coat off in here," Li shot back, smiled. "No offense."

Grant's brows lifted; she stared at Li. "Detective Vera Li."

That was all she said, but she said it in a way that sounded to Foster like Grant was putting Li's name on a list. She cleared her throat, hoping to break the spell. "Highly unlikely?"

"We ran labs and tests like the fate of the world was at stake. Ask me why?"

"I'd rather not," Foster said.

Grant's eyes narrowed. "Political pressure. Politics. *Clout*." She spit the words out like they were expletives. "I've got at least half a dozen bodies waiting to be autopsied. People. With families. That I had to put on hold. You know I don't play favorites in here. This room is the great equalizer, and everyone gets the same respect and attention. But we all have bosses, don't we? It galls me, but I won't belabor the point." She blew a breath out, reined herself back in. "You've got your notepad, grab your pen."

Foster lifted her hand so Grant could see the pen already in it.

"Good."

Leonard's face, empty of life or spirit, looked chalky under the harsh, bright lights, her hair tucked neatly around her ears. This shell of humanity was all that was left of her. Foster moved around the table to the other side to see the entry wound now that it had been cleaned and probed by Grant's instruments. "The round was cause of death?"

"Most definitely," Grant said. "And the gun found in her hand was the gun that killed her." She reached for her report. "Rush job, but striations are consistent. Federal 230 grain FMJ round, if you want to get into the weeds. One round missing." Grant looked up, peered over her glasses again. "But she didn't fire it. There's simply not enough residue to account for that being the case. Rosales hinted at such. Nothing abnormal in toxicology. Fairly healthy woman. Fifty-seven. No cancer. No heart disease. Some minor plaque in the arteries, but you'd expect a certain amount in a woman her age. Evidence of childbirth. She could have lived for decades more."

Foster stepped back from the table. "You said there was something we needed to see?"

"Her x-rays." Grant reached over and grabbed x-rays off a rolling cart and walked them over to a light box, then clipped the hazy pictures to the surface and flicked on the light. Foster made out little disks lodged in a milky area below what she recognized as the lungs. She was no doctor. She looked over at Grant, stymied.

"Dimes," Grant said. "Found in her stomach, along with remnants of a salmon dinner." She padded back over to the table and lifted a small Ziploc bag off the instrument tray, the tinkle of coins echoing in the cavernous space. "Thirty of them, to be precise."

"She swallowed dimes?" Li asked.

"Voluntarily or involuntarily."

Li stared at the bag of shiny coins. "That's . . . odd."

"Thirty pieces of silver," Foster said. "A traitor's payment."

Grant nodded. "Bonus points for Foster. I can't tell you whether she swallowed them before she died or after, but it would likely have been easier for whoever you'll be looking for to have her swallow them rather than try to force them down her throat after the fact."

Li was confused. "Wait. What are we talking about here?"

Grant shook her head. "Looks like somebody missed vacation Bible school. We'll get back to you, Li. I'm pressed for time and have others waiting. Dimes look silver, but they're not really. In case either of you are ever on *Jeopardy!* and it comes up, dimes are copper, actually layers of copper and nickel alloy, seventy-five percent to twenty-five percent ratio. Makeup's probably not significant here, the number could be, but I like to be precise in all things."

"So, she was killed," Foster said, "by someone who stuffed dimes down her throat."

"Or made her swallow them first," Li clarified.

Foster let it sink in, envisioning the enormity of their suspect list, from family to political adversaries to unhappy constituents. Somebody. Somebody who? "Prints on the gun, besides hers?"

"No," Grant said. "And Rosales didn't find any of note in the car. Doesn't appear she drove that many people around in that Mercedes."

Foster scribbled in her pad. "Anything significant about the dimes? Were they all minted the same year or something like that?"

"Random, everyday dimes." Grant studied them. "And because I'm thorough, no prints on the dimes, which weighed sixty-eight grams total, that's about two point four ounces to you two. That's all. My final report should be completed by the end of the day, tomorrow morning at the latest, since now I'm backed up. Anything else?"

Foster slid a look at Li, who shook her head. "No. I think we're good for now."

"Then good luck." Grant stood by Leonard again. "Hope you find the bastard."

They stood staring at their car in the lot, cold and ice boxing it in like an ingot of metal left to become brittle in a frigid wind. "Alderman Deanna Leonard. Judas," Li said. "Thirty pieces of silver. The dimes threw me for a second, but I get it." She shoved her beanie onto her head. "Harsh."

Foster wrapped her scarf around her neck, prepared to push the door open. "More like evil."

# CHAPTER 10

Marin sat across from Zoe in the psychologist's office, feeling small and ashamed of herself. Her heart raced. The potted plants, the earth-toned carpet and walls, the framed art depicting bucolic forests and calming waterfalls she knew were meant to give patients a sense of peace and safety, but it wasn't working for her. Paintings of forests and waterfalls weren't going to assuage her guilt.

Zoe had asked for her to be here, the message relayed by Will in a cold, short phone call the night before. The doctor, he'd said, thought it was a good idea too. There was no doubt she would come. But she'd barely slept agonizing over this, worrying about what she'd say. Marin had been a half hour early for the noon appointment and was sitting nervously with Dr. Wendi Bettleman when Will had dropped Zoe off. And now she waited.

Her daughter was beautiful. Those big green eyes, her light hair streaked with gold. The small dimple on her left cheek. What could she say? What words could erase the things she'd done?

"Zoe?" Dr. Bettleman asked gently, her pen poised over her notes. "You asked your mom to be here. What would you like her to know?"

Marin barely breathed, she couldn't, as she sat in the cushioned chair, her knees shaking, her palms sweating. She wanted her baby back. She needed this to work. She needed Zoe to forgive her, to let her back in. If there was any control in the room, none of it was within Marin's grasp. It was Zoe who would say how things would go.

"I don't know," Zoe answered, her chin to her chest.

Marin didn't want to speak. She didn't want to move too much for fear anything she said, or even a simple crossing of her legs, would upset Zoe, shut her down. Marin waited for Dr. Bettleman, the expert, glancing over at the petite redhead in the slacks and turtleneck sweater, her horn-rimmed glasses pushed to the top of her head, hoping irrationally that she had some magic something that would fix things.

Bettleman watched them intently, noting their silence, the reluctance on Zoe's part to speak, and the fear on Marin's face. She leaned forward, her elbows on her thighs, focusing on the wounded child. "Zoe?"

Tears began to trickle down Zoe's flushed cheeks, each one a dagger to Marin's heart. She'd done this. Not Will, not Deanna Leonard, not the others, *she* had done this.

"You're a criminal," Zoe suddenly blurted out. "That's what they say at school. They call me a criminal too. My mother's a prisoner. Even the teachers think it. I know it. Why couldn't you just be normal, Mom?" Zoe broke down, the crying intensified. "You left me. You did it."

Bettleman's eyes, which felt like they could pierce Marin's skin and dig out all her dark secrets, held Marin's. "Marin? Would you like to respond?"

She'd practiced what she'd say, what explanations she would offer, but in the moment, as she sat here undone by the hurt in her daughter's eyes, words failed her. It was as though she had forgotten what words were. She stared in stunned silence at Zoe's dimple. It had delighted her to no end when Zoe was a baby when she grinned and gurgled and smiled up at her. Thank God, Will had insisted on therapy for Zoe while she was away. It was one thing he'd gotten right. Away. Like she had been on a long trip and not in a cell. Away. Like it had been her choice.

"Marin?" Bettleman said again.

"I forgot what was important. Zoe. So much of my life was like a game of chess. Everything at stake. Right moves, wrong ones. Deals. More deals. Negotiations. Wins. Losses. My job became like a drug, and like a drug, I needed more and more of it. Higher stakes. Trickier deals. So, when they . . ." She caught herself. "So, when *I* made the wrong choice, everything just blew up. It didn't help that I was also drinking. You may not know that part. I hid it very well, or at least I thought I did, and for a long time. I wasn't happy with your father, or he with me. Things had been unhappy for a long time." Her eyes met Zoe's and held on for dear life. "You were important, Zoe, and I lost sight of that." Marin gathered herself up before she broke into a million pieces. "I'm so sorry. But I know sorry isn't enough, is it? No. How could it be?"

For a moment all was silent. Marin could see Zoe draw away from her, look away.

Dr. Bettleman sat back. "Zoe?"

There was nothing, and the nothing broke Marin's heart again. She squeezed her eyes closed. "I love you so much, Zoe. I loved you before I even met you. I love every hair on your head, your dimple, your smile. You. And I always will whether you forgive me or not." She opened her eyes but didn't look at her daughter; instead her eyes fell to her lap, to her wringing hands that had gone ghostly white. "Whatever I have to do, Zoe, to—"

It was as far as she got. Zoe bounded over and drew her into a hug, tears and snuffles, the vise grip, salve to her soul. Marin hugged back, the sting in her throat, her own tears, relief, redemption, a way forward. They talked about everything, like they used to, and with Dr. Bettleman's help, Marin even eased Zoe into the divorce that was coming. Zoe took it all well, and by the end the stone in Marin's chest formed by guilt and remorse felt less deadly.

Marin was smiling when she walked into the lobby of her condo building, a weight lifted off her shoulders. She'd walked the whole way from Bettleman's office, not even feeling the cold. Even the sun had felt brighter somehow, more like April than February now that she and Zoe were going to be all right.

There were two women standing at the front desk with Roy, the lobby attendant, one Black, one Asian, both in dark clothes and sensible shoes. Police. Marin knew it from the way they stood, authoritatively. Marin ducked her head and walked toward the elevator, holding her breath, praying to whatever god was up there that they weren't there for her.

"There she is," she heard Roy say behind her. "Ms. Shaw. Ms. Shaw? These detectives are here to see you."

Marin stopped but didn't turn around, mortified by the callout. She glanced around the lobby, relieved to see none of her neighbors in it. There was just so much shame a person could take. Roy, the poster boy for average, was new on the desk, or at least new to her. She hadn't liked him from the start. He gave off a predatory air that he tried to mask with an ingratiating smile. His eyes never stopped moving, shifty, sizing up. Before she went away, Sam, a retired lineman, had been on the desk. Sam would never have done what Roy just did.

The praying hadn't helped, but she really hadn't expected it to. She'd lost faith in all that so long ago. But the cops were real. She could hear them approaching. The last time people with badges had come to see her, she had been marched out of her city hall office in handcuffs into a waiting unmarked car. Her walk of shame, her downfall, witnessed by everyone, including those who had been just as guilty as she was. It took no time before her stricken face, the shock and defeat on it, was plastered all over the evening news and the morning papers.

Marin tried not to shake as she swallowed over the fearful flutter in her throat. *Police. Again.*

Marin slowly turned around to face two badges held up in front of her. Two badges and two sets of serious dark eyes set in unreadable faces. Marin's gaze drifted down from the badges to the lethal-looking guns at the women's sides. Almost as a Pavlovian response, she began rubbing absently at her right wrist, recalling the feel of the metal handcuffs, the clang and thud of her cell door.

"I'm Detective Foster," the Black cop said. "This is my partner, Detective Li. We'd like to ask you a few questions about Alderman Deanna Leonard."

# CHAPTER 11

Foster watched as Marin Shaw wore a circle into her living room carpet. Not a large circle, though the room could easily have accommodated a decent lap. Shaw's circle was small, she noticed, tight, six feet by eight feet, if she had to estimate, about the size of a prison cell.

Shaw hadn't said a word since the lobby. She'd reluctantly invited them up, away from Roy, the lobby bigmouth, who, with very little prompting, had told them far more than they'd asked about. Even in a nice, high-end place like this, loyalty and discretion couldn't be bought by a couple of twenties slipped into a pocket.

Shaw's fear made Foster uncomfortable. She didn't like being feared. She didn't like the feeling that she could elicit this kind of reaction in a person. But it was the badge, she thought, not her. It was the gun and the badge and the ability to take a person's freedom from them that brought the fear on. Though she'd come to accept it, to separate fear of who she was from the job she did, it still unsettled her. She and Li had decided with a look not to push the questioning, to let Shaw ease into things, at least for a time. The woman had just spent three years in prison being monitored and lined up, told when to sleep, when to wake, when to shower, when to eat. Giving her a little time to calm down wouldn't hurt anyone.

Li padded over to the floor-to-ceiling windows overlooking the lakefront and Navy Pier, its massive Ferris wheel stilled for the season. "Nice view." Small talk. Easing in.

Shaw stopped and faced them. "What's she saying? Deanna?"

Li turned her back to the window, a confused look on her face. "Saying?"

"That's why you're here, isn't it? Some kind of accusation she's made?"

"Alderman Leonard was killed," Foster said. "Tuesday night." She flipped to a fresh page in her notepad. "That's what we're here to talk about."

"It's been all over the news," Li said, incredulity dripping from every word. "Every hour on the hour. And in the papers."

For a moment Foster thought Shaw might faint. The woman went pale; she didn't appear to be breathing much. "Maybe you should sit down?"

Shaw eased down onto the couch. "I haven't been . . ." She began wringing her hands. "I've been reading and listening to music, enjoying the quiet . . . I haven't been following the news, for obvious reasons. Reporters call nonstop, hoping to get an interview. I have no interest in that."

"Roy didn't mention it?" Li said. "He strikes me as a guy who'd jump at the chance."

"He's just the guy at the desk," Shaw said, brushing her off. "I didn't know anything about her death."

"Could you tell us where you were Tuesday night between seven and midnight?" Foster asked.

Silence followed, a silence that stretched for almost a minute until Shaw slowly rose and broke it. "I'd feel more comfortable having my lawyer present." She scanned the apartment as though she might not see it again. "I'll get my coat."

Foster closed her notepad, exchanged a look with Li. "That's your right." She eased down onto the couch; Li joined her there. "But we can do it here. We'll wait for your lawyer." It was a courtesy that cost them nothing.

Relief flooded Shaw's face. "Why?"

Li smiled. "I like your view better than ours."

It looked like Shaw might cry. "Thank you both." She grabbed the receiver on her landline from a side table and moved away to make her call, their eyes tracking her every step and movement. Neither of them wanted Shaw disappearing into another room and coming back with something lethal.

"Something to hide?" Li whispered.

"Nothing wrong with being cautious."

"Hmm. Easy question. Where were you. I'd have answered it."

Foster slid her a look. "No, you wouldn't have."

Li shrugged. "I'd have at least thought about it. Now I'm suspicious."

"You're always suspicious." Foster slipped her phone out of her pocket and began punching numbers. "I'm dialing the number I called from Leonard's phone. Listen out."

She dialed and waited, but no ringing sounded in the apartment where they could hear it.

"Doesn't mean it isn't here," Li said.

Thirty minutes passed in relative silence before there was a brisk knock at the door and Shaw let in a fast-moving white woman in her midforties. They stood. Introduced themselves.

"Charlotte Moore," she said. "Ms. Shaw's lawyer." She dug into her designer briefcase and handed them her business card from a decorative enamel card holder with filigree and delicate songbirds etched into the top. "Let's all take a seat?"

Foster and Li remained standing. "We're good," Foster said. "And we'd like to begin."

Moore moved past them to the couch, set her bag there, then turned back to face them as she twisted out of her designer coat. "I appreciate the courtesy of waiting here instead of inviting my client down to the police station. Decent of you. I'll have to admit, though, I anticipated this visit."

Foster's brows lifted. "Oh?"

"*You* knew about Alderman Leonard, then," Li said.

Moore gave Li a sly smile. "Of course. It's everywhere. But you're not here to talk about what I know." She straightened her blouse cuff. "The papers said she died of an apparent suicide. I saw no reason to share that information with my client. She wasn't involved. This is a difficult time for her, getting her life back on track. She's looking forward, not backward, so I honored that. And Leonard, God rest her tortured soul, was looking back." She held her hands up. "All I'll say."

Foster addressed Marin. "Ms. Leonard's death has now been ruled a homicide. I'll ask the same question I asked a half hour ago. Where were you Tuesday night between seven and midnight?"

Moore put a hand up. "Stop. You think Marin killed Deanna Leonard?"

"You know how this works," Foster said. "Ms. Shaw was a known associate of Alderman Leonard's. They were former colleagues. Friends. That association was complicated. But there's no singling out here. We'll ask the same question of everyone we talk to."

"You're on a fishing expedition. But we'll give it to you. Marin?"

"I was here alone after seven. I'm still not used to being able to walk out of a door and go where I want, so I stay put."

"What about before seven?" Li asked.

Shaw lowered her head. "Dinner with my daughter, and soon-to-be ex-husband."

Foster jotted the information down. "Where?"

"Our house."

Shaw didn't elaborate. They let it go.

"When's the last time you saw Leonard?" Li asked.

Shaw checked with Moore and got a nod. "At my trial."

"So, you'd have no direct knowledge about any current situation she might have been in," Foster said.

Marin shook her head but didn't speak.

"What about emails, texts, phone calls?"

"What reason would I have?"

"Old business," Li said. "Unfinished."

Moore jumped in. "There it is. You guys trying to work up some vendetta as motive. Nice try, but no dice. I'll just say this, save us all some time. My client has nothing to do with Deanna Leonard. There's been no contact. None. If you're looking for suspects, well, good luck narrowing that down, because Leonard wasn't exactly *Mr. Smith Goes to Washington*, okay? This is Chicago. You'll have an easier time counting the politicians who haven't gone to prison than counting the ones that have. I won't rehash Marin's case. If you're interested, look it up, but there was more than one fish caught in that net, but only one made it to the frying pan."

"Reason enough to hold a grudge," Li said, unmoved by Moore's defense. "Three years is a long time for resentments to build up."

Foster watched Shaw. "You didn't contact Leonard. How about any of your other council colleagues? Maybe a few of those other fish caught in the net?"

"Nope," Moore said. "Who she talks to is her business now. Unless you have some good reason why it isn't?"

Marin looked over at Charlotte. "I can answer. I haven't had any contact with anyone. All that's behind me now."

Charlotte grinned. "See? My client is uninvolved. In summary, she was here alone Tuesday night. Never left her apartment. She hadn't set eyes on the woman in years, and she hasn't spoken to anyone else since her release. End of story. And we're done."

Foster studied Shaw. "Do you have a cell phone, Ms. Shaw?"

"I haven't needed one in years."

"But you have one," Li said. "Practically everyone does."

"Somewhere. Maybe."

"Did you make any phone calls Tuesday night?" Foster asked.

A beat passed. "I didn't."

Foster watched Shaw breathe uneasily around the lie she'd just told her. "Thanks for your time. We'll be in touch."

"Nuh-uh," Moore said. "Any touching from here on out goes through me." She ushered them to the door. "My take? Leonard was a real operator. Shrewd. Maybe she just got outplayed. Whatever it turns out to be, Marin Shaw's the wrong tree you're barking up."

"You knew Leonard personally?" Foster asked.

Moore appeared surprised by the question. "Met her once or twice. Social events. She knew how to work a room, let me just say that. Knew everybody and everybody knew her. A little shady. You know the type."

"One of the fish that got away?"

Moore offered a slight grin. "I'm not at liberty to say."

Li buttoned her coat. "You and Ms. Shaw seem to be close."

Moore shrugged, then opened the door to show them out. "Marin and I are old friends, so if you guys are even thinking about roping her into Leonard's murder, you can forget it. I guarantee you, CPD doesn't want me on its case. I'm a shark, and I bite hard. Good day, ladies."

The door closed behind them with a resounding *get lost*.

"Lawyers are special, aren't they?" Li said, her low voice carrying in the empty, narrow hallway.

"*Special*'s not the right word."

"Well? The phone was a bust, but you heard her up close."

Foster pushed down for the elevator, then plucked her hat from her pocket and put it on. "One deflection. One lie. Not needing a cell phone and not having one? Two different things. And she made at least one call Tuesday night." They stepped into the elevator car. "Because it was her voice on the other end of Leonard's phone."

Li clapped her hands together. "Yes. And *her* call prompted the ones Leonard made to Meehan, Valdez, and Franklin. I smell connections. Let's start with Meehan."

"Why him?"

"Because I like a challenge."

Foster inhaled, then blew the breath out slowly, getting ready to meet the cold. "Then city hall, here we come."

# CHAPTER 12

Chicago's city hall at 121 N. LaSalle sat like a child's wooden block plopped down in the middle of a long-running Monopoly game. The city center's high-rise and low-rise buildings of steel and brick surrounded it on a tight, neat grid bordered by Randolph, Clark, LaSalle, and Washington streets, each one clogged half the day with Yellow cabs, cars and Ubers, buses, Divvy bikes in narrow bike lanes, double-parked FedEx and UPS trucks, delivery vans, and city vehicles defiantly left in no-parking zones with hazard lights flashing, all but daring city tow trucks to haul them away.

Given city hall's eleven stories of Greek Revival ostentatiousness, Foster had pegged the building as the place where city bureaucracy ran amok from the top floor to the bottom, from the city side on the west to the county's on the east. The office of the mayor on the fifth floor was the axis in the wheel that kept the whole jumbled, inefficient machine lumbering along, top heavy, reactive, and often tone deaf. The golden doors, the marble walls, the ornate arches, and the gold filigree accents prettied it up, but walking into city hall with business to get done was like voluntarily offering yourself up to a running woodchipper.

There were news crews planted outside the building, all the affiliate channels claiming their tiny patch of sidewalk. A murdered alderman in a town where half the population would gladly dispatch their own city representative for a decent tax break and a year-round parking pass was media fodder of the highest order. Foster recognized the reporters, all of whom had hounded CPD and her many times for information not for public consumption. Notable among them was Soren Hastrup, the irascible reporter from channel 5, who always seemed to be front and center on any big story. Tall, bespectacled, a graying goatee, but with the rabidity of a cub reporter half his age out to make a name for himself, Hastrup darted over, mic in hand, beckoning excitedly for his saggy-panted cameraman to follow. "Detective Foster. You here on the Leonard case? What do you know? We're hearing it was suicide, so why're you on this? Was it something else? A robbery maybe? A targeted hit? Any suspects? Can I get a statement?"

The other reporters on the street, not to be outdone or scooped by Hastrup, rushed to join him. If she and Li didn't disengage quickly, they were going to be caught in the middle of a scrum and end up on the evening news. Foster sidestepped Hastrup and his cameraman, keeping an eye on the other reporters racing over, mics and cameras and running feet threatening a trap she and her partner didn't have time for.

"Any details on how she was found? Who found her? Can I get a name?" Hastrup shoved his mic in Foster's face, but the withering look she gave him quickly compelled him to draw it back, though Hastrup continued to pepper her with questions. "Or some kind of domestic situation? You going in to see the mayor? Were you two summoned? What's going on?"

By now all the reporters had made it over. Foster barreled past them, following Li, and the two slipped inside the building without a word to Hastrup or anyone else.

Li looked over at Foster, smiling. "Not even a 'no comment'?"

Foster pulled off her gloves and stuck them in her coat pocket. "It was implied, I think." They badged their way up past the cops on duty in the lobby; she and Li badged again on two for the PO stationed in the hall outside the aldermanic suites before being allowed into Meehan's inner sanctum. There was another cop sitting at a metal desk across from Meehan's secretary.

Li leaned over to whisper in Foster's ear. "Somebody stepped up security."

Standing at the secretary's desk, Foster could hear Meehan's booming voice as he tap-danced with someone on the phone. They'd called ahead to arrange the time. Meehan knew they were here, yet it took five minutes before he ended his call and appeared in the doorway of his office, larger than life, in an expensive blue suit, yellow tie, and clean white shirt, freshly shaved and as fastidiously dressed as a Vegas mobster. Foster doubted Meehan would have appreciated the comparison.

"Detectives, come in. Sorry to keep you waiting." They followed him in. "Can Helen get you anything? Coffee?"

They both declined the offer, so Helen, a sturdy white woman in a powder-blue sweater set who appeared to be in her late fifties, glasses hanging from a bejeweled chain around her neck, backed out smiling, closing the door to leave them to it.

"Have a seat." Meehan was loud, gregarious, confident, his wide face open yet closed at the same time. An odd trick. Foster got a whiff of strong aftershave, something mixed with cloves. "Busy day, like always. Harder today for our loss, for sure. I just can't believe what happened. This city, huh? Tragic. Just tragic. Deanna Leonard was such a force of nature."

"You knew her well?" Foster asked.

"I knew her okay. As good as you can know somebody you work with, huh? Sit. Sit."

She and Li sat in the two office chairs facing Meehan's big desk, which was neat and orderly, meticulously appointed. Foster wondered if it was Meehan's or Helen's doing.

The office was as she would have expected of a career politician, one ensconced on his power perch for decades. There were honorary plaques and awards, photographs with celebrities and politicians, flags and medals in frames all along the shelves and on side tables. Meehan was an important man, he knew it, and he wanted everyone else to know it too. His big chair creaked just a bit when he eased down into it, the leather exhaling with a prolonged hiss as if to protest the assault. Foster scanned the room again, finding framed photographs of Meehan with the last four mayors, which broadcast a message to whoever got in this far that mayors come and go, but John "Cubby" Meehan would always be here.

"News update now says Deanna was killed? Unbelievable. I don't know if that's any better than suicide, which they reported first. I mean, one way or the other, it's awful, awful news. What was it, a carjacking? Robbery of some kind? You know, this city really is a dangerous place these days." He pointed a scolding finger. "Not enough police. And a tight budget that keeps us from adding more on. You guys are heroes in my book, though. You got my respect. Big time. So, how can I help Chicago's finest? You're talking to all the council members, are you?" He folded his hands on his desk and looked at them eagerly.

Foster let a moment go so the room could quiet. "Did you work closely with Alderman Leonard?"

Meehan adjusted in the chair. "I don't know what you mean about close. We sat on a few committees together. Cosigned on a few things. I had no problems with her. You think what happened had something to do with the job?"

"She called you the night she was killed," Foster said. "Did she say anything about what she was doing? What her plans were?"

"Maybe she was meeting someone," Li added. "Or working late, which might explain why she was in that garage?"

"Nothing like that. She called about the agenda for an upcoming housing meeting. We compared notes, agreed on a couple of line items, and that was it."

Foster's eyes swept over him, her appraisal thorough. "Who else is on the Housing Committee?" She was thinking about Valdez and Franklin.

"We got about twenty on it. You want me to name everybody? Why's that important to this?"

"Leonard might have discussed housing business with someone else other than you," Li said. "Or something else."

Foster pressed. "Would it be possible for us to get a list of members?"

Meehan's eyes narrowed, and he took a moment to assess them. "I don't think I like the angle you're taking. Why are you two looking here for answers instead of out there where the thugs are?"

Foster could tell Meehan wasn't a man who rattled easily, but he looked a little wary. "Is that a no on the list?"

He took a moment, his eyes gliding from Li to Foster and back, then called out to his secretary. "Helen?"

The door opened, and Helen popped her head in.

"Print out a list of Housing Committee members for the detectives, please," Meehan said. "They'll get it on the way out." Helen disappeared again. Meehan smiled at them. "There you have it."

"So, Leonard called you Tuesday to talk about a housing agenda," Foster said.

"Unexciting, but yeah. But now, out of respect, of course, we'll definitely cancel that meeting."

Meehan grinned back at them, cunning playing in his eyes as though he were contemplating a chess move or plotting a military maneuver.

"Where were you Tuesday night when Leonard called you?" Foster asked.

Meehan's brows lifted. "That sounds like a question you'd ask a suspect." A beat passed. "Are you saying I'm a suspect?"

"No." Their eyes locked. "You know how this goes, Alderman. We're establishing a timeline. Nothing personal. We'll ask Helen, too, if it'd make you feel better."

Meehan thought about it, ever the cautious man, then decided to answer. "I took the call in the car on my way home."

"You drive yourself?" Li asked.

"I have a driver. Tony."

"We'll need his last name and number, if you don't mind," Li said.

Meehan scowled, but picked up his cell phone and jotted down a name and number on a piece of City of Chicago notepaper and slid it across the desk to Li. "I do know how this works, but it doesn't mean I have to like it. You guys want to bark up the wrong tree, that's your business, but you're wasting your time. I didn't get this far being stupid."

"No, sir," Foster said. "You didn't. What'd you do when you got home?"

He sat back, exhaled. "I had dinner, spent time with my wife and kid, then went to bed like a normal person. Lights out about eleven, before you ask. You can check with my wife, but I don't want cops talking to my kid."

He stood, signaling that he was done talking; the jovial mood he'd started with had long since gone. Now Meehan seemed tense and hard and humorless. "You got all you need here."

They stood, prepared to leave. Home alone with his wife and kid, Foster thought, and the name and number of Meehan's driver. All neat and tidy. Easy to check. Easy to manipulate. They had nothing connecting him to Leonard's death—he was just their first stop—but still she sensed something in his demeanor, something that didn't smell quite right. "One last question," she said. "Did Alderman Leonard have any enemies on the council? Rivals. Or off it, as far as you knew?"

"She could be tough, but she got along with everybody. There was no bad blood or feuds I knew about. You guys ever think about checking closer to home?" The smile was back, the cunning. "I don't want to tell you how to do your jobs, but if you're not looking at random killing here, nobody hates you enough to kill you more than somebody close."

Foster studied the big man as he stood in his $1,500 suit and cloying aftershave and mansplained Investigative Practices 101 to them. "Oh?" she said.

"Yeah, Deanna didn't talk a lot about her personal life, but she did mention the son. I got the impression he was a real pain in her ass. Underachiever. Not exactly setting the world on fire, and it bugged her big time. Maybe that bubbled up."

Foster didn't check with Li but didn't have to. There was no way Li was taking Meehan's attempts to direct their investigation any better than she was taking them. She waited for Li, curious as to how she would handle it. Would she bristle back or barrel on to get the whole thing over with? She was still learning a lot of Li's tells and tendencies, and Li was doing the same with her, but she had a good idea how it'd go, and stood waiting for confirmation.

"Thanks," Li said, coldness dripping from the word. "I'm curious. Leonard called you around seven. That's after normal business hours, isn't it? This place closes down tight earlier than that. City hours."

Foster smiled. She'd been right about Li.

"And Leonard had your cell number, which you picked up. Hints at a certain level of familiarity."

Meehan's blue eyes hardened. "First off, aldermen are always on the clock. Like you guys. And Deanna wasn't the only one on the council with my number. Bottom line, this is a tragic situation. Nothing to do with me. We'll have to put together a nice memorial service for Deanna. Thank her for all her hard work and dedication to the city. Now, if you'll excuse me? Helen."

The office door popped open, and there Helen stood with a couple of printouts. She handed one to Foster, one to Li. Foster held up a finger, indicating they'd need one more minute, and Helen eased out again, shutting the door.

"Just one more minute of your time," she said. "Have you had any contact with Marin Shaw recently? Or know if Leonard had?"

Meehan went a deeper shade of red. The smile long gone now. "Shaw? Why would we?"

Li folded the printout into halves, her eyes on Meehan's reddening face. "Your name was batted around in that fed probe she got caught up in. Maybe Shaw wanted to talk about it. Clear the air."

"I wouldn't know. And I'd be very careful, Detective, about what you're trying to say. Very careful. Marin Shaw is a convicted felon, and I would think she and you two would have more important things to concern yourselves with right now. Like finding the murderer of one of the city's public servants?" He opened the door. "Or I can call and talk to your superintendent about it?"

Foster stared at him, taking full measure. "Thanks for your time."

Meehan padded over to his desk. "Just a second." Reaching into the top drawer, his megawatt smile back and blinding. He plucked up two black pens, handing one to each of them. Meehan had his name, office number, and political slogan written on the side: *John "Cubby" Meehan, Chicago through and through, fighting for you!* "For the road, as they say." He then shook their hands like he was stumping for votes at a Rotary Club picnic. "If you have any other questions you think I may be able to answer, call me. My door's always open. Helen, please show these hardworking detectives out."

They nodded at the cop at the desk in the outer office as they passed him, then stopped at the other cop's desk in the hall, letting all Meehan's nothing settle in.

"See ya got a pen," the cop said, his receding hairline, paunch, and world-weary expression broadcasting that he was on the back slope of a long career. "And not much else by the look on your faces."

"He always like that?" Li asked.

The cop, Vaughn, by the brass nameplate on his uniform blouse, nodded. "All day, every day."

"Uptick in blue shirts," Li commented, noting the cop inside by Meehan's door.

"Big guy, big noise. Friends in high places." Vaughn smirked. "Guess he ain't taking no chances."

They walked away and left Vaughn to it. Foster checked her printout, running her finger down the list of the twenty names. Li tucked hers into her pocket. One set of eyes was sufficient. Foster's head popped up. "Leonard's here. Franklin and Valdez aren't."

They padded toward the elevators. "So, maybe Leonard didn't call the three of them to talk about housing. Coincidentally, after getting a call from the just-released-from-prison Marin Shaw."

"Maybe."

Foster stared at the cheap Meehan pen with the hokey slogan written on the side. Li did the same. "What a load of bull crap," Li said.

"Which part?" Foster asked.

Li twirled the pen in her long fingers. "Everything after 'have a seat.'"

Foster punched the down button, waiting at the elevators with a handful of city hall staff moving from floor to floor. "We'll have to prove it." She tossed Meehan's pen in a marble trash receptacle.

"Story of our lives," Li answered, tossing her pen in after Foster's.

# CHAPTER 13

"First, Meehan's crooked, but he don't strike me as being a killer. He might hire one, though," Detective Al Symansky, their resident curmudgeon, announced to the team as they sat huddled around the little information they had so far. Foster had set up her whiteboard, but they hadn't yet made any connections. Leonard's photo was tacked to the board, along with the times they had so far and the sequence of the calls she'd received and made, but they were still waiting for the in-and-out footage from the garage, the city cam captures from the streets surrounding it around the time of death, and a lead to pull at.

The office was cold, the heat wonky as always, but only Lonergan sat with his parka on, complaining nonstop, as though someone had dropped his bulky frame into the middle of the Alaskan tundra. Foster and Lonergan had had a rocky start, and four months in, after partnering for a time, then being reassigned to others, there was some lingering prickliness on both their parts. But she prided herself on being able to work with anyone, even though he had declared himself an "old-school cop" and appeared resentful of working with female cops, especially female cops of color, and definitely female cops of color who refused to sign off on his good-old-boy crap and let him run it. They were cordial. Foster was used to working with cops she didn't mesh with, Lonergan too. It was a big department, more than eleven thousand sworn officers at last count. You weren't going to gel with every last one. Besides, they weren't being paid to be tailgating buddies; they were paid to do a job, so she took cordiality as a win.

Foster stepped over to the board. Running cases this way worked for her, though it hadn't been how Bigelow, Lonergan, Kelley, or the others had done it before. It helped her to see the leads laid out in black and white, to be able to visualize the timeline. She circled Marin Shaw's name. "Home alone Tuesday night." Then Meehan's. "Home alone Tuesday night." She pointed the marker at Leonard's photo. "Killed Tuesday night. Our choices." She scribbled on the board. "Random. Familiar. Professional. Personal." She turned to the group. "Motives."

Bigelow spoke up, his beefy hands warming on a coffee mug. "I vote personal, and I vote for that bastard Parker. He's got to be looking at some insurance payout right about now."

Kelley leaned his lanky body back in his squeaky chair, his arms crossed over his chest. "Sounds like you have something against the guy."

Bigelow squinted over at him. "Where'd you get that?"

"I have eyes, and ears."

"Yeah? Well, keep them over on your side of the office."

Symansky held up his arms. "Children, children, can we get through this? Or are we forgetting the heat that's waitin' for us out there? We're not gonna get a lot of rope on this, okay?" He looked over at Griffin's closed door. "I've heard rumblings, and they ain't happy ones. And we all know how this is gonna go." He ticked it off on his fingers. "Mayor bites the superintendent's ass, he bites the asses of the brass, they bite Griffin's ass, and the boss bites our asses. Clock's tickin' on that first chomp."

Kelley nodded. "Amen, brother."

"News is calling it murder now," Li said. "So game's on."

Foster sighed. "Especially with Hastrup sniffing around."

Li studied the board. "The phone calls are important. Have to be. Shaw gets out, she calls Leonard? Why? And whatever they talked about, it worried Leonard enough that she called the others."

Foster circled the names Valdez, Meehan, and Franklin, then dragged a line from their name bubbles over to Marin Shaw's. "We talked to Meehan already. Got nothing. Valdez and Franklin weren't in their offices, and Li and I haven't been able to reach them by phone yet. Either we've just been incredibly unlucky, or they're avoiding us."

"Can't blame them for lying low," Lonergan said. "One of theirs gets taken out. They don't know what this is yet, any more than we do. Makes sense, though, to start inside out."

Lonergan slid a look toward Bigelow. "Anything with the daughter? Or did Leonard have another guy she was seeing? Maybe that went bad."

Bigelow came back. "Since when's going out with a person a crime? And who told you, anyway?"

Lonergan smirked. "Your voice carries, man. And cop ears are good."

Bigelow flipped him the bird. "Carry this, then."

"The coins down Leonard's throat," Li said, "kind of puts us on a different level."

Foster turned back to the board and underlined *30 DIMES*.

Symansky rolled his eyes. "So now we got to think biblical? Figure out who Leonard mighta cut off at the knees? And her being an *alderman*? That's gonna be like runnin' down one clown out of a whole circus of 'em. I hate the sick ones."

"I'm with you, Al. So, we take it like we take all of them. By the numbers. Step by step." Foster flicked a look at Lonergan. "Inside out. Alibis. Timelines. We try to find out what Leonard was into." She checked her watch, feeling the long day take its toll. It was just after five. There was nothing else they could do tonight. She put the marker down. "I'll give the boss a quick report, then we hit it again in the morning, all right with everybody?" She got no complaints. She turned to her partner. "Li? Anything?"

Li stood, stretched her back. She had a cat-drowning kid to get back to. "Sounds like a plan."

The group dispersed, and she and Li briefed the boss. At change of shift, she made one last stop at the coffeepot and sink, where she rinsed out her CPD mug, her mind still on Leonard and the dimes. It was an odd add, overly dramatic and unnecessary, in her mind. And she hoped it was a one-off. There were fifty aldermen in the city. If someone out there was going after all of them, they were going to have a problem.

She noticed then, in the trash bin by the sink, a half-dead plant in a small flowerpot, more brown leaves than green ones. It hadn't been there earlier. She hadn't noticed it the entire day, though she'd passed the coffeepot, the sink, and the bin several times. Who'd thrown it away? After lifting the plant out, she set it on the short counter and pressed her fingers into the parched dirt. She then filled her mug with water from the tap and slowly poured the water into the pot, watching as it soaked the dirt. After she'd plucked away the dead leaves, there were very few viable ones left on the scraggly limbs. She was no gardener. She didn't know the first thing about plants or flowers, about what made them grow or what didn't. But she knew that half-dead wasn't dead.

Foster gave the plant another thorough drink, then carried it back to her desk and set it on a leftover Burger King napkin in case the pot leaked. She took one last look at the whiteboard, grabbed her things, and went home.

A half hour later, Foster stepped through her front door into a silent house, dropping her bag on the table, the echo of her activity bouncing off stark white walls that hadn't a single photograph, painting, or adornment. There was a chair by the front window that faced the street, an empty coffee table, a floor lamp, carpet, and a whiteboard on a stand, much like the one at work.

She'd lived here for five years, and that was as much as she cared about the space. But the house wasn't what mattered or the things inside. It was the location. The tree outside. Her son had breathed his last breath leaning against it, thanks to Terrell Willem.

Everything sane told her that she should never want to see the tree again, yet she had bought the house overlooking it. Now she watched the tree get covered in snow and ice in winter, come to life in spring, shade the lawn in summer, and go to sleep again in fall. It was Reg's tree.

So, she lived with the sound of gunshots in the night, the revved motorcycle engines, dogs barking incessantly. There were arguing neighbors next door whom she hadn't met and quiet retirees down the block who tended their lawns and painted their houses every spring. The smell of weed wafted out of windows somewhere close. It was difficult being a cop here, deciding which battles to fight and which ones to let go. There were other places she could go, easier places, but nowhere else she could be.

She plucked a blue marble out of a box of hundreds and dropped it into the tall glass vase sitting outside the kitchen she rarely used. One marble per day. At the end. Every day since Reg's death. There would come a day when she wouldn't need to add another marble or live here watching a tree that couldn't care less if she lived or died. One day something would happen, and she would find a place somewhere else. Maybe she'd even be able to let Terrell Willem go. Someday.

She grabbed an apple from the refrigerator. There were three more inside, along with a half gallon of milk, a pint of orange juice, a premade salad from the local grocery store, and a box of cornflakes. It was enough. Nothing inside required any great commitment or time expense. Just enough to feed a shadow life. But she didn't brood over it. It was what it was. Unpacking her bag, getting her notes out, she began to set up her board, jotting down alibis, timelines, details like she had at the office with the team. When everything was up, when she could see it all in front of her, she stepped back to study the setup, to see if anything popped out at her that hadn't before. Deanna Leonard's death was her top priority now. A violent death in a violent town, but with a kink. Thirty pieces of silver.

Foster drew a circle around Marin Shaw's name and added a question mark, then finished her apple.

# CHAPTER 14

"I can stay if you want," Emelda Rodriguez told Alderman George Valdez as she locked up her desk for the night. "If there's something important you need to get out?"

Valdez hadn't slept or eaten since news of Deanna Leonard's death hit. He'd known the woman, not well but well enough. He knew what she knew—they were chained to a bloodthirsty sociopath—and they'd crossed him to his face over a tomahawk steak and expensive scotch. The *what if*s and the *could he really*s had been spinning around in his brain since then, and he had no idea where to turn, what move to make to protect himself. Could he go back to Meehan and smooth things over? Should he follow through and break ties, go to the feds? If he made the wrong move, he was as good as dead. He had known right away it hadn't been suicide, so when the news was updated, when homicide was confirmed, a knowing chill had gone through him. Deanna had been defiant at Dino's, as defiant as he had been. Hours later she's dead?

He checked his watch. "No, Emelda. It's already past six. I'll be here for at least another hour. Go home to your family. See you in the morning."

"All right, then. Don't stay too late. Sheila will worry. See you in the morning." Her car was parked right out front of the small storefront aldermanic office in the heart of Little Village, Valdez's ward on the Southwest Side. She gave him a playful wink. "I'll bring conchas."

He chuckled. "The chocolate ones, huh?"

"Of course. I know they're your favorite. Night."

He watched as she left, got into her car, and drove away. Now alone in the office, only the lights in back on, he returned to his work, worn down to the bone with guilt and fear and shame. He'd betrayed the trust of his people, his own ideals, by aligning himself with Meehan. His wife, Sheila. Just the thought of her, how crushed she would be, so disappointed in him. His children. What would they think of him? But there were things he could do. He could make good, at least a little, so that when everything came out, and it always did, they would see that he'd tried to make things right. He'd protected the money he'd gotten. It was offshore, waiting, secure, and it was for Sheila and the kids if the feds came calling, if he couldn't fix things before they did. The fear, the sinking feeling in the pit of his gut, was that Meehan had cards to play and a hand in Deanna's death. That it was a solution and a message to him. Was he smart enough to outmaneuver the man? Could he think three moves ahead in this twisted chess match he'd gotten himself in?

He paced the floor for a long time, his button-down shirt soaked at the pits though it was February. Valdez thought it through. The possible moves. The consequences. His chances for not only political survival but real survival, and he couldn't believe it had gotten to this point. That he'd sunk this low and gotten in so deep.

He turned at the knock at the door to see a dark figure standing on the other side of the glass, the person's face hidden by a hat with a wide brim. When had the bulb over the door burned out? He'd have Emelda get someone to change it in the morning. Valdez flicked a look at his watch in the soft light of his desk lamp. Nearly eight. Lost in thought, he'd stayed past his time and needed to get home.

"We're closed, my friend," Valdez called out. "Office opens tomorrow at nine."

The person knocked again. In no hurry it seemed. Persistent, though. The person was dressed in dark clothing, nondescript, a long dark coat. Valdez couldn't discern gender or race. But something looked familiar. The height. The thin frame. He stood in front of his desk, cast a look at the phone sitting there. He repeated what he'd said, in Spanish this time and a little louder so the person could hear. The figure didn't move. Strangely familiar. But it was the stillness of the person that flooded Valdez's sweating body with alarm and sent a bolt of ice down his spine. Danger. He felt it in his chest. It was like a fist pounding out an ominous beat. Valdez padded back around the desk. No time for the phone. He kept a gun in a lockbox in the bottom drawer. He had enemies. This was a tough neighborhood. Not everyone respected his office or liked him.

It was then that he heard the scrape of a key in the lock. The sound undid him. His brain began to cycle. Who had a key to his office except him and Emelda? Diaz, the maintenance guy, and the building manager, Easterly. "Diaz?" Valdez called just as the door eased open and the person stepped inside. He would never get to the drawer or the lockbox, Valdez knew it. The phone. If he could get to it. He reeled and lunged for the receiver. He needed the police. Grabbing the receiver up, he got as far as *nine one* before the person was on him. He turned to fight, to stand his ground, but only got halfway around before he felt a searing pain in his side that doubled him over and stole his breath. Valdez watched in horror as his shirt, the one his wife had given him last Father's Day with his fancy monogram on the cuffs, flooded with blood. His blood. White light danced behind his eyelids as shock overtook him. A million images flashed before him—his kids, his wife, his mother, Deanna, Meehan, Dino's, his first Holy Communion, his long-dead father, his sisters, their kids, his first car, a used 1994 Ford Taurus.

He dropped to his knees. "Stop," he pleaded. "Please."

The stranger's knife plunged into his back, then plunged again. Valdez could literally hear his lungs collapse. He was going to die. Here. For what? For money? For greed? For *things*? He wanted his wife, his mother. He wanted to live and atone and see his kids grow. Though his eyes could no longer focus, he could sense the stranger move away from him as Valdez toppled over onto his back, helpless. He didn't feel anything now that he knew he was going. This death wasn't peaceful, like others. It was . . . he couldn't find the word. He was cold. Conchas. The chocolate ones flashed behind his eyelids. The beating of his heart sounded like a runaway freight train. There was a tug at his pockets as his vision faded. What was that awful gurgling sound? Sheila, his mother, his kids seemed so very far away now. They would be gone in a moment, or at least he would be. After a prayer he muttered to God so that his sins would be forgiven, he recited his full name for the last time, knowing that his parish priest would likely be the next one to utter it.

"Jorge Guillermo Flores Valdez."

# CHAPTER 15

The soul food restaurant three blocks from the station had a small motel in back and a parking lot just off the street. It was close enough to the office that it got a fair amount of cop traffic all hours of the day, dining in or picking up carryout orders, which didn't appear to bother the regular clientele, made up mostly of sociable retirees and snappily dressed octogenarians who came in to eat but also to share a meal with friends and longtime staff, boldly claiming their regular tables to pass the time over smothered pork chops or hot bowls of grits and gravy before getting on with their day. Even the weather, midthirties this morning with a promise of snow flurries by noon, hadn't kept them away.

Foster and Li sat at a table off to the side against the rear wall, their heavy coats slung over the backs of their wooden chairs, real coffee in sturdy mugs steaming in front of them, menus open. The chatter around the room was lively. No one paid them any attention. Foster glanced around the dining room, noting who was sitting where, picking up bits of conversation, checking that all was well. She sipped her coffee, having decided on a simple omelet with sausage on the side. The waiter, Lewis, had set a plate of hot biscuits on the table, and Li was already on her second one. The first one she had downed straight. The one in her mouth now she'd dabbed with strawberry jam and butter.

"Leonard had a lot of things going on," Foster said, consulting the notes she'd made overnight. Instead of sleep, or a lot of it, she'd dug into Deanna Leonard's career looking for anyone, other than Marin Shaw, who might have wanted her dead. "She had a hand in starting up an arts center and a medical clinic in her ward. There were food drives and job fairs, too, that she organized regularly. By all outward appearances she was doing the right things for the right reasons. One interesting thing. Her son was involved in that arts center, though his exact role was kind of vague. There was some trouble with that. It folded a couple years in. Financial difficulties it looks like. But Aaron Parker's name keeps popping up when the trouble does. Maybe there's something there we can pull on."

"No good deed goes unpunished," Li said, wiping sticky fingers on a white paper napkin.

"Then there's that fed probe that swept Shaw up. It had to do with zoning. They found Shaw guilty of accepting bribes for helping to loosen zoning restrictions for businesses wanting into a particular area, ones not zoned for whatever it was they were peddling."

"You have to grease the palms," Li quipped. "Or the city's goody truck stays away."

"And something like that doesn't happen unilaterally. Several wards were targeted for rezoning. Want three guesses which wards were on the list?"

Li slid the last bit of biscuit into her mouth, her brows lifted. "I think I can make the leap."

Foster took a sip of coffee, needing the caffeine. "Like Moore said, Shaw wasn't the only fish caught in the net, she was just the only one to hit the skillet."

Li eyed Foster's notepad. "You got all that last night?"

"I gave it a couple hours."

"More than a couple, it seems. Know what I did?" Li didn't wait for Foster to answer. "I had a talk with Wynton about how it's not okay to drown cats."

Foster's mug stopped halfway to her mouth. "A talk? He's two."

"Never too early. I'm thinking, he was just playing with the cat. Oh no. Want to know what he told me?"

"I'm not sure."

"He said to me, his mother, but also a sworn police officer with arrest powers, that he was not *playing* with the cat, that he was *punishing* the cat for scratching him. Only I didn't see a scratch on him anywhere. Then he gives me this Damien look."

"Damien look?"

Li's face went demonic, a blank stare, stern set of her jaw, malevolence incarnate; then it was gone in a flash. "Damien look." She grabbed another biscuit. "I'm eating my feelings. I've got a demon child living in my house. Don't judge me."

Foster closed her notepad, took a deep breath. "When Reg was two, he managed to scoop the goldfish out of the bowl, walk it to the toilet, and flush it. We were at work, my ex-husband and me. The babysitter had a fit. When I asked Reg about it later, he told me the goldfish was lonely and he was sending it back to the ocean to live with the other goldfish." She pushed her menu away, smiled slightly, the memory both sweet and painful. "Circle of life? In your case, the lying part . . ." Foster left it there, playing with her partner just a little. "But, again, he's only two."

Li's mouth hung open. "I'm ordering pancakes."

Foster didn't think the pancakes were going to work, but that was Li's decision. "We need to talk to Shaw again. We'll have footage this morning. If we see her or her car anywhere on it . . ."

"We need to check her condo too," Li said. "Garage, exit doors, time stamps. If she left the building, we'll know. But something's been bugging me. If Leonard knew she'd crossed Shaw, why would she agree to meet her? And in a dark, deserted garage no less. Friend or no friend, she'd have to be nuts. I mean, she was worried enough to bring her gun with her."

"We could be wrong," Foster said. "Maybe Shaw *has* put the past behind her. Maybe her call wasn't what it looks like. Maybe we won't find her car on any of that footage. Doesn't mean she wasn't there, does it? She could easily have rented one, borrowed one, or hired an Uber. Someone could be in this with her, and they drove." Foster reached for her phone, sent a quick email. "I'm pushing on the street-camera dump at least. We might get lucky." She glanced over at Li. "How fast can you eat pancakes?"

Foster watched Lewis approach. A tall white man in a bow tie and half apron who'd worked at the restaurant for many years. "Morning, Detectives. What can I get you both this fine mornin'?" His Louisiana drawl was as warm and buttery as the biscuits sitting on their table. "The fried catfish and grits is lookin' mighty fine back there."

Li's hand went up like a star pupil in school. "Pancakes, please."

Foster's phone rang. She hoped it was an answer to her urgent email. Lewis stood by, used to cops in the place. "Uh-oh, hold up."

Foster answered, listened. "We'll be right there."

Li was already moving. She'd laid a napkin on the table and was placing the rest of the biscuits from the basket in it to take away. "Rain check, Lewis. We gotta bounce."

Foster placed a twenty-dollar bill on the table for the biscuits, and Li slid a ten out of her pocket for Lewis, then grabbed her coat. Breakfast on the run.

"Who's dead?" Li asked as they pushed out the door to the street, a biting cold hitting them in the face like a barrage of metal spikes.

"Alderman George Valdez."

"*What?*" They slid into the car and buckled in, Li stowing her napkin of biscuits beside her. "Leonard, Valdez, Shaw, Franklin, and Meehan. You think somebody's working off a list?"

Foster pulled out into traffic, made a U-turn, and sped down State Street. "Don't even think it."

———

Valdez's ward office was in Little Village, a predominantly Latino neighborhood on the Southwest Side. It was housed in an old storefront wedged between an H&R Block pop-up office and a T-Mobile store, a block from the landmark Little Village arch designated as the gateway to the Mexican capital of the Midwest.

The crowd that had gathered outside in the cold stood quiet, solemn, their respect for the man's passing obvious. That solemnity was not mirrored in the frenzied attention paid by the news reporters and cameramen who stood beside them, jockeying for sound bites from passing CPD personnel, a money shot of the body being carried out, or an exclusive statement from somebody authorized to give one in time for the midday news.

Foster scanned the crowd. There he was. Hastrup. He gave her a single nod, a knowing grin on his face. Hastrup smelled a good story, and he was coming after it. "Great," she muttered.

Li looked where Foster was looking, saw Hastrup, and sighed resignedly. "He's *everywhere*."

They badged their way into the cramped space crowded with police. Strangely the office smelled of sweet pastries and strong Mexican coffee, and not so strangely blood.

Vibrant Mexican artwork was tacked up on the walls, alongside political posters with Valdez's face all over them. There were also city maps with ward boundaries clearly marked, and others that showed garbage pickup schedules. Along the back wall, a big Chicago flag hung next to a Mexican flag. Bookshelves held various pamphlets on city programs for seniors, homeowners, students. POs stood guard at the door, admitting only the authorized, but Foster's eyes shifted to the hub of plainclothes detectives crowded around a back office. That's where she and Li needed to be, so they made their way back.

Of course, Rosales was there squatting over a body, the soles of a man's shoes peeking out from between him and two large detectives in wool coats standing alongside him. There were more posters of Valdez in here in which he looked earnest and honest, his shirtsleeves rolled up to the elbow as though he were ready to pitch in to clean up the streets, clear a crack house, or plant a community garden. VALDEZ GETS THINGS DONE was the tagline.

"Detective Tennant?"

The Black detective wearing a wool coat and standing next to the white detective in a wool coat turned around. "Detective Foster. Detective Li. You called us?"

"Yeah. Hold on," he said.

They stepped back, taking in the weeping Latina, about fifty, sitting slumped in a metal folding chair off to the side near an alcove with a coffee maker and small refrigerator tucked in it. The woman sat clutching a white pastry box, her heavy mascara streaking her wide face, her head shaking in disbelief, shock.

"Is she the one who found him?" Li asked the female PO standing watch over the woman, to assist if needed, but also to make sure she stayed put until she could be interviewed and released from the scene.

She nodded. "Office manager. Ms. Emelda Rodriguez. She called it in about nine."

Li and Foster both checked their watches. It was now just past ten thirty. The huddle of cops shifted, and Tennant and the white cop snaked their way past the body and joined them. Both men were formidable looking, big, solid, besting Foster and Li by several inches. Tennant took them in, nodded. "Tennant. My partner, Pienkowski. You're working the Leonard case." His voice was deep, slow. "This is alderman number two."

Foster stared past him at Valdez, getting a clearer picture. He'd been dressed for work in a pair of black slacks and a pale rose-colored button-down, which blood had soaked. His eyes were open, his mouth twisted, frozen in a rictus grin. His had been a violent death. "A stabbing?"

"Nasty one too," Tennant said. "Three strikes, according to Rosales here. One in the side, two in back. Bled out right where you see him."

"Robbery?" Li asked, looking around, though she'd have no way of knowing if anything was missing. That would be Rodriguez's job.

Tennant's eyes lay on Li's and wandered up and down. "Thought it might be. Wallet was missing. His cell phone too. He was working in here late last night, the office manager says. She left him here alone about six."

Foster's eyes drifted over to the alderman's desk. It didn't look like anyone had rifled through it. None of the drawers were open, and there was nothing strewed across the floor.

"No 911 call?"

"Doesn't look like he had a chance."

The hub of cops in the small office shifted, and she and Li, Tennant and Pienkowski rotated back in to stand by Rosales.

Rosales glanced back and saw them there. "Gang's all here, then? Okay. Three wounds. Difficult to say which came first." He pointed a gloved finger to the gaping slash on Valdez's right side. "Deep, though. Whoever did it meant business."

"When?" Li asked.

"TOD, of course, is tentative. With rigor, yada, yada, yada, won't bore you with the science, we're maybe looking at eight or nine last night?"

Li turned to Tennant. "You said his phone and wallet were missing? So, robbery."

Pienkowski shook his head. "POs found both in a trash can up the street. Money still in the wallet. That right there's a miracle."

Tennant sighed. "So, that part's just somebody jerking our chain. It looks like the stabbing was the main event."

"I didn't notice the door broken in," Foster said.

"Wasn't," Tennant said. "We found a key sitting on his desk. One key. No key ring. We bagged it. Maybe we'll get a print. The manager says they only had three keys to the place. She's got hers; Valdez's is on the key ring in his pocket. Third one belongs to the maintenance guy. We'll check with him forthwith."

"And you think your case links to ours because they were both aldermen?" Li asked.

"Not only." Tennant lifted up a small plastic bag with dimes in it. "When Rosales found this stuck in his pocket, he mentioned you found something like it on Leonard?"

"*In* Leonard, to be precise," Li said. "Coins were in her stomach."

His face blanched. "That's why you're here." He lowered the bag. "Looks like somebody's trying to say something."

Rosales stood, took a step away from Valdez, shook his head somberly. "I wish he'd stop."

---

Griffin paced behind her cluttered desk, glaring at Foster and Li each pass she took. "Two murdered aldermen. Both killings connected by pocket change. And we're supposed to figure out who might have wanted politicians dead? In *Chicago*? Who the hell do we look like, Professor X?"

"Are we supposed to know who Professor X is?" Li asked, turning to Foster. "Seriously?"

"Marvel character," Foster whispered as an aside. "Comic books. Let it go."

"Dimes? *Fuck!*" Griffin ranted as though they weren't there. "I hate the weird ones. I really do. I mean, when did murders start having to have a theme? Why's everybody got to get clever and leave stupid messages and calling cards behind?" She stopped pacing, faced her detectives. "Lieutenant Beatty has already gotten a half dozen calls from the mayor, which means I've gotten a dozen from him. I don't like Beatty. Beatty doesn't like me. So, a dozen calls do not make either of us happy." She flopped down in her chair and took a slow exhale. "There are news crews outside of city hall. They're hyping this like the entire city council is on some killer's to-do list. There are forty-eight more aldermen, who are now likely hiding under their beds thinking they're next. Run it. What do we have? Connections?"

"The calls are a thread. We're working on tracing the number on Leonard's phone to Shaw, so far, no luck. The number didn't immediately come up with an established account."

"Burner?"

"Could be, but even still there's information we can get from it, right?"

"So, are we thinking Shaw comes out of prison loaded for bear, determined to knock off everybody who turned on her, because this is how this is starting to look. She's out, and suddenly Leonard and Valdez are dead? Otherwise, it's mighty funny nobody starts dying with dimes on them until she's out." She looked at Foster, Li. "Well?"

Li smiled. "My partner and I don't like to jump to conclusions, boss. We follow the evidence. Step by step with open minds."

Griffin glared at Foster. "You did this."

Foster had no problem holding up to the glare. "We talk to Franklin and Meehan, and Shaw again. We backtrack on Leonard and Valdez. We scour whatever footage we can get our hands on. Shaw fits, but we can't ignore other possibilities."

"Like?"

"Like somebody else knew Shaw was released and took that as their starting gun. They'd have to know she'd be the first one we looked at."

The phone on Griffin's desk rang. She pointed at it. "How much you want to bet that's Beatty."

Li shrugged. "I could take it."

Griffin scowled. "Get out." She picked up the receiver and shooed them away. "Yes, sir, I was just about to call with an update." Griffin rolled her eyes and braced. "Absolutely, sir. We're making progress."

Foster and Li eased out and headed back to their desks. The team had nicknamed the office the Pen and designated it the home of the Area 1 Big Dogs, of which Foster was now, after four months, an accepted member. She'd settled in, and it was now as though she'd always been there. Symansky had even gone so far as to have T-shirts made for them with an image of a jowly English bulldog on the front under the words *BIG DOGS OF AREA 1* and their names stenciled on the back. Perfect to cheer on their side at the next CPD versus CFD charity softball game.

The team met at the whiteboard.

"I made some calls," Kelley said. "Shaw served her time at Logan without a single hitch. No disciplinary actions. Straight through. Head down. Even completed a full rehab program, then kept it going the whole time. She went in dirty, came out clean."

"Don't mean she wasn't pissed about bein' there." Lonergan played with the stress ball from his desk. "Keepin' it all in . . . till she can't."

"Besides Shaw," Foster said. "She's a possibility, but we can't close ourselves off from seeing other angles. Someone else who'd want to see Leonard and Valdez dead."

"I hear you," Li said. "But look at the calls. There's a definite chain going on. And that leads right to her."

Foster glanced at the board, seeing it, but not trusting it. "Maybe. And I'm not saying she isn't our number one, only that we can't let her blind us to whatever else might be going on."

"You say maybe, but it smells like more than that," Symansky said. "Look at the exchanges. Leonard gets a call at six fifty-two p.m. from the number you called back. You get a woman who hangs up on ya. Then that sets off the rest."

Foster underlined the notation on the board. "Right. The call to Leonard lasted thirty-three seconds. A few minutes go by, then she starts making calls. Valdez, then Franklin. At two minutes after seven, she calls John Meehan." She underlined the time, turned back to the others. "Three hours, give or take, she's dead. It looked like suicide, but I don't think the killer meant to confuse us or pass it off as that, otherwise the dimes wouldn't have been stuffed down her throat."

"So, we look for who Leonard and Valdez double-crossed," Lonergan said. "I don't think that's gonna be a short list."

Bigelow nodded. "True point. Anybody get anything on that case that got Shaw locked up?"

Foster reported what she'd learned about the fed probe, scribbling the important details on the board below Shaw's name and driver's license photo. "Logically the thing would have required more hands than just Shaw's. But in court it's about evidence and what you can prove. So, though the names of the others were whispered, obviously deals were made, and Shaw loses."

Symansky shot a finger gun at the board. "And that, my friends, is the Chicago way."

Li folded her arms in front of her. "You have to love this town."

Foster pointed to the names of Parker and his sister, Jeniece. "Family. Money issues? Rifts? Same for Valdez, though Tennant and Pienkowski are running lead on that. Their case clearly connects to ours." Foster scribbled the name of Valdez's wife on the board, then circled it. "Marriage problems, enemies? Something completely independent of Shaw."

"We know why Shaw's stuck down in some condo instead of being home with her husband and kid?" Lonergan asked.

"There's some marital trouble." Foster scribbled the word *marriage* on the board and put a question mark beside it.

"She had to see that comin'," Lonergan grumbled.

Foster ignored him. "If she's headed for divorce, she'd be worried about losing custody of her daughter. Which leads me to ask, Would she jeopardize all of that for revenge? What rational person would risk going back to prison, this time for life?"

Lonergan shifted in his seat. "Prison coulda changed her. It does most people. Maybe she's not thinkin' straight."

Kelley squinted at Lonergan. "You're being particularly cooperative today. What's going on? You sick?"

Lonergan sneered back. "Fuck off, Kelley."

"And he's back," Symansky muttered facetiously.

"Lonergan's right. Maybe she's not so concerned about custody or the divorce," Kelley said. "Revenge, if that's what we're looking at, is like a beast that eats you from the inside out. Like in *Hamlet*. '*O, from this time forth, my thoughts be bloody, or be nothing worth!*'"

Symansky fixed Kelley, his overeducated nemesis, with a steely glower. "*Hamlet?*"

Kelley grinned, pushing his gum from cheek to cheek. He knew he was needling Symansky. The old street cop was an easy get. "It's true, though. Every word."

"That's what's wrong with college. They spit out eggheads one after the other like they're loaves of bread on a conveyor belt. Me? School of hard knocks. Cut that *Hamlet* shit out."

Lonergan chuckled. "I met Al at that school. It was on the corner of Brass Knuckles Boulevard and Beatdown Way."

The room erupted in tension-relieving laughter. Needed, appreciated, even by Foster. "All right. Can we get back to the bodies we have lying on the ME's slab?"

"'You owe me.' That's what she said when she thought she was talking to Leonard and not to you," Bigelow offered. "So, if you're sure it was Shaw on that phone, she either didn't know Leonard was dead, or she's one hell of an actress. We got to nail that down one way or the other, right? Until then, she's looking good. Besides, I don't think Parker's got it in him to shoot his own mother in the head. That's just my feeling, knowing who he is."

"She said 'You *all* owe me,'" Li corrected. "But Bigs is right. Shaw seems to be the strongest pull here. And she had three years to perfect her acting abilities."

Bigelow took a sip from his mug. "If that's the case, a whole lot of people out there should double up on security."

Foster studied the board. "So, Shaw. We track where she's been since walking out of Logan." She turned to the team. "Franklin and Meehan too." She glanced over at Bigelow. "And Aaron Parker. But not you, Bigs. Kelley, maybe. Soft shoes. All of it neat and steady. We don't want to scare people off or force them underground, especially Shaw. Meanwhile, let's talk to her husband. But again, lightly. We good?"

"I think if Shaw's the one dropping coins all over town," Lonergan said, "we can drop the kid gloves, can't we? She's an ex-con. A thief. Why's she getting the princess treatment?"

She stared at Lonergan sitting there with his buzz cut and burly body leaned back in his chair with confident ease. "She gets what everybody should get, the presumption of innocence." Foster pushed the cap back on her marker and set it down, signaling the end of the rundown. "Thanks, everybody."

Squeaks and creaks from office chairs, the sound of gunky casters sliding across institutional tile followed as everyone got up and prepared to move out or hit the phones. Behind her, Foster heard Kelley recite more Shakespeare, knowing full well what was coming next. Kelley was no fool. He knew right where to poke to get Symansky going. It was a form of bonding or psychological torture writ small, depending on how you looked at it. The only one who didn't find it amusing was Detective Al Symansky, graduate of Hard Knocks University.

"Kelley," Symansky hissed, "I swear to all that is holy, if I hear anything else from *Hamlet*, they're gonna find your body floating in Bubbly Creek."

# CHAPTER 16

"So, you want to try Franklin next?" Li asked.

Foster plopped down into her chair. "I'd rather start with Shaw's husband. Check on that dinner she said they had. Then Franklin."

Li shrugged. "Sounds like a plan."

Foster checked her phone for email. "Finally. We have movement on the street cameras. We'll have it up in an hour or so."

"Great. I'm going to hit the little cop's room, then we'll head out. We can check in with Tennant and Pienkowski after. See if they've come up with anything on Valdez."

Foster nodded and eyed her adopted plant, though it appeared just as sick as before. She gently massaged one of the green leaves, then made sure the soil was damp. "Sure."

"Tell me somebody didn't sell you that thing."

Foster looked up. "I found it in the trash."

Li waited for more, but that was all that was forthcoming, as Foster shifted her attention from the plant to her notepad.

"That's it? No backstory?"

Foster picked up the phone on her desk and started dialing. "It's a plant. I don't think it has one."

Li walked away, grumbling. "Smart-ass."

A man picked up on the third ring. Will Barrett. Foster introduced herself, noting the immediate irritation in his voice.

"Mr. Barrett, I'd like to ask you a few questions about your wife, Marin Shaw."

"Great. What's she done *now*?"

———

Barrett didn't want them coming to his home or office, so instead he came to them, and they were surprised to see that he brought his young daughter with him, who stood morose, frightened, and visibly overwhelmed at his side, though Barrett appeared unaware of the girl's discomfort. She was small, petite, a waif of a thing, Foster thought, as she watched her, the child's eyes very rarely lifting off the floor. The girl should have been in school. Why wasn't she?

The two sat at the table in interview room three. Not a place for a kid, but the young PO who'd showed them in hadn't come to that conclusion. Foster glanced over at Li, who stood beside her. Li's expression was as hard as stone. "You brought your daughter," Li said, her voice tight. "Here."

Barrett's chin lifted, his cold gray eyes lasered in as he got a whiff of Li's condemnation and reproach. "I kept her out of school today. She has a right to hear. So, if her mother's into . . ."

"No." Foster stopped him. "Li?"

"Yep. Got it." Li pulled a chair out opposite Barrett and sat facing him while Foster beckoned to the girl to stand up and come with her.

"Zoe, isn't it?" Foster asked, guiding the girl out of the room. Zoe looked shell shocked, zombielike, but nodded at the mention of her name. "I'm Harriet, but you can call me Harri if you want. You like doughnuts? Are you allowed?" The girl nodded again. "Good. No better place for doughnuts than this place. Follow me." She scanned the office, looking for a cop who might be good with frightened children, but she came up empty; then her eyes landed on Griffin's closed door.

She placed a gentle hand on Zoe's shoulder as they walked over to the break room and the doughnut box. "Chocolate?" Foster asked. Zoe nodded. "Good choice. Grab it, and I'll introduce you to one of the coolest people I know. She's a sergeant. My boss. Then I'm going to go back in and talk to your dad, okay?"

"Is he in trouble?" Zoe's voice wobbled. She'd lost her mother for three years and was obviously afraid of losing her father too.

"No," Foster said. "We'll just be talking."

"Is my mom in trouble?"

Foster noticed that Zoe's breathing changed, her heart seemingly beating a mile a minute. "No one's in trouble, honey. You don't have to worry about that."

Zoe took a bite of doughnut. "What makes your boss so cool?"

Foster guided her toward Griffin's door. "She's like a superhero. She could probably take down everybody in here. Smart, too . . . also, hopefully, very forgiving." Foster pushed Zoe forward, knocking on Griffin's door, praying nothing profane came back.

"What?"

Zoe was startled by Griffin's gruffness. "Don't go by that," Foster said as she stuck her head in the office. "Need a favor. Need it now. And I don't have time to explain. Fifteen minutes tops. You can kill me later."

"What are you talking about . . . favor? Do I look like I'm in the favor business? Do you see that sign on my door? Does it say 'Favor Fairy'? It does not. And then the *now* just chaps my—" Foster pulled Zoe and her doughnut inside, and Griffin fell silent. She stared down at the girl, then up at Foster.

"This is Zoe Barrett. Daughter of Marin Shaw. We're talking to Zoe's father in interview," Foster said. "He brought her along." The two women shared a knowing look. "So maybe she can sit in here for a few minutes where it doesn't look so much like a police station." Foster scanned all the Irish stuff and family photos. "With someone nice."

Griffin stood, tugged her shirt down, then plastered a warm smile on her face, one Foster had never seen before. "Zoe Barrett. Nice name." She came around her desk and stood in front of Zoe. "Doughnuts. Nice. You know why cops like doughnuts?" Zoe shook her head, took another doughnut bite. "Because we're busy people and you can eat a doughnut fast, they go well with coffee, and they're cheap." Griffin showed Zoe to a chair. "Park it. I'll tell you about the time I almost got mauled by a black bear."

Foster mouthed a thank-you as she backed out of the room, but by the time she got back to the interview room, her fists and jaw were clenched and her mood dark. She pushed the door open to find Barrett and Li facing off silently across the table.

"Where's my daughter?" he asked.

Foster took a seat next to Li. "She's with Sergeant Sharon Griffin, our boss. Having a doughnut and a friendly talk about bears." No intelligent person could have missed the icy tone or the contempt in her delivery.

"Some conversations aren't for children," Li said, her eyes dark, broadcasting a warning Barrett would be foolish to ignore.

Barrett sneered. "Fine. So, what has Marin done now? She's barely out of prison and she's got us embroiled in something else already? I'm trying to be understanding and supportive, but . . ."

The detectives waited. "But what?" Li finally asked.

"I've reached my limit," he said. "What this has done to Zoe, well . . ."

Foster flipped over the cover of her notepad and slid a pen out of her pocket. She doubted it was his daughter he was concerned about. Otherwise, the girl would be in school and not here. "We'd like to confirm that your wife was with you and your daughter Tuesday night. Can you tell us from when to when?"

"I'd normally ask why, but I already know. It's Leonard and Valdez. You think she has something to do with that."

He crossed his legs, right over left, and rested his hands on his thigh. His wool trousers and blazer looked expensive, the silk tie too. He oozed pomposity. Will Barrett was superior, at least in his own mind.

Foster noticed there was no wedding ring, not even an indentation or lightness of skin to show where a band had once been, so he'd taken it off and kept it off a long time ago. And his nails were perfectly manicured. She jotted down a note. "We're not at liberty to say. Please, from when to when?"

"Dinner ended abruptly. Zoe was upset, naturally. She hadn't seen Marin in years. Now suddenly she's back?" He checked his nails, then his watch, though Foster suspected that was only to show them how expensive it was. "I had to ask her to leave. I'd say between six thirty and seven?"

"You didn't take your daughter to visit her mother?" Li asked.

"Of course not. A prison's no place for a kid."

Together they let the moment hang, waiting to see if Barrett caught the irony. He did not.

"Was your wife driving that night, Mr. Barrett?" Li asked.

"She was. I'm driving the Lexus. Marin's driving the Audi that we keep at the condo. It's an A6. Black. If she's wrapped up in anything, I have a right to know. For Zoe's sake. I don't have to tell you what her going to prison has done to our daughter and to me. The scandal, the humiliation. We've had news crews sitting out in front of our house for days since her release. And that doesn't hold a candle to the crap we had to endure during her trial and sentencing."

Foster's eyes locked onto his. "So, you asked her to leave her home between six thirty and seven, you said. Because she upset Zoe."

"This whole thing has upset her, obviously. You saw her. She's a shell of herself. Marin is unstable, I'll just say that. She's an alcoholic, and now a felon, for Christ's sake. I don't think our marriage is salvageable."

"Is that why you stopped wearing your wedding ring?" Foster flicked a look at the naked finger. "Some time ago, it appears."

"What's that got to do with this?"

"Is that why your wife's living at your condo, and not at home with her daughter?" Li asked.

Barrett dialed into the frostiness at last. "Look, the state of my marriage has nothing to do with either of you, or with what you're supposed to be about. Marin's done some damage, all right? I'm the injured party, and right now my job is to protect Zoe."

Foster smiled. Li smiled. They weren't sunny smiles.

"Have you had any contact with your wife since Tuesday night?" Foster asked. "Phone calls, visits?"

"No. I've nothing to say."

"Has Zoe seen her mom since Tuesday night?" Li asked. "Talked to her?"

"No."

"Where were *you* Tuesday night, after you asked your wife to leave her home?" Foster asked.

Barrett's eyes narrowed. "You keep saying that. It's *our* home. And Zoe couldn't handle it. Both of us want what's best for our daughter."

"So where were you?" Li asked.

"Home the entire night. I got some work done, then went to bed around eleven thirty."

"Anyone else in the house besides you and Zoe?" Foster glanced down at the ring finger again, her eyes traveling down to the cuffs of his designer pants and shoes and up again to the tie and worsted wool blazer, past the clean-shaven chin to judgmental eyes that Marin Shaw had the misfortune of coming back to after her release.

"Of course not," he said.

Li leaned forward. "And to be clear, you've had no contact with either Alderman Leonard or Alderman Valdez recently." It was a statement, not a question, anticipating his response.

"I barely met them. Cocktail parties, social events I was forced to go to. Politics was Marin's thing, not mine."

Li followed up. "Can you think of any reason your wife would be in contact with Leonard or Valdez so soon after she got out of prison?"

"Aren't you getting an idea about that already?" he said lightly, as though it was a joke. "Old business in need of settling. Marin's never been good at letting things go."

Foster had been watching him closely the entire time. Watching his body language as he sat composed in the chair, always making sure that his pants leg was straight and that his shirt cuff came right to his expensive watch, but never covered it. Precise. Designed to impress.

"Politics isn't your thing, you said, so what is?" Foster already knew. She'd looked him up, but she wanted to hear what he said about himself.

"I'm in real estate."

"Buying and selling it?" She asked it to needle him, having a good idea what reaction she'd get. She was not disappointed.

Barrett massaged his watch and glowered back at her as though she'd slapped him across the face. "*Developing* it. High-end real estate. Top of the line all the way."

"Having a wife in prison couldn't have helped there." The man's entire body appeared to clench.

"You have no idea what deals I've lost out on, the connections. Her greed, her recklessness sank us both."

There it was, Foster thought. She'd hit on the thing that stuck in Will Barrett's craw and had turned him against his wife—loss of status, loss of prestige, loss of business, all of it hitting him squarely in the ego. He had been found guilty by association and branded a thief. And now he wanted to get his own by serving Marin Shaw to them on a platter.

"I see," she said.

Barrett sneered. "I doubt you do. And I'm not here to talk about me. If Marin's up to her old tricks, I need to know. To protect my daughter."

For a moment no one said anything. Then Foster stood. "I think that's all we need for right now. We appreciate your coming in."

Li stood. "We'll be in touch."

Barrett's eyes widened in surprise. "That's it? I haven't even started telling you what you're dealing with. Marin's volatile and unpredictable, completely different when she's drinking. Like Jekyll and Hyde. I don't even think she's capable of taking care of herself, let alone Zoe."

Li stared at him. "You know, most times, Mr. Barrett, we have to pull information out of people we talk to. You're a real gift."

"I'm not doing it for you guys, it's for—"

Foster cut him off. "Zoe. You said."

"Right, so if she's dangerous, I can't take the chance, and neither can you."

"We appreciate your time," Foster said. "If we have any further questions, we'll be in touch."

Left unsatisfied, thwarted, Barrett lashed out with a curt demand. "Where's my daughter?"

From a window, Foster and Li watched Barrett and Zoe walk out of the building and get into a maroon Lexus parked across the street. Zoe walked slowly, like a kid doomed to a fate worse than death. Barrett paid her little attention; instead he was on a call, his cell phone to his ear, his face animated, angry.

"Do you think he's talking to his wife?" Li asked.

Foster's eyes were trained on Zoe, on her slow amble to the car, her shoulders slumped. "No."

They moved away from the window.

"Prison or life with him?" Li asked.

Foster thought about it. "I don't see much of a difference."

# CHAPTER 17

Marin couldn't say that she hadn't wished them all dead. She had years to sit and hate and blame. The detectives would be back, she knew it. She could tell they hadn't believed her. When they traced that call, they would be back, and Marin would have to admit what she had done, what she had planned to do. And it all meant more trouble, more trauma for Zoe.

Up since dawn after a fitful night, she was finding it difficult to sleep without the noise of the prison. It had taken months to get used to the clanking and clattering, the crying, and the menacing voices, and now having it all behind her, she was having to get used to the quiet and the stillness of being alone.

Even the view of the lake from the couch where she rocked to soothe herself failed to calm her. Because she knew it was there. She felt it looming over her. She could just see it out of the corner of her eye. Will's bar. It seemed to breathe. It felt like it was watching. The bottles of scotch and whiskey, the expensive bourbons, the bitters stared at her from the glass shelves. Above the shelves Will had even had his name spelled out in green neon—**BARRETT'S**. Had he stocked the bar because he knew she would be here? Had he hoped it would entice her to drink again? She hated to think so, but he was a petty man, a small man, not a good man. It had taken sobriety and a cell for her to realize it. If she needed any more proof of that, or that there was nothing left between them, the bar was it. But she'd held through the night, through all the nights. Here on the couch watching her enemies in the bottles. Sleep may have eluded her, peace, too, but her resolve so far had not. She was stronger than he knew. And she was done torturing herself. She'd just been waiting for the morning light, she'd told herself, only it had come hours ago, and she was still sitting here.

"Get up. Do something." She prodded, willing herself up. "Now."

Up on her feet, she took a second to acknowledge the victory, then got to work pulling flattened banker's boxes out of the storage closet, dragging them to the bar and assembling them one by one. Bottle by bottle, she cleared the shelves and filled the boxes, pulling each box through the living room, down the hall, through the kitchen to the back service door. It took eight trips, eight filled boxes to clear the shelves, each time, her bare feet squeaking on the hardwood floors, the boxes brushing across the slats, bottles clinking. If she was going to live here, BARRETT'S couldn't. All of it had to go, including Will's monogrammed swizzle sticks and cocktail napkins, even the neon sign. She unplugged it, then unscrewed it from the wall. Everything went into a new box, the last to go out.

At the end when everything was gone, Marin stood sweaty and exhausted in front of the empty shelves, her eyes squeezed shut. "One day at a time." The words came out as a prayer, an affirmation. "I will not drink today. I will allow myself to feel today." She showered and dressed and then headed to a morning AA meeting. She'd feel stronger afterward, strong enough, she hoped, to tell the detectives what she should have before. "Move."

———

It had taken two meetings back to back before Marin was ready to meet the day. She emerged from the church basement, fortified, the cold wind off the lake putting energy in her stride. Despite the cold and wind, she decided to walk home; it was just a few blocks. It would give her time to think. In the basement, she'd found a little grace, a little empathy for Leonard and Valdez, though not quite forgiveness. That was movement forward; it was growth.

At the crossing light, Marin stood on the curb at Superior and Michigan in a small huddle of pedestrians waiting to cross, heavy traffic slushy and sliding along at 10:00 a.m., people racing to offices and the hospital nearby, double-timing it trying to get out of the cold. Marin was in no hurry. There was no one expecting her anywhere. She had no job, no prospects, no tasks to perform. Hidden behind dark sunglasses, her hat pulled down, and the collar up on her long dark coat, she was unrecognizable to those around her, unmarked. She was just one woman among nameless others.

Marin watched the seconds tick down on the crossing signal. Seven, six, five . . . cars and cabs sped up instead of slowing down, hoping to beat the light before it turned red, fast tires spitting up the city salt laid down over the black ice beneath it.

Marin felt a hard shove at the small of her back. Her feet launched off the curb. There was time for a gasp, but little else, as the fear of falling into the street, into oncoming traffic, sputtered her brain. Her world went from fast to slow, every second painfully prolonged, as the inevitability of disaster hit. Falling. She was falling. Marin's arms flailed as her legs and feet fought for purchase, but there was none to be found. There was nothing she could do. Car horns blared, honked, screeched. She could hear the crunch of tires, the squeal of brakes, the hum and womp of thick rubber on half-melted dirty snow. Someone on the curb yelled out, "Oh my God!"

Marin didn't want to see the car that hit her. It was enough of a horror to hear the tires approaching as she landed in the street helpless, bracing for pain and oblivion. She squeezed her eyes shut, and saw her daughter's face, her smile.

*Zoe.*

# CHAPTER 18

Alderman Sylissa Franklin paced around her office in city hall, the morning's paper glaring up at her from the desk. *Alderman Valdez Killed in Office Break-in*, the headline read. Franklin flipped the paper over. She couldn't look at Valdez's photo yet again.

She grabbed her cell phone, made a call, not bothering to wait for a greeting when it was picked up on the other end. "What the hell's going on, John?" She walked over, checked the outer office for eavesdroppers, but found it empty; still she closed her door and locked it. "Deanna, now George? Something you want to tell me?"

Meehan's voice came calm and unrushed through the line. "What are you talking about? None of that's got anything to do with me, or you."

Franklin's lips pressed closer to the phone. "This is me you're talking to, remember? Are you doing this?"

"I'd be careful with that."

"Or what? I'll be next? They both made themselves very clear at Dino's, now they're dead. I don't believe in coincidences, John, especially when you're involved."

"You must be losing it, otherwise you woulda known better than to call me with this bullshit." She could almost feel the heat coming through the line, but it was quickly gone, as Meehan got himself under control again. He was a master at it, she knew, and could blow hot and cold, go from friendly to deadly almost in an instant. "I'm torn up about this. Two trusted colleagues cut down in the prime of life—"

"I'm not wearing a wire, John. Not because I wouldn't, but only because it's not in my best interests right now."

There was a moment's silence before he spoke again. "Good to know where we stand, Sylissa. As for the rest of it, my hands are clean. My eyes are on a different prize. I got nothing but sympathy. Besides, you were a lot closer to Valdez than I was, weren't you? Maybe something went wrong there, hmm?"

"I don't know what you're talking about."

Meehan chuckled. "Yeah, you do." She could hear him readjust in his executive chair, the sound of his body against the leather projecting over the phone. "But I'll bottom line it for you. I'm not in this."

Franklin didn't believe a word Meehan said. She knew the man. She knew he hadn't an ounce of concern for anyone but himself. Meehan had gotten rich off his crooked deals and had his hooks into so many dirty pockets he barely had time to run his own ward. The power he wielded, the connections he'd made, high and low, made him dangerous. Treading carefully would be wise, prudent, Franklin knew, but what if she were next? What if Meehan were cleaning house?

"I'm not stupid enough to think you got your own hands dirty," she said. "At least not with this, but if you had it done. If you're trying to intimidate me . . ."

"Sylissa, I'm going to do you a favor and forget you just said that. I'm going to chalk it all up to your being confused from the shock. That's what I'm going to do. What *you're* going to do is keep your fucking mouth shut, and for once in your greedy little life grow a spine."

It was as though Meehan's hand had flown through the receiver and grabbed her by the throat. What had she done? How could she have forgotten who she was talking to? Her eyes slid toward the door. Still closed. Franklin lowered her voice even more, fighting hard to keep the shake out of it. If she showed weakness now. If Meehan sensed she was afraid and unsure, there was nothing he wouldn't do to crush her.

"I can ruin you just as fast as you can ruin me. And you have more to lose, don't you?"

Meehan let a moment pass. "I do, and I'm not about to lose it."

"Then you'd better think long and hard about what you do next."

"Funny, I was just about to tell you that." Meehan's voice was slow, deliberate, free of all intonation. Like a robot, a sinister, unfeeling, inhuman machine. "You forget, Sylissa, I own you. I flip the switch and everything you've got disappears. So, I'm going to have to hear from you right now where you're at."

Franklin felt sick to her stomach, her head so light it felt like it might float away. This was John Meehan she was talking to. She wet her lips. "Nothing's changed. You protect me. I protect you. But John? If you come after me, you'd better not miss."

The laugh he gave her chilled her bones. "If I do, I won't."

The line went dead. Franklin hung up, then paced her office, the armpits of her silk blouse soaked through with sweat. Had she just made the biggest mistake of her life? The second biggest, perhaps. The first was getting pulled into Meehan's web. Now she found herself in too deep. Was there a way out?

"Shit. Shit. Shit. *Shit.*"

# CHAPTER 19

Foster ducked her head inside the back of the fire department ambulance, its lights flashing, a steady snow falling out of an ominous gray sky. Six more inches of snow had been predicted by nightfall. Marin Shaw lay on a gurney, a female EMT attending to a deep gash on her forehead. Shaw's palms and knees were bloodied, her eyes dazed, but she wasn't dead, which was what Foster was used to rolling up on. Li slid in beside her, and they watched as Shaw got a gauze bandage applied to her head. She was refusing to be taken to the hospital, which was why the ambulance was idling in front of the Neiman Marcus on Michigan. Uniformed cops were moving pedestrians along, the traffic heavy but flowing behind them. Ambulances weren't an oddity in the city. Not even in the heart of the Mag Mile. They'd been heading out to speak to Sylissa Franklin when they got notified of Shaw's accident.

"I don't need a hospital," Shaw insisted. "Nothing's broken."

The EMT rolled her eyes, gave them a heard-it-all-before look. "Only an x-ray can confirm you don't have a skull fracture, ma'am. This gash is deep. You're going to need stitches at least. The hospital's just up the street."

"I want to go home."

"Well, that's dumb," Li whispered to Foster.

"Then if you don't want medical attention," Foster said, "you can come take a ride with us. We have more questions for you. If you want to call your lawyer, you can do that on the way." Shaw's eyes widened and began to dart around the ambulance as though looking for a way out. "I think there's more you can tell us, isn't there?"

It took only a few moments, which Foster had anticipated. She'd given Shaw a clear choice, and she knew when she'd done it which option the woman would likely take. Nobody wanted to talk to cops, especially when they had something to hide.

"I'll go to the hospital," Shaw said.

"Good, but first, briefly, what happened this morning?" Foster turned to the EMT. "Would you mind giving us a minute?"

The EMT scowled. "We don't have all day, you know."

Foster nodded. "This won't take long. Three minutes. Tops."

The EMT reluctantly climbed out and Foster climbed in. Li stood at the back doors, protecting the space.

Shaw leaned her head against the pillow, her face contorted in pain. "I had nothing to do with what happened to Deanna."

"We'll get to that. How'd you end up in the street?"

Shaw dabbed at the bandage on her head, blood already beginning to seep through the gauze. "Someone pushed me."

"You see who?" Li asked.

Shaw shook her head, then winced at the pain the shake had caused. "I had a feeling someone was following me, a sense. But I didn't see anyone."

"Following you from where?" Foster asked.

"Church. AA meetings are held in the basement. I attended two this morning. Afterward, I decided to walk. At the crosswalk, just as the light started to change, someone shoved me." She stared at Li, then Foster. "Someone tried to kill me." She searched their faces, but only stoic cop faces came back. "You don't believe me."

"Why wouldn't we?" Foster asked.

Li was skeptical. "You only had a sense someone was following you?"

"See?"

"Who'd want to hurt you?" Li asked.

Shaw snorted derisively. "Half the city. I'm a crooked ex-alderman, a felon, or haven't you heard?"

Li held up a black cashmere hat and a pair of broken sunglasses. "The POs found these in the street. Hat, glasses. Plus the scarf and heavy coat you're wearing. How would anyone even recognize you?"

"Whoever followed me obviously knew who I was."

Foster scanned the busy street. "You walked south?" Shaw nodded. They could check the cameras. She took a deep breath, watching Shaw for a time. "You're the woman I talked to the morning after Leonard was killed." Shaw stiffened. "Can we at least establish that?"

"Yes. But I didn't do anything."

"You were angry with her, though?" Li asked.

Shaw stared down at her shaking hands, blood dried on her fingers, gauze wrapped around her scraped and bloodied palms. "Of all the knives stuck into me at my trial, Deanna's was the one that plunged the deepest. We were friends, or I thought we were. When everything went bad, she just disappeared. I did call her. I wanted to talk. She listened, surprisingly, then she did something I didn't expect. She apologized. That should've been enough, but it wasn't. How could it be?"

"You two didn't meet?" Li asked.

"We were supposed to, but I didn't go. Nothing good could have come from my being there. It's time to make smart choices, right? When I got the call from her phone, the anger roared back. I told her she owed me, but it was you on the other end. I knew instantly I'd made a mistake and hung up. That's the truth. And none of that has anything to do with the fact that someone out there just tried to kill me."

"You said they *all* owed you." Foster's eyes lasered in. "Want to explain?"

"I misspoke."

"You're sure about that?" Li asked.

"I've been under a lot of stress. I need to go to the ER now. I'm bleeding."

Foster could feel the EMT standing outside the rig behind Li getting restless. Shaw wasn't sitting in a limo hired just for her. It was an ambulance, and an ambulance had calls to make, people to save. Foster turned to the EMT and held up one finger, indicating how much longer she'd be. "Last question. When's the last time you saw Alderman George Valdez?"

"George? Why?"

"He was killed in his ward office last night."

Shaw paled. "What?"

Li pulled a face. "C'mon, there's no way you can't know that. It's all over the city. Even if you're not reading the papers or watching the news, there's no way you could have missed it."

Shaw covered her face in her hands. "I didn't . . . I couldn't . . ."

"Where were you between the hours of six p.m. and approximately nine p.m. last night?" Foster watched as Shaw's entire demeanor changed. She went from languid, resigned, to hyperalert and frightened.

"I haven't laid eyes on George Valdez in over three years."

"Not what she asked," Li said.

"I was home. And I was mistaken about the push. I slipped on the ice. It was an accident. I don't have anything else to say."

"So, no one followed you?" Li asked.

"I was covered up, like you said. Who could know it was me?"

"Have you been to the bank lately, Ms. Shaw?" Li asked.

The woman's brows furrowed in confusion. "No. Why?"

"Just curious." Li eyed the hat in her hand, dirtied by slush and mud. She handed it to Foster, who laid it on the side of the gurney next to the bleeding woman. For a moment, no one said anything, and then Foster climbed out and the EMT got back in.

"Have a good day, Ms. Shaw," Foster said before closing the back doors.

They slid into the unmarked cop car, staring out the windshield at the grayest, ugliest, gloomiest day you'd ever want to see, Foster's mood matching the atmosphere. They watched the ambulance pull off and head north. The street quickly reverted to normal, no big deal, just another shitty day for somebody else; the rubberneckers had nothing more to look at. The squad cars pulled off, too, the POs on the lookout for the next disturbance. The city was a tinderbox of random violence and impromptu idiocy as opportunists emboldened by ineffective policies and dwindling police numbers took their shot whenever they could to smash and grab, strong-arm or carjack at a moment's notice. The once Magnificent Mile was now far less than that, half the stores and businesses having picked up and moved out when the cost of doing business grew too great, leaving behind shuttered storefronts, down-market retail enterprises, and a brooding sense that irrelevancy was just around the corner.

"She'd be a fool to go to her bank and ask for a bag of dimes, wouldn't she?" Foster said.

"Absolutely. I just wanted to see her face when I asked her."

"So?"

"The bank didn't register. Valdez's death did. I had a thought that maybe this little accident could have been her idea of throwing us off the scent. That old I'm-a-victim-too thing we've seen a million times. Sometimes they think we're just that dumb. But did you see how she froze up when you told her about Valdez?"

Foster started the car. "I did."

Li settled back. "She knows more than she's saying. And she's for sure afraid of somebody."

Li buckled in, ran her cold hands across the heater vents. "So, if not a bank, where else can you get your hands on sixty dimes?"

Foster cranked up the heater. "Good question. We can add it to the list of all the others we have to get answered."

# CHAPTER 20

"We finally got the street cams around the garage up," Foster announced to Symansky and Kelley hours later. "Where's Bigs and Lonergan?"

Symansky slid his chair over to Foster's desk. Kelley padded over with a can of Diet Pepsi. "City hall talking to Franklin," he said. "We're lookin' for in and out."

Foster cued up the video on her monitor, and they all watched as grainy black-and-white images of cars whizzing up and down Dearborn Street played across the screen.

"They send up Randolph too?" Kelley asked.

Foster nodded. "Hours of Tuesday night. We'll never be able to put eyes on all of it. Like Al said, we concentrate on in and out around Leonard's time of death and see what we get? If we need to expand out, we tackle the rest then."

"Try an hour before, and work forward," Li said. "I can't see her sitting alone in a garage for more than that, even with a gun in her bag."

Foster kept her eye on the time stamp and forwarded the tape to 9:00 p.m., then slowly let it run, watching the cars pass the garage, noting the license plates of the cars entering or exiting the garage. There were more exits than entrances. Late workers presumably.

"Hey, there's no sense in all of us looking over Foster's shoulder," Kelley said. "Did we tap the camera from Shaw's place too?"

Li backed up to her computer, her hands flying along the keyboard. "Yeah, but we haven't had time to crack it open yet. I'll send it to you. Hold on. There."

"On it." Kelley tossed his empty can into a wastebasket and went back to his desk to get started.

"Hamlet's got it right. We got to divide and conquer here." Symansky pedaled his chair back to his desk. "Li, send me something. The more eyes we get on it, the better."

The problem as Foster saw it was that there weren't enough eyes. The department was woefully understaffed. There weren't enough cops to cover the entire city well. She knew attrition, early retirement, frustration, and burnout had claimed some of the best cops they had. Those who were left were being asked to take up the slack with crime numbers rising. Now they had the high-profile murders of two city leaders. They didn't have the luxury of studying every frame of footage. That would take days. They didn't have days. What they did have was time of death, and Foster was grateful for it. It narrowed their search window.

She checked her watch. Two p.m. There was so much to do, so much ground to cover, so little time. She grabbed her notepad and went to the board to scribble down the makes, models, and license plates of the people they'd already interviewed, those connected directly to Leonard. That was their starting point. "If we find anything, and it matches with whatever Tennant and Pienkowski find, we'll be onto something."

"You put Meehan up there?" Symansky asked. "He's as big as they come in this town."

"So?"

"So, you really see him stuffing dimes down somebody's throat?"

Li thought it over for a moment. "I can see it."

"We look at everybody," Foster said padding back to her computer. "We see what we see."

Foster consulted the list she'd written on the board. "Leonard's Mercedes, Barrett's Lexus. Shaw's Audi. Top three."

"We're going to need good coffee," Li said.

Symansky snorted. "Lot more than that."

Kelley grinned mischievously. "I say we make this interesting. Me and Al, you and Li. First team of eyes to spot something that moves the needle gets a free dinner on the other two. Deal?"

Li raised her hand. "I'm in. Harri?"

She knew what they were doing. They were breaking down the difficult by bringing lightness in. It's what cops did when faced with the worst kind of death, the evilness of people. It didn't mean they were callous or uncaring; it just meant they were people and needed a release valve. She managed a smile, her eyes already focused on her screen. "Real dinner at a table, not leaning against a counter with a hotdog wrapped in wax paper."

Kelley nodded his appreciation. "That's what I'm talking about. Game. On."

Li pumped a fist in the air. "For surf and turf."

"I'll take the turf," Symansky said. "You can keep the surf."

The enthusiasm of game on and surf and turf lasted about an hour before the drudgery of tired eyes on moving pixels and hundreds of passing car plates morphed into an endless bunch of nothing. Even with the window winnowed down, two more hours passed before they got their first hit.

Kelley called out, "I got Shaw's Audi pulling up in front of her house at five twenty-six p.m." Everyone got up and gathered around him, watching as Shaw got out of the Audi, hesitated on the sidewalk, then went up and rang the bell. "That's her. I started reviewing at nine Tuesday morning in case there was some activity. This is the first time she's picked up."

"She told the truth," Li said. "Dinner with her kid."

"The dinner didn't work out, though," Foster added. "She said she was gone before seven. Barrett said the same."

Kelley fast-forwarded the tape to when Shaw exited the house.

"She looks upset," Li said.

Everyone stared at the time stamp. "She told the truth about the time she left too," Foster said. "Six forty-eight."

They watched as Shaw walked to her car, then stopped to stare back at the house. "What the hell's she lookin' at?" Symansky asked.

Li pressed a finger to the screen and the figure standing in a second-floor window. "That's Zoe."

Shaw waved up at the window, then pulled her cell phone out of her pocket and made a call. "And that's when she called Leonard," Foster said. When the Audi drove off, they each straightened up, and Kelley freeze-framed the tape.

"Now we need to know if she went home, like she said." Foster went back to her desk. "That time of night, it wouldn't take her more than twenty minutes to get back downtown."

"We'll have to access those cameras, then."

"Might be quicker to check the security office at her building. They're bound to have the garage covered. Shaw would likely have to key in and out. There'd be data. But look at this. Here's Leonard's car driving into the garage at nine forty-five."

Li drew closer to the monitor. "That's definitely her driving. Good shot of her face through the windshield."

Symansky shook his head. "Drives in at a quarter to ten, then fifteen minutes give or take, she's dead."

"Whoever we're looking for didn't take a lot of time explaining himself, did he?" Kelley said.

Foster froze the image, then sat back in her chair. "None of the cars that came in anywhere close to when Leonard did fit anything on the board. Next step, match them to anyone she might have known."

"What about anybody leaving after ten?" Li asked.

Foster ran the tape forward, but there were no exits. "Nothing. Maybe he walked in instead of driving in."

"Then he'd be on the elevator," Symansky said.

Kelley's brows furrowed. "Or he took the stairs."

"Which means more footage," Li said.

Symansky sighed. "The hole we're in just keeps gettin' bigger."

Foster checked her watch. It was almost six. "We're going to get nothing else tonight. We go back to Shaw's condo. We go back to the garage. We find out when Shaw got home Tuesday and who was walking around that garage at the time Leonard was killed. And we're going to have to work closely with Tennant and Pienkowski, so we don't all work at cross purposes."

"I don't like working with strangers," Symansky said.

"When's my birthday?" Kelley asked Symansky, getting a blank look back. "Or the name of my firstborn kid?"

"What? How the hell should I know?"

"See? You work with strangers every day. Get over it."

Symansky's face bloomed red, and his eyes narrowed. "One of these days, Kelley. One of these days."

Kelley grinned. "We'll see."

Foster stood, turned her computer off. "Yeah, I'm out. We come back tomorrow. Fresh eyes."

# CHAPTER 21

Foster sat across the table from her older brother, Felix, their mother, Annemarie, at the head of the table in their father's chair. Her chair, at the other end of the dining room table, was empty, no place mat set out in front of it.

Their mother sitting in their father's chair was not usual. Foster looked over at Felix for an explanation, but he avoided her gaze. She didn't have to be a detective to know that something was up.

The chair beside Felix was empty, as was the one next to her. This was their immediate family now, minus its patriarch, not counting Felix's wife and two kids, or Foster's ex-husband, RJ, and her lost son. She lifted the fork to her mouth and swallowed her mother's meat loaf. The dinner had been impromptu, or so she'd thought. Heading out of the office, she'd made the mistake of picking up the call from Felix, who had swiftly guilted her into dinner. She had declined at first, citing work, which wasn't a lie. They were nowhere yet on either Leonard or Valdez, and there were still miles of tape to go through, but Felix knew where to turn the screws. He was a psychologist and her big brother by three years and knew more about her than she apparently knew about herself. It wasn't that she'd been avoiding these family dinners, exactly. It was the house, not the people in it, she had decided. It was the memory of those who'd once been here and now weren't. Her father taken by stroke, Reg by a bullet, and those who fell away afterward, her ex. The empty chairs now sat like headstones.

The house smelled the same as it had when she and Felix had grown up in it, like lemons and homemade corn bread, and the furniture hadn't changed either. It was dark and heavy and overly fussy but well cared for. There was heirloom china tucked away in a massive cabinet that was older than Felix and her. But the house felt like a shadow of its former self, like it was slowly fading away to nothing.

And the chairs. The spot next to her where Reg used to sit, first in a high chair, then in the chair there now, close so that she could cut his meat when he was little. The empty chair, the quieter house, the people missing almost burned like fire against her skin, consuming the comfort and peaceful feeling that had once been there and leaving the fading feeling behind.

"I've been reading about those aldermen," her mother said. "Do you have anything to do with that?"

Foster nodded. "Yes. We're working them. I have to get back to it in a few hours, which is why when Felix—"

"He told me," she said, cutting her off.

Her mother's smile warmed her, and there was nothing but love in her brown eyes, which searched hers now, gathering all manner of vital information only a mother could glean. Annemarie Foster was a good-looking woman for seventy-two. Bright eyes, brown hair graying gracefully, an open heart and mind, a soft place to land. She was a retired social worker with a full life and a thing for crossword puzzles. There were a million of them around the house in books and in folded-over newspapers. And then Felix, the spitting image of their father, now graying at the temples and sporting a beard and moustache, a Black Freud.

"I meant to get over here sooner, but things got busy."

"Hmm. You do important work. I'm so proud of you."

She studied her mother for a time, taking stock, checking. She looked well. "How're you feeling, Ma?"

She smiled. "I'm seventy-two, Harriet. Everything creaks or cracks or doesn't do what it's supposed to. You've missed a lot of Sunday family dinners."

"Sorry. I got caught up."

"Hmm." Her mother rested her elbows on the table and steepled tapered fingers under her chin. "Felix."

At the mention of his name, Felix got up from his chair, lifted his plate off the table, and walked it into the kitchen as if on command.

"We need to talk," her mother said.

Foster glanced back at the kitchen door, then over at her mother. The dinner was a setup. She put her fork down gently, thoroughly caught in the trap. Fighting it would be of no use.

"I'm all right, Mama."

"You look a little tired, and there's no joy in your face." Annemarie folded her hands on the table. "RJ told me about that boy."

"Willem. There was no reason for you to be there, so I didn't tell you about the hearing. I can just imagine what RJ had to say."

Her mother stared at her. "Hmm. Moral support's always nice, though."

"Yes, but I didn't need it. It was fine. He didn't get what he was after. RJ shouldn't have bothered you with it."

Her mother let silence hang in the air for what felt like an interminable amount of time. Foster slipped her right hand into her blazer pocket and felt for the paper clips she knew were there. Her mother didn't miss it.

"I need to see more of you, Harriet Louise. I'm old. Nothing's promised. You call, you check in, but you don't come around a lot, and I need to see your face. I helped make it; I think I should get to see it more than once in a blue moon."

Foster pushed her plate away. "I'll do better. It's just work—"

"It's just a house, Harriet. They're just chairs. Wood and varnish. Things. In a hundred years none of this will be here. You, me, Felix . . .

we'll all be gone. But we're here now. Now's all there is. I'm sitting in your father's chair. Because it's just a chair. I've said this before to you, and I'll keep saying it until you hear it. You've wasted too much time holding on to what's already gone. That's not living. You keep doing that, you're going to miss the life that's here."

Foster shifted in her chair, uncomfortable. She was a grown woman, a cop, but not in this house. "I don't want to talk about this."

"I know you don't." There was a moment of silence as her mother focused on her, those knowing eyes emitting a compassion and an empathy that nearly stole her breath. She didn't want to cry, for fear that if she allowed herself to start, she might never stop.

"If we accept folks coming into our lives," Annemarie said, "we also have to accept them going when their time comes. That's life. You see death every day. The waste of spirit. I know it bothers you. It bothers most people. I can't sit by and watch my own daughter waste hers. You don't want to talk to Felix, even though me and your daddy paid good money for him to get that fancy doctor's degree, I get it. But he's got people you can talk to that'll help you get through all this. It's time for you to get through, Harriet. You hear me?"

Foster was too stunned to speak; the little bit of meat loaf she had consumed before the snare snapped shut sat like a brick in her stomach. "It's not that easy."

"I didn't say it was easy, I said it's time." Her mother rose, walked over, and wrapped her arms around her from behind. "You're thinking right now that it's not for me to say when. Normally, that'd be true. But I'm old, Harriet, and I'm your mother, and I will not go to my grave knowing you're lost and unhappy." She kissed her on the top of her head. "So, it's time. Now finish your meat loaf. Felix."

She padded back to their father's chair and sat down again. Felix came in from the kitchen as if on cue with three slices of red velvet cake on a tray. "I brought dessert, figuring we'd need something sweet." He put the tray on the table and handed a saucer to her. "Your favorite.

Made by Mama just for you. And I'm here for anything you need, you know that."

Foster took the cake. It was her favorite, only when her mother made it, because it tasted like love. She dipped a spoon in the cream cheese frosting, still stunned at the openness that had gone before. Her mother, of course, was right, but she was also wrong. Getting through, how and when, was still up to her. Her mother had just given her a reality check and words of wisdom. None of them would live forever. Nothing was promised. Memories she could keep when those she loved were gone. And a house was just a house, and a chair just a chair.

She looked across the table at her brother. "Felix?"

He stopped, a fork to his mouth. "Hmm?"

"It's never a good idea to lie to the police."

He pointed his fork at her. "First, I didn't lie. I just didn't tell you Mama had something to talk to you about. Second, I wasn't talking to the police. I was talking to my baby sister who I love and worry about, and who used to eat paste in the first grade, so obviously has a history of not knowing what's good for her. Now eat your cake, and let's talk about something else."

She narrowed her eyes. "I have handcuffs in my bag."

He grinned. "I outweigh you by at least sixty pounds."

She took a bite of cake. "Forget you, Felix."

He chuckled. "Right. Like I'm going to let you."

Hours later, Foster stood at the board in her living room eating another piece of cake, her eyes on the notations. She zeroed in on the lone key that had been sitting on Valdez's desk, wondering if Tennant had accounted for it yet. It was too late to call and ask now, but she made a mental note to do it first thing in the morning.

She backed away from the board, ready to call it a night, though there wasn't much left of it. Turning the lights out on her way upstairs, she took the cake with her.

# CHAPTER 22

At nine the next morning, Li came in and tossed the morning's paper on Foster's desk as she sat busy at her computer.

"See this? The headline's bad enough—*Second Alderman Killed!* But inside, the small piece on Parker? He's already jockeying for his mother's aldermanic seat. She's not even buried yet. Little skeevy, if you ask me."

"Saw it. I also saw Hastrup's report this morning. Already dinging us for not doing our jobs fast enough. He'll keep it up until the whole city's turned inside out. Listen to this, it's the preliminary report from Grant on Valdez's autopsy. The wounds are consistent with the use of a long, slender knife, like a fillet knife she says." She looked over at Li. "You ever see a fillet knife?"

"No, who do I look like, Julia Child?"

Foster googled it, then sat back in her chair. "Thin, long, flexible. It's used to cut fish. Why a fillet knife? I'd think you'd want to come at Valdez with something a lot sturdier, something that means business."

"Like your standard hunting knife," Li said. "Serrated for maximum damage. So maybe the fillet was a weapon of opportunity. The killer got the impulse, looked around, saw it there, and grabbed it."

"Do you have a fillet knife in your kitchen?"

Li snorted. "No idea. My mother does the cooking in our house. The kitchen's not my room. Bet you Shaw's got one. She's just out of prison. She likely wouldn't have had time to get to the sporting-goods store for anything better."

"You're so convinced it's her. Like Lonergan. But if a woman Marin Shaw's size comes at a man Valdez's size with a thin little fish knife, the guy's not just going to stand there and let her stab him three times."

"But what man's going to come at a guy with a fish knife? And remember two of those strikes came from the back. He likely never saw it coming."

"Which would make the third strike a lot easier," Foster conceded.

"Fillet knife. A weapon, maybe, for someone not used to killing. These aren't perfect kills."

Li frowned. "But they are planned kills. And good enough works."

Neither spoke for a time, but the wheels turned. Finally, Foster stood, grabbed her coat. "Let's go see if we can talk to Aaron Parker."

"Not Shaw?"

"Not until we can place her *not* where she says she was on either night."

"Ugh. The footage."

"Or eyewitnesses. So far, we've got her at dinner with her family. That's not enough."

Li grabbed her coat and her coffee mug. "You think Parker killed his mother for her job? Might be a motive. But it doesn't explain Valdez."

"We'll see."

"You keep him talking," Li said. "I'll check his kitchen for a missing fillet knife."

Foster smiled. "We're not doing that."

Li shrugged. "Missed opportunity."

———

Parker let them in, but he didn't look too pleased to be doing it. The house was empty, except for him, all the mourners from before gone, the front room filled with flower arrangements that inevitably showed up when a person died. The place smelled like a funeral home, flowery, but also like something industrial, something out of place. Parker was out of his suit and dressed in a pair of dark jeans, tasseled loafers, and a blue button-down shirt. He didn't offer anything, not even a seat. Foster and Li weren't guests. This was business. Foster's eyes swept the room searching for the source of the incongruous smell, quickly landing on a box of campaign leaflets with Parker's face on them. Printer's ink. Had Parker gone right from the mourners to the printers and asked for a rush job?

"You're lucky you caught me," Parker said. "I'm just here getting things in order. Jeniece's coming later to help. My mother never threw anything away. Do you have something new?"

Foster watched him, still wondering about the leaflets, noticing he wasn't as off putting as he'd been during their first encounter. Maybe it was because Bigelow wasn't with them this time. "Mind if we ask you a few more questions, Mr. Parker?"

Li smiled, then surreptitiously craned her neck to get a look down the long hall that led to the kitchen in back.

"All right," he said, gesturing toward the couch. "Forgot my manners. Sit, please. Did you find anything? Some new evidence?"

"We're pursuing all avenues," Foster said. She sat on the edge of the couch, Li beside her, Parker across from them in an easy chair. "We're trying to piece together your mother's last movements, who she saw, where she might have been. You said before you hadn't talked to her in days and hadn't seen her the day she died."

"That's right. Jeniece checked in more than I did. That mother-daughter thing. Besides, I've been extra busy lately. I'm an insurance executive. I was at the office most of that Tuesday, then went home. I was asleep when you two showed up at my door." He twisted the gold band on his finger. "I guess other cops went to Jeniece's." He ducked his head. "A part of me still can't believe this is all happening."

"I think we asked you this before," Foster said, "but you aren't aware of any enemies or conflicts your mother might have had at the time of her death? Professional or personal?"

Parker sighed. "It's no secret my mother was outspoken. That could rub people the wrong way. She had her battles in the city council. She even ticked off a few people in the press and in her ward. But nobody who'd go this far." He straightened his collar. "But first, I'd like to apologize for how I acted last time. It was a tough day. A lot of people. And then when Bigelow walked in. I . . ." He held out his hands in mock surrender. "He really did leave her high and dry, I felt. But before that even, he overstepped, in my opinion."

"Overstepped how?" Foster and Li asked the question in unison, and the double echo hit the room like the amplification from a megaphone.

Parker drew back slightly. "Me and him didn't exactly see eye to eye, and I had the feeling he was trying to wedge himself in where he didn't belong. In family matters. I don't want to get too specific. I was all right with him picking up and leaving, don't get me wrong, only he could have done it with some class."

"You're running for your mother's seat," Foster said. "Sudden decision?"

Parker flicked a look at the leaflets. "No. I told my mother weeks ago I planned on running. Nothing against her, but it was time for some new blood."

"How'd she take that?" Li asked.

Parker rolled his shoulders as if sloughing off the question. "It wasn't personal. I felt . . . *feel* the people in our ward need somebody in there fighting for them, not playing the game. My mother leaves big shoes to fill, but I'm committed to the community."

"What game?" Foster asked.

"Politics. I'm an outsider. I'll get things done."

Foster was unimpressed with the campaign pitch. She was more interested in how Parker's discussion with his mother over his coming after her job might've gone down. "And how *did* she take it?" Foster offered a little smile. "You didn't say."

Parker glanced over at the leaflets. "She was upset, but it was nothing serious. We're both adults. Let the best man win, right?"

"Is that how your sister feels too?" Li asked.

Parker dipped his head again. "It's got nothing to do with Jeniece. It's me making the run, not her." Parker's head lifted; he stuck his chin out. "Public service is in my blood. My mother would want me to carry on her legacy."

There was a short silence, one neither Foster nor Li felt compelled to break for a time, but that didn't mean they weren't getting any information from Parker. His body language, his discomfort, spoke volumes. "So, you were home asleep the night your mother died," Li said.

"And you can't think of anyone who'd want to do your mother harm?" Foster finally asked.

Parker shook his head. "That's right."

Foster scribbled in her notepad. "Your mother have any connection to Alderman George Valdez, besides sitting on the council with him?"

Parker's eyes widened. "Valdez. I heard about that. Someone broke into his office. Some coincidence. God, this city is really going to the dogs. Another reason I'm running. I can really get in there and make a difference. But, no, my mother wasn't close to Valdez, as far as I knew. Both were battling progressives, though, as I will be."

"*You* ever meet Valdez?" Li asked.

Parker shook his head. "His ward's in Pilsen, right?"

Li smiled. "Little Village."

Foster slid a glance down at Parker's hands. Unmarred. No nicks, no cuts. Not even a single callus.

"Would you know who has a key to your mother's ward office?"

"Key? What's that got to do with anything?"

"The more information we have, sir, the better."

"Eh, all right. Let's see. My mother, obviously. The office manager. The owners of the building and the maintenance guy. There may be a spare here in her desk somewhere for emergencies. She kept it pretty tight. I'll do the same." Foster made the notation. "Thank you. Anything else you think we should know?" Foster asked, putting her notepad away. "Mr. Parker?"

He held his hands out. "I've told you all I can. My mother was a great woman. She was obviously caught in the wrong place at the wrong time. A tragedy. A great loss to the city."

Foster stood, Li too. "Thanks for your time, then. We'll be in touch."

"And, again, condolences to you and your family," Li added.

They stood on the front sidewalk watching the gloomy street for a moment as a cold wind blew through their winter coats, their breaths visible when they hit the air. They hurried to their car at the curb.

"Nothing wrong with being ambitious," Foster said.

Li blew out a few puffs of air, watching as they disappeared like smoke from a chimney. "Unless you kill your mother for her job."

Foster slid her a look. "And Valdez?"

"There's that. But she let *someone* she knew into her car. I don't care what kind of family you have, you never in a million years think your own kid's going to kill you. You asked about the key to her office?"

"The one found on Valdez's desk bothers me. Just wanted to see if limiting keys was a usual thing. I suspect it would be."

"So, more on Parker."

Foster nodded. "Yep."

"Want me to drive?" Li asked.

Foster lobbed the keys to her. Li caught them, then just stood there gawking at her. "What?"

"You know how many cops I've ridden with who refused to cough the keys up? Insisted on driving?"

Foster smiled, opened the passenger door, and slid inside. "Men?"

Li slid in behind the wheel. "Every last one."

***

They pushed through the door back at the office a half hour later, glad to be out of the cold.

"Yo, Foster, you got a visitor," the desk sergeant called out in a gruff tone. Hammermill was beach-bally around the middle, the buttons straining on his uniform blouse, but his eyes were keen, and he knew his job. He thumbed a chubby digit toward a row of chairs off to the side. Foster turned to see her old partner's husband sitting there, his elbows on fidgety knees.

She signaled to Li to go on. "I'll meet you up there." Then she walked over to where he sat. "Mike?"

He popped up, gave her a long, tight hug. "Harri." He pulled back. "Sorry to just drop by like this, but I need to talk to you. It can't wait."

"Sure, no problem. Hold on."

She went over and spoke to Hammermill, then cleared Mike to go up. Easing him into a small interview room, she closed the door behind them and gestured for him to take a seat. He looked nervous, agitated. Not like him, not at all. Glynnis had been dead now six months, leaving behind Mike and their two sons. Maybe things weren't going well? She kept in touch, checked in regularly, but maybe that wasn't enough? It likely wasn't, given her mother's loving rebuke the night before.

After pulling out a chair, she sat beside him. "Mike?"

He looked exhausted, like he hadn't slept for years. The tired breath he let out sounded of misery as he squeezed his green eyes shut, then reached into the backpack he held in his hands and pulled out a manila envelope. Placing it on the table without explanation, he pushed it toward her. "You were the only one I could come to. You're family. It was in our mailbox two days ago. I haven't slept since. I don't know what to make of it or what to do, but I know what it looks like."

Foster picked up the envelope, opened it, and drew two eight-by-ten black-and-white photographs out. It took a moment to realize what she was looking at, but when she did, her breath caught. It was a photo of her former partner, Detective Glynnis Thompson, with a man, not

Mike. It wasn't an intimate shot, but evidence of an exchange. The two looked to be outside, somewhere isolated, industrial; there were brick buildings in the background and chain-link fences, like an old factory or manufacturing yard. Foster's eyes focused on a white envelope caught in freeze-frame passing between them with no way of knowing who was passing it and who was receiving. Either way, the pass looked shady, problematic, and completely out of character for Glynnis, who'd been as honest and as straight up as they came. Foster stared at Glynnis's grainy images, focusing on her face and the expression on it. She recognized the look. Glynnis was dialed in, not playing. Whatever was going on, whatever *this* was, it was serious. Glynnis's goofy side, her love of a good prank, and her wicked sense of humor were not on display. She'd obviously stuffed all that.

Foster had never seen the man in the photograph before. He was white, middle aged, dressed in black pants and a checked blazer, his face visible only in profile, his hairline receded practically to his ears. He looked like an old gangster past his prime, an old-time hit man whose eyesight had gone and who was now too fond of hard drink. Was Glynnis paying him? Was he paying her? What was this?

A faint time stamp, top right on both images, read August 9, 7:02 a.m. Foster's stomach roiled. Her blood raced. She turned the photos over to find a telephone number on the back of one of them. Lower right-hand corner. Local area code. Nothing more. Checking the envelope next, she found no postmark. No evidence that the envelope had been mailed and delivered. Someone had physically placed it into Mike's mailbox. They knew where he lived.

"Two days ago, you said?" Her voice was heavy, deliberate.

"Thank God I found it before the kids did. This looks like a payoff. Doesn't it look like that? Was she dirty? Please, Harri, tell me she wasn't dirty."

"She *wasn't* dirty."

"But these photos . . ."

"There's a number on the back. Did you call it?"

Mike shook his head, his eyes on hers. "To tell you the truth, I was afraid to. Afraid of what I'd hear. It's an exchange. You can clearly see that."

Foster shot up from her chair. "She *wasn't* dirty, Mike."

She said it, believed it, but she was worried all the same, scared. She wanted to burn the photos, the envelope, push it away, stuff it, anything to get it as far away from her as she could get it. She had known Glynnis. The woman in the photograph bore no resemblance to what she knew for sure about her, so she held to the partner she'd known, the one she'd trusted.

August 9. Seven a.m. She was sure Mike had missed it, or else he would have caught the significance and mentioned it. The photos would have been taken right before Glynnis's shift. But that wasn't what made Foster's hands shake now or her head begin to throb; it wasn't what snaked a ribbon of dread through every sinew and tendon in her frightened body. August 9 was the day before Glynnis, her partner, her friend, had driven into the staff lot at their old station, idled for a time, according to cops who'd walked past her car, and then drew her service weapon to her head and pulled the trigger.

Every cop in the building had heard the shot. Foster had come running out with everyone else to see a crowd around Glynnis's black Nissan with the Blackhawks decal on the back bumper. She had thought at first Glynnis had been ambushed. Some in the city held no love for cops, but a frantic sweep of the lot revealed no one who *wasn't* a cop. Stillness followed, silence. No cops on radios, no one running toward a fleeing suspect. Just a stunned, solemn crowd of blue around a dusty Nissan, an eerie, reverent hush, which said everything and would later become the marker between before and after.

Certain images were seared into her brain as a result. The shattered driver's side window. The way Glynnis's right hand, still holding the gun, lay on the middle console lifeless. She remembered that her nails had been painted pale pink, freshly done, Foster knew, by her favorite tech, named Maggie, who worked at a salon around the corner from the station. Glynnis's blue eyes were at half-mast. She was gone. The contact burn on the right side of her head, the hole the round had made, the blood, thick, angry, too much of it, soaking her forehead and cheek. The smell of death. The heaviness of the air. The desolate feeling it all gave her. And then the gasp. And the scream. Both hers. She remembered lunging for the car door and being pulled back by someone. CPR, she had thought as her brain clutched for an action she could do, assistance she could give. There was still a chance, her fear had convinced her irrationally, despite what her eyes told her. Not again, she remembered muttering before she shut down, walled up, and turned to stone.

Foster backed away from the table, away from Mike. She had no idea what it all meant, but she'd known Glynnis. They'd had frank and honest talks about every aspect of their lives, marriages, kids, politics, aspirations, goals. They shared holidays, vacations. Their families had blended, and they'd closed cases together. Glynnis had been the rock on which Foster had depended when Reg was killed and her marriage disintegrated, weighed down by grief and loss and assigned blame. Foster had been the same rock for Glynnis when her mother died of cancer. More than friends, family, sisters. Foster swallowed hard, then dug for the cop. She picked up the photo with the number on it, slid her phone out of her pocket, and dialed.

"What are you doing?" Mike said, slowly coming out of his chair, his face a sheet of stunned white.

She turned her back to him and waited for the pickup. She didn't have to wait long. Two rings. Then nothing on the open line. "Who is this?" she asked, angry now, livid. Nothing came back for a moment, and then it did.

"I knew he'd come to you," the man said. His voice was low, unhurried. He sounded playful, slightly amused. "Though I hadn't expected it to take him two whole days."

"Who's this?"

"Detective Harriet Foster. CPD's finest."

Foster moved back to the table, sat, and got a pen and notepad out of her pocket. "What do you want? What are these photographs?"

"We'll get to all that later. This is just to open the lines of communication. To establish our working relationship."

It would have been easier to put the call on speaker and have both hands free to make her notes of the call, but she didn't want Mike to hear. He was spooked enough, so she held the phone in her left hand and wrote down what she could in a hurried scrawl, noting the tone of voice and anything else she thought was salient. No background noises, she noted. No indication where the caller might be. Working relationship?

"I don't work for you," Foster said.

"That's what Detective Thompson said at first. Then we made a deal. She gives me what I want when I want it, and I won't kill her kids."

Foster's pen shook. She stopped breathing.

"I'll make the same deal with you, Detective Foster. You give me what I want when I want it, and I won't kill her kids. I know this is a lot to process now, so I'll give you a little time to get your mind around it. I'll be in touch."

The line went dead, but Foster couldn't move to end the call. She held the phone and the pen just as they were.

"Harri? Who was that?" Mike asked. "What's wrong?"

It wasn't until he shook her arm and brought her back that she put her phone away and closed her notepad. "Have you noticed anything strange around the house? Anyone hanging around? Any weird phone calls?"

"Nothing, until this envelope showed up. What's going on. Who *was* that?"

She stood. Picked up the envelope. It was hers now. "Where are the kids, Mike?"

"I dropped them off at the movies. Why?"

"Can you pick them up?"

"Pick them up? They usually walk. We're only five blocks from . . ."

Her eyes met his. "Can you pick them up, Mike? When the movie lets out."

He caught on. "They're after our kids?"

"I'll handle it," she said. "If anything else shows up, let me know. If anyone calls you or contacts you, call me right away, okay? Now go home."

He looked down at the envelope in her hands. "What about those?"

"These stay with me. I'll take care of it, Mike."

She walked him out, then watched him go, the envelope in her sweaty hand burning a hole in her soul. How a thing looked and what a thing was, she knew, could be quite different, a matter of perspective. One thing she knew with certainty was that Detective Glynnis Thompson had been a good cop, and she would go to her grave believing it.

The voice on the phone. The deal he had hinted at. *What I want when I want it.* Of course, Glynnis would have done whatever she needed to protect her kids, but why hadn't she come to her? She could have helped. Had Glynnis felt as trapped as she did now? Had the strain of it become too much?

The man on the phone knew who she was and knew that Mike would come to her. How? Did he know her? Did she know him? He had sounded overly confident that she'd fall in line, as Glynnis appeared to have done. What was he after? What game was he playing?

Fuming, rageful, Foster stormed past her desk and into the women's restroom, where she flung the envelope into the sink and then paced the floor wanting to hit something, wanting to hurt someone, wanting to punch out at the world and everyone in it. She couldn't scream, or else the entire building would come running, so she ate the fury, screaming inside so loud that her organs felt like they shook from the vibration.

"Jesus." It was part lament, part entreaty. "Help. Jesus. Help me." It had been five years since she'd asked for help, prayed for it. How could she pray to a God who'd taken everything from her? But she reached up now, for Glynnis. Her eyes lifted to the ceiling, a glare, a threatening glower. "Don't make me beg you."

The door opened. It was Li. "What's going on?" Her eyes drifted to the sink and the envelope, then back to Foster, standing visibly shaken in the middle of the room, her equilibrium gone. "What the hell happened?"

Foster took a breath, then reached over and grabbed the envelope. She trusted Li, respected her. She was her partner now, but she still felt the pull to protect Glynnis. And she didn't know yet what she was dealing with. How could she, in all good conscience, drag Li into it? "Everything's good. I just needed a minute." She pushed past her with a bogus smile that she dragged up from somewhere. She hoped it was convincing, but how could it be? "What's up next?"

She could feel Li's eyes on her back and knew the smile hadn't worked. But she couldn't worry about that now. They had two dead aldermen to deal with, and now she had hooks in her, put there by a voice on the phone.

# CHAPTER 23

Marin stood at her window staring down at the bandages on her palms, the sting of the scrapes and cuts throbbing underneath. Nothing broken, just the bruises and the cuts and the sinking feeling that someone was out to hurt her.

"Marin, you should rest," Charlotte said from the couch. "That bump you took to the head is no joke. And why didn't you call me before talking to the police? How many times have I told you not to say a word to anyone without me there? Lawyers really are the worst clients."

"Someone had just tried to kill me."

Charlotte rose. "Sit. I'll make you a cup of tea." Marin didn't move. "Marin. *Sit.*"

When Charlotte returned from the kitchen minutes later with tea mugs on a tray, she found Marin sitting on the couch gazing off into nothing. "Drink. Breathe. You're sure you were pushed? Absolutely sure?"

Marin lifted the mug, took a sip. "I felt their hands on my back. I don't think the police believed me. I can't blame them for looking at me. I knew them both, didn't I? I go away, nothing happens. I get out, and both of them are dead? If I were the police, I'd suspect me too."

"Did you kill them?"

"What?"

"Did you kill them? I have to ask."

"Of course not."

Charlotte leaned back, took a sip of tea. "Good. Consider this, then. It's likely that Leonard and Valdez, who clearly crossed you, also crossed somebody else. Their shadiness didn't start and end with you, is the point. And that someone, not you, finally called them on it. Some would call that karma."

"This isn't funny, Char."

"I'm just stating the facts. They cost you three years. You don't seem to be pissed off about that, so I'm pissed for you. I make no apologies for my feelings here."

"But why now? If it's nothing to do with me, if it's somebody else, why this moment?"

Charlotte shrugged. "Because, like you said, now makes it look like it's got to be you. Lucky for us, cops need solid evidence, and they haven't got any because there's none to find, so relax."

"I can't be involved in this. With the impending divorce . . . custody? I can't be on the police's suspect list. You know Will. He'll take this and twist it, use it against me. He'll make me out to be some crazy murderer, and I'll never get Zoe."

"No one's taking Zoe. I won't let them."

Marin stood again, padded over to the window. "You don't know everything."

"What don't I know?"

"George Valdez."

Charlotte chuckled. "So, you *did* kill him?" Marin turned to face her, an odd expression on her face that worried her. "What about him?"

Marin stared at Charlotte sitting there in her lawyer suit, her designer heels kicked off. It was 2:00 p.m., but Marin doubted her friend had business in the office on a Saturday. Charlotte was senior counsel in her firm. The position had its privileges.

Charlotte held up her hands. "Wait. Stop. Are you talking to me as your friend or as your lawyer?"

"Hopefully, both."

Charlotte stood up, straightened the hem of her blouse. She then ran her fingers through her hair and took a breath. "All right. Go. Lawyer first."

"I didn't kill him," Marin said.

Relief appeared to flood over Charlotte, and she slumped over at the waist, her hands on her knees. "Oh, for fuck's sake. Thank God. I thought I was about to hear a confession."

"But we did have an affair. A *brief* affair."

Charlotte plopped back down on the couch. "Not a crime. Half the world's having an affair with the other half."

"But it *is* a connection," Marin said. "I was all over the place back then, drinking, stealing, gambling my life away. It was like I was someone else. You remember. It didn't last long, but the fact that it happened at all and that it ended the way it did . . ."

"Have you spoken with Valdez since you got out?"

Marin shook her head. "No. Purposefully."

"No calls, texts, DMs, skywritten messages?"

Marin hesitated.

"Marin, I know your secrets, most of them anyway, and you know mine. You're safe with me." Marin shook her head. "Then you're in the clear." Charlotte looked around the apartment lasciviously. "Did he ever come here?"

"Once or twice."

"And you went to his place?"

"No, his place had his wife in it. We'd meet in his office. He even gave me a key. It all felt so dangerous and illicit. We eventually came to our senses, or he did."

"Will know about this?"

Marin shook her head. "Too self-absorbed. But I didn't care then, and I don't now. He had his own affairs to worry about, didn't he? Look, the important thing here is, I can be linked to two murder victims, and

151

now someone's targeting me in a really frightening way. I don't want any of this touching Zoe. What should I do?"

Charlotte sat up, slipped back into her pumps. "Let me think about it. What we don't do is throw ourselves on the funeral pyre. You're not obligated to help the police with their case. If they suspect you, they're going to have to work to prove it, and then they're going to have to go through me. That's number one. Meanwhile, we get this divorce rolling. Will's going to make that difficult enough, not because he loves you and doesn't want to lose you, but because he's angry and a vindictive son of a bitch." Their eyes held for a time. "Full custody's going to be an upward climb, Marin, but I'll do my best for you and Zoe."

"Thank you." Marin took a deep breath, relieved she had an advocate on her side. "I'm ready for it. What about what happened today?"

"Well, we can hire a bodyguard to tail you."

Marin shook her head adamantly. "I've had enough guards."

"You can stay indoors for a while. Lock the doors."

"And I've had enough jail cells."

Charlotte picked up her coat lying over a chair, grabbed her bag. "Any idea who might want you dead?"

Marin let a beat go. "Yes."

"But you're not going to tell me, are you?"

"Better if I didn't."

"At least give me a hint where to tell the police to look if you turn up dead."

Marin grimaced. "Nice."

"Well? You're leaving me nothing to go on here, Mar. You're scaring me, to tell the truth. Someone following you, pushing you into the street. Somebody's trying to send a message." Charlotte buttoned her coat and leaned in to give Marin a peck on the cheek. "Just be careful, will you? Don't borrow trouble. Call me if you need me, night or day. Promise?"

Marin hugged Charlotte again. "You're the best."

"I know. I'll check in later. Lock this door behind me. And cut down on the long walks, huh?"

Marin locked the door, then stood there for a moment before padding into the bedroom to lie down. Her palms felt numb, and she could feel the angry abrasions made by the potholed street and rock salt. She wanted everything to go away: the gray, the push, the cops, Will, all the mistakes she'd made, the disappointments she'd caused. She wanted to be clean, new. For Zoe and herself.

Bypassing the king-size bed she'd shared unhappily with Will, she walked into her closet and over to the sliding drawer where she kept her expensive jewelry. Middle drawer, left side there was a small Limoges trinket box her grandmother had given her on her twelfth birthday, pale green with a purple violet in full bloom on the top. The box wasn't expensive, but it was priceless to her. It's where she kept the diamond earrings her grandmother left her, which she wore only on special occasions. Grandmother Rose had been the only one who'd really seen her. Marin had faltered under her father's dictatorial roof. Her mother's compliance and insistence on conformity had nearly suffocated her. There were rules and limitations, a narrow path. The right school. The right clubs. The right dress. The right man. The right look. That's how she'd gotten stuck with Will and the rest of it. When the dam eventually broke and the right everything didn't work any longer, that's when Marin imploded. She could see that now. Echoes.

She lifted the lid on the box, ran her fingers along the earrings shining inside, then slid them aside, looking for the key she'd hidden there years ago now. It was the key George had given her. The key to the office where they'd meet. It hadn't been George she'd wanted. He could have been anyone anywhere, as long as he wasn't Will, as long as it was forbidden and wrong. The truth was that he hadn't wanted her, either, not really. They were just treading water, hiding from hard things.

Marin lifted the box, moved the earrings around again, the sinking feeling growing.

It wasn't there.

The key to George's office was gone.

# CHAPTER 24

Foster read over the ME reports for the fifth time, but the information just wouldn't stick. She glanced up at the clock on the wall. It was after three. She'd checked. The early show let out at two thirty. Mike would have picked up the kids by now, and they'd be safe at home. Needing the confirmation, she sent him a quick text and waited for the response, which came back almost immediately. Just two words. We're home.

The office buzzed with activity around her. She could feel the energy, the static, the rush of smelly cops moving behind her niggling at leads and parts of leads, making calls, slamming phones, the *fuck*s and *bullshit*s and *goddamn*s giving voice to their growing frustration. She had to focus. Though she and Li hadn't been called into Griffin's office all day, she knew the pressure was still on. Pressure rolled from top to bottom, she knew, but they weren't magicians, or Supermen. Cops didn't often get miracles.

She flicked a look at her watch, willing the second hand to stop, freezing time, just long enough for her mind to stop racing, just long enough to catch a breath and get a handle on her fear, long enough to process what had happened and find a way out. Had Glynnis done the same? She must have. She'd have done anything to keep her boys safe. Foster ran a hand across her forehead. Where had she been? Why hadn't she noticed Glynnis was going through something? More guilt. More blame. Useless.

Pushing the autopsy report away, Foster grabbed a bottle of aspirin from her top drawer. She consumed far too much of it but needed the relief. She couldn't work, couldn't think with her head pounding. She thought of the Valdez scene. The weapon hadn't been found at the scene or anywhere near it. Not a break-in. Not a robbery, though it had been staged to look like one. A single key left on his desk. No information yet from Tennant or Pienkowski on whether they found prints on the key, so at the moment it was just a key, unimportant until it became important. Why were the dimes in his pocket and not down his throat, like with Leonard? Foster downed the aspirin with a gulp of cold coffee, her eyes locked in a faraway stare. Did the killer run out of time? Had something gone wrong?

"Ready to run the case?"

Foster startled and looked up to see Li standing over her with a legal pad and a bag of potato chips. She slipped her phone into her pocket and gathered her notes. "Sure. Give me a second?"

Li's eyes narrowed. "You okay? You look like you've seen a ghost."

Foster eyed Griffin's door. She should report the photograph and the phone call she'd had. That was what was required. But then Glynnis would be out of her hands and in someone else's, someone who didn't know there was no way her partner could have done anything wrong despite what the photo suggested. She was still Glynnis's backup. She could fix this. She could make it stop.

Foster grabbed the reports and tucked them in with everything else, not wanting to have this conversation or any other. It wasn't that she didn't trust Li. She did. But the drive to protect Glynnis overrode even that.

Monitoring time was becoming a compulsion. Another nervous, fidgety check of her watch proved fruitless. Only a minute or two more had passed. Watching time crawl, wanting it to stop or pass more quickly made her desperate to move, to do, to go, and the aspirin wasn't working yet.

She headed for the whiteboard at the front of the room. The board. She knew a lot of cops who didn't work that way, but for her it helped to see everything laid out in black and white. That way it was easier to see connections when they formed. "Anything new on Parker?" Foster asked Li without breaking stride.

"Oh, we've changed subjects then?"

"For now, please."

"Okay. I did some digging. Parker's a liar, but we kind of knew that already?"

Symansky and Bigelow saw them coming and pulled their chairs up to gather around Foster's board. Kelley and Lonergan weren't there. Symansky anticipated her question. "Mr. Shakespeare and Lonergan are on their way in now. They went to talk to Leonard's daughter, since you guys already took the son. Bet you five dollars Lonergan walks in here with lunch only for himself."

Li pulled up a rolling chair. Foster went to the board and picked up a marker to begin filling in what they had so far. "Vera?"

Foster's use of her first name appeared to throw Li for half a second. She consulted her notes on the legal pad. "Parker told us he was an insurance executive. Half right. He *sells* insurance. He's an agent who works out of his house. No arrests. No warrants. His car's been repoed twice in the last eighteen months. Divorced a year ago. One kid. A boy. Ten. He's behind on child support. The financial instability could be another motive for him killing his mother, besides him wanting her job. They didn't exactly have the best relationship, according to Bigs. She dies, he's bound to inherit something—a share in the house, at least."

Foster scribbled the information on the board. "Might fit. But while Valdez is connected to his mother's death by the dimes, Parker's got nothing to do with Valdez, or am I wrong? What motive would he have for killing *him*?"

"He wouldn't be the first idiot to try and cover up a murder with another one," Symansky said. "Never works, but these mopes always try it. I blame television."

Foster scribbled the theories on the board, though that one didn't scan. They hadn't released information to the press on the dimes. Parker couldn't have known about them unless he'd killed both victims. There was something deeper going on, she was sure of it. "Bigs?" She turned to face him. "You know him. Is Parker capable of shooting his mother in the head and stupid enough to try and make it look like she did it?"

Bigelow crossed his arms over his bulky frame. "Look, it's no secret I can't stand the little weasel, but you'd have to be a special kind of asshole to do something like that. And look at Valdez. He was way bigger than Parker and a lot fitter. He could easily have gotten that knife away from him." He shook his head. "Nah. Parker doesn't have the stones. I think if he'd done it, he'd either be halfway to the Dominican Republic by now or he'd have pissed himself when you came at him again at the house."

"And he looked dry when we left him," Li said.

"I don't think the piss factor is going to hold up in court," Symansky said dryly. "We gotta come up with something that puts him either in that garage or at Valdez's office, and so far, we got nothin'."

"You mentioned him being a liar," Bigelow said. "That's true. When I worked for Deanna, she was always chastising him for not living up to his potential, not trying hard enough. There was something going on, but it was personal, and she didn't clue me in to it, so I never found out what the real issue was. He never mentioned Valdez either."

Foster circled the words *THE KEY* on the board. "The key is odd." She wrote the word *PRINTS*, followed by a question mark. "Waiting for this."

"And the footage from Shaw's condo, the adjacent parking garage, and from around Valdez's office should be in soon. And we've got tons of street-cam stuff to still get through."

"And we're sticking with betrayal?" Symansky asked. "The thirty pieces of silver?"

"Hard not to," Bigelow said. "I'm wondering why Valdez's were found outside of him instead of inside."

"Maybe it went down too fast, and the killer had to kill him quick," Li said. "It'd be hard to get a dead man to swallow anything."

"He could have shoved the dimes into his mouth," Bigelow said. "Afterward."

Symansky blanched. "All right. All right. Can we move the fuck on from this particular point? We got dimes on the board. Let's just leave the sick scenarios to ourselves, okay? We're dealing with somebody who's obviously yanking our chains. These freaks just *love* to get cute."

"And none of that sounds like Parker, according to Bigs," Foster said, giving him a look.

"Not as far as I know him, but like I said, we didn't hang out. I only got a whiff of him in passing. What I do know is he resented the hell out of Deanna and his sister, Jeniece, him being such a fuckup. He thinks he's the smartest thing going, but personally, I don't think he can blow out a candle without three people showing him how to do it. The fact that his mother had a class A job, and he's stuck in the background shoveling crap, galls him. Resentment could get him to think she betrayed him and him to feel some kind of way about it."

All eyes turned to the bustle caused by Lonergan and Kelley strolling in, peeling off overcoats, knocking wet off their wool like they'd just come out of a sleet storm. Lonergan tossed a Chick-fil-A bag on the desk, soggy from the elements. Symansky smirked, nodded, proved right again.

"God, I hate fucking February," Lonergan said, flinging his coat and hat onto a chair. "When I clock out for the last time, I'm packing my shit and moving south. Key West. Or Miami. Get me some of that rum, sit on the beach all day. This Chicago-winter bullshit is for the birds."

Kelley grinned. "You wouldn't last two seconds on the beach before somebody harpooned you."

"True dat," Bigelow said over a chorus of chuckles. Foster didn't join in. Her mind was on the voice on the phone and on the threat to the kids and on what she was going to do about it.

She turned to see Li staring at her, then hastily turned away to take the board in, giving Kelley and Lonergan a second to settle down. She looked over her notations, the driver's license photos of Leonard and Valdez tacked to the board, a line drawn connecting them with a question mark below it. Foster approached again and wrote down the names *Franklin* and *Meehan*, then circled them both.

"The phone chain the night Leonard died. Leonard and Valdez are gone. That leaves Franklin and Meehan." She turned to face the team. "Li and I talked to Meehan briefly. He says he was home with his wife. Let's follow up. Franklin's up next."

Kelley studied the board. "I see you've got Parker still an open question up there. We might be able to close that one off, at least. We talked to his sister. She didn't want to get him into any trouble, but we finally got her to admit that he's got a major gambling problem. That's what broke his marriage up. He routinely hit his mother up for cash until she got to the point a year ago when she cut him off. As to his alibi of being home alone?" Kelley shook his head. "She said there was a good chance he was at an OTB in Lansing where he likes to go. We went out there. The manager confirmed he's a regular. The night Leonard was killed, Parker dropped fifteen hundred. The guy said Parker looked like somebody had tased him."

"The place closes down at ten," Lonergan added, biting into his chicken sandwich. "Parker stayed till then. All this is on security tape. Him sitting there losing his shirt, the shock on his face, him walking out at closing like he was going to the gas chamber. So, unless he's magic, there's no way he could be in two places at once."

Bigelow crossed his arms against his chest. "He ain't wrong."

"So maybe this *is* Shaw settling up," Symansky said.

Bigelow shook his head. "She went overboard with the dimes, though. Too freaky."

Lonergan swallowed a mouthful of sandwich, reached for a fry. "She's definitely who we should be looking at."

"We're looking," Foster said. "But why would she risk everything to settle an old score?"

Lonergan's brows rose. "What everything? What's she got? Her name's freaking mud anywhere she goes. She's got a felony record. Don't look like her marriage is too strong with her living one place and her hubby someplace else."

"What about her daughter?" Li said before Foster could. "There's her everything."

Symansky stood to stretch, his eyes on the board. "Killers are single minded, Li, we all know that. They're like one of them horses with the blinders on. They want what they want how they want it. Three years laying on a smelly cot, burning with hate for the people you think put you there, you're not thinking about anything else but that."

Foster put the marker down, walked away from the board. "Interesting theory. Right now, we don't have anything but question marks. Shaw, Shaw's husband, Franklin, and Meehan again. Maybe Li and I will take Franklin?" She glanced over at Li, who nodded in the affirmative. "We need to check to see what Tennant got from Valdez's staff, his wife. Maybe there's something there we can ping off of. I guess that's it." She gathered her notes and files before padding back to her desk.

"I'll call Franklin," Li said. "See if we can set something up."

"Set it up for first thing Monday, will you?" Foster checked her watch again. It was nearing four thirty. Dinnertime. Ticking seconds. "I've got to leave a little early today. Personal time. Not much we can do now anyway until we start getting some images in." She stuffed her bag with notes and files, eyeing the manila envelope already there, almost teasing her. "Bright and early?"

"Sure. Go," Li said. "Need help with anything?"

"No. I've got it. Thanks." She grabbed her coat and went.

"You're sure?" Li called after her, getting only a wave back.

"Monday," Foster answered. "Early."

———

The downstairs lights in Glynnis's house went out at 10:08 Sunday night; then they went on in the master bedroom and stayed on for another hour. The boys' lights had extinguished at nine, ensuring them both at least ten hours of sleep before school the next day. For the second night in a row, Foster burrowed into her coat, a blanket over her legs and her hat pulled low over her ears. It was cold. Thirty-six degrees, according to her phone, but she wasn't going anywhere. This wasn't her first stakeout. With hand warmers inside her gloves and double socks on her feet, she had come prepared to watch the house for as long as she needed to. She would figure out what to do next in due time.

Mike had no idea she was outside. Neither did the kids. It was better that way. There was nothing unusual on the block, no abnormal activity. She was sure no one was watching Glynnis's house but her. She didn't want to alarm Mike, but the voice on the phone had made it clear that all of them were targets, depending on what she did when the voice came at her again. That's where the conflict bit. She couldn't turn. She couldn't dishonor her badge or the oath she'd taken. The job wasn't perfect, nothing was, but she believed in it. She considered her sacrifices, her commitment, all going toward a noble cause. The voice was asking her to pit that against the lives of Glynnis's children. She was sure this was the dilemma Glynnis had struggled with, only the pull would have been a million times greater since the children were hers.

"Damn it," she muttered, puffs of warm breath hitting cold air. She didn't dare turn the ignition and start the heat. She wasn't supposed to be here. No one was supposed to see her. It was going to be another long night.

There was nothing she could do but watch and wait. She couldn't run the number she'd called because it wasn't connected to any case she was working. She couldn't even submit the photographs to be analyzed for prints or to see if it could be blown up to capture information about the man or the envelope he was holding without justifying the request or connecting it to an active case. The laws about what she was allowed to do were clear. She could lose her job. She could go to jail. How far could she go? How far *would* she go?

Hours later, Monday morning dawned bright, but the sun offered nothing in the way of warmth. Every inch of her body was stiff and numb, despite the blanket and the warmers. At seven, she started the car, relieved to have heat at last. She checked the street again, for the millionth time. It was still quiet, as it had been the entire night. When the light switched on in the master bedroom, and then in sequence in each of the boys' rooms, she waited a half hour more, until a light turned on downstairs, before getting out of the car and walking up to the front door to ring the bell.

Mike opened quickly. "Harri? What're you doing here?" The surprise on his face turned to worry. "Everything okay? What's happened?" He stepped back and waved her in. He glanced behind himself toward the stairs, making sure the kids were still in their rooms. "What now?"

For a moment, she said nothing, letting the heat of the house warm her up. The tips of her fingers and toes stung and were slow to warm. "Nothing yet. I was just in the area, heading in to work, thought I'd drive the kids to school. Spend some time." The look on his face told her that he didn't believe a word she was saying, but she had every intention of sticking to it. "They've got to be there at eight fifteen, right? Plenty of time. Got coffee? It's cold out there this morning. But first. Bathroom?"

She left him at the door, walking back toward the kitchen and the small bathroom halfway there, the aroma of fresh-brewed coffee pulling her forward, her needing the coffee more than wanting it so as not to die.

"You staked out the house," Mike said when she joined him at the kitchen table. He handed her a mug of coffee and slid a plate of warm danish toward her. "All night, didn't you?" He searched her face. "No, longer. I was married to a cop, remember? He threatened the kids, didn't he?"

"I know about as much as you do." She warmed her hands on the mug, then lifted it up to her nose to savor the aroma before taking her first greedy sip. "But I promise I'll get to the bottom of it."

"Harri, this shouldn't be your problem."

"I made a promise to G."

"That didn't include something like this, and you can't watch us twenty-four seven."

"No, I can't. You'll all have to keep your eyes open, be extra cautious about where you go, who's around you. At least until I know more." She took another sip. Mike pushed the danish closer to her. "Glynnis never said anything about someone approaching her?"

Mike shook his head, grabbed one of the danish himself, and bit into it. "I've racked my brain, but there's just nothing. She was normal with me, with the kids."

It had been the same with Glynnis at work. There had been nothing Foster had noticed that was different about her. No strain or worry. She'd hidden everything from everyone.

"And then we didn't talk work a lot in the house. We wanted the kids not to have that in their heads, you know? Then . . ."

The children bounded down the stairs, all noise and youth and energy. Foster stood, taking one last sip of the coffee. She slid Mike a warning look. "We'll talk later. For now, I'll drive the kids to school." She heard them in the front room getting their school stuff together. She lowered her voice. "Glynnis's gun is still in the house?" Mike nodded.

She knew he knew how to use it. Glynnis had made sure. There was nothing else she needed to say.

Jamie and Todd, fourteen and ten, respectively, tore into the kitchen, surprised to find her there. Todd, her godson, rushed over and hugged her, his curly brown hair a mop of confusion, his brown eyes the very picture of innocence.

"Harri? What're you doing here?"

Jamie, too cool for school, smiled and high-fived her. "She's here to take us all to jail, right?"

"Actually, I'm here to drive you both to school."

Todd's eyes lit up. "In a police car?"

"Sorry, bud. My car."

He deflated. "That sucks."

She waited while they ate their breakfast, got their coats on, and then they were off. There was only a little tug in her chest at the memory of getting Reg out the door for school.

"I'll pick them up after school," Mike said.

"Right at dismissal," she said. "Eyes open. When I know something, I'll call you."

Mike squeezed her arm. "Thanks, Harri."

She nodded, then met the kids at the car. "Let's go. You don't want to be late."

"I'm okay being late," Todd said, grinning.

Her eyes narrowed. "I already know that about you. Get in the car."

# CHAPTER 25

Marin walked into the back entrance at Dino's, nodding at the manager and threading her way through the kitchen and staff toward Meehan's table in his private room. She'd been here many times before, of course. This was Meehan's lair. It's where he planned his dirty politics under cover, protected, over lunch or dinner with a bourbon or whiskey. The only thing missing was a fat cigar, but smoking was the only vice that Meehan didn't partake in.

He was expecting her, and when she met him at his table, the sight of it and him reminded her instantly how low she'd once gotten. How many times she had sat there selling her soul for dollar bills. It didn't surprise her that nothing here had changed while she'd been away. The white tablecloths remained, as did the dark wood, brass fittings, and attentive staff who pretended plotting politicians in their back room were normal and legal. Meehan hadn't changed much. Maybe ten pounds heavier, mostly around the middle. She knew his twinkling blue eyes could go from impish playfulness to killer cold with very little provocation. He fixed her with a sly grin, the one that told her he had a secret he wasn't about to share.

She eased down in the leather chair across from him. Meehan was a devourer, a vampire, much like a Venus flytrap, still, open, seemingly harmless until an unwitting fly got too close. She had known it before but knew it more fully now. Meehan was a taker—he didn't give—and the more he took, the more he wanted. Marin stared at the flag pin on the lapel of his blue suit. A light-blue silk tie had a gold tie clip with the word **CHICAGO** etched into it. Meehan, ever the politician. None of it real. Meehan didn't care about the country or the city. He cared about Meehan, and his avaricious tentacles spread far and wide. He knew people who knew people and had the dirt to turn the wheels where others couldn't. Marin knew he wanted to be mayor. She could almost smell it on him under his cloying cologne.

He amped up the grin, but all Marin saw was the threat behind it. John Meehan was a rattlesnake, unpredictable and deadly.

"Marin, you look good. I was surprised to hear from ya after three years, is it?"

She cringed at the sound of his voice, his South Side accent like long fingernails on a chalkboard. The plate in front of him held a steak and baked potato, beside it a glass with two fingers of Irish whiskey, the bottle left at the table for him to draw from as he saw fit. Power lunch on the city's tab. His usual. It didn't matter if Meehan went back to city hall inebriated. No one would comment. No one would dare.

Marin didn't want to prolong this. She was under threat, and it had to be Meehan. Who else would be so desperate to have her out of the way? She, Deanna, and George knew where the bodies were buried, now two of them were dead. That left her and Franklin. With them gone, Meehan's path to the top job would be effortless and clear of impediments. But Marin had other ideas.

She reached into her bag and pulled out a folded piece of paper and slid it across the table to him. He flicked a look at it but made no attempt to pick it up. He didn't even look curious, just slightly amused. He eyed her bandaged hands. "Trouble?"

"I was pushed into oncoming traffic. I'm also being followed."

Meehan adjusted his tie, his gold Rolex glinting off the silver cutlery. The revelation didn't appear to move him. "Sheesh. A lot of crazy people in the world, huh? I hate to hear that."

"Deanna. George. Then me?" she asked, leaning forward, her voice low. "Franklin goes last? I always suspected she was your favorite."

He picked up his glass and took a sip, his eyes piercing hers over the rim. "Not sure I get what you're tryin' to say."

She knew he wouldn't admit to anything. Meehan was always careful, fearing that whoever he conversed with might be working with the authorities and wearing a wire. But that wasn't what this meeting was about. Marin was here to send a message, to make things clear, so she could walk away clean for Zoe.

"I took full responsibility for what I did, and I kept you out of it. I wanted to make up for what I'd done and get it over with. But I'm no fool, John. I know what you are, how far you'll go. This is business. I have audiotapes and photos and enough documentation to send you away for a very long time. I dotted every i and crossed every last t. I figured three years was doable. I considered it my penance. But getting rid of me opens the vault, John. And when the vault opens, the mayor's office goes away for good." She pointed at the paper between them. "That's just a taste to prove I'm not lying. Read it, or don't. It doesn't matter. But I have what I say I have."

"This sounds like a shakedown."

"I learned from the best. I know there's a tape recorder hidden behind you. The switch is under your chair. I know you turned it on the moment I stepped into this room. If you want to record what I'm about to say and run the risk of there being a record when the feds come calling, by all means, keep it running." For a moment neither of them moved a single muscle; then Meehan reached under his chair to flick the machine off.

"Okay?" she said.

Meehan nodded. "Your show, it looks like."

"It's simple. Leave me and my family alone and you get what you want. Come after me again and I bury you. After today, I don't exist for you, John, or the clock starts ticking on your political career." Marin could see the wheels turning in his head. "There are duplicates of every-thing I have all over the place, not just here, so a fire or an explosion or a robbery won't do it. I may have been dumb enough to get tangled up with you and the others, but I've never been stupid. And I'm doubly dangerous now because I'm as sober as a judge."

His eyes hardened. "I don't know what you're talking about. I mean, if a person had all that, I would think she'd use it during her trial."

"I made a choice at trial. To serve the time and keep the leverage, hoping I'd find peace at the end. You're going to give me peace, John. You're going to let me walk away."

He smiled. "You got a lot tougher in the can. Only you got the wrong end of the stick." He leaned forward, his whiskey breath revolt-ing her. "You're no threat to me. None of you are." He flicked a look at the paper between them. "You got paper. I got paper. I blow up, everything blows up. I was curious about what you were thinking when you walked out, but it looks to me like you're not in the axe-grinding business, so to speak." He sat back. "Smart move on your part."

She stood up. She'd had enough. "I'm walking away. I stay safe, you'll stay safe. It's not complicated." She glanced down at his lunch with disdain. This was what Meehan's constituents were paying for at the expense of pothole repairs and streetlight maintenance. "Enjoy the taxpayers' steak."

He pressed an index finger on the paper sitting in front of him. "Just curious. What's this?"

"An attention grabber," she said. "I've flooded the universe with copies, and they're locked away with instructions for what to do with them if I die anywhere other than in my own bed by natural causes."

He glared at her. "A sword hangin' over my head?"

Their eyes locked. "That's up to you."

For a moment Meehan said nothing. Then a slow smile bloomed, and he took another sip from his glass, savoring the spirit as it slid smoothly down his throat. "Funny thing, though, this whole thing.

You're thinking it solves your problem, only it don't. I got far too much juice to squander it on killing. I got pull in this town, real power. You're lookin' at your next mayor. Leonard, Valdez, you? Small potatoes compared to that. Unfortunate what happened, but I can't say it ain't good for me in the long run." He tapped the paper. "I also made backup plans. What you call redundancies? I guess that keeps us both in check." His eyes went cold and bored into hers. "So, if I was you, Marin Shaw, I'd be real careful out there. Because you got a target on your back . . . and I ain't the guy who put it there."

———

He was lying, of course. He had to be lying. Just to freak her out, just to screw with her head. But what if he was telling the truth? Then that would mean she was back where she'd started. Who? Why, if not for her connection to Meehan?

And as much as she tried to shoehorn Meehan into her troubles, he couldn't explain the missing key to Valdez's office, Marin thought, as she padded around the condo worrying the problem. It had to have been Will who took the key, but why? He would have no idea what the key was for. How could he? He had no idea she was having an affair with Valdez, did he? She stopped pacing. Was anything else missing? She hadn't thought to check. Turning around in a slow circle, she scanned every inch around her. Nothing looked different, but she could feel now that something was. There was a different feel to the place, suddenly, like it wasn't hers, like the place had eyes. The cleaned-out bar sat there desolate. The couches were the same, the curtains, the tasteful accent pieces and artwork scattered around, purchased to impress and validate. The same. But something wasn't. She turned for the master bedroom. Will had taken the key, and now George Valdez was dead. It was a leap. It was her perhaps trying to make a connection that wasn't there, but her husband was a selfish man, and she could feel the "something."

Her eyes scanned the bedroom, the walk-in closets she'd insisted on, the king-size bed she was certain Will had shared with half the city's women in the years she was locked up. None of that mattered now. There was something different, and she was determined to find it.

# CHAPTER 26

"One of those mornings?" Li asked when Foster rushed in at nearly 11:00 a.m.

Foster, of course, had texted Griffin and Li to say she'd be late. After she'd dropped the kids off at school, she had gone home for a shower, a change of clothes, and a long sit with her case notes. She was running on no sleep, but she was warm, wired, and ready to work.

"Slept through the alarm. Sorry. Anything new come up?"

Li leaned back in her chair, skeptical. Foster wasn't the kind of person who slept through alarms. "Nothing. Still waiting on . . . everything, actually. We've got Franklin up in an hour if you're good? She seemed pretty antsy on the phone."

"Antsy how?"

Li pulled a face. "I don't know. Like I'd just told her I was auditing her returns for the past twenty years."

Foster shoved her bag in her bottom drawer, slipped out of her coat. "Nothing from Tennant. We should talk to Valdez's wife too. I'll give him a heads-up. I don't want to step on any toes." Foster spotted a wayward thumbtack on her desk, likely dropped by the last cop who occupied the desk on an earlier watch. She plucked it up, dropped it into her blazer pocket, knowing Li saw.

"Sounds like a busy day," Li said. "Let's do it."

"Anything from the boss?"

Li glanced over at Griffin's closed door. "Nope, but she's in there. She's *always* in there. I think there's something brewing, though. All this coverage this case is getting, you know the heat's on."

Foster looked around for Symansky, Bigelow, Kelley, Lonergan. "Where's everybody?"

"They're all out pulling leads. Even Lonergan, the old dinosaur."

"Okay, a minute to get situated here, and then we'll head out?"

Foster's cell phone buzzed. Unknown caller. She answered it, holding her breath.

"Good morning, Detective Foster."

She stiffened her spine but said nothing to the voice on the other end. Sliding a look over at Li, she held up a finger to tell her she needed a minute, then slipped down the hall for privacy.

"I won't keep you. I just wanted to say that I admire your loyalty, I really do. But watching Thompson's house all weekend is not going to cut it. You must be exhausted, what with the no sleep and the cold. You can't keep that up forever, you know that, right? You'll crack up." He laughed, and the playful sound of it burned a hole right through her chest.

She closed her eyes, listening for any information she could glean from his end of the line—a thump, a tick, a scrape, anything that would identify a location.

"Relax. The deal's between you and me. I only mentioned the kids to get your attention. Unless you force me to elevate things?" There was an ominous pause. "Cat got your tongue?"

"Your show," she said. No lisp, no speech impediment. Tenor, not bass. White, most likely. No discernible accent. Not old. Not too young.

"So right. It is. But it doesn't have to be unpleasant. Look, go home tonight. Get some sleep. You have my word the kids are safe." He let a beat pass. "Harri? You still there?"

Her eyes popped open. A mistake. He'd called her Harri. He knew her. How? From where? Did that mean she knew him too? She ended the call, then checked the incoming number on her call log. It was a different number from the one she'd called yesterday. He was generating random numbers, difficult to trace. Two different area codes. He was watching her. His word that the kids were safe meant nothing.

When she returned to her desk, Li took one look at her and said, "All right. What the hell's going on?"

"Family problems," she said, and it wasn't exactly a lie.

"Sorry, Harri. Anything I can help with?"

For a moment she considered telling Li everything. Two cop heads were always better than one, but this looked like something capable of blowing up a career. She couldn't do that to Li. "Thanks. No. It'll be okay. Ready to go?"

"If your family needs you, I can—"

But Foster was already moving. "I've got it under control."

The cameras and reporters outside city hall had increased in number, despite the cold, despite the threat of snow. To Foster, it looked like every station, paper, and online media outfit had sent a representative. Each reporter, knowing the drill, was bundled up in a heavy parka and woolly hat. Station vans were lined up at the curb, engines running. Blue riot horses had been set out to keep the madness away from the doors and allow pedestrian traffic to get through. But the officers assigned to the cordon could do little else but hold the chaos of media cables, lights, and reporters back behind the line. The reporters looked amped up, dialed in. The violent deaths of two city aldermen were a big story, and they all wanted it first.

In the front, as she knew he would be, was Soren Hastrup. He nodded as she and Li strode past but didn't try to pepper them with questions this time, which didn't feel like the blessing it should have been.

"Not sure which is worse for us," Li whispered as they pushed inside the building. "A loud and pesky Hastrup, or a quiet one."

Foster sighed. "Both are equally bad."

Franklin was standing behind her desk chair when they were shown into her office. Meehan had greeted them in his seat of power as though they had been granted an audience with the king. Franklin's office was much smaller, which indicated where she fell in the pecking order, yet it felt to Foster like she struggled to command even this tight space. Franklin's blue eyes held steady on them as they stood in the doorway, her gripping the back of the chair as though it might fly away and leave her exposed. Foster flicked a look at her watch. Needing to be somewhere else yet bound by duty to be here.

"Alderman Franklin. I'm Detective Foster. My partner, Detective Li."

A smile. Franklin's hands let loose of the chair, and she smoothed down the front of her navy-blue business suit. She looked to be in her early sixties, shorter than average, stout. The gold statement jewelry around her neck and on her fingers stood out, as did the clunky brooch pinned to her small chest fashioned in the shape of the Chicago skyline. Ever the politician. But it was the eyes that Foster focused on, the caution in them.

Franklin sat down in her chair and gestured for them to take the seats in front of her desk. "Please, I expected this. You'll want to talk to everybody on the council, I assume?"

Foster flipped open her notepad and stared at Franklin. "Not everybody. You got a call from Deanna Leonard the night she died. Can you tell us what that was about?"

"Right to it. All business."

It was obvious Franklin was trying to cut the tension in the room, slow things down. "If you don't mind."

"She called to beg off of an event she was to speak at. I arranged a youth forum at a community center in my ward. Deanna said she would have to miss it."

"Did she say why?" Li asked.

Franklin's eyes moved to Li. "A last-minute schedule conflict. Something she couldn't move around."

Franklin reached into her top drawer and came out with a flyer, which she handed to Foster. She read the list of names of invited attendees and sponsors. Leonard's name wasn't on it. She handed the flyer to Li.

"Last-minute back out," Li said. "And her name's not listed."

"She was a late entry. Things happen. But that's why she called."

"The call lasted a few minutes," Foster said. "Canceling out on an event sounds like it'd be quick."

Franklin's hands flew up. "Ah. Yes. There was some mention of an agenda item for the next council meeting. Only briefly. To make sure we were both on the same page."

"Which agenda item?" Foster asked.

"More red-light cameras, yea or nay. There's a faction in the council that would like to ban them completely in certain areas and another that believes we need more of them. The debate continues. Deanna wanted a quick confirmation that I'd be there for the quorum. To think that would be the last time I spoke to her . . . and then right on the heels of that tragedy, George Valdez. I can't believe it. The violence. I have an initiative proposed to the council—"

Foster held up a hand to stop the stump speech. "Were Alderman Leonard and Valdez close on a personal level? Besides being on the council together?"

"Personal level?"

"Seeing each other," Li said. "Romantically. Or otherwise connected?"

Her brows lifted. "I wouldn't know. We were just colleagues. Coworkers."

Foster leaned forward. "Were they, to your knowledge, involved in any initiatives or agendas they might have been working closely together on? Maybe something controversial that might have gotten the wrong kind of attention?"

Franklin balked. "Something illegal, you mean. Not all politicians are corrupt, Detective. Some are in this for the right reasons."

"I'm sure. So, that's a no?"

"It is."

"Do you get a lot of angry mail from constituents, Ms. Franklin?" Li asked. "People unhappy with how the city works or how you do?"

"Of course. You're not a good alderman if you don't upset *some* people. We all get our fair share of feedback. Some more vitriolic than others. Some more rational than others. Why?"

"Someone targeted Leonard and Valdez," Li said. "We're looking for a motive."

Franklin shrugged. "I wish I could help you, but I can't think of one. I worked with them both, but how well can you ever know the people you work with? You don't follow them home, do you. I can say that both Deanna and George were committed public servants who served their constituents well. It's horrible what's happened."

"Despite what the papers hinted at a few years ago?" Li asked. "In the Shaw case, in fact."

Franklin's expression turned dark and disdainful. "Papers can say anything, and they do, in my experience."

"What about Alderman Meehan," Foster asked. "How'd he and you get along with Leonard and Valdez?"

"Meehan?" her eyes widened, and her hands flew to her jacket buttons. "Meehan's a member of the old guard. Neither Valdez or Leonard, or me for that matter, could be lumped in the same category. They were colleagues. Nothing more." Her eyes shifted from Foster's to Li's and back. "But you talked with him, so you know that already."

Foster's brows lifted. "You two discussed our conversation?"

"I didn't have to. It's not every day city hall is visited by homicide detectives. Word quickly got around. There are more police officers in the building than usual. Everyone wants to be protected."

Foster's eyes stuck to Franklin's. "Can you think of any reason why Leonard would call Meehan the night she died? Or Valdez? I don't see either of their names on that flyer."

"I can't say. How would I know?"

"Where were you when you took Leonard's call?" Foster asked. She checked her notes. "At seven oh five p.m. The day she was killed."

Franklin's shoulders relaxed, and the tension seemed to leave her face. "At Saint Stanislaus's church. A community meeting. There were at least fifty people there who can corroborate that, including the pastor, Father Kozlovski."

"Remember where you were when Valdez was killed?" Li asked.

Franklin took a moment. "This sounds like I'm a suspect. Am I?"

Foster's attention didn't waver. "At this point, everyone is. So? Where were you?"

Franklin hesitated. "In bed with a migraine. I live alone, so no one can verify that, but it's the truth."

For a moment no one said anything.

"Marin Shaw," Li said finally without context.

Franklin stood, signaling the end of their interview. "I've had no contact with Marin, and unfortunately, this is all the time I have."

Foster rose; Li followed. "One more question . . . for now," Foster said. "Can you think of anyone who'd have it in for Leonard and Valdez? Someone who'd consider them disloyal or a threat? Someone they both knew who would have been able to get close enough to kill them?" Foster watched as Franklin flinched.

"I can't think of anyone."

A lie. Foster closed her notepad. "Thanks for your time. We'll be in touch."

They stood in silence at the golden elevators waiting for the car.

Li sighed. "Well, that was the biggest snow job we've gotten since Meehan dumped twelve feet on our heads. Do these people go to snow job school, or what? They talk, but nothing but hot air and lies come out of their mouths. It's like all circles, and the circles lead to other circles, and none of the circles go anywhere because, duh, they're circles, and then by the end of it, you just want to knock their teeth out and shove them into the lake."

Foster pressed the elevator button again, watching as the numbers changed on the panel above the doors. "It wasn't what she said, though, was it? It's how she said it. She's afraid of Meehan, the big dog. She wasn't about to say a thing that would contradict what we got from him."

"And they've been in contact," Li said. "They discussed us asking questions. They're trying to keep their stories straight."

Foster looked over at Li. "We need to talk to Marin Shaw again. But Saint Stanislaus's first?"

Li shrugged. "Sure, but the fact that she gave it up so fast probably means it's solid, or that she figured out a way to make it look that way." Li zipped up her parka. "See? Circles."

The elevator arrived. They got on. Foster checked her watch.

"I'm good with family issues," Li said. "Wanted you to know that."

"Thank you, Vera. I appreciate that."

"So, whenever."

"Yep."

Silence.

"I should run for mayor," Li said. "I bet I could whip this city into shape."

"You'd have to learn how to talk in circles."

Li snorted. "The hell I would."

Foster's phone buzzed. She stiffened, but relaxed when she saw the number had a City of Chicago exchange. "Foster." It was Detective Tennant from the Valdez scene. She listened. "I appreciate the heads-up." Tennant had more to say. "Ah. Mind if we stop by? Great. On our way." She ended the call. "Saint Stanislaus's is going to have to wait. They've got updates on their interviews, and a partial print off the key they found by Valdez's body. Want to guess who it—"

"Marin Shaw," Li said, grinning.

Foster nodded as she wiggled into her leather gloves, prepared to hit the cold again. "You're good at a lot of things."

# CHAPTER 27

Tennant and Pienkowski were at their desks, cops milling around an office that looked pretty much like theirs, everything city issued, everything old and utilitarian. Tennant saw them coming and flicked a chin toward his partner, and they both rose to greet them.

"Welcome to the nuthouse," Tennant said facetiously, his shirt-sleeves rolled up to the elbows, his tie loosened. It looked like he'd been at work for three days straight, and he smelled a little ripe. Pienkowski looked about the same, his five-o'clock shadow looking like it had seen three five o'clocks since the razor met it last.

"Let's take it somewhere quiet," Tennant said, grabbing his paperwork and heading down the hall. Pienkowski snatched up his mug and followed.

"Sit?" Tennant asked when they entered the small interview room. This too was much like theirs. There was no mystery, no innovation needed for police stations. They were city property. Stark. Perfunctory. Both she and Li declined the offer to sit. They also declined the offer of coffee. They were focused on what Tennant and Pienkowski had come up with. The key with Marin Shaw's fingerprints on it could be a game changer.

Tennant placed his fisted hands on his hips. "First, people are coming out of the woodwork to tell us what a great guy Valdez was. Fashioned himself a real man-of-the-people kind of dude. Prounion.

Builder of playgrounds. Real champion in the council. Everybody loved him."

Tennant slid photos from his file. "Then we found these when we pulled his security tape." Tennant turned two photographs toward them, and Foster and Li closed in on the table to get a better look. One photo was of Valdez kissing a half-naked woman, her back to the camera. The other was of Valdez walking a woman to the front door of his office. "This is the bad part."

"I knew it," Li muttered. "There's always a bad part."

"This was a couple months back," Tennant said. "We're thinking he got into the habit of turning off the cameras or wiping them clean. This one he missed, apparently."

Foster picked up the first photo, studied it. "Valdez and I guess *not* his wife?"

"You guess right. Wife says she didn't know."

"When was this taken?"

"Right before Christmas. Nice, huh? The office manager, Emelda Rodriguez, said Valdez managed the cameras. Wouldn't let anyone else touch them. We see why now. He kept them off while he was working in the office alone. He told her he didn't like the sense that someone was watching him."

Pienkowski took a slow sip from his mug. "Rodriguez had an idea what was going on, but she wasn't about to say anything. I got the impression she had some major puppy love going for Valdez. She talked like the sun rose and set on him. But whoever that is, she knows she's not the first."

"Far as we can tell," Tennant added. "He had no beef with anybody in his immediate circle. Wife's clear too. It was parents' night at their kid's school. Witnesses put her there till about eight thirty."

"She could have hired somebody," Li said. "Wives usually have a feeling about these things."

"My gut tells me she's clean," Tennant said. "But, of course, we're still digging."

"Rodriguez said Valdez got a few angry letters from people crabbing about garbage pickup and potholes and whatnot, but none of that looks serious enough for somebody to want to stab him. Still, we checked them out. Harmless. Accounted for on the night."

"And it doesn't explain the key," Foster said, "which you say has Marin Shaw's fingerprints on it."

Tennant drew out a photo of the key in question and laid it on the table, taking the others back. "You already know the office door wasn't broken in to, which meant he either let whoever in or they got in on their own. Rodriguez swears, as far as she knows, there were only three keys to the place: Valdez's, hers, and the one the maintenance guy had." He tapped the photo. "This key isn't any of those. She had hers, and the maintenance guy had his on his key chain. We got Rodriguez leaving Valdez around six, and she went straight home to her kids. That's confirmed. The maintenance guy, Diaz, hasn't been on the premises in over a week and was halfway across town, again accounted for, when all this went down. Valdez's key was on the key ring in his pocket, along with the bag of dimes. We got no idea how *this* key came to be or if it's the only one floating around. Maybe he gave one to each of his . . . dates?"

"No way of ID'ing the woman?" Li asked.

"So far we got nothing," Tennant said. "Valdez ran a smooth operation. But we're running plates on the cars parked around that office on the night these images were taken. Might come up with something still on that."

"So, one of Valdez's women might have gotten angry when she found out he wasn't exclusive," Pienkowski said. "Leaves the key as a final FU."

Li's brows rose. "With Shaw's prints on it, not hers?"

"Then we're back to Shaw," Tennant said.

"Who'd be fool enough to leave the key with her prints on it next to his body?" Foster said.

"Two theories," Tennant said. "Either Shaw made a beeline for him when she got out because they were a thing before she went in, or she was pissed at him for something and was coming to confront him about it. Second theory explains the dimes."

"He knew her," Pienkowski said. "Worked with her. Likely knew her better than that, if we're looking at past behavior. He'd probably let her in, no question, or she let herself in. Something goes wrong. Things get heated. She pulls out a knife and . . ."

"A fillet knife," Li said. "From a kitchen."

"That's what the ME's report said," Tennant offered. "Not something your average street thug's going to carry around in his pocket."

"No video inside, but what about outside?" Li asked. "Any sign of Shaw or any other mystery women coming or going?"

"Nothing yet," Tennant said. "Lot a dead spots on the street and in the alley. But the prints make Shaw somebody we got to talk to. The key alone's not enough to charge her, but she's definitely going to have to explain it. What've you two got on your end?"

Foster sighed. "Not much. Everyone we've talked to is cleared the night Leonard was killed, except Marin Shaw, who claims she had dinner with her family and then spent the rest of the evening home alone. The dinner we confirmed. The home-alone part, not yet. And then there's that threatening phone call she made."

Tennant threw his hands up. "She's looking good for it, you ask me."

"It does look neat and clean," Foster said. "Maybe too neat?"

"No such thing, you ask me," Pienkowski said.

Tennant gathered up the photos and closed the file. "Well, she's next steps. I figure we take her. The key's at our crime scene."

"I get that," Foster said delicately. "But the cases are linked, and we've already talked to her. Wouldn't it be simpler for us to follow up?"

"I'm used to doing my own talking, Foster," Tennant bit back. "Courtesy's one thing, you two grabbing the reins—"

Foster stopped him. "We ask her in. We work together. Your boss is getting the same heat our boss is getting. The quicker we solve this, the better off we'll all be."

Tennant took a moment. "Yeah, okay. But no soft soap. We go hard."

Pienkowski lifted his mug. "Sludge for the road?"

Li pulled a face. "Nah. We're good. Appreciate your keeping us in the loop."

Foster nodded. "And we'll do the same."

Back at the car, Li glared at Foster over the roof. "Is it me, or do you get the impression they think we're little petal pickers who just happened to stumble upon a couple of toy cop badges?"

"It is what it is," Foster mused, checking her watch for the trillionth time. "Mind if I make a call before we go? Two minutes."

"Course not. Take your time. I'll warm it up for you." Li got in the car.

Foster slid her phone out of her pocket and moved away for privacy, bursts of air puffing around her in the cold. She dialed Mike's number to check on things. But she also had something she wanted to try.

# CHAPTER 28

Marin stood at her window looking down at the street fourteen floors below. The wind rattled the windows, the sound of the wailing whistle squeezing through the tempered panes. She had checked the entire apartment, and one of her long coats wasn't there. Black, long, wool with a red heart on the chest. It had been made by a local designer, and she'd only worn it once. Maybe she'd left it at the house and had forgotten?

Will wouldn't have taken just one coat. Why would he? If he were trying to unnerve her, scare her, wouldn't he flick the lights or cut the brakes on her car, or at least take something she'd lament the loss of, like her grandmother's earrings? The coat wasn't particularly expensive. There would have been no good reason to take that coat over any of the others in her closet. It had to be at the house, she finally decided. She was making too much of far too little. Still, the feeling that something wasn't right remained. It was just a little niggle at the nape of her neck, a pall of dread embedded in the center of her chest.

"I don't trust him," Marin muttered.

"Who?" Charlotte asked.

Marin turned from the window to stare at Charlotte at the table, notes on the beginnings of the divorce spread out over the surface. Charlotte wore her lawyer suit but had kicked off her business heels underneath. How long had they been friends? More than twenty years, though it seemed somehow longer to Marin. "Lawyer," she said, letting Charlotte know that this wasn't a friend talk, but a lawyer-client talk.

Charlotte winced. "I don't have to put my shoes back on, do I? My feet are killing me."

Marin shook her head, then sat down at the table. "John Meehan. I went to see him because I believe he's the one who's having me followed."

Charlotte blew out a breath and took a moment to let Marin's words settle. "Not exactly the smartest thing you could have done. I mean, isn't that a little like the hen walking out of the hen house and right up to the fox? In fact, that was a very dumb thing to do. Dangerous, Marin. Why didn't you call me?"

"It was something I needed to do alone."

Charlotte shook her head. "He's a snake, you know that, right? Zero redeeming value. You're lucky you walked away."

"I'm tired of hiding," Marin said. "Tired of waiting for things to work out on their own. He said it wasn't him. That he had no intention of jeopardizing his career by killing anybody."

"John Meehan hasn't told the truth about anything his entire life. He's the one who should be in prison."

"But he's not stupid. He knows I can hurt him. If anything happens to me, he loses everything." She turned to Char. "But he has insurance of his own."

"That won't help him," Charlotte said. "You've served your time. And if anything happens to you, he'll have to deal with me." She angled her head and stared at Marin. "Is that it, or is there more you haven't told me?"

Marin shook her head. "Whatever he's got could only embarrass and humiliate me further. I guess I'll know if he's lying when I walk out my door. If something happens, as my lawyer, you have instructions. Above anything else, Zoe gets taken care of. Everything goes to her."

Charlotte leaned over and placed a comforting hand on Marin's arm. "Friend." Marin nodded at Charlotte's shift in roles. "You never,

*ever* have to worry about Zoe. You have my word." She pulled back her hand. "Lawyer. I think we should go to the police, fill out a report so that we have this all on record. Second, I know you don't want protection, but I think it wouldn't be a bad idea to have someone shadow you for a while. Third, we get this divorce started and finalized as quickly as possible, so that you can move on with your life."

Marin looked over at Charlotte. "What if it's Will? He'd want to know what I was doing so he could use it against me. He would think he'd benefit from my death. I haven't told him I've changed my will to leave everything to Zoe."

Charlotte laughed, realizing too late that Marin hadn't joined in. "Sorry." She held up a hand. "Friend now. We both know Will's too hung up on himself to give two nickels about what you're up to. He's angry, sure. He blames you for scuttling his business. He slept around to get back at you for becoming an alderman and showing him up. You did it for the thrill." She sat back. "Dysfunctional as hell, but so's a lot of things. It's not Will."

"One of my coats is missing." Marin didn't mention the key. Although she and Charlotte were close, she hadn't told her about Valdez. She'd been too ashamed, too out of her head and moving in the wrong direction to give voice to it even to her closest friend. "Who else would take it?"

"Fur?" Charlotte asked.

Marin shook her head. "Just a coat. You don't think Will gave it to one of his mistresses, do you?"

"Lawyer. I can't speak to that. Friend. I wouldn't put it past him."

Marin shook her head. "Me either. And you would tell me if you knew who it was? If he exposed Zoe to anything . . . he shouldn't have? As a friend?"

"Will's sleazy, but he's never cheated out in the open. You have to catch him at it. And I would tell you as a friend *and* as a lawyer."

"I may have misplaced it, then. I wasn't exactly in a good place during the trial. The drinking. I don't remember half the things I said or did."

"I remember. I had to do a lot of sobering up to get you into court. You were in a bad way. I hated seeing you like that. No blackouts, thank God, but a lot of sloppy, drunken conversations where you made no sense. But that's behind you now." She tapped the papers on the table. "You're back, and this is a new beginning."

Marin said nothing for a moment. "No police. No bodyguard. Not yet."

Charlotte sighed. "All right. Your call. But if you die, Marin Shaw, I will *kill* you."

"Lawyer or friend?" Marin asked, a slight smile on her face.

"Both."

Marin was suddenly cold and wrapped her arms around herself to warm up. Charlotte stood. "You're shivering. I'll go get you a sweater. Breathe."

Charlotte padded into Marin's bedroom. "Breathe," Marin muttered. "It's all I can do."

The sun was out, temperatures balmy at forty-two degrees as Marin strolled out of the church basement later that day to head back to her apartment. She didn't feel that cloying cloud of menace behind her, but that didn't keep her from turning around every few yards to check to see if anyone was there. Maybe her confrontation with Meehan had done the trick. She'd known who she was dealing with, of course; the man was a thug in an expensive suit, a dangerous thug. But she'd stood her ground and made things clear. Neither was innocent of anything, but there could still be an understanding between them.

Quickening her steps, she headed east, then turned south to walk down Lake Shore Drive. She wanted to see the lake, the traffic, the life. There could be a future beyond prison. She felt the hopefulness inside her. Marin Shaw, for once, was moving in the right direction.

That feeling stalled as she stepped into her lobby to find Detectives Foster and Li standing there, grim of face. Her future, which had seemed bright just seconds ago, dulled and shriveled into a lump of coal, and she was back where she'd been—treading stagnant water with a boulder on her back.

Marin scanned the lobby. There was no one there but the detectives and Roy, the pock-faced lobby attendant at the desk in his blue blazer and tie. He stared at her with a mixture of pity and excitement. News of this would be all over the building by the end of the day. The detectives walked over, assessing her as they got closer.

"It isn't me," she offered feebly, with barely enough energy to form the words. "It's not."

# CHAPTER 29

They put Shaw in an interview room with a paper cup of weak coffee and a patrol officer standing at the door. She'd turned down the opportunity to call her lawyer, which Foster thought was odd.

"How long are we going to let her sit?" Li asked, leaning back in her chair. "It's been an hour already."

"I already called Tennant and Pienkowski. They're on their way. They should be here when we talk to her."

"I don't know. Suddenly, she doesn't feel right for this. She'd have to be a real dunce to leave her prints at Valdez's. And she's not a dunce."

"You're right." Foster glanced down the hall toward the interview room. "Something's going on with her, though. Why hasn't she asked for her lawyer?"

Li flicked a look at her monitor, and her face brightened. "Hey ho. Garage video's in." She scooted her chair closer to the computer. "From the garage company's lawyer." Foster got up to stand behind her. "Time of death, approximate, ten p.m." Li's fingers flew across the keyboard, her eyes glued to the screen. "A little before . . . and a little after . . . and maybe we get lucky."

"Let's hope we do. Street cams so far are getting us nowhere. No plates around the garage match those belonging to anyone on our board."

Li's fingers stopped moving. "Okay. Here we are at level six. All kinds of cars at seven p.m. *Jersey Boys* started at seven thirty, which explains the traffic." Li's fingers moved across the keyboard, her eyes glued to the monitor. "We already pinned Leonard's entrance at a quarter to ten. She's dead soon after." Li advanced the footage. "Here she is pulling into the spot a minute or so after she comes in. The picture's really muddy. This angle doesn't give us a clear view of the passenger side either. I can't tell if she's by herself." Foster leaned in, and Li advanced the tape a little further. "Closer to ten, no movement. Car's just sitting there. Whole right side of the car's out of frame." A few more keystrokes, another advance. "Uh-oh. Interior light comes on. It's the passenger door opening."

Li tried to zoom in more, but lost resolution, the inky images degrading to even inkier shadows. "Ugh. This is a bunch of crap." She zoomed out again and ticked the tape forward one frame at a time. She stopped at the flash. "There it is. The shot." A short violent burst of accelerant as the round left the gun. She turned to Foster. "We missed it. He slipped in and out. The camera got nothing."

Foster focused on the screen. "Advance it, huh? Slowly."

Li advanced the tape. The interior light went on again. "There," Foster said. "Door opens again, and look, whoever it is comes toward the camera, not away from it."

A figure in a black coat and a hat obscuring their face strode past Leonard's car, head down. Foster held her breath and suspected Li did the same.

"What are those on the front of the coat?" Li squinted at the screen. "Red circles?"

"That looks like a woman's coat," Foster said as they watched the dark figure turn and stroll casually down a level, hands in their pockets. "Shaw?"

"Can't see the face, but body type looks similar. But truthfully it could be anybody."

Kelley walked over and joined them. "That the security video?" He leaned in. "That's the guy?"

"Or woman," Li said. "Walking down. Right after killing Leonard."

Kelley turned to Foster. "No way somebody's walking down six levels."

"You're right. Someone would notice," Foster added. "We need tape from the elevators."

"The elevators are wired," Li said. "No way he or she's going to stand in front of those cameras and risk being ID'd."

"Covered up like that?" Kelley asked. "All they'd have to do is keep their head down and turned away from the lens. The elevator hits the lobby, they waltz out, mix in with the theater geeks, and they're gone."

Li leaned back. "Or she, or he, goes down a level or two, gets in their car, and drives out in the jam at the exit. But not without paying. And if they paid by credit card . . ."

Foster went back to her desk. "Unless they had a transponder."

Li rolled back up to her computer. "Way ahead of you."

———

Foster and Tennant sat across from Marin Shaw. Li had wanted to stay on the garage captures, a promising lead. Pienkowski had found the coffeepot and the chocolate doughnuts.

"What's changed?" Marin asked, her voice barely above a whisper, defeat in the tone, exhaustion in the delivery. "Why am I here?"

Foster slid Tennant a look and got a nod back, so she started. "Just to make sure. You don't want a lawyer, and you are fully aware that you are speaking with the Chicago Police Department about two homicides we're investigating?"

"I know who I'm talking to. I want to get this over with so that I can be left alone."

Foster watched Shaw for a moment, then flipped the cover open on her notepad. "When was the last time you saw George Valdez?"

"When he testified at my trial. He testified that I was a 'hardworking and dedicated public servant . . .' and that he was 'devastated and disappointed that I chose to abuse my power in such an egregious way.'" She shook her head. "I didn't kill him. I didn't kill Deanna."

"How do you explain us finding your fingerprints not two feet from his body, then?" Tennant asked gruffly.

"You found the key."

Foster and Tennant sat up straighter. "What key?" Foster knew full well already, of course, but needed Shaw to explain it.

Marin looked like she might be sick. Her face blanched, and she doubled over and rocked for a bit, her arms wrapped around her middle. "That's it. That's what this is. That *bastard*."

Foster's eyes narrowed. "Ms. Shaw?"

She lifted up. "It's my husband. He's trying to send me back . . . or kill me. I know how that sounds . . . I know how it looks."

Tennant said, "You think your husband killed two people to get at *you*?"

Foster watched silently as Shaw broke. There were no tears; she was too proud a woman for that, but there was a visible release. She could see it in the lowering of Shaw's shoulders, in the clasping of her hands in her lap as though in prayer, as the lock on her secrets, which she'd guarded both times they had spoken, appeared to ease open.

"All we want is the truth, Ms. Shaw."

"I didn't kill them. My husband wants me out of the way. The truth. George and I had an affair. Short, reckless. Obviously, Will found out about it somehow. I had a key to George's office because we would meet there. I kept the key in a box at the condo. It was there, hidden, when I left for prison. It wasn't there when I looked for it just yesterday. One of my coats is also missing. He's setting me up."

Tennant smirked. "We didn't find *his* prints."

"If I go back to prison, he gets everything, he gets my daughter, the house, the money, and the satisfaction of knowing he ruined me. Payback. Revenge. Use whatever word you want."

"You having an affair with Deanna Leonard too?" Tennant asked facetiously, his contempt unmasked. Foster glared at him until he looked away.

Shaw stared up at Tennant. "That was cruel." Tennant shifted on his feet and cleared his throat, chastised. "But the answer is no, and I never told him about George, not consciously. I can't explain how he knew where to find the key or how he found out what it unlocked. He wouldn't kill George himself. He'd find someone else to do it . . . I know I look like the perfect connection between them both, but I swear to you, I didn't kill them. I have too much to lose, too much to get back."

"Tell me about your call to Leonard," Foster said. "That was you, not your husband. From a pay-as-you-go phone. Like a street thug."

Marin lowered her head in shame. "It was one of the tricks I picked up during my time of idiocy. Disposable phones." She looked up again, her resolve firmly planted. "I threw it away that night. Down the garbage chute. When I realized what I'd started . . . and then when I got that call from the police, from you, I just lost it. It was a mistake calling in the first place, but I was so angry. I wasn't thinking. I told her I wanted to meet to clear the air. Surprisingly, she agreed. But I never went. I changed my mind. I never left my apartment that night. And I haven't set foot in George's office or touched that key in years. *That's* the truth."

"But nobody can confirm any of that," Tennant said. "You being by yourself."

"I'd have to walk out of my building, wouldn't I? There are cameras in the lobby. There are cameras everywhere. In the elevators, in the parking garage, the storage room. I never left." She searched each of their faces, pleading for understanding. "I. Never. Left. I want this over. I want this behind me." She looked around the room as though she were destined to live the rest of her life in it. "I don't want this."

Foster, despite the cop part, the part that was hardened and circumspect, felt for Shaw. "Why were you the only one to go to prison?"

Shaw took the question in, resigned to it. "Because I was the low-hanging fruit. I was the one spiraling out of control. And because they were better at covering their tracks. I won't get more specific."

"Are we going to find a knife missing from your kitchen?" Tennant asked bluntly.

Shaw looked at him, seemingly confused by the question. "My kitchen?" Her eyes widened. "Oh, no. Did you find a knife with my prints on it too?" She began to panic. "Oh my God. Will."

"Back to Will," Foster said. "Would either Leonard or Valdez have felt comfortable enough to let *your* husband get close to them?"

Marin shook her head. "How can I answer that? The fact is that the key was hidden away and now you've found it somewhere it had no business being. Who else benefits from that besides Will?" She turned her head away. "I lied about not being followed and tripping into the street. But you know that. I confronted the person I believed was responsible. I won't tell you who, but the threat was real."

"That your husband too?" Tennant asked.

"You don't have to believe me, but I think *she* does." Shaw glanced over at Foster.

"You mentioned a coat missing from your apartment," Foster said. "Can you describe it?"

"Black. Long." Her hands went to her chest and made circles. "Two hearts on either side. It was made by a local designer I was supporting. It's not overly expensive, but I know where I left it."

Foster stood, her chair scraping loudly on the floor. "I'll be back in a minute."

She raced out of the room and straight to Li's desk. Her partner was still at it, her fingers flying, her eyes glued to the monitor. "Li.

That garage video. Can you go back? Isolate the person coming out of Leonard's car? We need a printout of that coat."

"Why? Got something?"

"Marin Shaw's telling us that the key we found at Valdez's was hers, but that it was taken from her condo, along with a long black coat with two red hearts on the front."

"Whaaaaat?" Li cued it up, scrolled through, and found the clearest image of the figure she could find, then sent it to the printer. Foster was already moving in that direction to snatch it out of the printer tray before heading back to Shaw and Tennant.

"Follow me. I need you in there," she said as she passed Li's chair. "Tennant's not helping." She looked around the room. "Pienkowski?"

Li shrugged. "No idea. He's a restless wind."

Back inside the interview room, Foster placed the photo on the table and turned it so Marin Shaw could see it clearly. "Is that your coat?"

Marin leaned in, then turned even paler. "It looks like it might be. I can't say for sure." She looked from Foster to Li to the scowling Tennant. "But it looks like it. Whose car is that? Is it . . . is it Deanna's? Is that the person who shot her? Wearing *my* coat?"

Foster sat down again, and Li pulled up a chair and sat beside her. Tennant looked a bit uncomfortable being outnumbered by women, but he said nothing.

"We're going to go over this again," Foster said. "All of it. Your husband. Your affair. Who knew about it. Who had access to your condo. Everything."

"You believe me, then?"

Li stared at Shaw. "What can you tell us about thirty pieces of silver?"

Shaw looked confused. "I don't know what you mean."

"You're not a religious person, then, Ms. Shaw?" Foster asked.

Shaw sighed. "I was raised agnostic. It stuck. That makes AA a little more difficult, but I'm managing."

Foster's eyes held Shaw's for a time, searching for the truth. "Let's move on."

———

"Well, that was a bust," Symansky groused later as they all sat around the board. "Hate it when we gotta just let 'em waltz out the door."

"I looked her straight in the face," Foster said. "She didn't know a thing about the dimes."

"But her husband." Li shook her head. "I don't see him putting in all this work unless he's just off his head nuts, and I didn't get that vibe."

Foster eyed the board. "Neither did I." She tapped the garage photo tacked to the board. "Okay, let's run through it again."

Griffin eased out of her office to stand to watch as they ran what they had for the hundredth time. Shaw's missing key wasn't enough, and her prints hadn't been on the knife that killed Valdez.

Tennant paced around the room. "Tell me you two aren't believing that damsel-in-distress nonsense? Is she serious? Her *husband* is setting her up?"

Symansky, Kelley, Lonergan, and Bigelow sat at their desks, their chairs facing the center, watching Tennant wear a path in the cracked linoleum. Li leaned on the corner of her desk, eating a bag of barbecue chips, sneering at Pienkowski, who'd found yet another doughnut that didn't belong to him.

"She called Leonard," Tennant went on. "She planned to meet her." He turned to the photo tacked to the board. "That's her coat! And Valdez's key has her prints all over it. Maybe he dropped her. She took it bad. Figured he crossed her. That's where the dimes come in. She had three years to work this thing, too, let's not forget that. She plays victim, poor me, the whole nine, then while we're spinning wheels, bending over backward thinking it can't be her because she's so weak and pathetic, she's out there clearing the board."

Kelley raised a hand. "All circumstantial. We don't know it's the same coat. Looks like it. A lot of things look alike. And her husband *could* have taken that key and killed Valdez, hoping to jam her up."

"He wear her coat too?" Lonergan asked snidely.

Kelley shrugged. "Why not? If he's into this, why wouldn't he wear the coat? It would explain how he fooled the victims. Dark garage, dark street. You see somebody you think you recognize wearing a coat you've seen before, so you let your guard down."

"Makes sense," Bigelow said. "And in that case, we don't have to link him to either victim for him to be the guy, since he was masquerading as his wife."

Lonergan scowled. "We're in Hollywood now? Killers got costume changes all of a sudden? I think we're moving in the wrong direction here."

Symansky tapped pudgy fingers against his stomach as he leaned back in his chair. "Yeah, I'm with him. Too showy. Plus, even with the coat, we got nothin'. The state's attorney would laugh us out of her office."

"Shaw's got motive," Pienkowski said, "and opportunity." The whole room turned to look at him, as though a rock had suddenly burst into song. "And if that knife came out of her kitchen, which we don't know it didn't, since we haven't searched, she's got means."

Tennant pointed to his partner. "See? There you go. Cop 101."

"We ain't gonna find that knife missing from her kitchen now, though," Lonergan said. "She's had all kinds of time to replace it with one just like it. And, if it's her we're seriously looking at, the knife she used on Valdez, unless she's dumber than lint, is either buried, tossed, or melted down by now. We moved too slow on this ticking all the boxes, scribbling on that board. In my experience, the faster you strike, the more you get."

Foster knew that was a dig at her, but she turned her back to him and let it go. "Timelines." She drew long black lines on the board and then wrote the names of Shaw, her husband, and two remaining coconspirators, Franklin and Meehan. "Aaron Parker's clear. He was gambling his life away at the OTB. There's also no connection to Valdez."

"Jeniece. Also out," Li said. "Sticky relationship with her mother but she'd have no way of getting into Shaw's condo for the key or coat. She'd have had no problem getting into her mother's car at the garage, but without the key, she couldn't have gotten Valdez."

Li held up a hand. "Unless he let her in."

Symansky sighed. "So now what?"

"We put Shaw in her apartment for one," Kelley said. "We eyeball the cam video. If she lied about being home, we prove she's a liar. And since we're talking about motives, wouldn't Franklin and Meehan have the same reason for wanting Valdez and Leonard dead? They were all in whatever that thing was together. That'd explain somebody shoving Shaw in the street. Maybe we need to turn this and look at it from a different angle."

"Tight little circle, in any case," Bigelow mumbled. "What you'd call incestuous. Makes me worry about Franklin maybe being next."

Li turned to him. "Why not Meehan?"

Bigelow laughed. "Because John Meehan is a cockroach. He'll outlive us all."

"They'd have to change it up, though," Kelley said. "An accident. A fall in her shower. Something that wouldn't look like it belonged with the other two. Leonard was supposed to look like a suicide, remember? And Valdez some rando attack."

"But they weren't," Foster said. "They were always meant to be connected. You're forgetting the thirty pieces of silver down Leonard's throat, the dimes in Valdez's pocket. Were we really supposed to believe she swallowed each one before she killed herself? Or that Valdez was accusing *himself* of betrayal?"

Kelley looked over at Tennant. "What about the wife? Valdez was a cheater. Maybe she got tired of it. Maybe Leonard was one of the women he cheated with. The dimes would fit then."

Tennant shook his head. "Not her. She was completely clueless. Pienkowski hated to break it to her, but she had no idea. Besides, she's covered for both killings. Some cookie-bake bullshit at the kids' school when her husband died and her tucked at home with the family the night Leonard was shot. Both alibis check out."

Foster drew a line through the wife's name. She checked her watch, stuffing the worry down for the millionth time today, moving on.

"Someone tried to kill Shaw too," Li said. "Which one, since we're thinking closed circle? Husband or the aldermen?"

"Or somebody an alderman sent?" Symansky pointed a finger at Li and squinted. "You don't always have to get your own hands dirty."

"Or we got it all wrong," Lonergan said, "and there's somebody we're not even seeing yet."

The statement, true as it was, brought the entire room down. Griffin, her arms folded across her chest, glowered at them from the corner. They hadn't made much progress.

Foster stared at the jumble of disparate notations and the tight gallery of persons of interest on the board, the lines leading nowhere. She capped the marker and put it down on the desk.

"We keep at it."

If not Shaw, then somebody else, Lonergan had said, and it made sense to her. Who? What angle had they missed? She turned back to the board. "Shaw's lawyer, Charlotte Moore. We haven't talked to her." She padded over and wrote Moore's name on the board. "She might know something without realizing she knows it."

Li frowned. "We're not going to get anything out of her, especially when she finds out we spoke to Shaw without her being here."

Foster glanced at Li. "We offered her the opportunity. She turned it down. That's not on us. And she'll talk to us if it clears her client."

"Right. A lot of holes on that board," Griffin said, quieting the room. "Fill them in while I still have the will to live." She turned and walked back into her office, closing the door behind her. Everyone waited for what they knew was coming. "Somebody out there's killing people, people! The husband's sketchy! And Meehan's an asshole." Griffin's words shrill, strong, flew like angry rounds through the thin walls.

"Boss ain't happy," Symansky muttered.

"And if the boss ain't happy . . . ," Bigelow said, leaving his statement unfinished.

"*Though she be but little, she is fierce*," Kelley offered with a knowing nod.

Symansky reeled, his eyes angry, burning darts. "One more line of that fucking Shakespeare and your name goes up on that board."

# CHAPTER 30

Foster called Mike right before the start of her shift the next morning. There'd been no trouble. He and the kids were safe, though he sounded tense on the phone. "This is insane," he'd said.

"Just a little longer, Mike. I'll figure it out."

They'd agreed that Mike and the boys would go someplace they felt safe, that even she didn't know about. Out of the field of battle. Hopefully beyond the voice's reach. She'd driven by the house on her way in, just to assure herself that no one was scoping it out, but even knowing Glynnis's family was safe and no one was watching, she couldn't shake the feeling of impending doom. It hung over her like a heavy shroud.

Adding to her misery, Lonergan was the only one at his desk when she walked in. It was odd. He was never early. She nodded, acknowledging the morning. He nodded back. She hadn't been at her desk ten seconds before Griffin's door swung open. Griffin looked around the office, her eyes landing on the only two detectives at her immediate disposal. "You two, with me. Superintendent's called a news conference with the mayor. Downstairs in ten."

"Us?" The word came out with far more panic than Foster would have wanted to convey. "Li or Kelley or somebody should be here any second."

Griffin's ice-blue eyes, freakish in good times, narrowed like two slits of frigid demon ice. "You two are who I see, you two are who I got. Downstairs. Ten. And for God's sake, try to look like you know something."

Foster glanced over at Lonergan. They exchanged a look of panic. She could work with anyone, she told herself. *He's a cop. You're a cop. Be a cop.* She stowed her bag in her bottom drawer, then plucked a pen top from the desk and quietly slid it into her right pocket.

Her eyes swept over her struggling plant. She had no idea what variety of little plant it was, but she was now attached to it and invested in its survival. Polly. She decided just then that's what she'd name it. For her comfort as much as Polly's, Foster reached down and massaged one of the green leaves between a thumb and index finger.

Griffin swept out of her office, glowered at the two of them still standing there, her gaze offering up a dangerous challenge before she headed downstairs, tugging at her blouse sleeves under her jacket, making sure she was camera ready and inspection worthy. "In eight," she said before heading out.

Lonergan stood watching her, a sly grin on his wide, ruddy face. "Looks like we're partnering again, huh?"

"I don't have a problem with it, if you don't."

He shrugged. "I don't."

"That's a change."

"You're sure of that, are you?"

"Seven!" Griffin's voice came from somewhere.

Lonergan groaned. "What's she doing, waiting on the stairs?"

The shrill voice came again. "Yes!"

Lonergan straightened his tie. "Showtime."

The small meeting room was packed. Nothing brought out public frenzy like the violent deaths of prominent citizens, Foster thought. A kid gunned down in a playground by gang bullets? Barely a ripple in the air. But here she was standing at attention, resentfully, beside Lonergan, her boss, her boss's boss, and the mayor and her people. A united front. A show of unity and strength meant to convey the message that CPD and the City of Chicago were on the case and on the job, committed to finding the killer of two of the city's leaders. Optics. Theater. Wasted time.

As the police superintendent attempted to calm the waters and assure the citizens that the department had a plan, that their best detectives were on the case, that finding the killer was everyone's top priority, Foster looked out over the sea of cameras, mics, and reporter notepads and spotted Soren Hastrup. It wasn't a surprise. She sighed but kept her face expressionless. She was here for the show of competency, for the politics. Here they all stood in the small stuffy room with a replica of their CPD emblem hung on the wall behind the podium, dutiful public servants hard at work.

The head man, a seasoned cop in a white shirt and gold braid, fielded the rapid-fire questions, giving as many details as the department had to share. But the answers were insufficient because the city demanded a suspect in custody, and they didn't have one. They *could* have a suspect soon, maybe, she thought, if they weren't all standing here like tin soldiers when there were leads to follow. The questions came fast and loud, the reporters' voices both low and high pitched, but all insistent, like the amplified call from a murder of crows.

Foster resisted the urge to check her watch. It would give the wrong impression, make it seem like she was bored or preoccupied, though she was truly the latter. Was Marin Shaw playing them? Playing her? She stood ramrod straight, pondering the questions, her face unreadable, her eyes focused on a single point on the back wall. A soldier awaiting orders.

When the superintendent stepped aside from the podium to let the mayor speak, Foster zoned out. Politics wasn't going to find their killer. In her experience, nothing they ever needed to solve anything came out of the fifth floor of city hall. Foster quickly clocked back in at the mention of her name. Her keen eyes scanned over the sea of reporters. *Hastrup.*

"So, we *don't* get to hear from the lead detectives?" he asked. "The boots on the ground, so to speak."

The mayor didn't bother looking behind herself to where Foster and Lonergan stood with Griffin. "Everybody's lead on this. We have the whole city on this, Hastrup, as you well know. All hands are definitely on deck. My office . . ."

Hastrup raised his hand to interrupt the preelection speech, but the mayor ignored it and hurriedly shut the Q and A down. Calming the waters was one thing; offering yourself up for a public bloodletting was quite another. "Okay, that's all we've got time for now. We'll keep you up to date on new developments as they come in. We're going to catch this guy. Meanwhile, our streets are safe, our city is secure. Go out there and have a good day." The reporters rose to shout more questions at the mayor, but the woman, well practiced at evading unpleasantness, just smiled, gave a hearty tone-deaf thumbs-up, and then filed out, taking her entourage and the top brass with her.

Lonergan cleared his throat and cocked his head toward the reporters. "Looks like you got a fan."

Foster watched as reporters rushed out to file their stories, all but Hastrup, who stood watching her, his cameraman by his side. "You more than anyone, Detective Foster, know how dangerous a city this is. Off the record, how close are you *really* to solving this thing?"

Hastrup had covered her son's murder all the way up to Willem's trial and sentencing, and he hadn't been gentle about it, much like now. It was the job—she knew that intellectually—but emotionally he felt predatory, almost gleefully so.

Without a word, she turned and left the room with Lonergan.

"No worries," Hastrup called after her. "I'm not going anywhere."

Lonergan caught her at the door. "You gotta hit those vultures back, you know, or they start thinkin' you're an easy touch."

She looked up at him. "Or you can choose not to engage, which I just did. Not everything has to be a fight."

He brushed past her. "Nothing wrong with a good dustup once in a while."

Li was at her desk when Foster and Lonergan got back. Lonergan branched off, back to his desk, while Griffin stormed into her office and slammed the door. Li held up her cell phone with a replay of the news conference running with the sound muted. "Oh. My God. What. The. Frick."

"The boss needed bodies. Ours were the only two here. Any other day you'd be here hours before me." Foster plopped down into her squeaky chair, reaching for the top drawer and her bottle of aspirin. "Not today."

Li leaned over and held up a greasy bakery bag. "I stopped for jelly doughnuts. The good kind, not those hockey pucks in the break room."

Foster glowered at her partner, then popped the aspirin in her mouth, washing the caplets down with cold coffee from her mug. Li wiggled the bag enticingly. "Strawberry."

Foster took the bag. "This doesn't make it okay."

Li grinned. "It makes it a *little* okay."

"One doughnut." Foster reached into the bag and flicked a look at Polly for reassurance. "Then we go."

———

They waited for Marin Shaw outside her house in an unmarked car around noon. Her husband was inside waiting for them but hadn't appeared too happy about the whole thing when they'd arranged the meeting on the phone. It was a two birds, one stone situation. They'd ask him some questions; Marin would check around for the black coat she claimed was missing from her condo.

"We only have her word for it that the coat was at the other place and not here," Li said. "This could be her way of putting Barrett in the mix."

Foster checked the rearview. "True. But if it was her, she'd be a fool to keep that coat anywhere, so not finding it helps her more than it hurts him."

Li slid her a sideways look. "You're distracted."

"I am not."

"You're distracted but trying not to act distracted. You check your watch a lot. You're worried about the time. Family issue, you said. It started with that envelope you shoved into your bag the other day."

Foster fought the impulse to check her watch again upon being called out by Li's killer observation skills. First, the press conference, now this. She glanced behind them in the driver's side mirror. "I'll figure it out." Li got quiet, and Foster worried she might have hurt her feelings, so she faced her. "I don't want you thinking I don't trust you. I *do*, Vera. I trust you with my life, obviously, as I hope you trust me with yours. Something's come up, and I'm worrying the problem to death until I figure out what to do about it . . . I'm not a big sharer."

Li snorted. "Oh, I've noticed, believe me."

Her eyes narrowed. "The point here is. Yes, I'm working through something, but I've got it. And I appreciate your concern, as a partner and as a friend."

"Friend? I've never seen your place."

"I've never seen *your* place."

"All right, I'm inviting you over. Come for dinner once we wrap this up. Meet my family. Bring wine."

Foster turned back around. She'd gone too far and now was stuck with an invitation she couldn't turn down without looking like a jerk. "Fine."

They were quiet for a time, but she could tell Li was satisfied with herself. And the more she thought about it, the more she had a feeling she'd somehow been maneuvered into the entire thing.

"You ever think about how some people get together?" Li asked.

Foster scanned the house, checked the street, the rearview, the side mirror. "No."

"I mean, look at Shaw and look at him. They don't seem to match. He's like a brat, and she's got more to her, you know? I just wonder how that whole thing happened. For sure she could have done a lot better."

Foster checked her watch. It was exhausting living her life second by second, ruled by the hour and minute hands of a clock. But she was worried about the kids and Mike. She dreaded the next call. Her entire life now seemed to be nothing but worry.

Li was watching her.

"Don't."

Li smiled. "I wasn't going to. Red wine."

Foster looked at her. "What?"

"When you come to dinner, bring red wine. And don't go cheap, I'm your backup, remember?"

Foster had opened her mouth to respond when she saw Marin Shaw drive up and park in front of the house. "Later."

Li unbuckled her seat belt. "Here we go. The mother of all domestic calls."

"We stay calm, they stay calm," Foster said getting out of the car.

Li eased out on her side. "Yeah, when's that ever worked."

They'd already discussed with Shaw how they hoped it would go—Marin going through her things upstairs, looking for the coat, she and Li downstairs with Barrett, asking him questions once Marin was done and gone again.

As they sat in the living room with Barrett, sullen and grouchy opposite them, they could hear drawers opening and closing, and doors doing the same as Marin searched for what she obviously couldn't find. They hadn't told him what she was looking for, but if he was the one terrorizing his wife, he likely already knew, and if he had half a brain working, if the coat had ever been there, he'd have gotten rid of it by now. It took Marin about half an hour before she came down without a coat but with lingerie instead. The detectives stood, watching as Marin walked over to her husband and threw the frilly things in his face.

"These aren't mine." Her face was an angry, menacing mask of red. "In my house. With *Zoe*."

Barrett hadn't even the decency to look ashamed, the smug grin on his face infuriating even to Li and Foster. Without another word, Shaw walked out of the house, slamming the door behind her.

Barrett gathered the lingerie up and threw it on the couch beside him. Li and Foster sat down again. No one spoke for a moment.

"She's got no right to play the victim here. She's done far worse."

"Meaning?" Foster asked.

"Corruption. Drunkenness. *Prison*."

"That it?" Li asked.

Barrett's brows rose. "Are you serious? Isn't that enough? Our entire lives ruined because of her?"

Foster looked over at the lingerie. "Your friend here the night Leonard was killed?"

"That's none of your business." He stood. "And I'm done talking. You want to know anything else about this whole thing, you can buy a paper in the morning. I've given my side. A look into the *real* Marin Shaw. We'll see how *she* likes being humiliated for once. Now, I'm busy. You'll have to leave."

Foster hadn't thought it possible, but she disliked the man now more than ever. "Your wife is our prime suspect in these murders. You might be able to help us close these cases."

It was a lie she and Li had agreed on before they came in, motivation to get Barrett talking too much. If he truly wanted to hurt his wife as they headed for divorce, what better way to do that then to offer her up to the police in a murder investigation?

"She's an angry woman," Li added. "We all saw that just now."

Barrett eased down again, suddenly eager to talk, as they both knew he would be. He smiled slyly. "You have no idea. I worry about

Zoe, though, not myself. About what all this violence might do to her. Marin's unstable. She always has been."

Foster nodded. "Yes, as you've said, I wanted to ask about your condo. When's the last time you were there?"

"What's that got to do with anything?"

"We're wondering who had access to the apartment, prior to her being there, so when we find something, say a weapon, we'll know *she* put it there, not someone else. You see?"

His eyes brightened, and he grinned. "Yes. Well, I was there on the odd evening or weekend when Zoe was at an overnight, or something. Check with the lobby guy. Ray. Roy. Something. If I worked late or had an important client to get ready for, I'd stay there instead of driving all the way home, and I'd arrange for a babysitter for Zoe. I also stopped by sometimes to check on the place. If you're talking about weapons, we do keep a gun there for security. It's in a lockbox in the walk-in. Both Marin and I have the code. I haven't touched it in years."

"And I'm sorry." Li shot him an apologetic grin that aped embarrassment. "Just to clarify. The night Alderman Leonard was killed, you had dinner with your wife and daughter, and then you were home alone. Your wife, then, had hours unaccounted for." She watched as Barrett's eyes danced at the possibility of Marin being their prime suspect. "What about the night Alderman Valdez was killed?" She consulted her notes, flipping through pages, though she already knew the date. The appearance of a bumbling, disorganized, overworked cop was meant to give Barrett the idea he had the upper hand.

Will emitted an aggrieved sigh, then reached into his back pocket for his iPhone. Swiping, scrolling, he finally answered. "Business." His finger moved down the screen. "Six p.m. dinner with a client. I got a sitter for Zoe. I was home, I think, by nine." He put the phone away and fixed them with a self-satisfied look.

"The client? Just for the record." The last she added hurriedly when it appeared Barrett might resist.

"Damon Woodrich, Woodrich Realty Inc. I had salmon, he had steak. I paid, and I have the receipt."

Li's eyes held steady, the pretend forgetfulness and the fake apologetic smile now gone. "And the sitter?"

"College kid. She lives down the street. Amy Dyman. Charged an arm and a leg."

Foster asked, "So, no one else but you and your wife could have been in the condo to access your gun? You didn't hold any company parties, or anything, in three years?"

He scoffed. "I haven't exactly been in a party mood, have I? My wife was in prison, for God's sake. And I haven't exactly been tops on anyone's invite list either. Our circle of friends pretty much disowned me after Marin's implosion. It's like I've been in prison right along with her."

"That has to be terrible," Li said, feigning sympathy. "What a mess all this has made, huh?"

Will rolled his eyes, missing the sarcasm. "Tell me about it."

Foster watched him. "When did you decide your marriage was over, Mr. Barrett? Before your wife went to prison or after she got out?"

"It was over the minute she was arrested. The embarrassment. Even still, I stood by her for Zoe's sake. What a mistake."

"Who does the lingerie belong to?" Foster asked.

Barrett bristled. "That's none of your business."

"It might be," Li said, "if she can vouch for where you were at critical times."

"I don't need anyone to vouch for me. I've done nothing untoward."

Foster angled her head. "How's your daughter dealing with all of this?"

"How do you think? She's devastated. A mother in prison? Her friends at school? If it wasn't for Char stepping in to help, taking charge of Zoe and getting her through with all the girl talk and the girl things, I don't know where I'd be. I mean, it's not like *I* was equipped for all that."

"Char? Is that Charlotte Moore, your wife's lawyer?"

"She's Zoe's godmother." Barrett brushed nonexistent lint off the crease in his slacks. "She and Marin have been friends since Columbia Law."

"Your wife believes someone's been following her," Foster said. "That they tried to hurt her. Any idea who'd want to do that?"

He scoffed. "No one. Marin likes playing the victim, but believe me, she isn't one."

"You saw the bandages on her hands," Li said. "But you didn't ask about them."

"If there are any real victims here, it's me . . . and Zoe, of course." He stood. "Now, go out there and do your jobs. Lock her up. I'm done talking." After moving toward the door, he held it open for them. "I'm done with all of this. I'll see her in divorce court."

The door slammed behind them, and Foster and Li stood for a time on the icy porch scanning the tony street. "That family is so damaged," Li said.

"Luckily, not our job to fix." Foster held up the car keys. Li took them, and they bounded down the steps and raced the windchill to the car and got in.

From the driver's seat Li glared up at the house they'd just come out of. "Brrrr."

Foster peered out the window, too, at the front door to the unhappy home. "The coat's not in the house. It's not at the condo. The key to Valdez's office isn't at the condo but was found near his body." She was talking to herself, ordering her thoughts. "Corruption. Drunkenness. Prison." She looked over at Li. "When he was ticking off Marin's faults, he never once said, 'Oh, and she had an affair with George Valdez.' He's the kind of person who would have."

"Definitely."

"They own a gun," Foster said. "Either of them could have used it to incriminate the other, yet Leonard was shot with her own gun."

"If he didn't know about the affair with Valdez," Li added, "he'd have no idea about the key."

"Well, somebody knew about it."

"Shaw."

"Then why tell *us* the key and the coat were missing?"

"Running us around." Foster looked over at Li, who shrugged. "I'm playing devil's advocate. You heard him, she likes playing the victim."

"No, it's something else. Woolrich we can check, but if Barrett gave him to us so quickly, he's likely a no-go." Foster sighed. "Motive. Maybe we're looking at the wrong one? We've been hanging on the alderman angle. Shaw taking the hit."

"Lonergan said it," Li said. "I kind of see it."

"That's her going after them, but what reason would anyone have for wanting her out of the way? Back in prison, if we can prove she's a killer. Or dead. *Someone* pushed her into the street."

Li flicked a look to the house. "So he doesn't have to sneak around."

"I think he enjoys sneaking around. But he's going to be alibied by Woolrich. And, according to Shaw, Barrett didn't know about the key, which meant he couldn't know about Valdez, so he'd have no reason to go after him."

"He could have found out and kept quiet about it. Biding his time," Li said.

Foster thought for a moment. "He doesn't strike me as the type to bide his time. Too vindictive. Too entitled."

Li started the car. "Then it could be literally anybody."

"Not so sure about that," Foster said. "One other name. Mentioned just now. It's on our board, but we haven't chased it yet."

"Charlotte Moore." Li pulled away from the curb.

Foster took a final look at the house. "Charlotte Moore."

# CHAPTER 31

The day hadn't been fruitful. Standing at her board at home, Foster struck a line through Damon Woolrich's name. He'd verified that he and Will were together Thursday until almost eight. It had taken a visit to the restaurant on Huron to get their copy of the credit card slip for the meal and the time stamp of when the table cashed out. Even Amy Dyman confirmed that she'd sat for Zoe that night until almost nine. Barrett couldn't have been in two places at once to kill Valdez. Foster and Li hadn't been able to contact Moore all day. In court, her assistant kept telling them. Moore's name rose to the top of their interview list.

Stepping back, studying the lines and circles and cross outs, Foster searched for patterns and gaps. Franklin's alibi had also checked out. Saint Stanislaus's priest had put her there at the time she'd claimed she was. That left the big dog, John Meehan, who'd told them he had been home with his wife, which she, too, confirmed. But Meehan hadn't been the dark figure easing out of Leonard's car in the black coat, and he wouldn't have had access to Marin's closet. Maybe Valdez would have let him into his office after hours. Maybe there were more than three keys floating around.

"Too many maybes," Foster muttered, putting down the dry-erase marker and rubbing her tired eyes.

Her cell phone buzzed on the counter. She padded over, checked the screen, another unknown number. It was nearly eleven o'clock. She swiped right and waited.

"Detective Harriet Foster." The menacing voice no longer came as a surprise to her. "What have you done? The Thompsons are not at home. You've hidden them. It's an interesting move in our little game. One I don't like a whole bunch."

"It's only a game if both sides play," she said.

"But we are playing, aren't we?"

"What do you want? I'm tired of asking."

"Not yet. Go to bed. You're working way too late. You know, you really should decorate your place. It's so . . . lifeless the way it is."

Foster reeled around to face her front window. The blinds were open, the street dark.

"How would you know?"

He laughed.

She grabbed her gun from the table and rushed out the front door to stand on the porch, scanning the block. Dogs barked their heads off down the street, but everything else was quiet, dark, save for one or two houses where the faint blue glow of television screens flickered through partially opened curtains.

Across the street, an inky figure walked slowly away. Long coat. A knit cap. Could be anyone. She ran across the street, shadowing the figure, half a block behind him, her gun at her right side, her phone to her left ear. "Is that you? Walking away?" He didn't answer. Pulling the phone away from her ear, she yelled. "Stop." The figure ignored her. She pulled the phone back to her ear. "I will shoot you."

"How can you be sure it's me?" His tone was playful, almost giddy with excitement. "You won't shoot, Harri. You don't have enough information."

The figure stopped at a car parked at the corner. The taillights flickered as he unlocked the vehicle.

"And you won't get it tonight," he said as he opened the car door. "Next time." He got in. "Promise."

Foster ran for the car, cold air burning her lungs, warm desperate air puffing out into the night. She'd run out without a coat, the T-shirt and jeans she wore wholly inadequate for the temperature. Her footing faltered on the ice and slush, but her eyes stayed on the taillights.

"You won't make it in time." The taillights flickered as he tapped the brakes. "All I have to do is make one little gear shift, and you're still so far away."

Foster hit speaker, shoved the phone into her back pocket without breaking the connection and sped up, her eyes focused, needing to get close enough to at least get a plate number. She was closing the distance, almost there, when her foot caught a patch of glassy ice and she went down hard, her elbows, hands, and knees scraping against rock salt, her left cheek skidding against the same. Panicked that her tormentor would pounce while she was down, she took no time to assess her injuries and scrambled up to her feet, gun drawn, head slowly clearing, ignoring the pain in her knees, elbows, and face. The car door never opened. It looked like he wasn't interested in killing her, just taunting her.

"Be careful, Detective. It's icy out."

She took off running again toward the car, this time slower and limping. Only a few yards to go.

"You know, I played this game with your partner. You two are a lot alike. Chicago's finest."

She ignored him. She was done talking. Almost there. But he had been right. She never had a chance of getting there in time. Just as she'd gotten a few yards from the taillights, the car bolted out of the spot, its wheels spinning on ice, snow, and rock salt, then sped off. Dark, four-door sedan. Blue or black. Ford. No back plate. No back fender damage, no decals. Nothing to distinguish it from a thousand other sedans running the streets.

"Good night, Harri. Sleep tight."

The line went dead.

Her chest heaving from exertion, Foster stumbled back and flumped down in the snow to catch her breath. Her elbows were bleeding, and she'd torn the knees in her jeans, blood seeping through the rips. She ran her fingers along her left cheek and pulled them back bloodied. After a time, she got up and limped back to her place. She needed a plan, she thought, a way through. He'd elevated things coming to where she felt safe. He meant for her to feel less so by doing it. If he knew who she was and where she lived, what else did he know? Who was he?

# CHAPTER 32

Foster showered, dressed her scrapes, and then changed back into work clothes—slacks, blouse, jacket, solid boots. She was going in to work at midnight because there was no chance of her sleeping. As she walked into the office, easing through the handful of detectives sitting around on the midnight shift, she gave them each a nod. No one questioned her being there off shift. Nobody cared. She had texted Li to tell her she was coming in to spend a little extra time on the footage only because on their first case together she'd made the mistake of following a lead solo and had caught Li's ire. Li had been right. They were partners, and their cases, whether they involved scut work or active leads, had to be shared. The text was simple. **Working late on footage. Hoping to get a break. No need for you to come in. Keep you posted.**

She then booted up her computer to get started. But even fueled by caffeine and cheap food from a drive-up window on the way in, even with the clock ticking on both the Leonard and Valdez cases, her fingers just hovered over the keyboard.

He knew where she lived. How? No one gives out a police officer's address. Had he followed her? If so, for how long? Since Glynnis's death? Since their first call? Intimidation. That's the case she could make. The voice was attempting to intimidate a police officer. Justification enough for the computer run. She picked up her cell phone and found the numbers he'd called from and typed them into the search field, her hands sweating, her lips dry. It didn't take long for the numbers to come back unattached to any registered users. She'd hoped for better results, but these results didn't surprise her. Obviously, she wasn't dealing with a stupid person. He didn't want to be tracked. Burners didn't have GPS chips. That was that. The numbers were as much as she had so far. What had he said to her? *You don't have enough information.*

He had been right, but it wasn't something a regular person would say. It was something she would think, as a cop, before taking a potentially lethal act. Could he be a cop? The sickening thought sputtered her brain for a moment. He'd called her Harri. He'd claimed an arrangement with G. Could he really be one of them? She had no idea where to start. The numbers were a bust. What next? Where next? *She didn't have enough information.*

Foster had no idea how long she'd been sitting there before Li's voice startled her.

"Hey."

Foster's head snapped up to find her partner standing over her, travel mug of coffee in hand, a concerned look on her face. She'd been sitting, thinking, not going through footage, for half an hour. "I didn't mean for you to come in. No good reason for both of us not to get any sleep tonight."

"You said there was no *need* for me to come in."

A beat passed. "But you came in."

She grinned. "I felt the need. We're working a case. That wager on free dinner is still on. What happened to your face? Looks like road rash."

"I fell on the ice. No big deal." Foster closed her notepad on the burner numbers, but there was nothing she could do about the feeling of doom hovering over her other than try to ignore it . . . for now. "I'm on the street cams around the garage Leonard was found in. You okay with the captures from Valdez's office?"

Li lifted her mug. "Let's do it."

Foster put the voice away again, for now but not forever. Four hours later, she paused the tape she'd been reviewing, her eyes on a front plate that matched one she'd put on their board days before. "I've got a plate match."

Li's head popped up. "Who?"

"Jeniece Eccles."

Li got up and padded over to stand behind Foster's chair. "Get. Out."

"Look. Her car comes into the garage the morning her mother was killed. Two minutes after ten." She advanced the tape. "Comes out again seven minutes after eleven that same night. That's an hour after Grant puts approximate time of death." She turned to Li. "You'd think she would have mentioned this."

"We can't make out who's driving."

Foster said, "She hasn't reported her car stolen."

Li's brows furrowed. "She did say she was in and out of city hall all the time. That garage is close. Working late? Coincidental crossing?"

"It's odd. And not much. But it's something."

"It might be more when it's matched with mine." Li walked back to her desk. "I ran the plates on our board against any around Valdez's on the night. Nothing, like we got before, but also against this." She swiveled her monitor around so Foster could see it. "That photo Tennant showed us of Valdez and his December mystery date? The one where he's walking the woman to the door? I blew it up, and it got part of the street through the front window. The car parked right in front. A dark Tesla. You can see the recessed door handles. Not saying it's hers, but late at night, the neighborhood being what it is, if it were me, I'd park right in front."

Foster stood and approached the board. Circled the matching plate number, then drew a line from it to Jeniece Eccles's driver's license photo. "Jeniece owns a 2022 Tesla Model 3. Black."

Li joined her at the board. "She could get close to her mother. And if that's her in the photos with Valdez, we can see how close she got to him. Bottom line, though, if she matches, she lied to us about not knowing him. And if she lied about that—"

"Everyone lies to us." Foster stared at the photo of the key tacked to the board. "And Jeniece doesn't explain the key."

"Unless she also lied about not having any contact with Marin Shaw. City hall, remember. Lawyers. Her mother working with her. No reason they couldn't have connected at some point."

Foster stepped back. "So, we talk to Eccles again." She was exhausted, and her eyes felt like they had ten pounds of sand in them, but she had no choice except to push on. Common sense told her that running on fumes was not the ideal way to get the work done, but she always managed to find herself pushed well past E. She plucked her coat off the back of her chair, ready to go.

Li frowned. "Maybe we wait until the sun comes up? I suggest a couple hours' sleep first."

Foster blinked, checked her watch. Five a.m. Their shift didn't officially start for another few hours, and they'd already done a half day's work. "Right. Sleep, then Eccles. Thanks for coming in. We got somewhere." She grabbed her bag, shot Li a tired smile. "See you in a few."

Li watched her go, knowing there was something going on that Foster refused to share. "Harri?"

She turned back. "Yeah?"

Li decided in that moment it wasn't the time. They had a conversation to have, but she didn't want to start it here and with so much to do. "Watch yourself on that ice."

"Thanks. One fall per winter's my limit. See you in a bit."

———

They were all in at nine, despite the slushy commute, a result of three inches of fresh snow and a sideways sleet that defied the laws of decency. Coffee was brewing. Symansky had arrived with pączkis from his favorite bakery on Milwaukee Avenue, and Kelley had already consumed two with a mug of oat milk hot chocolate.

"We're gonna need something more than some nameless Tesla in front of Valdez's," Bigelow said as he rubbed his big hands together to warm them. "And I'm with Li on that garage. No crime in her parking there, and it's close to where she's got to be. She might even be a monthly. Might want to check."

Kelley took a bite of pączki, some of the jelly oozing out the side. "And we can't say that's her naked with Valdez. You can hardly see anything other than the fact that the person's obviously female and definitely not his wife."

Lonergan shook his head. "This whole thing reeks."

"He ain't wrong," Symansky added.

Foster stood at the board. "Anything else?"

"Woolrich checks out." Symansky fiddled with his ugly dad tie, a monstrosity of purples and blues and yellows . . . with red dots.

Kelley picked up the story. "Yeah, Bigs and me found the guy at his club, if you can believe that. A club in this day and age. Says he and Barrett did have dinner, which we already got from that receipt, but he confirmed how long with an Uber receipt that says he got into the car about eight, so unless Barrett spliced himself, he couldn't have gotten to Valdez to drop the dimes. And if he didn't kill Valdez, and the two deaths are linked . . . but he did say Barrett was distracted the whole night. Checking his watch, eyeing the door like he was expecting somebody, like he couldn't wait to get out of there. He didn't ask why. I would have."

"Maybe he was waiting for the hit man he hired to report back," Bigelow said. "So he could settle up. If we pulled his financials . . ."

Symansky shook his head. "Nope. We ain't got enough to make that play."

Foster scanned the board. Franklin. Meehan. Aaron Parker. Jeniece Eccles. Marin still a question mark. Barrett now alibied, but not above hiring out. Her eyes moved across the board and landed on a notation from their first visit to Marin Shaw's. Her lawyer. Charlotte Moore. Foster turned to Li.

"We still need to talk to Moore."

"She's never going to give Shaw up," Li said.

"But she's an unanswered question."

"She links to Shaw, but her name didn't come up with Leonard or Valdez," Symansky said. "What question?"

Foster reached for her notepad. "She's Shaw's close friend. At the very least, she'll have some insight."

Lonergan frowned. "She might have it, but she's not gonna give it to us, you know that, right? Her job's gettin' Shaw out of jams, not puttin' her in 'em."

"That doesn't mean we don't have the conversation. Moore, then Jeniece. Both today."

"Nobody wants to say it, so I will." Symansky pointed at the board. "You know we could be dealing with somebody not up there?" He looked around the group but found no takers willing to sign off on his theory. "That'd put us back at square one, with the boss, the top guy, and the mayor clawing down our backs."

Foster shook her head. "Not random. The circle's too tight. Who we're looking for is up there."

He threw his hands up. "Well, we got nothing but the daughter's car coming into the garage and then a car that looks like hers in front of Valdez's."

"Don't forget Leonard circling Shaw's release date on her calendar," Li said. "Another reason this revolves around Shaw. What'd Leonard intend on doing? Whatever it was, maybe Shaw got to her first. Valdez hits close too."

"We need a break. We need a slam dunk," Bigelow said.

Symansky frowned. "We ain't got it."

An incoming call on Foster's desk phone cut off the conversation. "Foster." It was Tennant. "Hold on, I'll put you on speaker. Go ahead."

"We got more prints in from Valdez's office. We lifted a good one. Want to guess who?"

Li leaned over the phone. "Jeniece Eccles."

There was a long pause from Tennant's end. "Is that Li?"

Symansky smirked. "You know it is. What'd you think? We were over here being a bunch of do-nothin's?" He gave Li a thumbs-up, which she gleefully returned.

"How'd you get Eccles?" Tennant asked.

"We have her car entering the garage where Leonard was found," Foster said. "And a car much like it parked outside Valdez's place the night he spent time with his December date. Now we have her inside the office."

Symansky slapped a hand on his desk. "That's more like it."

"Yeah, well, first one to her makes the next call." Tennant sounded put out; then the line disconnected.

"Since when is this a competition?" Kelley asked.

Bigelow scoffed. "Since Li burst Tennant's bubble."

Lonergan scoffed, his feet up on his desk. "So, this Eccles is a liar *and* a home-wrecker."

Kelley blinked, a pączki halfway to his mouth. "Home-wrecker? What year is it in your head?"

Lonergan folded his arms across his chest, smiling. "Just sayin'. Sometimes it's not so big a jump from screwin' around to killin' around."

Bigelow didn't look like he was buying it. "Nah, no way I believe it's her." He pointed at the board. "I know her. She couldn't kill her mother like that."

"People kill their mothers every day on the regular," Lonergan said. "Fathers. Brothers. Sisters. Cousins. Nieces. Grandfathers . . ." His voice trailed off.

"All right. Change of plans." Foster turned from the board, eyed Li. "Eccles first, *then* Moore. Not to beat Tennant to it, but because her being in that garage and her print in Valdez's office trump the fact-finding expedition with Moore. Agree?" Li nodded, gave her a thumbs-up.

For a moment no one said anything. Then Symansky broke the silence. "Okay, I'm just gonna say this. Am I the only one who has a problem with us sharing with Tennant and that lamppost he partners with?"

"It does kind of feel itchy," Li admitted. "How many players does it take to run the ball?"

"Two victims?" Foster said. "I'll take as many as I can get. But I'm not waiting around for a call from Tennant." She gathered her things, stopping to slide a paper clip off her desk to tuck into her pocket. "We've got trouble on that board, and we've got to fix it." She met every set of eyes. "So let's fix it."

There were head nods all around as everyone moved away to get back to it, except for Kelley, who studied Foster's face. "What happened to your cheek there?"

Before she could answer, Li answered for her. "She fell on the ice. No big deal. Move along, Matt."

He jabbed a half-eaten pączki in her direction. "There's something very weird about you, Vera Li."

"That's it? I don't get Shakespeare?"

Kelley's eyes narrowed as he fought a playful grin. "Nah. No Shakespeare for you." He walked away.

Foster glanced at her watch, anxious about the time they were losing. Almost nine thirty. She needed to check in with Mike and the kids. Staying away from their home, school, and place of work wasn't a long-term solution, and she couldn't keep them safe on her own, especially when she had no idea yet what they were dealing with. Her late-night visitor held all the cards, and she hated that. But fear and shock after last night had morphed into a burning resolve and anger. She slammed her bottom drawer shut harder than she intended, then turned to Li. "Best shot at finding Jeniece, work or home?"

"I'd say it's a toss-up." Li eyed the drawer Foster had just slammed. "That face have anything to do with your personal matter?"

"No." She managed a weak smile. "Ready?"

Foster's phone buzzed in her pocket. She grabbed it. Him. Two calls in two days. He wasn't going away, losing interest; he was escalating. She stood with the phone in her hand and looked over at Li, who was watching her with concern.

"I'll step away so you can take your call," Li said.

Foster held up a hand. "No. Stay." She answered. "What?"

"No good morning? I thought we were friends now?"

Foster said nothing.

"Did you get my delivery?"

"What delivery?" She checked her desk and spotted an 8½" × 11" mailing envelope with her name written in black marker on the front. How had she missed that? When had someone dropped it into her inbox? It had no postmark. It hadn't been delivered by a mailman. No one off the street could have placed it there, only a cop with access to the building. She grabbed it. "What is this?"

"Open it."

She tore open the seal. There was a photograph inside; this time it was of her, taken last night when she'd chased after the dark figure watching her house. The photo showed her in full run, gun at her side. She turned the photo over to find a name written on the back. *Elan Dreyer.*

"Who's this?"

"Your first get. You're going to lose me some evidence."

Foster scoffed. "You're dreaming."

"And you're not going to say a word to anyone about it. I'll be in touch."

The line went dead.

Foster dropped her phone back in her pocket, then stood there holding the photo.

"What the hell is going on?" Li asked. "Who *was* that?"

Foster turned to the room, held the envelope high. "Did anyone see someone drop this off on my desk?" She got a lot of head shakes, no answers. "No one?"

Foster handed the photo to Li, then eyed Griffin's door. She would have to go in.

Li stared at the photo. "Where's this?"

"Outside my house. Last night. Before we head out. Come with me? I'll explain."

They walked into Griffin's office. Foster placed the photo on her boss's desk and calmly, orderly, without emotion, explained to her and Li what they were looking at. When she'd finished, Griffin had turned an unhealthy shade of pink and steepled rigid fingers under her chin. She'd heard every word, and so had Li. A prolonged moment of silence filled the room.

"And this is the first I'm hearing about any of this," Griffin said.

"I felt I had to protect Glynnis. She wasn't dirty. I'm as sure of that as I'm sure Li isn't. And I needed to protect the kids. This guy? Whoever he is? I—"

"A cop," Griffin said. "That's what you think. He's one of us."

"I think so . . . or maybe pretending to be?"

"And now you're supposed to do his bidding? Tamper with evidence? This, this . . . Dreyer? And he expects this to be an ongoing arrangement? And he thinks you'll actually do it?"

"Then maybe he doesn't *really* know you," Li said. "Just thinks he does."

"He knows enough. He knows my name. He knows where I live. He knows where G.'s family lives."

There was silence in the room as the three women watched each other. Foster knew Li would be angry at being left out of the loop for so long. She needed to explain. "I didn't tell you, Vera, because this has career suicide written all over it. Fouling up my career is one thing. I don't have the right to foul yours up too. Glynnis was clean. I'd stake everything on that. But what I might have to do to prove it, I—"

Griffin shot up from her chair. "That would be *nothing*, Detective Foster." She tucked the photo under her desk blotter. "You'll give me those numbers. You'll write me a full report on every encounter you've had with this son of a bitch, and that is all. Understand?"

"I'm not just going to leave it. She was my partner. I have a responsibility here."

"Not anymore. You're out of it. You do not touch it from here on out. You get another call, you bring it to me *immediately*. He contacts you any other way, the same thing happens. Understood?"

Foster hesitated, unwilling to turn Glynnis over to the CPD machine to get chewed up and managed. Foster knew for a fact that nobody would fight harder to clear G.'s name than she would. "He could be any cop, *anywhere*." She stared at Griffin, willing her to get her meaning. "You know what I'm saying here. He's got eyes somewhere."

Griffin was unmoved. "Tell me you understand what I just said."

Foster let a beat pass. "Understood."

Griffin sat down and leaned back in her chair. "Good. We have two dead aldermen and a city about to burst into flames. Back to it."

Foster didn't move. "With all due respect—"

Griffin leaned forward, eyes hard. "Nuh-uh. Drop it. Drop it now. There will be no career suicide on my watch. If he's a cop, we'll fry his ass. If he's not a cop but pretending like he is, we'll fry his ass *twice*. Bottom line. This one-woman game you've been playing has now become a game with more than eleven thousand players. *Nobody* threatens one of our own. *Nobody* threatens our kids. Back to work."

Back at her desk, Foster grabbed her jacket from the back of her chair, aware that Li was staring at her. "Okay. Let me have it."

"In the bathroom." Li turned and walked toward the restroom. Foster put her coat down and followed, and as soon as the door closed behind them, Li reeled around. "What the fuck?"

"Getting tangled up in this, whatever it is? You could lose your job, Vera, your pension. Your *life*, for God's sake. He targeted me, not you. Me? I can handle. I can't be responsible for you going down with this or, worse yet, getting on his radar."

"How long do you think you can go holding the whole world up by yourself?"

Foster's brows knit together, confused. "What?"

"You're white-knuckling it. Everyone can see it. I can see it. This, whatever this turns out to be, is something you share, Harri. It's something you get help with. Partners. It's more than just riding in a car together, chasing leads together, at least for me. I need to know right here and now if it means the same for you. I'm talking trust here. Bottom line. In or out. Partners, or not. That means sharing the weight, good or bad. That means *all* the lousy parts, or none at all." Li took a step closer, her eyes blazing. "It means, he comes for you, he comes for me."

If she had closed her eyes, she could almost believe it was G. scolding her. Li was right, of course. So, was she in or out? Foster thought it through. She studied Li, letting time pass, then slowly held her hand out to mend the rift. "Partners."

Li nodded, took Foster's hand, and shook it. "About damn time. We'll catch this creep for sure. But for now, back to work?"

"Sure." Foster reached for the door.

"One more thing," Li said. "That Charlie Brown plant of yours needs more than water. I brought in some fertilizer and new potting soil. We replant that sucker and feed it right, it'll take over this whole place in a couple months."

"Anything else you want to help me with, Li?"

Li grinned mischievously, letting the tension dissipate. "You seeing anybody? Because I know the sweetest guy who would be just right for you."

"Vera? No."

"Harri? *Yes.*"

# CHAPTER 33

Marin stared across the breakfast table at her daughter, smiling, at last doing something normal, something motherly, something right.

"Pancakes good?" she asked.

Zoe angled her head. "Are there bad pancakes?"

Marin chuckled, then bit off a chew of bacon. "You're absolutely right."

"Do I really get to stay all weekend?" Zoe asked, excited.

"Yep. So, what should we plan to do? A movie? The zoo? Maybe the planetarium. You love the planetarium."

Zoe pulled a face. "When I was ten."

Marin turned serious. "Oh. Right. Sorry."

Zoe got up and put her arms around Marin, gave her a kiss on the cheek. "It's all right, Mom. We have a lot of time to do stuff."

The guilt lay on Marin like a brick, but she willed herself not to show it, not to cry for the time she'd wasted. "Your pancakes are getting cold."

Zoe retook her seat and tucked in again. "Museum, I think. It's nice in there when it's cold outside. Besides, Auntie Char took me to the zoo and stuff plenty of times when . . ."

"It's okay. I'm glad she was there for you when I couldn't be." She watched Zoe enjoy her breakfast. "Zoe? Was Char around a lot?"

"Sure. She makes good pancakes too. She made it not so bad, and I can call her anytime. That's cool."

"What else did you two do, besides the zoo?"

"She took me to see *Wicked*, *The Lion King*, and we went to the Saint Patrick's parade every year. Shopping. She never forgets my birthday or Christmas. The fireworks at Fourth of July are always fun." She pointed at the windows facing the lake. "Sometimes, if I closed my eyes, I could almost make myself believe she was you." A giant smile brightened her face. "But now you're back."

"I am." Marin got up, started clearing plates, a ball of jealousy roiling deep in her gut, and something else. A prick, a stitch of something else she couldn't name. She was grateful to Char, yes, but she wasn't big enough or evolved enough to deny the resentment or the bitterness. "And this weekend, we'll start with the museum. But for now, school."

# CHAPTER 34

Instead of racing around in the cold from Eccles's home to her office, hoping to find her, Foster called Aaron Parker, who told them that he and his sister were at the funeral home making arrangements for their mother's service. It wasn't the time or place to ask Jeniece what they needed to ask, but they had little choice. The best they could offer was brevity, delicacy, and respect.

They waited for Jeniece in the Peaceful Slumber Chapel of the Dixon Funeral Home on the South Side. Harri stared down at the navy carpet, the sickly-sweet smell of flowers tickling her nose, watering her eyes, itching her skin. She knew this room. Everyone who'd lost someone knew rooms like this. Rooms like this were meant to be quiet, comforting to those left behind, and they were, to a point, but mostly they drove home the finality of loss. This room, and rooms like it, were the last stop before the coldness of the grave. Pretty flowers with cloying fragrances, chairs with velvet cushions, drawn curtains, and calming paintings of empathetic angels were temporary distractions for what came next. Too many rooms like this, Foster thought as she focused on her shoe tops, fighting back funereal gloominess. It was funny, but not really, how she could stand over a dead body, the remains of someone's loved one, and do her job, but a chapel, a quiet, peaceful mourning chapel, made her uneasy.

"Tell you the truth," Li whispered, her hushed tone in keeping with their surroundings. Nothing moved fast in a funeral home. No word was uttered in anything but a subdued voice. "If we'd known we'd end up here, we should have let Tennant take it. Funeral homes? Not my fave."

Foster drew in a breath, her right hand fishing around in her pocket to feel for the small silver paper clip she'd dropped there earlier. "Don't think anyone likes them much." She let go of the clip and pulled her phone out to send a quick text. "But that reminds me. We don't want Tennant and Pienkowski wasting their time driving all over the city looking for Eccles."

Li frowned. "They'll swear we poached them."

Foster completed the text and slipped the phone back in her pocket. "Not a competition."

Their eyes tracked a somber Black man in his sixties as he moved past the open doorway. He was dressed in a black suit, his head lowered. One of the staff. He made not a single sound. Not even his footfalls registered on the carpet. "Bet *he* likes funeral homes." Li paced around for a bit, sliding side looks at her partner. "You ever wonder how Grant can work on dead bodies all day long, then go home and fix dinner and watch Netflix? She hangs up her knives and scalpels, clicks off that big machine with the god-awful light beam on it, washes up, changes into her street clothes, then drives home to what? A teriyaki steak and a baked potato? Maybe some late-night ice cream?"

Foster glanced at the paintings on the wall. There was one of Black Jesus looking heavenward, a look of absolute peace and certainty on his face, and then a few of heaven itself, a nirvana of clouds and placid sunbeams. The eternal homeplace. One's final destination. Anywhere but here would be nice, she thought.

She knew Li was trying to distract her with talk of teriyaki steak. Li never missed anything, she'd come to learn over the last few months. That came in handy when following leads, but was slightly invasive on a personal level. She didn't like that she was apparently so easy for Li to read, but there was nothing she could do about it. Glynnis, too, had found it easy. *You're written all over your face,* she'd told her at times when she'd least wanted to hear it.

"No different than what we do, is it?" Foster said. "The gun and badge aren't glued to our bodies. We weren't born with them."

Li scoffed. "Sure feels like it sometimes. Did I ever tell you about the time when . . ."

Jeniece appeared in the doorway, her eyes rimmed with red. Her brother, Aaron, stood behind her but didn't appear affected by grief so much as irritation that seemed to be directed at them.

"Is there a break in the case?" Jeniece asked hopefully. "Did you catch him?"

Aaron pushed past her into the room, the man taking charge. Jeniece followed, her hands clutching a wad of facial tissue. "Even if they did, this is a lousy place to come and tell us about it. We've just picked out a casket for our mother. This couldn't wait five seconds?"

"We apologize for the timing," Foster said, meaning it. "But we'd like to talk to you, Ms. Eccles. We promise to be brief."

Aaron's eyes narrowed. He moved in to act as a buffer for his sister. The great protector. The gambling addict now running for his murdered mother's aldermanic seat. "What's this about?"

Li stood at her partner's shoulder. A team. Unmistakable. "We'd like clarification on a couple things. We won't take long, Mr. Parker."

Jeniece took them in. "It's fine, Aaron. Maybe you can go check on that flower package we talked about?"

Parker stood for a moment, not moving, not happy about being dismissed yet again, but there was nothing he could do in this hushed place but cause a scene or comply with grace. He shot the detectives a sour look before reluctantly choosing the latter.

There were fancy white chairs and settees with crushed velvet cushions arranged around the room. Foster offered one up to Jeniece, who declined, choosing instead to stand.

"Just a few questions, then," Foster began. "You told us you were home with your family the night your mother was killed. What time did you get home from work?" She consulted her notepad. "And you said you called your mother to possibly have lunch, but it didn't work out. So, you didn't see her."

"I worked late. I got home sometime after eleven."

"A big case?" Li asked.

"Not particularly. Just a lot to do."

"How'd you get home?" Foster watched the tissue as Jeniece twisted it into a rope.

"I know how you all work. You've obviously found something that brought you here." She met their eyes. "But whatever it is, it doesn't mean what you think it does. I didn't kill my mother."

Li drew closer, took a second to study Jeniece, a defiant yet worried look on her face. "So, you worked late and drove home sometime after eleven."

Jeniece eased down into the chair she'd refused minutes ago. "I had no idea my mother had been shot dead in that garage. How could I? That's why you're here, isn't it? This is only a tragic coincidence."

"Which you knew about the first time we talked to you, but failed to mention," Foster said. "Why?"

Jeniece let out a little laugh. "Isn't it obvious? You're here. Both of you looking at me like I skinned my mother alive. What? Am I now your prime suspect because I parked my car where my mother parked hers?"

"Who'd you work late with?" Foster asked.

"I worked alone." Jeniece's tissue started to fray as her damp wringing hands broke it down. For a moment no one spoke.

"You said you knew how we worked," Foster said finally. "In a second, we're going to ask you about George Valdez, but first the details that brought us back to you." She stared at the younger version of their victim, Deanna Leonard, her eyes holding. "The Tuesday your mother was killed, we have your car entering the garage in the morning and driving out again late that night, less than an hour after the ME places your mother's time of death. If working late is what you're giving us, we will check up on that. Alone or not alone, there will be security cameras, maybe even a cleaning crew, that can place you where you say you were." Jeniece appeared to stop breathing. "No stone unturned is what I'm saying. So, if there's something else you need to say, now's better than later."

"I didn't kill my mother."

Foster and Li shared a look. "Let's talk about George Valdez, then," Li said. Jeniece emitted a short, shallow gasp, hardly audible, but neither detective missed it.

"I have nothing to do with—"

Foster broke in. They didn't have time. There was more to get to, the security cams, the lawyer, so much more. "Your fingerprints were found in his office. Lies make this worse. They also waste time we don't have. Please, do us the courtesy of not wasting our time, Ms. Eccles?"

Jeniece's shoulders sagged. She sighed. "Show me what you have."

Li opened the folder she carried that held copies of the Tesla plates and the December photos of the half-naked woman in Valdez's office, and the walk to the office door. As Li held them up one by one, the detectives stood watching as Jeniece's face went from shock, to fear, to silent resignation in no time at all.

Foster stood ready to take Jeniece's true statement, knowing it was coming, knowing Jeniece knew, as she and Li did, that she had no wiggle room, nowhere to go but with the truth, especially with Black Jesus looming over them and her mother's body lying somewhere in the building.

Jeniece stared at the photo of the half-naked woman with Valdez, at the one that caught her Tesla parked outside his office, the ones of her car driving into the garage and out again, both fixing the times. Jeniece gently handed the photos back to Li. "Not enough for an arrest."

"But with your prints, this is more than enough for a conversation," Foster said. "Or we can keep digging. There are street cameras everywhere. Every public building has a security system with cameras of their own. With more time, we can pick you up from the second you left your house on Tuesday morning, track you down every street you drove, every sidewalk you walked, every building you entered. We can do the same for the night Valdez was killed. Are you going to make us do that?"

Jeniece lowered her head, then slowly lifted it again after a settling breath. "It's personal."

Foster took a step back, glanced up at one of the painted angels, then at Black Jesus. "Murder usually is," she muttered more to herself than anyone else.

"Just tell us," Li said.

For a long time, Jeniece sat thinking, and then she finally made a decision. "I was with George. He has . . . *had* . . . an apartment his wife doesn't know about. Afterward, I got an Uber back to my car and drove home. I never saw my mother."

"An affair," Li said. "How long?"

"About three months."

"Did your mother know?" Foster asked.

"Not at first. She found out a few weeks ago. She didn't approve, and that's putting it mildly. We argued. Things were said. She confronted George, threatened to tell his wife. It got ugly. She accused us of sneaking around behind *her* back, like she was the injured party."

"So, what happened next?" Li asked.

"She ordered us to stop. We didn't. She hated being defied."

"Did she follow through on her threat to tell Valdez's wife?" Foster asked.

Jeniece shrugged. "George never mentioned trouble at home, so I'd say no. My mother, though, would have wanted to keep the information to herself . . . for leverage. She was a politician through and through."

"Leverage against Valdez?" Li asked.

"Against both of us. I'm married. Not happily, but I have a family, children."

Foster poised her pen over her notepad. "Where's Valdez's apartment?"

"I'd rather you didn't," Jeniece muttered. "The affair had nothing to do with what happened. If this leaks . . . look, my marriage isn't perfect, obviously, but this will kill it. George is dead. This needs to die with him. You check your cameras. You'll see I'm telling the truth. I picked up my car. I drove home. I never saw my mother. I had no idea what had happened to her until the police showed up at my door the next morning. If you keep on this, two families will be destroyed, innocent kids will suffer. The whole thing will blow up in the press, and you know how cruel they can be."

Foster had to concede that Eccles was right, and she was sympathetic to her predicament, but it didn't negate the fact that they needed to fix her whereabouts by time, date, and duration. "I'm sorry. All we can do is promise to be respectful."

"You'll ruin me—my marriage, my kids' lives, my job, you know that, right? You *know* that?" They waited. Eccles slumped. "His apartment's in Old Town. On Sedgwick."

Foster scribbled down the address she gave them. "Thank you." There was the sound of activity outside the chapel door, and she knew who it was, sight unseen. Tennant and his partner had made good time, which meant the tenor of their interview with Jeniece was about to change. "That'll be our colleagues. You'll be asked to go over everything again. You may be asked to join us at the district to do that, given your prints and your connection to both our victims. Do you understand?"

"And my mother's arrangements?"

"They'll have to wait," Li said. "Sorry."

Foster thought of Jeniece's prints at Valdez's and the key on his desk with Marin Shaw's prints on it. Affairs. "How are you connected to Marin Shaw?"

Jeniece bristled. "Why are you still trying to shoehorn Marin Shaw into this? She's been in prison for years. Out of the picture."

Foster wanted to get things moving. "Your connection?"

Jeniece glared at her. "Acquaintances. Through Mama but also through professional circles. We're both members of the Illinois State Bar Association, and other things. I know her, okay? We've had drinks. We've run into each other places. Friendly, I wouldn't say friends."

"Have you ever been to her home? Her condo downtown?"

Jeniece's brows furrowed. "Once or twice. For get-togethers, parties. Why?"

There was a heavy knock at the door; male-cop energy practically punched its way in under the crack. "Detectives Tennant and Pienkowski will want to ask more questions."

Jeniece stood. "It's been months since I've set foot in George's office." She searched their faces for any give or leeway, but there was none either detective could give. "This is going to ruin everything for me. You both know that."

Foster flipped the cover of her notepad closed. "We'll do everything to prevent that from happening."

"But you can't guarantee it, can you?"

Foster let a beat pass. "I can't. No."

Tennant and Pienkowski stormed in, neither looking happy to be the last ones asked to the party. The walk out went smoothly, once Aaron caught on that his bluster and threats of legal action weren't going to save his sister from a ride downtown in the back of an unmarked police car.

Foster and Li watched as Pienkowski put Jeniece in the back seat, then stood at the passenger door waiting for Tennant, who made an aggrieved beeline for them as they stood on the sidewalk.

The ride didn't require four homicide cops, and they'd already taken their first bite at the apple. They had confirmation of an affair, a secret love nest, and a good reason Jeniece might have wanted her mother dead.

"Uh-oh," Li said as an aside, watching as Tennant approached. "Gird your loins."

Tennant loomed over them, his arms akimbo, cold air puffing out of his mouth like smoke from a chimney. "You knew we were out looking to talk to her?"

"We are on the same case," Foster said, a little put out. Tennant's competitiveness was getting old. "We had an idea, we followed it up and found her."

"We coulda got a heads-up sooner."

"You got it pretty quick," Li said.

Tennant glowered at them. "What'd she say?"

Foster filled him in, but it didn't appear to satisfy him much. "It's not like we're bogarting anything, Tennant. We get it, you get. We're all on the same side. A question. You cleared Valdez's wife, you said? You're sure? Her husband was a serial cheater with a private meeting spot. Leonard threatened to tell her about his affair with her daughter. There'd be plenty of reason for her to have a problem with that. Not unreasonable either for the wife to maybe want to do something about it."

"Not her. We checked her up and down and back, and she's clean. This whole thing wrecked her. According to her, Valdez was the hardest-working man in America and loyal as the day is long. Anyway, Eccles's prints at *our* crime scene means *we* get her."

"Actually, it's CPD's crime scene," Li said. She pinched an inch's worth of distance between her thumb and index finger. "Little difference."

Tennant's hard eyes lasered in on Li. "Foster texted me, at least. Don't think you would have."

"You're probably right. But I still respect you."

He shook his head, bewildered. "I don't know about you, Li." He pointed at her head. "Something ain't right up there." He backed away. "We'll take it from here. You can sit in if you want, but we're lead." He turned his back to them, headed for the car. "And respect, my ass."

"Be nice. You're ruining it," Li called after him. Tennant flipped her the bird. "Ah, there it is. The official CPD salute. Right back atcha."

Foster turned for the car. Li followed. "Valdez had an affair with Shaw, then Jeniece, likely others."

"Maybe even Leonard," Li said. "Mother and daughter. There's reason right there for Jeniece to lose it. Take it out on her, and Valdez. Betrayal. Dimes. Perfect fit."

"Maybe." Foster stood at the car door and watched as the cop car with Jeniece in it pulled away, a very heated Aaron Parker following behind in a two-door Chevy covered in street salt.

They slid into the cold car. Foster started it up and blasted the heater. "Let's keep it moving."

Li glanced over at her. "Moore, our gap on the board."

"Then Shaw again."

Li clicked her seat belt and settled in. "As long as we beat Tennant."

Foster's phone buzzed in her pocket. She slid it free. Unknown number. The voice. "Give me a second." She climbed out of the car and walked a short distance away before standing in the cold, her back to Li.

"Detective Foster, what a night, huh? You almost had me."

Anger rose in her chest like a fire-breathing thing. "We're done. You stay away from my house, you stay away from Glynnis's family, or you'll regret it."

He chuckled. "I don't respond well to threats."

"Neither do I. Game's over."

He paused for a moment. "Let's talk about—"

Foster ended the call, switched her phone to vibrate, and slipped it into her pocket before getting back in the car. It didn't take long before the phone began to shake, but she refused to answer. Instead, she started the car and pulled away from the curb toward Moore's.

Li didn't say a word, just looked out the passenger window. "We're supposed to get more snow tonight. Two inches at least."

Foster's grip loosened on the wheel. They weren't going to have to talk about the call. "Seems manageable."

"Guess you're right."

For a time, there was only silence.

Li shook her head, her eyes surveying the street. "Cops."

# CHAPTER 35

Marin knew Will was a creature of habit. He rose every morning at six fifteen, he fixed himself an energy smoothie in that wildly expensive French blender he bought himself just because, and then he'd head to the gym. It was Marin's job to get Zoe up and ready for school, pack the lunches, check the homework, and navigate the drop-off lane. She wondered how he'd managed without her, but from all outward appearances, it looked like he had. Will loved his gym. He never missed. Not because he was ever that dedicated to health and fitness, but because his gym was *the* gym, the costliest one in town, the place to see and be seen, to move and shake alongside those who reeked of money and power. Yearly membership cost more than a small economy car, but it was the place where deals and connections were made, where fortunes were won or lost.

When the door to her house opened and Will and Zoe bounded down the front steps, her daughter weighed down by an overloaded backpack, headphones slung around her neck, Marin slid down in the driver's seat so only her eyes cleared the doorframe. Zoe wasn't wearing any gloves. Obviously Will hadn't noticed. Parked a few doors down from the house she used to live in, her car idling for heat, she stayed slumped, watching, until Will drove away and the street was clear before she sat up.

Taking a minute, she looked up and down the block of expensive homes. Judges, surgeons, lawyers, and CEOs lived here. Though they were technically still in the city, this part of it, the well-heeled part, had always felt like a world unto itself. Marin saw it differently now. Now, she saw it as an illusion of separation, the barriers to entry invisible to the human eye, but as strong as iron ore. It wasn't real, and she didn't want Zoe to grow up here anymore.

She still had a key. She knew the alarm code. This was her house, after all. It took no time to enter the house, disengage the system, and lock the door behind her. The lingerie that wasn't hers was one thing, but she knew there was more to find. Will wasn't discreet. It wasn't that he didn't have the capacity for discretion, but that he never felt he should have to bother being subtle. His feeling was always that if he wanted a thing, that whatever he had to do to get it needn't be hidden. Women. Lingerie. Money waste. Her drinking, her affair, her risky behavior, she knew now were meant to take the sting out of it. None of it had worked.

There was no plan, no line of attack. Marin just needed to see what was different in the house, what had changed since she'd been gone, to find what Will had found no reason to hide. She no longer cared who he was sleeping with; neither did she care overmuch that he was sleeping with anyone. But before she put a lid on this part of her life, she wanted all the information.

Marin walked the house, remembering the years she'd lived there, some happy, some not so much. It smelled the same—of rich coffee and sandalwood, a faint floral note. The decor a vibrant splash of deep crimsons and golds and earthy tones. Lived in. Interesting. The master bedroom a bust, nothing there that she hadn't found before. She stood at the threshold to Zoe's room, a lump in her throat, regret in her chest so strong it nearly stole her breath. She backed away and turned for the stairs.

Black-and-white photos of Zoe from birth to present lined the walls leading to the kitchen. Pretty baby, pretty girl. The kitchen was clean, the counters neat. She knew Will hadn't done it. He must have hired a housekeeper. Marin eyed the large silver coffee maker, top of the line with all the bells and whistles, which Will had insisted on. Pretentious then, pretentious now. She ran her fingers along its surface. Chances were good, she thought, Will cared more about that machine than he'd ever cared about her.

Zoe had mentioned pancakes, which had started her thinking. Marin checked the cabinets. Nothing unusual. Zoe's favorite granola, the spices, imported jam. The fridge was next. It was full, Will's Stilton, an acquired taste, front and center. For her, a lot had changed in three years, but it didn't appear that Will had changed much of anything. She found the bag of French coffee beans on the second shelf toward the back. Almost thirty dollars a pound, imported, if she remembered correctly. There had been a glimmer of hope that she wouldn't find it, but now that she had, there was little surprise. In fact, it seemed almost fitting.

She slipped out of the house just as quietly as she'd slipped in.

# CHAPTER 36

Charlotte Moore sat staring at Foster and Li from a leather chair behind a desk that looked like it had rolled out of a Regency palace somewhere. The rest of the space looked like a Monet painting. On side tables, bouquets of fresh flowers sat full and vibrant, their subtle aroma a pleasant antidote to the dead of winter outside. Moore's long, tapered fingers steepled under her chin, her steely brown eyes amused, playful, her toned legs crossed one over the other at the knee. It was almost lunchtime, but Foster and Li's day didn't have a second of give in it. The press was going apoplectic, the entire team was out on the streets, and Griffin had taken to texting them for hourly updates.

Moore's office overlooked the bogged-down traffic along the LaSalle Street Bridge, the ice-topped Chicago River below it, hulking skyscrapers canyoning it all in. They weren't far from city hall or their first crime scene, just a short taxi ride, Foster noted. Moore was dressed in a black suit that looked like it might have cost as much as a beat cop's mortgage payment. Along with the blingy jewelry and the designer shoes, Charlotte Moore appeared to be worth every dollar she charged per billable hour.

"You two do know that attorney-client privilege is a real thing?"

"We hoped you'd want to help your client," Li said.

Moore's brows lifted as her smile broadened. "Believe me, I am. What are *you* trying to do? I don't mean to be a cop basher, but in my experience people with badges don't usually sit at the defense table."

"We have two murder victims," Foster said. "Both connected to Marin Shaw. I think that at least warrants a conversation, don't you?"

Moore reached over, picked up the morning paper, and held it up for them to see. The headline read, *The Real Marin Shaw*.

"*This* is what your investigation has warranted. Will has unburdened himself. The ultimate payback. Good thing she's no longer on trial for anything, because she'd be hard pressed to get a fair one in this town." She tossed the paper aside. "Your person of interest."

They'd been so busy they hadn't seen the morning's paper, though Barrett had hinted his take was coming. "That's unfortunate," Foster said.

"It is," Moore said. "I may even sue the bastard. Won't that be fun."

Foster glanced around Moore's office. There were a lot of ego-driven photos with VIPs and city leaders, but none appeared to be of family. On a shelf were small sculpted bookends hemming in lawbooks. Interesting ones, Foster noted. Roman gods? Norse warriors? An angel? They looked like characters from a TV show or video game, which didn't quite fit with the little they'd learned about Moore. Single, never married. Net worth impressive. A sophisticate, cosmopolitan. No criminal record, tax liens, no hint of controversy. Clean. Maybe the fantastical stuff was meant to entertain Shaw's daughter.

"What about that conversation?" Li asked.

"Conversation? With police." Moore pulled a face. "Not always the smartest move, is it?"

Li took offense. "We're not the enemy."

"No. You serve and protect. We know this because you've written it on the side of all your little cop cars. I admire the ideal. In principle. In practice?" Moore shook her head. "Some fall a little short." She angled her head, assessing the cops in front of her. "Maybe not enemy, but definitely not friend."

"Marin Shaw. How did she handle three years in prison?"

"Straightforward. I like that." Moore stood, pulled gently on the cuffs of her jacket to neaten her look, then padded over to the window and turned back to face them. "She handled it like a real trooper. After the shock wore off, of course. Marin is a very strong person, one of the strongest women I know, actually. She got sober inside. More importantly, she's staying sober outside. She's done her time. There's nothing more she owes the state. And she's *not* a murderer."

"She has no alibi for the nights of the murders," Li said.

Moore stiffened. "Innocent people don't require them."

Li's eyes narrowed. "She had history with both victims."

"She had history with all forty-nine aldermen on the council."

"But she didn't call all forty-nine when she was released," Li pushed back. "She called Deanna Leonard. Who is now dead."

"Means nothing," Moore responded. "We can do this all day. What's your endgame here?"

"You can't deny her connection to these deaths," Foster said.

"Her connection isn't significant. My client wouldn't have done anything to jeopardize her freedom or her family. Again, she is not a killer."

Foster could tell Moore meant that to be the end of the discussion by the woman's definitive lift of her chin and the set of her shoulders. But she was only beginning. She thought back to Leonard's desk and the circled date that coincided with Shaw's release. "Who knew when Shaw would be released?"

"The court. The prison. Me. No one took out an ad in the *Daily Planet*, if that's what you're thinking. Prisons leak like sieves, as do law firms, newsrooms . . . and police stations, I'm sure. In fact, I know this to be true, because there was a crowd of reporters waiting for her when she drove through the prison gates."

"You were there?" Li asked.

"Of course. I came to pick her up, to welcome her home."

"What about her family?" Foster asked.

Moore shook her head. "Marin didn't feel it would be good for Zoe to be there. As for Will, he didn't like the optics." She stood behind her seat of power. "Is there any actual evidence linking Marin Shaw to either crime?" She waited for an answer, but none came. "Ah, I see. Cops ask and ask but never ever tell."

"Did you know Leonard and Valdez?" Foster asked.

"I deposed them. Before Marin's trial. I won't go into the details of all that. It's public record now. The rest is none of the city's business."

"Can you think of anyone else who'd want either of them dead?"

"Both of them had questionable entanglements that I couldn't bring up at trial. Marin refused to go down that road. My hands were tied. I wouldn't be surprised if you found a laundry list of suspects, if you really went looking. Instead, you're here trying to put my client back into a cell. Which I will not allow."

Foster stared at Moore. "Marin Shaw had reason to want Leonard and Valdez dead."

"*I* have reason for wanting people dead." Her eyes held Foster's. "So do you, Detective." She slid a look at Li. "So do we all. That's human nature. It isn't evidence, but you know that already. This is a fishing expedition, isn't it? Only you've got no bait on your hook and you're not dealing with a dumb fish."

"This is like talking to a stone wall," Li said.

Moore grinned. "As it should be. Anything else?"

"You're Zoe Barrett's godmother." It wasn't a question, but Foster threw it out, wanting to see if it got them off the back-and-forth and onto something significant, something they could use.

"Not a question, but yes."

"You stepped up while Shaw was out of the picture. How was that? Couldn't have been easy with your schedule."

The grin was back. "I'm not exactly Mary Poppins, but we made it work. It was a sense of normalcy Marin wanted to maintain, or as much as I could offer. I don't have kids, unless you count some of my clients." Moore smiled. "Zoe's the daughter I never had."

"And Will Barrett?"

Moore laughed. "The man I would never in a million years have married?"

"Because of the affairs?" Li asked. "Even while his wife was in prison."

Moore turned serious. "I was there for Zoe. The rest of it . . . was not my concern or my business."

Foster scribbled a note in her pad. "Normalcy. Continuity."

"Exactly. From Christmas on down. Marin missed three birthdays, three Fourth of Julys, three Thanksgivings, but also the little confidences, the quiet moments, the bonding. I . . . *we* . . . wanted to make sure Zoe didn't suffer unduly. There was never a question that I would step up."

"But back to Barrett just briefly," Li asked. "No pushback on you taking up the slack with his daughter?"

Moore smirked. "Will didn't have a clue what to do with Zoe on his own. He was relieved to have me step in."

"Stepping in," Li said. "That's what family does. You know, speaking of the Fourth, we got a look at that awesome view of the lake from Shaw's condo." She let out a whistle of admiration. "That's some sweet spot to catch the fireworks. Add to that you're not fighting the crowds or paying a single parking fee. Really nice."

"That first year without Marin, even the view couldn't rouse Zoe from her depression. She'd lost her mom for all intents and purposes. Staying close, being there proved to be the key. Subsequent years were better. Zoe has come out all right on the other end of this, I think."

Foster's shrewd eyes swept over Moore. Her smile was slight, slow to form. "What's your take on Ms. Shaw's stalker? She doesn't feel safe. Any idea why?"

Moore considered the question, then began to pad around her office. "I believe she is safe. That there's nothing to worry about there."

"You believe she made it up," Li said. "Some imaginary bogeyman?"

Hard eyes met Li's. "My client is not suffering from mental defect, if that's what you're hinting at."

Li stood her ground, unbowed by Moore's heat. "It wasn't. Simple question. And it's more like *you're* hinting at it, not me."

"You don't know for sure she was home alone the nights Leonard and Valdez were killed?" Foster asked.

Moore turned back. "If she says she was home alone, I believe that to be true. Marin isn't a very good liar."

"Did you know she had an affair with George Valdez?"

Moore paused a moment. "Having an affair isn't a crime, and bad marriages shouldn't be a death sentence."

Foster pushed. "Is that a yes?"

"That's me lawyering, Detective. My job is to protect my client at all costs."

"Where were you the nights of the murders?" Foster gave Moore the dates to refresh her memory, then waited for her to answer. If a pin had been dropped, all three women would have heard it.

"Me?"

"Just to be thorough."

"You think I'm running around the city killing people?"

"Just dotting the i's."

"I'd have to check my calendar."

Foster waited. Li, too, both stern of face, until Moore walked over to her desk and accessed her phone. "A social engagement on the night Leonard was killed. Nothing for Valdez. A rare occurrence, for sure. But the doorman at my building can tell you I never left." She tossed her phone on the desk. "Satisfied?"

"What kind of social engagement?" Li asked.

Moore turned to Li. "A date."

"With?"

"Someone I just met. Bill or Burt. Burt. Don't ask me for a last name. I don't think I asked. Ah, here come the judgmental faces. I can literally see the wheels turning in your little cop heads. It's simple. I'm single. My free time is limited. I swiped right, and it was a good enough evening. If I'd been out killing people and needed a good story, I'd have at least made sure to get a last name?"

Foster closed her notepad. "I'd think you'd want to get that anyway, alibi or not."

Moore grinned. "So casual sex is *not* your thing? Because I'm getting a whiff of disapproval."

"Then you whiffed wrong. It's concern for your safety. This is a big city. A lot of things happen."

"I'm a big girl. I can take care of myself. Have been since I left home for college and never looked back. Best decision I ever made."

"Where was home?" Li asked.

Moore began to fiddle with her watch, almost as though she were assuring herself it was still there, still real. After a second, her face brightened again. The lawyer was back. "Home is *here*. On the Gold Coast. With a doorman and a housekeeper and my name on my office door." She sat down at her desk. "I'll wrap this up for you nice and tight. Marin Shaw is no murderer, and you have no evidence proving that she is." She slid a look out the window, then turned back. "That's the lawyer. Here's the friend. Marin's all about Zoe now. She's left the past behind her, and she hasn't a murderous bone in her body. So, if either of you are thinking about railroading her into some half-baked murder charge, just forget it. You come for her, you come for me, and if you come for me, I'll burn this entire city down and you two with it." She smiled, but there wasn't a single ounce of mirth in her expression. "Enough?"

"One more question," Foster said. "Interesting bookends. Where'd you find them?"

Moore glanced at her shelves, then shrugged. "I don't remember. Some antique store. Antiquing is one of my hobbies. If you're really interested, I'll work you up a list of my favorite spots."

Foster pointed her pen toward the statues. "Eclectic. A Viking, one's some kind of god—Greek or Roman? And an angel with wings."

"I just needed something to keep the books from falling over, and they tickled my fancy. Unless you think I'd use one to bash someone's head in?"

Foster looked at her. "I hope not. Thanks for your time."

A minute later, Foster and Li rode down in the elevator.

"Bookends?" Li asked.

"Felt out of place. Maybe they weren't casual buys? Everything else felt carefully selected to send a message."

"The message being she'd go for your throat in court?" Li asked.

Foster nodded. "Smart cookie."

Li slid her a look, topped off by a devilish smirk. "Yeah, you are. You got her to admit to having access to Shaw's place while she was in prison. That makes her and the husband. Either one of them could have stolen that coat or the key. Means. Opportunity."

"Motive's still cloudy," Foster said.

Li zipped up her coat. "Slow and steady wins the race, Harriet Foster."

# CHAPTER 37

"So, there's no way anyone gets through the lobby or out of the residential garage without getting picked up by these cameras?" Li asked as she and Foster loomed over Trev Bonner, the security manager at Marin Shaw's condo building. They were standing in front of a bank of security cameras in a tight little room that smelled of hot wires and someone's lunch. Pastrami, if Foster had to venture a guess.

"And how long do you keep the captures?" She looked over at the slight little man with a mass of curly red hair on his narrow head. The blue blazer he wore had the management company's logo over the left breast pocket. Bonner's brown eyes were jumpy. Nervous about the badges? She wondered if he was the building's only security, or if he just managed the beefier guys employed to handle things if they went bad.

"Being digital, we don't have a space problem. We keep 'em. Because you never know, right? Just like you guys being here. Who could have anticipated? These people are paying top dollar to have all their worries taken away. So, we got cameras all over. We pick 'em up before they even get through the front door. That circular drive out front? Covered. We even got cameras on the outside of the building around back. All four corners, really. They get the grounds and even a slice of the streets. We got a guy at the garage doors twelve hours a day. After that we got automatic readers that lift 'em if your car's registered or if you made arrangements for a guest. Cameras are in every row and at the front. So, what I'm saying is, we got whoever comes and goes."

"Everybody knows about them?" Li asked.

"Residents know the place is secure. We don't share the details. We got cameras where they'd expect them, and then in places where they might not."

"Can you cue up the night of February twelfth?" Foster asked. "We want to know if a certain plate left the garage." Bonner had already kept them waiting almost a half hour while he got the permission of the building's management company. If they hadn't gotten it, a warrant would have been necessary. Still, she registered hesitation from Bonner, who appeared uncomfortable with her request. "You did hear us when we said we were *homicide* cops? That hints at a certain urgency."

"Yeah. Sorry. So used to keeping things private." He cued up the digital files. "February twelfth."

Foster and Li exchanged a look while Bonner's fingers flew around the keyboard, coaxing files out of the system.

"The whole day?"

Foster realized this was a daunting task. "Wait. Is there just one way in or out of the garage?"

"Just one."

"And either the cameras or the reader clock everybody in and out. Do you have that information stored?"

"Sure, but you got permission for the footage, not the garage logs. I might have to—"

"What if we gave you a plate number and you looked?" Li asked.

Bonner thought for a moment. "Just me? I guess that would . . ." His voice trailed off.

Foster scribbled Shaw's plate number on a page from her notepad, then ripped it out and handed it to Bonner. "In or out. February twelfth. If we find anything, we can cut down the search time on the footage. We'll have a pinpoint."

Bonner went back to the keyboard, switching his focus from the camera bank to a computer screen. It took a few minutes before he had something. "Yes. The car went out a little after four. Came back at nearly eight? Isaac would have seen it go out. The reader would have picked up the return."

Foster exhaled. The times fit with Shaw's account. She'd had dinner with her family, confirmed by her husband, the night of Leonard's death, then returned home after seven. She checked her watch. It was almost four now. "Is Isaac working today?"

"Yeah. He works six to six. But don't you want the other times?"

Foster froze. Li too. "What other times?" Li said.

"The car goes out again after nine and comes back a little before midnight."

"Check another date?" Foster gave him the date of Valdez's murder and watched him hit the keyboard anew. She and Li backed away in the small office and lowered their voices.

"Her alibi's shot," Li whispered. "She was definitely in play when Leonard was killed."

"Let's not jump yet."

"Car went out at seven," Bonner said. "Back at nine thirty."

Foster searched around the tiny room and found two chairs slid into a tight corner. She grabbed one, Li grabbed the other, and they pulled them up to the monitors. "All right, Mr. Bonner. Let's look at that footage. Then we're going to want to talk to Isaac."

With the dates and times narrowed, it took less than an hour to see what they needed to see. A dark figure in a dark coat and hat pulled down walking into frame from a side door leading to the residences and easing into Marin Shaw's car before driving out of her spot.

"Looks like her," Li said. "Height. Frame. The coat. If it's not her, how'd she access that door?"

Foster turned to Bonner. "Can you give us lobby footage right before this picks up?" He tapped the keyboard, and another monitor engaged. "Start maybe a half hour before this person shows up in the garage?"

They waited. Foster's breathing was steady, despite the fidgeting coming from her more excitable partner. "Ugh. This is driving me nuts," Li muttered. "Just a shot of her face and we'd know."

The lobby monitor popped up with a still of the front desk with Roy standing at it. Bonner rolled back the footage to about forty minutes before the garage captures picked up, and they all three zeroed in as the tape ran at half speed. Nothing happened for a time.

"Doesn't look like this is going to pan out," Li said.

"Give it time," Foster said, eyes plastered to the screen.

The tape kept running, showing nothing, until ten minutes passed and a man walked into the lobby, waved to Roy, and headed for the elevators. Then two minutes after that a woman and two small children walked from the elevators, past the front desk and out, then nothing again for a time.

And then . . .

A woman came in the door wearing a black coat and a hat pulled low over her eyes. She stopped at the desk. Roy smiled. He knew her. She knew him. The woman reached into her pocket and pulled out a small envelope and passed it across the desk. Roy plucked it up and slid it into his pocket. Deal done, and the woman glided out of frame.

Foster scooched closer. "Roll that back, please. To the moment she walks in."

They watched it all again. The entrance, the glide over to the desk, the smile, the exchange, then the glide out of frame again. "What'd he take?" Bonner asked, his voice sounding a stressful octave higher. "What was that? *Who* was that?"

Foster stood. She looked at Li. "Mr. Bonner, would you ask Isaac and Roy to come in here?"

Li turned to the stricken-looking security guy as he stood to go out. "Without giving them a heads-up," she added.

"Oh my God," Li said when the door closed behind him.

Foster shook her head. "Wait."

"She lied to us. She's wearing the damn coat she told us somebody took from her. And she left that key at Valdez's." Li stomped around the small office. "Revenge. We pegged it right from the start. All that poor-little-victim crap. I hate when they do that, by the way. Trying to make us feel sorry for them when they're stone-cold killers. Ugh. She played me." Li shook out her arms. "I hate getting played."

Foster watched, a little amused. They were opposites in temperament. Hot and cold. Rash and measured. "All we saw was a coat and a payoff. If it's Shaw, and her car's in the garage, why's she waltzing through the front door to access it?"

"Because she's playing games, that's why. Sneaky little murderer."

Foster smiled. "Wait. And get ready for when that door opens."

Three minutes later, her words proved prophetic. The office door opened. Roy took one look at them waiting and bolted down the hall. "Stay here," Foster commanded Isaac and Bonner as she and Li ran after the fleeing Roy.

"Stop, police!" Li called out to Roy's back, but he was down the narrow corridor, through a door, and gone.

They reached the door. Foster pulled it open to reveal a set of metal stairs leading down to the lower level.

Li groaned. "Basement? Damn it. It would be, wouldn't it?"

Foster flashed on their last case, which ended for Li in a shadowy basement at the bottom of a flight of stairs. Had things gone differently, neither one of them would be alive today, so she understood her partner's reticence about descending into yet another basement quite so soon. "I'll go. You go around. See if you can catch an exit."

The withering look Li gave her told her she'd veered into dangerous territory. "Like hell I will." Li pushed past her. "C'mon."

The basement was well lit, big, and longer than it was wide. The churning, blowing, and whirring of the building's monster furnace almost drowned out the sound of their footsteps on the metal stairs. At the bottom, the concrete floor was smooth and clear of debris, the only clutter reserved for the chain-link storage cages assigned by condo unit. The basement smelled of oil; trapped heat; old, forgotten things left to languish in the cages; and laundry detergent, which made sense when Foster spotted a side room with five washers and five dryers set up inside.

They stood still for a moment, guns out, up and ready, eyes scanning the space, listening for the sound of Roy's running feet, but nothing came back. He was holed up somewhere in a niche or corner, like a trapped animal. Trapped animals were the most dangerous.

Foster and Li shared a look. They needed a plan, one where everyone came out of the basement just as they went in. "Roy?" Foster called out. "This is Detective Foster. I'm here with my partner, Detective Li. We met the other day? We just want to talk."

Nothing.

"C'mon, Roy," Li said. "What're we doing, huh? Down here in the basement." Focused eyes swept right, left. "We need to ask you a few questions, and then you're on your way."

Nothing.

They started forward, slowly, passing the cages with the dusty bicycles and stored luggage and overflow things not often needed stacked inside, the smell of dust and grease and compressed heat permeating the trapped air.

"Thing is, Roy." Foster tried again. "Us needing to ask a few simple questions has turned into a whole other thing now." They inched forward, eyes scanning for movement. She felt sweat begin to form on her forehead and dampen the back of her collar. "You running, leading us down here, see how that elevates things, Roy? We have to assume you're armed. Don't make this worse than it is."

There was the sound of a short slide off to their right, like the sole of a hard shoe repositioning on a dusty surface. They shifted in that direction. Could have been Roy, could have been something else, maybe even something in one of the cages settling. But it was nothing they could ignore. They resumed their advance and had almost covered the length of the basement when they spotted an emergency exit and a roll-up overhead door suitable for truck deliveries. Both entrance and exit points were covered in signs that announced that an alarm would sound if either were breached. No alarm had sounded. Roy was still in the basement with them.

"Back off."

The warning came from their right. Behind the cages. They reeled, braced. "Roy. Think about this," Li said. "Two of us. One of you. We don't want to hurt you, but we don't want you to hurt us either. Not to overshare, but I've got life plans. Pretty sure you do too?"

"I said back *off.*"

Foster tightened her grip on her service weapon and slid Li a look, noticing that she, too, had sweat on her brow. This was a situation she knew neither of them wanted to be in. Their badge came with a huge responsibility. It also came with the power to take a life under extreme circumstances. And no cop, no cop now or ever, wanted to be the reason someone didn't come home to their family.

"You know, Roy," Li continued, "neither one of us woke up this morning and said, 'Hey, let's go shoot Roy in the face this afternoon.' We want to walk you out of here, Roy, so you can go and live your life." They let a moment go, listening for another shuffle. "What do you say, Roy. Face or a simple walk out?"

For a moment there was nothing, then movement. They braced anew, and gripped their weapons tighter, prepared to react to whatever came at them from behind the cages, but it was only Roy, soaked in sweat, shaking arms held up over his head, tears streaming down his face. He was surrendering.

"Down. Spread eagle," Foster barked, the cop voice, harsh, clipped, fueled by adrenaline yet tinged with sweet relief. "Hands behind your head."

Roy complied. Li holstered her gun and cuffed Roy while Foster covered, and then they walked the crying lobby guy out. Nobody had to die, nobody did. It was a good day.

"Hold up," Foster said as they moved past the cages. "Shaw's unit is what, 12C?" She followed the numbers to the right cage. Lifting a small flashlight from her pocket, she then ran a light into the cage. Not much there. A kid's pink bike. A bag of golf clubs. A metal Coleman cooler. A half dozen plastic storage containers, contents unknown. The cage was secured by a large combination lock. She flicked off the flash. They'd need a search warrant to go further. "Let's go, Roy."

"I didn't do anything," he whined.

Li held him securely by the cuffs and shoulder. "Yeah, we know. Let's go."

"Face or walk out?" Foster whispered to Li as they mounted the stairs, Roy weeping.

Li grinned. "Who's going to ever choose face?"

# CHAPTER 38

Griffin glowered at them, her eyes piercing into their very souls like a spike of arctic ice. Foster glanced down at the boss's desk and found the phone off the hook. Beatty. "Thrill me," Griffin said.

Li cleared her throat. "Roy's lips are sealed. He went from crying like my little sister to asking for a lawyer. We're waiting for a public defender. The security footage clearly shows someone in a black coat paying him off. If we're making assumptions." She slid a glance over at Foster. "We could assume it's Shaw. But we don't assume."

"We didn't get much from Moore," Foster added. "Other than the fact that she's convinced her client and friend is innocent. But if we're looking for people who would have access to Shaw and access to her condo, Moore fits, but so does the husband. Tennant and Pienkowski cleared Jeniece Eccles. Once they found out about the affair and didn't find anything more recent that put her there the night he was killed, they let her go."

"And, of course, we're still looking to see if any one of our persons of interest pops up anywhere near either crime scene," Li said.

"And we've now added Moore and Roy to that list," Foster said.

"What about the guy at the garage?" Griffin asked. Foster knew Griffin hadn't missed a single detail in their thorough report. "Couldn't he give us an ID?"

"He saw Marin Shaw drive out of the garage the night of Leonard's death, but that fits with what she told us. She had dinner with her family and was home before eight. The second in and out that night he couldn't attest to since he was off duty. The cameras that took over only registered the plate, didn't ID the driver. Could have been Shaw. Could have been someone else."

"And we don't know if it was Shaw in that getup paying off the crying guy?"

They both shook their heads. "Waiting on Roy," Li said.

Griffin's eyes narrowed. "Any leverage?"

Foster said, "Bonner, the security manager, is scouring the tapes to see if Roy received any more gratuities, I guess you'd say? Maybe we'll get something more to press him on."

"Or else we'll just make something up. Tell him we have more than we do." Li grinned. "Sweat him a little. See what comes up."

Griffin thought for a minute. "The dimes. We've kept it out of the press, but those little prying buzzards are bound to latch on to that little detail and go to town with it. Anything?"

"My feeling is that when we find out who, we'll find out why," Foster said.

"I agree," Li said. "The dimes obviously tie to motive."

Griffin picked up the receiver, held it in her hand. "And this lawyer, Moore, why's she on our radar?"

Foster closed her notepad, the report complete as far as she was concerned. "Because she's connected to Shaw and knows the players. She also had access to her place. And because she's a gap on the board."

"And she's got bookends that don't fit who she claims to be," Li added without explanation. "I mean, they're cool and all, but something feels odd."

Griffin stared at her, then at Foster. Her eyes then narrowed. "Get out of the weeds."

Griffin put the receiver back where it belonged, and the phone immediately began to ring. Jabbing an aggrieved index finger at the offending device, she said through clenched teeth, "Hear that? Nonstop.

Here's the situation, in case I need to clarify it: We have two dead aldermen. Two dead aldermen in a town where there are literally two million potential suspects." She lifted the receiver to stop the ringing, then quickly placed it down again. "Coats, keys, Teslas, whatnot. I'm gonna need you to wrap this up." The phone began to ring again. "Find the son of a banshee."

"Son of a what?" Li asked.

Griffin lasered in on Li. "I'm cutting down on the swearing. I've been told by certain higher-ups that it can be off putting."

"You cussed out Beatty?" Foster asked.

Griffin straightened in her chair, appearing a little chastened by the accusation. "I may have used some flowery language, so I'm trying to be a little less flowery."

Li smiled. "Huh. Okay."

They stood mystified. A kinder, gentler Sergeant Sharon Griffin simply did not compute.

The phone stopped ringing, then began ringing again. "Fuck!" Griffin screamed, yanking the receiver up. "Griffin. Yes, sir. We're making progress." Her eyes narrowed at Foster and Li. It was their signal to exit quietly.

Foster threw her notepad on her desk and pulled her chair out. "May as well go back to footage while we wait for Roy's PD." She glanced around the room. "Symansky and Kelley are out, so are Bigelow and Lonergan. Looking for anyone on the council with a motive. No luck yet. Kind of confirms we're looking at a personal, not a professional one." She eyed the board. "Personal and angry. Resentful. Hurt feelings. Getting back in some way."

Li looked where Foster was looking. "That pretty much covers everybody up there."

"We never backtracked to Meehan or Franklin. Let's see if we can pick them up anywhere on the murder nights."

Li nodded. "Let's do it. With any luck we might get through everything by Memorial Day."

Foster heard the receiver bang down in Griffin's office. "Don't think we have quite that long."

They sat across the table from Roy Izarra two hours later and watched as he conferred with his public defender, a young Latina who looked all of twelve years old. Suzanne Rivera. She seemed nervous, unsure, her big brown eyes alert and focused. She wore a bejeweled headband that held her black hair away from her round, unlined face. Youth, Foster thought, a wonderful thing. When Roy was ready and Rivera was ready, they began. They'd not heard back from Bonner. It was a good bet that he was checking with his bosses before he went any further with them, which meant that they were going to have to tap-dance a little and hope Roy revealed more than he wanted to.

Foster placed a photo on the table they'd copied from the security footage of Roy taking something from the figure in the black coat. "Explain this exchange, please."

Roy glanced at the photo but didn't pick it up. "A tip for good service." He pointed a finger at it. "There's nothing illegal in that, all right? You guys come storming into my job and chase me like I'm some criminal." He pointed to Li. "She threatens to shoot me in the face." He turned to Rivera. "You need to get on *that*, okay? That's police brutality. They literally tried to kill me."

Rivera nervously consulted her notes. "Um. I don't have any of that here. I thought this was a straightforward statement. In relation to . . ." She flipped through the papers in a leather folder. Foster noticed it was monogrammed in gold—SHR. Suzanne's initials. Maybe the folder was a law school graduation gift from her proud parents.

"New to the PD's office?" Li asked gently.

Rivera looked up, frazzled. "Couple months. But I've got this."

"You do," Foster offered with a slight smile. "Take your time."

They waited for Rivera to confirm for herself that she had had no advance warning that Roy Izarra would be accusing CPD of police brutality and Foster and Li specifically of trying to gun him down in a condo basement among all the residents' detritus.

The lawyer looked up, stymied. "What happened?"

Foster leaned in. "It's simple. We're investigating homicide. Mr. Izarra was captured on security cameras exchanging something with someone we believe might be connected. A woman, it appears, in a black coat and a hat pulled down, concealing her face. We would like Mr. Izarra to tell us who that woman was."

Li's eyes held Roy's. "And what she was paying him for."

Again, Roy conferred with Rivera while they waited. It was getting late. Almost seven. This was a viable lead. Was the woman in the coat Marin Shaw? They needed Roy to spit out the answer.

Foster and Li had already checked with the building's management. Roy Izarra hadn't been on the lobby long, just under a year. Clean record. He did a good enough job. Accepting a gratuity wasn't a crime if that's all it was. But Shaw had told them she didn't know Roy well. That there'd been someone else on the lobby desk three years ago. So, if that was Shaw in the coat, what was the money for?

Foster sighed. "Mr. Izarra?"

"Hey, I stand at the desk. That's it. Nothing wrong with taking a tip for my services."

Li slid the photo closer to him. "Is this Marin Shaw?"

He shook his head. "No. I don't know her. I just did a service. She was appreciative. Not a crime."

Her hopes dashed, Foster pushed on. She should have known it couldn't have been that easy. "What service?"

His jittery eyes ping-ponged around the room. "No comment."

Foster turned to Rivera. "Please inform your client that we're about to arrest him on suspicion of—"

"All right. All right. I can't get locked up, okay?"

Rivera held up a hand to quiet her client. "Not so fast. On suspicion of what, exactly?"

Li stared at her. "Maybe she was buying drugs. Maybe information. Maybe Mr. Izarra here is the head of a robbery crew targeting the building. Maybe he's an accomplice to murder. Maybe—"

"That's a lot of maybes," Rivera said. "Do you have any definites?"

Foster nodded her approval. Rivera had found her footing. "We have evidence of a money exchange with an individual who may be involved in two homicides. We can hold your client for forty-eight hours." She turned to Izarra. "And we will. If we find he was complicit in those homicides, he'll be with us a lot longer than that."

Izarra and Rivera put their heads together and lowered their voices. It took about a minute before they broke apart.

"I had nothing to do with any murders," Izarra said. "She didn't want to sign in. Everybody's supposed to, but she thought her husband was stepping out and knew the woman lived in the building. Not my business."

"And *she* paid *you* to let her up?" Li's mouth hung open. "Do you know how dangerous that could have been? She could have killed somebody."

"She didn't look like the type. Besides, I don't control what people do."

Rivera looked like she was running through in her head all the things she'd learned in law school, running down a checklist for how to defend dodgy clients devoid of a moral compass.

"You know her name?" Foster asked.

"Didn't ask."

"How much did she give you?"

"Two hundred."

"Would you be able to identify her if you saw her again?"

"Don't think so. White. Not young. She wore that hat, and I was looking mostly at the envelope. The building doesn't pay much. A chance for extra? I took it. That's all I know, and that's all I got."

"So, why'd you run when we wanted to talk to you?" Li asked.

He glared at them. "Because your kind are always trouble for people like me."

Foster let a moment of silence go. "This isn't the first time you've taken a gratuity from this woman, is it?" She held up a hand. "Before you lie, know that this isn't the only footage that we accessed. Practically every inch of that building is covered by cameras."

"I get tips all the time. Those people don't want to do anything for themselves if they can pay somebody else to do it for them."

"I asked about *this* woman."

"Maybe another time. Same reason. That time she only gave me a hundred. She wanted to see if her husband's car was parked in the garage. I told her if she came back again, she'd have to make it worth my while. Still, no crime." He turned to Rivera. "Right? Tell them. Tips aren't a crime. And if I lose my job over this, I'm suing the whole city and you two cops specific."

"If you don't have anything other than that exchange, which he's explained," Rivera said, "then it's not enough to hold him, unless you can link it to something criminal."

It was true, but Foster didn't like the reminder. "So, to be clear, you can't ID her? You don't know who she is? But she paid you twice, no questions asked."

"That's it. She had light eyes. Blue or something. She smelled nice. That's all I got." He shoved the photo back across the table. "And that's all *you* got. And it's nothing." He leaned over to his lawyer. "Right?"

Rivera exhaled relief. "Absolutely right."

Foster stood and pushed her chair in. Li followed suit. "We'll be in touch."

Izarra shot up from his chair and readjusted his pants at the waist, cocky, like he'd gotten the best of a worthy opponent. "Yeah, well, don't, because I got nothing else for you."

They watched as he and Rivera walked out of the room, Izarra with a swagger that galled Foster on principle.

"So, *not* Shaw," Li said.

"He could be lying."

Li shook her head. "Nah. He's too much of a chicken to lie. It wasn't her."

"Bonner still might come through with something else. Roy seemed mighty cocky once that photo came out. Like he was relieved that was all we had."

"Leaving a spot open, for Bonner, then." Li gathered her things, yawned.

"Let's call it a day," said Foster. "Pick it up in the morning?"

Li gave her a thumbs-up. "Let's hope for a quiet night, huh? See you in the morning." She headed for the door, stifling another yawn.

"Night."

Foster's cell phone rang, but it wasn't an unknown number this time. It was Mike. She answered, bracing herself. "Mike, everything okay?"

"Harri, thank God you're all right."

"What?"

"He called my cell and said you'd been shot. We jumped in the car and headed right back. I tried calling. Your phone went to voice mail. I've been checking news reports, but there was nothing. I didn't know what to think. We're an hour out. I'm pumping gas while the kids hit the snacks inside. They don't know anything. They just think our trip's over."

"No. *No.* Mike, turn around. Go back. He's just playing with us."

"I'm done being played with, then." He sounded determined, defiant. "I'm not going to run and hide and let you take the brunt of this. She was *my* wife, and she wasn't what this guy says she was, and I'm going to prove it. The kids go back to school, with some precautions, and we all keep our eyes open and our heads on the swivel, as Glynnie used to say. That's it, Harri. That's how we're doing this."

She lowered her voice. "Mike, he might be one of us. How else would he have your address? Your cell number? That changes things, don't you see?"

"A cop?" For a moment he said nothing. "What the hell are we dealing with?"

"Go back, Mike. Take the kids and—"

"No. Harri, no. We do this together. We get him together."

She didn't know what to say, what to think, what move to make. The voice had them covered, and Mike's mind was apparently made up. She had nothing to offer on her end to ensure they would all be okay. An hour. That's how long she had.

She stood at her desk not knowing which way to go. She'd hung up on the voice the last time he'd called, hoping that would put an end to things. A game is only a game if both sides agree to play. But the creeping feeling in her gut told her she'd only delayed things, and maybe even made them worse.

"Harri, you there?"

She was standing in a room with cops in it, cops she couldn't tag for fear of exposing G. for something she didn't understand. Worse yet, maybe one of them, or maybe someone one of them knew, was the voice she couldn't identify. She was it. "I'm here. I'll meet you at your house. We need to talk."

# CHAPTER 39

John Meehan's black town car idled in the alley behind Dino's, waiting for the great man to exit and slide inside after a late dinner meeting with a few associates best suited for a clandestine gathering rather than a full-on audience at city hall. He'd waited for the two men to leave through the front door before he slid out the back. Standard op for him. He had a campaign to plot out, palms to grease, chits to call in. Easing into the car, sated by pricy beef and bourbon, high on the idea of one day soon being mayor of the Second City, he didn't bother even looking at the driver, his head lowered, the obligatory chauffeur's cap tilted toward the steering wheel. Asleep.

Meehan glowered. He abhorred sloth. The nuns had taught him it was one of the deadly sins. Though it was his usual car service, none of the drivers were noteworthy enough to be remembered by name. Besides, he was about to become mayor. What shit did he give about some driver's name?

He checked his watch, nearly nine p.m., then tapped the back of the driver's headrest. "Hey, buddy. Let's move it. Home." His blue, watery eyes dropped to the screen of his phone. His second phone. The one he kept secret from his wife and staff. The one he used to broker the deals that didn't hold up in the light or skirted the law in full or in spirit, the deals that reeked. There was a lot still to do before he announced. It would be a delicate dance.

It took him a few seconds to realize the car wasn't moving. That the nameless driver hadn't heeded his command. "Didn't you hear me? I don't have all night."

The front passenger door swung open, and Meehan recoiled when someone jumped in. It was dark. Things moved fast. The bourbon wasn't helping.

"What the hell? Who the *fuck*?"

The gun came up. He saw the glint of it under the murky alley lights. Then the face attached to the hand that held the gun took shape; he registered it, then began to laugh. "Seriously? C'mon. *This* is your play? What'd you do, slip that guy a mickey?" He waved a beefy hand, the gun not a threat. He was John Meehan. Big guy, soon to be mayor. You didn't survive in this town for as long as he had by losing your head over a peashooter. "Go on. Get out of here. Wake up that mope, and have him take me home. I don't have all night." Meehan's eyes turned devilish. "As to this, well, now I own ya, don't I? Flat out."

There was a smile. "You're right, and wrong. You don't have all night. You don't even have all minute. And you don't own me. You don't own anyone anymore."

Meehan got angry. "Wise up. You took your shot, and you lost. Let it go already. You really want to ruin your life over this?"

Nothing moved for quite a while, not even, it seemed, the air in the town car. Meehan suddenly reached for the door handle, but the door was locked. He checked the gun, found it still pointed at him, and tried sliding along the seat to the other side, but he was too big, too slow, and too buzzed to make the slide work. "You're crazy. Bent. Knew it the first time I laid eyes on ya."

The shot came next. Just one. Silenced. The round hit the Never Would Be Mayor, John Meehan, squarely in the chest. The shooter watched as blood blossomed out all over his expensive shirt, and smiled as the blowhard, the crook, the master manipulator, the means to an end doubled over on the black leather, groaning, dying.

No movement from the driver. Still out. He had said his name was Vince when he made the mistake of taking a hot coffee offered by the waitress from Dino's, who wasn't really a waitress anywhere. He'd wake in a bit, groggy, confused, but none the worse for wear. Not so for Meehan. Meehan was a strategy, a lit match on a pile of dry leaves. Two dead aldermen had captured the city's attention. What would three do? Three would connect to one, and then the powers that be would scream for an arrest. And the game would be won.

The shooter slipped the gun into the pocket of the black coat, then got out and walked around to the back passenger door and eased it open for the final thing. Meehan's breathing was labored, his eyes clenched tight, his right hand flattened under his protruding belly. He mouthed something that no longer mattered. Maybe a prayer. It was almost laughable that a man like Meehan would have the nerve to call on God, even at a time like this. But what was the saying, *There are no atheists in foxholes?*

"Were you reaching for your phone, Mr. Mayor, to call for help?" A small chuckle. "It's too late for—"

The bullet fired from Meehan's small-caliber handgun, and the burning that followed knocked the shooter back. The shock of both realizations was almost too intense to process. The smell of seared wool and the bitter bite of gunpowder, the pain ripping through the arm, the fog of incomprehension short-circuited everything, sending alarm bells through every vein, artery, and nerve ending.

This wasn't how this was supposed to go. Not how any of this was planned.

"You old goat. You son of a *bitch*," the shooter hissed. The gun was up, ready to finish him off, but Meehan's gun had fallen to the floor mat, his arm dangled over the seat, his eyes frozen at half-mast. No need. He was gone.

There was no time to assess the damage. Meehan's gun hadn't been silenced. The shooter dropped the gun into a pocket and plucked out the small bag of dimes, then leaned in and shoved it into Meehan's overcoat, seething, mindful not to bleed over his body and leave a trace behind. "Damn you."

Right hand clamped over left arm, the shooter backed away from the car and headed west almost at a run, holding in blood, cursing the dead man. No fear of cameras. There were none around Dino's. The late John Meehan had seen to that. Three aldermen should do it.

# CHAPTER 40

At eleven that night, Li stood at the open door of the town car, staring down at what was left of John Meehan crumpled over on the back seat. "This blows. Another dead alderman on top of the two we already had?"

Symansky, Lonergan, Kelley, and Bigelow looked over at her, somber, bundled in their coats in the cold, hands shoved into pockets, hats pulled low.

"This is gonna make some noise," Symansky said. "Meehan?"

Kelley groaned. "I heard he was planning on running."

Bigelow worked a wad of gum around in his mouth. "Don't think that's gonna happen now."

"The world's going to seed." Lonergan shoved his hands deeper in his pockets. "Somebody definitely took his foot off the brake." He flicked his chin toward the back seat. "I don't see any dimes."

Li checked the head of the alley, looking for Foster. She'd been called, same as them. It wasn't like her to be the last one to show. She then glanced over at Rosales and his crew preparing to get started. "Waiting on Rosales for that. Could just be robbery."

Lonergan scoffed. "Or a good old-fashioned hit. Meehan was no altar boy."

Kelley looked over at Li. "Foster?"

"On her way."

The alley had been cordoned off, and POs stood at the barriers. Still others were walking the perimeter, looking for anything that might be pertinent.

Rosales and his crew moved in, and Li and the others moved back to give them room. "We have to stop meeting like this," Rosales offered dryly. "Seriously, I mean it."

"Gun on the floorboard there," Symansky said.

Rosales looked back, narrowed his heavy-hooded eyes. "I see it."

Symansky shrugged. "If you see any dimes anywhere, call out."

Rosales glared at the group, Symansky most of all, and they took another communal step back for self-preservation.

"We all know this makes three," Bigelow said. "So, now what? Shaw's out here free as a finch."

"We keep dancing around her, that's for sure," Symansky added. "Might be time to stop."

Lonergan slid a sideways look at Li. "On her way, you said? Or maybe she decided to sit this one out for a hot date?"

Li glared at him. "Give it a rest already, huh? You're like a bitter old woman pissing on everybody's parade. The constant sniping? The grousing? If you think it's getting to her, it's not, so grow the hell up."

It was frustration and little sleep that caused the outburst. It was three dead alderman and no solid way forward, and it was Lonergan. His eyes fired. He opened his mouth to respond, but Li shut it down with a raised hand. "Think first. Then don't."

Everyone but Li suddenly found the tops of their shoes interesting. Lonergan fumed and stormed off, Li's eyes burning a hole in his back, itching for a fight on her partner's behalf after four months of Lonergan being a complete ass.

Bigelow let out a low whistle. "Damn, Li. Remind me never to get on your bad side."

"Not wrong, though," Kelley muttered. "He is a parade pisser."

"He just ain't made the full jump from the old days, is all," Symansky said. "Like me." Everyone turned to look at him. "What? You all got somethin' to say?" No one did. They turned back to the town car and the waiting.

Kelley glanced over at Lonergan, who was leaning against a squad car a few yards away. "Classic misanthrope."

Symansky glowered at him. "You always gotta get the last word in, dontcha? Plus I was just getting ready to say that."

Bigelow flicked his chin. "Here's Foster coming."

Kelley turned toward the opposite end of the alley. "And there's Tennant and Pienkowski. The gang's all here."

Li noticed right away that Foster hadn't changed clothes since she'd left the office hours earlier, which likely meant that she also hadn't rested. Under the glare of the alley lights, Foster looked tired and tense. Another body wasn't going to help.

"What have we got?" Foster stood back watching the techs.

Symansky spoke first. "Alderman Meehan. Expired. One shot to the chest, looks like. Blood on the shirt. No idea what went down. Maybe somebody tried robbin' him?"

"Wallet and phones are here," Rosales called out from the back seat.

"I said *tried*, didn't I?" Symansky fired back.

"Blind spot," Li said. "Perfect for an ambush."

She then watched as Foster moved closer to get a better look at Rosales working the body. "The gun on the floorboard is a .22." Tennant and Pienkowski slipped in beside Foster for their first look.

Tennant asked, "The pocket change?"

Li shook her head, pointed at Rosales's back, then tapped her watch to indicate the time it was taking Rosales to give them what they needed. "Zip."

"I saw that," Rosales said.

"Oh, you did not," Li shot back.

Li watched as Foster stepped back from the car and scanned the alley, her eyes landing on Lonergan holding up a squad car, his arms crossed over his chest.

"What's with him?" Foster asked.

"Li called him a parade pisser," Kelley said.

Foster turned to Li for an explanation, but she only shrugged. "He pissed one too many times. Meanwhile we have Meehan's driver over there. He's groggy and refusing medical attention. Claims he's fine. We haven't talked to him yet. Thought we'd wait for the fog to clear."

Foster pulled her notepad from her bag. "Then let's do it."

Li's eyes tracked Foster as she made her way to the squad car the driver was in. Something was up. Foster seemed distracted, off. "Not good," she muttered as she followed after her. "At. All."

Vince Bradford looked like he'd been on an all-night bender. His collar was unbuttoned, his tie loose. His eyes were bloodshot and his hair, thinning on top, was disheveled, as though he'd been in a fight.

Foster leaned into the car. "Mr. Bradford? Mind if we ask you a few questions?" Li stood beside her. Tennant and Pienkowski, like barnacles on a ship's anchor, loomed on the other side of the car.

Bradford took in all the cop heat and shrank a little in the seat. "Yeah, sure. Can't tell you much, though. Like I told the other cops, I was out."

Foster leaned out, spied the pod of waiting patrol officers nearest to her. "Who took his initial statement?" A stout Black woman in a CPD beanie raised her hand. "Don't go far." She turned back to Bradford. "Mind telling us again what happened? Take your time."

"I was waiting for Meehan behind the restaurant, idling. He's a regular with our car service, but this was my first time driving him. No big deal. It's cold as a mother out here. Last thing I remember, one of the waitresses from there is standing at my window with a cup of coffee. She says Meehan ordered it for me. I rolled down the window, took it, then . . . everything's blank after that. Next thing I know, I wake up, turn, and see him dead back there. I freak out. Call 911 and all you showed up."

"The waitress. How was she dressed? What did she look like?"

"I dunno. She was dressed for the cold. In a coat. Couldn't see much of her face because she had a face mask on and a hat."

"Eyes?"

Bradford seemed to have difficulty searching his memory bank. "I dunno. Blue. Green. It wasn't real well lit back there, and it was just a quick handoff. Fifteen seconds, tops."

"How'd you know she came from the restaurant?" Li asked. "Did you see her go in or come out?"

"Ah, I don't remember."

"Do you remember what you were doing while you were waiting for Alderman Meehan?"

"Nothing. Just waiting. Look, that's all I know."

"Were you sleeping while you were waiting?" Tennant asked. "So that's why you didn't see where she came from?"

"No way."

Li stared into Bradford's face. He'd answered too quickly, too adamantly. Could he have been asleep at the wheel? "This is an important point, Mr. Bradford," Foster said. "We're not interested in jeopardizing your job, okay? The information's just for us, so we can find who did this. Could you have fallen asleep, even briefly, while you were idling, and not seen where the woman came from?"

Bradford considered the question. His eyes narrowed, apparently suspicious of being lured into a trap. "I could have closed my eyes for a minute. Only that. And it doesn't have to get back to the job."

"Anything else you can recall?" Li asked.

"That's all I got. And my head's killing me. I just want to go home and sleep this off."

"Sure you don't want to go to the ER? Get checked out? At the very least to find out what she slipped you?" Li said.

"What you don't want is to be at home and have some kind of reaction later," Foster added.

Bradford held his head. "Maybe you're right. I got a mother of a headache now. All right. I'll go."

Li waved for a PO. "Good. We'll have a squad drive you over. Call your wife or someone? Let them know where you are so they can come and be with you."

"Yeah, yeah, that's the best thing. Thanks."

They backed away from the squad and watched while Bradford got driven away to the hospital.

"Yeah, she didn't walk out of that restaurant," Tennant said. "This was a setup. Take the driver out. Kill Meehan."

"Sure looks like it," Pienkowski said.

"Maybe," Li said. "We'll see."

The men snorted and shook their heads. Tennant spoke for the team. "Yeah, we will."

A PO ran up. "Detectives, we found blood."

They followed after him to stand in a semicircle around a droplet of fresh blood in the snow. "This the only one?" Li asked.

Officer Vaughn nodded. "So far, just this. We're still walking the area. There might be more."

Foster turned from the droplet to glance down the alley, then back to the street where they stood. Not far. "The killer walked this way and then went where?" She looked up for cameras, but the closest one was half a block up. "Bit of a blind spot." She turned back to the PO. "Good work, Vaughn. Thanks."

Rosales took well into the wee hours before his head popped up from the body with information he felt comfortable relaying. "You saw the gun. Recently fired. Ruger 22 LR pistol. One GSW to the chest. Looks like he bled out. Wallet, phones, all here, like I said, so there's that."

"And?" Tennant asked the logical next question, the one everyone had been waiting to ask.

Rosales held up a small bag. "Stuffed in his overcoat pocket. Thirty dimes. Again, we'll run them for prints, but don't get your hopes up."

"Shit," Symansky said. His frustration was shared by everyone around him. "All right. No sense standing here crying over it. Everybody find a hole, and let's get 'em plugged up."

Foster turned to Li. "We grab Shaw."

"No more maybes?"

"Very few."

# CHAPTER 41

They had placed Marin Shaw in the interview room to wait for her lawyer. This time, she had refused to say a single word to them until she was represented. Roused from a sound sleep, Shaw had come to the door in pajamas at 5:00 a.m. and had looked genuinely confused and bewildered to find police there. She asked no questions, made no comment; she simply got quickly dressed and came along, exercising with great resolve her right to remain silent.

It was nearly 8:00 a.m. now, and the coffee was brewing; doughnuts were on hand, and no one had spoken to the quiet suspect. Meehan had been dead approximately eleven hours, according to Rosales's estimations. Foster stared down at her cell phone, waiting for a return text from Mike. She needed to make sure that he and the kids understood how careful they needed to be. It had been hours since the last call from the voice, and worrying about why was taking up half the space in her brain, whether she wanted it to or not. If he was a cop, what did that mean? What was he after? If he wasn't, and she hoped that would turn out to be the case, he seemed to know enough about her and what she did to sound like one. None of it made sense, and she was tired of being toyed with. She'd gone to Griffin, as she should have, and she'd been ordered to stand down. Foster had expected that, but she wasn't off it. She couldn't be. She had no intention of letting the voice go. She needed to square that with Griffin, insist on being brought in.

Mike had let her look around Glynnis's things, her papers, her files, through the boxes with her personal effects that he'd packed up, stored in a back room, but hadn't yet had the strength to move out of the house. There'd been nothing in any of it that hinted at anything untoward. Foster had even gone through G.'s cell phone, which Mike had also kept. None of the numbers the voice had used to call her were on it. In fact, every number on it was well accounted for—work, doctor's office, dentist, accountant, her home and cell. Normal. Everything as it should have been. The phone cradled in her hand, waiting on Mike, she thought of sending another text, this time to the voice. Her fingers hovered over the device, but she couldn't think of what to say. What could she boil down in a text? What would engaging mean for her, for Mike and the kids? What risk would she be taking? Mike responded with a quick All fine. We'll be careful. You be careful too. Promise, Harri. She texted back. I promise. Be in touch. Then she slid the phone into her pocket.

Li had watched the whole thing, the text, the hovering, the worried look on her partner's face. Say something or not? Now or later? She decided later. After this was done. After the aldermen stopped dying with dimes on them. She eyed the door to interview three. "I'd have booked it. Three bodies hanging over my head? I'd be halfway to Canada by now." The lightness in her voice, the business as usual, was deliberate.

Foster sipped from her coffee mug, wide awake on zero hours of sleep and many hours of stress. "Instead, they found her in pajamas, completely bewildered to find police at her door. So, either's she's a psychopath, which doesn't *appear* to be the case, or she has no idea what's happened."

"Or she's a very good actress," Li said.

"Got hold of the owner of Dino's," Symansky yelled out from his cluttered desk. He looked even more haggard than usual, like a cop from a '40s black-and-white movie, grizzled, rumpled, world weary.

They were all working the phones on bad caffeine and empty calories, which wasn't going to do any of them any good in the long run. "It was like talking to somebody from the CIA, for fuck's sake. This guy, this Teo Mazza, don't know nothin'. Claims the place was closed last night for his ma's ninety-first birthday, so he swears up and down he's got no idea what Meehan was doin' there. So, of course, no waitress. Driver, though, said full out Meehan walked into the place and walked out. Mazza's lying through his crooked teeth."

Foster stared over at him. "How're you so sure?"

"You don't know Dino's?" Symansky looked from Foster to Li and back. "Seriously? Neither one of ya? And you call yourselves cops?"

Li's eyes narrowed. "Is this one of those back-in-the-day things?"

He smirked. "Back in the day and yesterday too."

"So the owner, this Mazza, had a connection to Meehan?" Foster asked.

"On the record, no. But rumor has it Dino's is more than a place where you eat. The important crap gets done under the table, if you get my meaning. It'd be right up Meehan's alley to slip in and out of there like a double-dealin' ghost. And if he did, and he did, Mazza's in on it and isn't goin' to say too much about it, even if the guy got popped and is now dead."

"The lack of cameras around the place is telling," Li said. "I wonder how Mazza worked *that* deal. And how the businesses around there are okay with it."

Symansky snorted. "Work what deal? You hand the cash out, Li. Grease the palms. No different than back in the day when you'd buy shit cheap on Taylor Street knowin' full well it got yanked off some poor schlump the day before. Mazza's a businessman. He knows what he's doin'. And Dino's is Meehan's place. So, Meehan gets the job done. No cameras. Those that start squawkin' get one of two things—a nice little payout or a beatdown. Either way, all you're gonna hear from then on out is the sound of silence."

"Sounds so … Chicagoey," Li said.

Symansky scoffed. "Damned right it does."

Li pushed away from her screen in frustration. "A woman in a face mask and a dark coat. We're toast."

"Not yet," Foster said. "We're just not seeing what we need to. It's all on that board."

Li sneered at the board. "I hate that thing. It's like it's laughing at us."

Foster managed a slight smile, then eyed Griffin's closed door, the gulf between doing what she was ordered to do and what she wanted to do as wide as Lake Michigan. "This is very simple, very personal. There haven't been a lot of bells and whistles, not a lot of showboating, except for the dimes. Specific. Tight. Targeted."

"And the only motive we've got fits Shaw. Revenge."

"Jeniece has a pretty good one. Her mother found out about her sleeping with Valdez and ordered her to end it. They argued. Maybe Jeniece even finds out she's not the only one? And we know Shaw's husband has a reason for offering her up. He wants her gone, but more importantly he wants the money."

"Parker's in debt, a hopeless gambler," Li offered. "Motive for killing his mother, seeing as he's after her job, but he's accounted for, and what does killing Valdez and Meehan do for him?" She looked over at Griffin's door. "Where's the boss?"

Foster dipped two fingers into the pot on her desk to check if Polly needed watering. The plant was looking a little better, stronger. "Upstairs." She looked over at Li. "With Beatty. What about Sylissa Franklin? There might be a reason she wanted her colleagues dead."

"She seems way too skittish for killing," Li said incredulously. "She was practically jumping out of her skin when we talked to her."

Foster stood and padded over to the board, where she picked up the marker and wrote the word *blood* under Meehan's name, then circled it. "Rosales didn't pick up any blood that wasn't Meehan's in the car or around it, at least preliminarily. The POs found fresh blood in the snow at the end of the alley headed west. Could be related. Could not be." She turned to Li. "One shot fired from Meehan's twenty-two. Let's say he hit his killer."

"A woman, presumed to be from the restaurant, drugs the driver and kills Meehan. The description Bradford gave us is close to the one we got from Roy Izarra. Long coat. Face mask. Hat pulled down. Roy told us it wasn't Shaw, but how could he be sure? I'd hardly recognize you in a getup like that, especially if you glamoured me with an envelope full of cash first." Li saw the skepticism in her partner's eyes. "Go with it, all right? Roy and Shaw aren't buds. She told us three years ago there was a different lobby guy on the desk. She doesn't know Roy from Adam, and that means he doesn't know her."

"He pointed Shaw out to us the first time we talked to him."

"He knows what she looks like when she's being herself. Plus, her face has been all over the news since she got out. But he wouldn't know sneaky Shaw, would he? If she's disguising herself? Nothing showing but her eyes? And let's face it, Roy isn't exactly the smartest kid in class. I'm only saying that we should not *assume* that wasn't Shaw paying him off."

"And she went through an elaborate ruse coming into the lobby and buying her way up in a building she already had full access to?"

Li pointed at Foster. "Bingo. That way she claims, '*That's not me. Roy knows me*,' blah, blah, blah. And it gets us running around like headless chickens looking for somebody else. While she works her get-'em list. The woman who drugged Bradford could be sitting in our interview room right now is all I'm saying."

Foster put the marker down. "Maybe she'll give us DNA. We match it to the blood we found."

Lonergan, who'd been sitting quietly at his desk, his back to everyone, overheard. "Ain't gonna happen. She's a lawyer. Lawyers don't give you jack without a court order, in my experience." He got up, walked over. "Only way you're goin' to get it is if you go in there and scare the hell out of her. But then what do I know, I'm just a parade pisser."

Li leaned back in her chair. "Truth hurts."

He crossed his arms over his chest. "Sometimes fear works, is all I'm saying. You don't bust out the rubber hoses, but you make it clear who's boss. We been dancing the tango with her for too long. There are three bodies now on the slab. What the hell are we doing, since you seem to be running things?"

Symansky nodded. "Hate to say this, but the pisser's got a point. Not about the rubber hoses, mind, but we kinda crossed the bridge on polite with three bodies piled up."

"I'm not running things," Foster said. She was tired, worried, over-loaded, and could feel herself slipping. "*We're* running things. All of us. Is that what you've been salty about since I got here? You feel *you* should be running things?" She looked around at the team assembled. "Did I come in and step on some toes? If I did, someone, please, set me straight." She got no responses. She turned back to Lonergan. "*Your* toes. Is that it? Go on. Say it." She waited for him to respond. He didn't. "Nothing? You'd rather grouse about it behind my back?"

Lonergan bristled. "If I got somethin' to say, I got no problem sayin' it to you, Foster."

She held her arms out, ready for it. "Then go ahead. Here I am. Let me have it. Just know I'm done with the sulking, the snide remarks. It's a waste of time and energy." She glared at him, realizing that she was giv-ing him what she wished she could give to the voice. Misplaced anger, frustration, helplessness, but Lonergan had been the one to choose the wrong time, not her. Maybe if she wasn't so spent, she'd have found a way to hold it all in as she had been doing for months, but her tank was low. "We work together, or we work around each other. I'm fine either way." She glared at him, awaiting his challenge.

Symansky cleared his throat and got everyone's attention. "Bottom line here is we're a team and we need to start actin' like one. Good point there, Foster. And since we're clearin' air, let me say somethin'. Me and Lonergan are about the same era. I've got a year on him. Bigs is right in there with us. Old guys closer to handing in our papers than you younger ones—Foster, Li, Mr. Shakespeare over there. Don't mean we can't learn something all the way around. And at the end of the day, all that needs to count for anything here is that we all bleed blue. So, let's get past this shit and get all our oars movin' one way."

"I don't like being bossed around by cops still wet behind the ears," Lonergan hissed. "It's got nothin' to do with what she's thinkin'. I got no problem with girl cops."

Li's brows lifted. "What'd you say?"

Symansky slapped his forehead, shook his head.

Kelley's mouth gaped open. "Wow."

Lonergan looked around at the stupefied faces. "What? C'mon, you know what I mean."

Foster's desk phone rang. It was the sergeant downstairs. Shaw's lawyer had arrived. She hung up, grabbed her things, and nodded to Li. "Ready?"

Li stood. "Right behind you." As she swept past Lonergan, she cut her eyes at him and shook her head. "*Girl cops.* Step into the light, you old hound dog."

When Foster and Li walked into the interview room, Foster was surprised to see that Shaw's lawyer wasn't Charlotte Moore but a white man in his fifties dressed in casual wear—jeans, sweater, collared shirt—like he was headed to Sunday brunch with his family instead of meeting a client at the police station.

He stood, extended his hand. "James Lindall. Representing Marin Shaw."

They introduced themselves, then sat across the table from the lawyer and their person of interest. Shaw appeared tightly wound.

"I expected Ms. Moore," Foster said.

Shaw ignored her. "You think I killed John Meehan. What evidence do you have?"

Lindall put his glasses on, picked up his expensive pen, poised it over a yellow legal pad. "That's a good start. What connects my client to Meehan's murder?"

"Can you tell us where you were last night between eight p.m. and nine?" Foster asked.

Lindall held up a hand to stop Shaw from answering. "Not so fast. Is she formally a suspect? Is this fishing expedition headed toward an arrest? If so, I advise my client to answer nothing until formal charges have been made and we know what we're facing."

Foster fixed steady eyes on Shaw's face. Three people were dead. All connected to her. Foster sat back in her chair, studied the nervous Shaw. "This is our third time talking to you, Ms. Shaw. Each time after someone you know has been killed. A key with your prints on it found at one of our crime scenes isn't an insignificant thing. An affair, you say. Your husband trying to get back at you. Plausible. Maybe. One thing is true. We're going to stop these killings. Now, for the purposes of elimination, it would help us to know where you were last night. If we can verify that, we get to move on and look elsewhere if that's what we're doing. If we can't, you're it until we can verify."

"We don't appreciate the heavy handedness, Detective," Lindall said. "My client is a law-abiding citizen who . . ."

Foster's eyes slid to his. "Again, three people are dead." She turned back to Shaw. "You understand the urgency."

Shaw conferred with Lindall, both keeping their voices low and mouths shielded by their hands. After a minute or so, Shaw started talking. "I went to a meeting at seven thirty. It lasted an hour. I walked home afterward. No one was with me. I popped popcorn, watched a movie, then went to bed. I slept until police woke me up and brought me here."

"No contact with anyone else?" Li asked.

Shaw shook her head. "Earlier, though you didn't ask, I was allowed to drive my daughter to school. I went to an afternoon meeting, then the grocery store. I came home, then made dinner for one. I felt I needed the evening meeting, too, so I went. I called my sponsor later. We talked for a while."

Foster clicked her pen. "What time was that call?"

"After the meeting. During the movie. I'm going through a divorce and the end of other things. I didn't kill Meehan, or anyone else."

"When's the last time you saw John Meehan?"

Shaw slid a look over at a wary Lindall. "Days ago. Unfinished business. Unrelated to this. He was alive when I left him."

Foster angled her head. "How do you know it's unrelated?"

Shaw stared at a point over Foster's left shoulder. "Personal."

"Where did you meet?" Foster asked.

"Dino's. John had his own table in back that no one sat at unless they got an invitation. He knew the owner, had his own key."

"Meehan was killed in the alley behind Dino's," Li said. "Someone shot him." It didn't appear that the news came as a shock to Shaw.

"John Meehan had more enemies than friends. I would be more surprised if you told me he had died peacefully in his sleep."

"There was blood found near the scene."

"It's not mine."

"Would you mind proving that? Voluntarily give us a DNA sample? And show us that you're not injured."

Lindall tossed his pen down. "Are you serious? No way. We're not in the freebies business. She's not under arrest. You've not charged her. How is any of that in her best interest?"

Li leaned forward. "If you weren't there, why's it a big deal?"

Shaw let a moment go. "You know the first thing you lose in prison? Trust. In everything and everybody. The second thing, the thing you try to hold on to the longest, is hope. You lose that? You've lost everything. Hope comes back. Trust never completely."

"John Meehan is at the ME's office," Li said. "If you didn't put him there, prove it. Roll up your sleeves."

"Meehan got a shot off," Foster explained. "We're looking for a bullet wound." Her eyes held Shaw's. "Or we can detain you. Get a court order. You know how it works."

Shaw conferred with Lindall again, who appeared adamant against any show-and-tell on Shaw's part, but when the conferring ended, Shaw rose from the table.

"Marin, I strongly advise you not to do this," Lindall said.

"They'll just keep coming, won't they?" There was a timbre of defeat in her voice, which barely rose above a whisper. "Whatever it takes."

Shaw slipped out of her yoga hoodie and lifted the sleeves of her T-shirt to reveal smooth skin on both arms. No wounds. "I'll go even further." She then lifted the legs of her jeans. No wounds. They hadn't asked for more, but Shaw then lifted the hem of her shirt and turned around slowly and back. No wounds. Foster watched the reveal, but also the expression on Shaw's face. There were no grimaces of pain, no gritting of teeth, no sweat on her brow. The presentation was not distressing her physically in any way.

"Satisfied?"

Meehan had taken his shot from the back seat, his killer presumably facing him at the door. The upper body would have been the likeliest contact point for his desperate round. Shaw was clear. "Your friendship with Charlotte Moore. Is that one of the other things ending?"

Shaw sat down again, smiling slightly. "You don't miss things, do you?"

"I try not to. I thought you two were close? That she was your number one lawyer?" She glanced over at Lindall. "No offense." Shaw didn't answer. "Ms. Shaw, this is the end of the line. Three deaths. Even one would be too much, but we have three unanswered for. We need the truth, all of it, right now. Think of your daughter."

Shaw lowered her head, suddenly exhausted by everything. "She's all I do think about. Which is why I can't be here. I can't be in this. You've met my husband. This is ammunition he'll use against me. But more importantly I promised Zoe I was done with police and trouble and . . . all of it. I can't disappoint her again."

Li leaned forward. "Then talk to us."

Lindall leaned over to confer again, but Shaw held him off with an upraised hand.

"We need all of it," Foster offered simply. "Every scrap, no matter how insignificant you think it is." Foster shot her a look that offered no compromise. "Every turn we make, we end up right back at you."

They waited, even Lindall, who turned a strange shade of red, his thin lips pressed tightly together in disapproval and frustration. Shaw lowered her head, exhaled deeply. "Why James and not Charlotte. That was your question?" She folded her hands primly in her lap. "When I went to the house looking for my coat, thinking Will had taken it, I found the lingerie and knew. I wasn't even shocked or angry. I didn't feel much of anything, really. Still don't. But I started to wonder how long it had been going on. Three years? Four? Longer? Was he with her when I was with George? Crazy, isn't it?" She stared at Foster. "She made my daughter pancakes. It sounds like a little thing, but it was *our* thing, and she knew it. She knows everything. Just like I know she only wears French lingerie, and that Will can never pass up an opportunity to stick the knife in."

"Charlotte Moore," Foster said. "Your friend."

Shaw nodded. "Had I been paying attention, I might have predicted it, but . . . there were other things going on."

"You're sure the lingerie is hers?" Li asked.

"Char flies to Paris at least twice a year looking for . . . someone. She comes back with frilly things from a tiny shop on Rue Legendre. Their name was on the label. The things were in her size. Our bedroom, their bedroom now, smelled of her perfume."

Li sat back. "Stabbing you in the back like that doesn't fit with what we heard when we spoke to her. She was all in with Team Shaw."

"Char's pragmatic in all things." Shaw let out a wistful breath. "I started to wonder about my trial, then. Whether she'd really done her best to defend me. I go to prison, and she gets Will, the house, and the daughter she never had. Crazy thoughts. Again, trust has gone. I see deceit everywhere."

"You believe she's setting you up," Foster said. "For murder? She wouldn't have to go that far to get rid of you, all she'd need to do is make sure you finalize the divorce."

"But she wouldn't get Zoe, would she? At least not completely. I would fight like hell for custody, and she knows it. I'd never give up."

Foster was sure skepticism was all over her face, but she said nothing for a time.

"You asked why Char wasn't here. I told you."

Foster thought it through. An affair wasn't a crime. Being a terrible friend wasn't actionable. Even motive wise Shaw's setup contention seemed a stretch. Moore was a successful lawyer with a corner office. What could she possibly want or need that she felt compelled to kill to get it? And not once, but three times?

Was Moore spinning some elaborate fantasy? A diversion? There was something about the woman that was off, though she couldn't put her finger on what that something was. Marin Shaw wouldn't be the first killer to try a double fake, thinking cops were too dumb to catch on. Foster sat watching the woman across the table, wondering how much of what she'd just told them was the truth.

"Is Moore a particularly religious person?" Foster asked, thinking about the dimes and the strange bookends, specifically the one of the angel.

Shaw almost laughed. "Definitely *not*. Char said she gave all that up the second she left home for college. Her mother was livid. Still is, I'd imagine. They're not close."

"Define not close," Li said.

"I don't think they've spoken in years. Char supports her, makes sure she's comfortable, but there's no real relationship. Char is a wanton woman. That's what her mother thinks." Shaw stared at Foster. "I guess Mother's always right."

Foster poised her pen over her notepad. All she had was procedure, process, and a murky road ahead. None of it was new.

"The name of your sponsor, please?"

# CHAPTER 42

They swept back into the office, making a beeline for their desks. "I'll try the sponsor," Li said, plopping down into her chair and reaching for the phone.

Foster turned toward the whiteboard, then approached it to draw a line running from Charlotte Moore to Will Barrett. The affair didn't explain three deaths. Moore and Barrett didn't explain the dimes left on the bodies. How had the victims betrayed Moore and Barrett?

"Foster, you had a call from Grant," Kelley called from across the room. "She's on the Meehan autopsy. She wants to see you and Li pronto."

"Thanks." She stared at the lines, the circles, the photos of the dead. An affair. Divorce. A life disrupted by prison. A child left hanging in the balance. A circle of suspects. Timing. *Timing.*

"Kelley? Do me a favor? Get a hold of the few street cameras there are around Dino's? The alley was blank and the front, too, but maybe the streets over?"

"Who're we looking for?"

She padded over to her desk, flipped through pages in her notepad, finding the license plate she needed. "Plates attached to a silver 2020 Mercedes S-Class. And if there are any other eyes free, maybe check it against the garage and the Valdez office too? We looked for Shaw, we looked for repeats, but we didn't look specifically for this car. Also check for Will Barrett's car."

Kelley swiveled around in his chair. "On it. I think I can pull Bigs and Al in when they get back."

"Lonergan?"

Kelley swiveled back around. "After that girl-cop dig? I figured he'd be persona non grata for a while."

Foster glanced over at her plant, then quietly plucked up a paper clip and slid it into her pocket and waited for the calming. "I see dead people on our board, Matt, what do you see?"

"Right." He swiveled back around and got to work. "Lonergan's got eyes. Might as well use them."

Li ended her call. "I got the sponsor, Ed Osterman. Shaw's telling the truth about talking to him. He says they talked for more than an hour while some movie played in the background." She consulted her notes scribbled on a legal pad. "From a little after eight to almost nine thirty. That plus she's not sporting any bullet holes."

Foster grabbed her bag, her coat. "Grant wants to see us about Meehan."

Li picked up her coat. "Still think it's Shaw batting us around. I don't know how she's doing it, but she's doing it."

"Shaw's eyes are brown."

Roy Izarra hadn't told them much, but he'd plainly stated the woman who'd paid him off had blue or green eyes.

Li stopped short, one arm in her coat. "Izarra."

Foster smiled. "Izarra."

Grant was waiting for them in her chilly autopsy room. The pukey green tile on the walls and all the metal tools and silver instruments, the plastic buckets used for lord knows what. The lights. The death. Normally when they found her here, she had music playing, everything from acid rock to show tunes. Today, the room was silent. Grant standing next to her autopsy table with the body of John Meehan covered up to the neck in a plastic sheet. Grant could have sent over her preliminary report. It wasn't often necessary that detectives, she and Li specifically, needed to stand over Grant's autopsy table with her and hear every little detail. So, if they were summoned, that meant the good doctor had something important to share. Foster hoped it would be something that would point them toward a killer. She also hoped that killer was not Marin Shaw.

They stood well away from the table. This was Grant's domain, not theirs. Foster needed the distance more than Li. Reg had lain on Grant's table, so had G. Foster didn't fear the table. It was just a table, after all. Still, she hated it more than words could say.

"Any closer to ending this?" Grant said finally, a stern expression on her dark, humorless face.

"We're working it as hard as we can," Li said. "No music?"

Grant's eyes narrowed. "Not in the mood."

Silence followed, disturbed only by a slow dripping from the faucet in the sink. Drip. Quiet. Drip. Quiet. Drip. Foster started things off. "You asked for us?"

"I could have sent an email with my report, but this you had to be here for. Breathe."

"Excuse me?" Li asked.

"Breathe. Deeply. In and out. Like a human."

They did as instructed.

"What do you smell?"

"Chemicals," Li said. "And dead Meehan."

Grant turned to Foster. "You?"

She took another breath, held it, then let it out. "Same. And sweetness. Some kind of scent."

"Familiar?"

Li and Foster breathed again, really pulling on the inhales and exhales this time. It was Foster who answered. "Yes."

Li stepped closer to the table. "Also, yes. I take it he wasn't wearing any perfume?"

Grant frowned. "Do I look stupid? You needed to smell it on the off chance it sparked a recollection and pointed you in a direction. Nobody's going to go into court, especially me, and testify this perfume is exclusive."

"I get that." Foster stepped closer, too, blocking out the memories as best she could.

Grant lifted the small bag of dimes that had been taken from Meehan's overcoat pocket.

"Nothing unusual about the dimes, like the others, but this time there's scent on the bag. Likely from prolonged contact with the source, the source presumably being your shooter. It's not aftershave, not musk." Grant put down the bag. "That's it. That's what I needed you for. Otherwise, this case is unspectacular. I retrieved the round. I'll spare you the science right now. Long story short. Somebody shot him in the chest, and he bled to death. Beginnings of cirrhosis of the liver, but that's a moot point now. And his arteries were an utter nightmare. Too much red meat, not enough walking. Again, moot. Preliminarily, no clean prints on the bag, only the scent was a new wrinkle. Good luck."

Li studied Grant. "You're an interesting person, Dr. Olivia Grant. But who are you when you're not here?"

Grant's eyes went to suspicious slits. "Detective Vera Li." The words were uttered slowly, distinctly, like Grant was handing down a sentence or committing them to a list for the Dark One. "The answer to that would curl your hair."

Li appeared more intrigued than ever by the enigma that was Dr. Olivia Grant, but left it there, instead offering the doctor a fierce thumbs-up on her way to the door. "Thanks for the Smell-O-Vision. It's been real."

They eased into the car and strapped in. Li smiled. "Want to bet that perfume's French?"

"We'll ask Moore when we bring her in. Office or home?"

Li checked her watch. Almost 10:00 a.m. "Assuming she's carrying around one of Meehan's bullets? Home." She grabbed her radio. "Maybe Bigelow and Lonergan can hit her office on the off chance. I'll get a squad for backup. Let's hit it." Li slid Foster a playful look now that their course was set. "That was fun with Grant, right?"

Foster drove out of the lot. "When? Before or after you came close to her coming after you with a bone saw?"

Li thought about it for a second. "Both."

# CHAPTER 43

Bigelow and Lonergan badged their way past reception at Moore's firm, planting two patrol officers in reception in case she tried slipping past them. But when they got to Moore's office, it was empty and the lights were out.

The receptionist, who'd followed them back on angry heels, said, "I told you, Ms. Moore is *not* in."

"When's the last time she *was* in?" Bigelow asked, towering over the petite gatekeeper. "Or you heard from her?"

Heads popped out of offices all around them as everyone came out to see what the commotion was about. Why were there cops in their building? "Nothin' to do with any of you here," Lonergan groused. "Go back to what you were doin'." Each head popped back in.

"Yesterday," the woman said. "She left right after lunch. She hasn't been in today."

"That unusual?" Bigelow asked.

The woman glared up at them. "I'm not at liberty to say."

Lonergan's brows rose. "Why not? Simple question. Usual, not usual."

The woman looked put out but begrudgingly answered, "Unusual."

"See? That wasn't so hard, was it?" They gave the office a quick scan, the receptionist one final look, and then left.

Bigelow called Foster from the car. "Yeah. She's not here. They haven't seen her since yesterday."

"Thanks. Li and I are walking into her building now. We'll keep you posted."

They badged their way past the lobby, leaving two POs by the main entrance in case Moore tried sneaking out behind them. The nervous man at the front desk called the manager to meet them at Moore's apartment door. When the elevator made it to the eleventh floor, the manager, an overweight, middle-aged Black man in an ill-fitting gray suit, was waiting at the door to 11C, looking jumpy and just a little bit nauseated.

"I knocked," he said when they got to him. "There's no answer. Unless this is some kind of emergency—"

"She may be hurt and unable to answer," Foster told him. "We need you to unlock her door."

The manager looked unsure. He clutched a small ring of keys. "We could try calling? We try not to invade our residents' privacy. I could contact the building owner if you need to speak with him?"

Li held a hand out. "Which of *those* keys opens *this* door?"

The man pulled the ring back. "You should have a warrant, right? To go into someone's place?"

Foster took him in. "You did hear me when I said she may be hurt inside?"

Li wiggled her fingers for the key. "That means no warrant needed. Mr. . . . ?"

"Townsend." He begrudgingly picked through the ring, found the key to 11C, and handed it to Li, who unlocked the door.

"What were your names again?" he asked. "I'll need them for my report."

They ignored him, unholstered their guns, and readied themselves to go inside. Foster went first, pushing the door open, gun up, Li right behind her following suit. Moore was an open question, maybe a killer. Safety first. Safety always. "Stay out here," Li instructed as she moved past Townsend.

He backed away. "Guns? Is all this really necessary? This is a quiet building. I'm definitely calling the owner."

But Li and Foster were already in the apartment, moving deliberately down a narrow entryway whose walls were lined with framed black-and-white photographs of the city's skyline and landmarks. Light flooded in from the floor-to-ceiling windows in the living room just ahead. No drapes, only raised security blinds. The apartment felt empty, sounded empty, but both knew assuming it was empty was a good way to end up in a body bag.

"Ms. Moore?" Foster called out. "Chicago Police."

No answer.

They moved down the hall, eyes sweeping. Foster flicked on the lights as she passed the switch, and the hall lit up from recessed fixtures above their heads. More light was always better than not enough, she reasoned. The living room was richly furnished, tastefully decorated, more French influences, pastels, flowers, froufrou vases, paintings of Parisian street scenes and dance hall girls predominating. "France much?" Li muttered, her eyes scanning right to left and back again. "Did you take a whiff?"

"Yep. It's the same perfume."

"Her signature scent," Li muttered.

They looked for signs of blood. Moore wouldn't have been able to rush into the hospital with a gunshot wound without having to answer a lot of questions or getting a visit from a city cop, Foster thought. And if she ran home instead, there should be blood somewhere, some evidence that she had tried to doctor herself up—bandages, antiseptic, bloody towels. Grant was right; the perfume on the bag pointed them in this direction, and it appeared to close a circle. But if betrayal had been a fake meant to implicate Shaw and send her back to prison, what had been the real motivation? Lust? Loathing? Envy?

Foster looked around Moore's place. It was gorgeous but cold and hollow, lifeless. What good was it to create the perfect nest and then have no one in it? Foster realized as she walked through the luxury that, unlike Moore, she'd chosen to go in the opposite direction. In her place, she'd added very little. There wasn't a bowl or a chair or a painting in all the world that held the least bit of interest for her. Not more in her hollow place, less. She shook off the comparison. Moore. Had she wanted what Shaw had and couldn't get it, so she found a way to take it? Somehow, it made twisted sense.

Foster poked her head cautiously around a corner, then drew it back quickly. "Kitchen. Dining room. An office it looks like."

Li checked the opposite direction. Another hall. Open doors. "Bedroom. Bathroom. First one to find her loses."

They split up, one right, one left, each picking their way through the apartment. Li moved down the hall toward the bedroom. "Chicago Police."

Foster found nothing in the kitchen or dining area except a lot of expensive pots and pans and dishes. The coffee maker was a work of art in and of itself, expensive, imported, if she ventured to guess. She checked the small broom closet, but there was nothing inside but brooms and a mop. She turned and moved back the way she came, toward Li.

"Nothing this side. Heading back your way," she called out. What she didn't want to do was come up behind Li unannounced and get a round to the face.

But Li was already heading her way, holstering her gun. "Don't bother. She's not here. No blood anywhere either. Her luggage is in the closet, and all her stuff's still in the drawers, so if she's running, she's doing it with the clothes on her back."

Foster's eyes drifted over to Moore's bookcases. Not lawbooks this time. Art books. Expensive-looking ones. She padded over to take a look at the bookends. One was a twin of the bookend she'd seen in Moore's office, an angel with wings and a sword; the other had her reaching for her phone.

"What?" Li asked.

Foster's thumbs worked overtime on the keypad, searching. "Bookends."

Li moved over for a closer look. "Angels. And that's definitely Jesus with . . ."

"It's Judas's kiss." Foster found it. "And the other is Raguel, an archangel. The sword, the book. He's the archangel of justice and fairness."

"Fits with her being a lawyer," Li said.

Foster looked at Li. "Also, vengeance. And the others we saw in her office?" Foster showed Li her phone screen. "Vidar, Norse god of vengeance, and Nemesis. Greek goddess. Three guesses?"

"I don't think I need them. I sense a theme here. But she's not out there killing *her* enemies, she's killing Shaw's. So that *we'll* give her what she wants. Shaw's life."

Foster dialed Bigelow's number. "But if Barrett doesn't go for the replacement . . ." She left the sentence unfinished. Bigelow answered.

She filled him in on the search, her thoughts about the bookends, and Moore's motives for wanting three people dead and her friend back in prison. "We need to check Barrett's. Moore could have gone there to hide."

"Bookends, great, but you didn't find a pile of dimes," Bigelow said. "A gun? Knife?"

He was right, of course, but Foster had a feeling there was something to it. "No. But it won't hurt to check Barrett's."

"On it. Keep you posted." Bigelow hung up. Foster turned to a worried Li. "I hope I'm wrong."

"I hope you're right," Li said, "because if you aren't, we've got nothing."

Foster's phone rang in her hand. It was Kelley. "Nothing from cameras, but patrol got a call on a car parked in a tow zone with blood on the seats. It's Moore's Mercedes."

"Where?"

"A couple blocks from her place."

"That's where we are now, and it doesn't look like she's been here."

Foster heard the tapping of computer keys through the line. "On it. I'll send it out. She has to be somewhere."

Li picked up one of Moore's tchotchkes from an end table, a small porcelain figurine of a ballerina in fifth position, delicate arms raised high. "Ballerina of vengeance?" She thought for a moment. "I don't think she'd go to Barrett's."

Foster slid Li a concerned look. "Then the only other place she'd likely go would be to . . ."

Li finished. "Shaw's."

They turned and raced for the door. Out in the hall, before the nervous Townsend could ask, Li slapped her business card in his hand. "Thanks for your cooperation."

They raced down the hall for the elevator, which had a young mom with a stroller just stepping onto it. "Hold that elevator," Foster called out.

# CHAPTER 44

Marin stood at her coffee maker, staring out her kitchen window at a gentle snow falling. The snow wouldn't amount to much. It was well above freezing today, a rare respite. The flakes would fall but die ruined on the dirty street below, but until they hit, while they fell, it was magic.

Marin had woken up in a good place, finally, with a feeling that she'd turned a corner. She was sure the detectives believed her this time. They had to. Why would she risk everything on an old grievance? She had her daughter, and that's all that mattered. She would be around to watch her grow; she could make up for lost time. After scooping coffee into the machine, Marin switched it on and listened to the comforting gurgle begin. Caffeine. Nectar of the gods. The marriage was easy to let go. The affair was nothing in the end. Endings didn't have to be sorrowful or leave a scar. Sometimes they cleansed and burned away the bad, making room for other things. Marin inhaled and filled her lungs with newness, freedom, coffee. Her life was good, solid, she could see a path forward.

The sound of her front door opening startled her, then angered her. She and Will had agreed that as long as she was here in the condo, he would never darken her door. Couldn't he even keep true to that promise? Tightening the belt on her robe, she reeled, ready to confront, storming down the hall to reclaim her space and set him straight.

"Will, you can't just barge in—"

It was as far as she got as she stopped in her angry tracks and pedaled back. It wasn't Will standing in her living room; it hadn't been him who'd let himself into her apartment unannounced.

Char turned to face her, dressed in Marin's coat, close enough in body type and features to be her sister. Yet there was something unfamiliar in her eyes, something Marin had never seen before. Shock prevented her from identifying the something by name, but as her eyes scanned her friend, she saw that Char's left arm hung by her side. Her right hand was deep in the opposite pocket, and her color was off. She was slightly sweaty and pale. The hairs stood up on the back of Marin's neck. A rapid pulse and a sickening feeling in the stomach told her that she was in danger. Char's thousand-yard stare chilled the air. She stood zombielike in the coat, saying nothing. Marin knew in that instant that it had been Char, not Will. Char who wanted her away from Zoe. *Zoe.*

Marin turned and raced back to the kitchen, to the knives in the drawer, to the phone on the wall, to the service entrance that led to the back stairwell, to Zoe. The coffee maker beeped. Coffee was ready. But Marin ran from the sound of slow footfalls on the hardwood floor behind her. She couldn't die here like this, not now. She would have to fight.

# CHAPTER 45

There was a woman in a blue blazer standing at the lobby desk instead of Roy when Foster and Li swept in, badged, and fast walked to the elevator, where an older white woman in a designer coat stood waiting for the car. She looked them over with a slight sneer of disapproval, but neither responded. Cops were used to dirty looks from those who held them in disdain until they needed them.

Foster's phone buzzed. Bigelow. "Yeah, Barrett's okay. We got him out of bed, if you can believe it. Big surprise, he wasn't alone, but it wasn't Moore. What a prick. Swears he hasn't seen Moore in a couple days."

"Thanks." She slid the old woman a sideways glance, aware she was hanging on every word she said. "We're here. Keep you posted."

When the elevator arrived, Li turned to the woman and politely said, "Ma'am, would you mind waiting for the next one? We don't have time to make a stop."

Surprised, the woman appeared taken aback, affronted beyond belief at being denied even this tiny thing. Cutting brown eyes glanced over the CPD stars hanging from silver chains from both their necks. "*I* live here. I need to get to my apartment."

"And you will," Foster said, "when you catch the next one." They got on the elevator, leaving the woman behind. As the doors began to close, she added, "We appreciate your cooperation."

The last word they heard before the doors closed and the car started up was a disapproving "*Well.*"

When they reached Shaw's door, it was ajar. They shared a look; then their guns came out, up, again. Foster pushed the door open with the toe of her boot, and the two waited a second to assess.

"Police," she announced.

There was no sound of activity from inside, so they pushed forward. They found nothing as they swept through the apartment but got unlucky the last place they looked—the kitchen. There they found Shaw lying unconscious on the floor, the side of her head bloodied, a shattered coffee mug beside her.

Foster checked. "Still breathing." Li stepped back and called for an ambulance. Foster continued her assessment. "No gunshot wounds, no stab wounds, just the head, it seems. Somebody whacked her good." She looked around the kitchen. "Looks like she fought back."

"Did Moore leave her calling card?"

Foster checked the pockets on Shaw's robe. "No dimes. And she's breathing, not choking, so there aren't any stuffed down her throat. She didn't kill her." She looked up at Li. "Why?"

"Who kills their best friend?" She punched numbers on her cell. "I'll call the team." She stepped back farther, then noticed tiny drops of what appeared to be blood. "Harri. We have blood." She pointed to the droplets. "Perfectly round. Like they dropped instead of got flung. Doesn't look like spatter."

"Moore's." Foster checked to make sure Shaw's pulse was still there. "Let's hope this isn't too bad. I don't want to have to tell that little girl her mother's dead."

"Moore's lost it." Li stared down at Shaw. "Which means she's twice as dangerous now."

They stayed with Shaw until the paramedics and the others arrived, filling the apartment with uniforms and emergency equipment, heavy shoes, and well-trained movement. Foster and Li hovered just outside the kitchen, watching as paramedics attended to Shaw. The head wound was deep. There was a lot of blood, but she was alive.

Symansky waved for them from the living room. They joined him there. "One of the POs found a couple more blood drops by the back elevator. Good guess that's how she got up and down without parading through the lobby. We got the whole department looking for her. She won't get far."

"How's she moving around? She ditched her car?" Li asked.

"Maybe that's why she came here," Foster said. "For Shaw's. She's done it before, right? We need to check if Shaw's car is still in the garage."

Shaw's bloodcurdling scream drew them all back to the kitchen, where they watched the frantic woman thrash around, fighting the paramedics trying to calm her down. Her eyes were wild. "Zoe. Let me *go*. I have to get to Zoe."

Foster stepped forward, hoping she would be a calming presence, someone Shaw recognized and hopefully trusted. "Marin, calm down. Let them help you."

Shaw's wild eyes met hers. "Char's going after Zoe. She's going to take her. I *have* to stop her."

Foster's heart skipped a beat. "Where's Zoe now?" It was Tuesday, almost noon. Foster assumed Zoe would be in school. "What school?" Shaw hadn't heard the question. She was too dazed, too confused, too scared. She got closer, knelt down. "*What school*, Marin?"

"Stanton Academy." Shaw erupted in sobs. "She's going to take her."

Foster stood and tried to exchange a look with Li, but her partner was already on the phone getting a unit over there. She found her team in the sea of cops. "It's the girl she's going after now." She could practically feel the chill that went through all of them.

"We'll check the garage," Kelley said, tapping Bigelow. "See if Shaw's car is gone."

"I'll keep on that unit rolling to the school," Symansky said. "She might not a gotten there yet."

Lonergan stood there, looking a little less obstinate than usual. "I'll contact the school. Make sure they don't let that kid outa their sight."

Stanton was twenty minutes away from Shaw's place, and Foster raced there with lights and sirens engaged while Li monitored the radio and her phone for any updates on Moore sightings.

"She wouldn't hurt Zoe," Li said as though trying to assure herself. "She could have killed Shaw, but she didn't. She's obviously working off some major conflicted feelings here."

Foster gripped the wheel tighter, hoping Li was right, knowing full well it could go the other way just as easily. Lonergan called in. "Yeah?" Li listened. Foster looked over and saw her partner's face fall and her jaw clench. "When? Yep." She punched *end*. "Moore picked Zoe up a half hour ago, supposedly for a dentist appointment."

Foster slammed a fist against the wheel. "They just let anybody walk into a school and take a kid out?"

"Moore's name was on the list of authorized contacts. They had no reason to think something else was going on."

"She's bleeding, for Christ's sake. They didn't notice *that*?"

Foster pulled over to the curb, her mind racing. Where? Where would Moore take Zoe? "Let's check with Kelley. Maybe he got something from the garage that might help us."

Li made a call, put it on speaker. "Matt, tell us you got something."

"Just about to call you two. Shaw's car is not in her spot. Garage guy saw Moore drive it out. She told him Shaw wasn't feeling well and she was doing her a favor driving it to the shop. Since he's familiar with her coming and going in the building, he didn't think anything of it, and he saw no reason to double-check."

"She's got the kid," Li said. "We have no idea where she'd take her."

"Shit." Kelley's voice came back tight and tense. "Bigs and I will go over to the hospital, see if we can get something more out of Shaw. Maybe Moore hinted at something."

They sat in the car idling at the curb, the radio busy with cop cars all over the city calling in, getting the details, cops everywhere scanning the streets for Shaw's car.

"It's not enough," Foster muttered finally as she stared out the windshield at a gray day and city streets covered in gray, depressing snow. "They could be anywhere."

"Favorite places," she mused, working it through, recalling the conversations she'd had with Shaw, with Moore. "The museum. Pancakes. Shopping. Shows. The zoo."

"Well, it's Tuesday afternoon," Li said. "She can't go anywhere too public. She's bleeding. And she wouldn't want to upset Zoe."

"Right. Right." Foster's brain worked overtime. She ran through their list of options. "The zoo's outdoors."

"Don't they move most of the animals inside during the winter?"

Foster put the car in drive. "Moore's not there for the giraffes."

"It's a gamble," Li said. "If we're wrong . . ."

Foster flicked her a sideways glance. "We can't be wrong. Moore's hurt; she's cornered. She's gone too far."

She pulled from the curb, hit the siren, and turned at the corner, lights flashing, back toward the Drive. "The zoo. Fingers crossed."

# CHAPTER 46

"Zoe has a cell phone, Moore too. We haven't tried calling them." Foster sped up Lake Shore Drive headed north. "Send us the numbers, huh?"

Symansky was on speaker. "Hold on. Sending them through." Muffled talking followed, but he was soon back. "Sent 'em to both your phones. We got cars followin' you up there. No bells and whistles in case she's there and jumpy."

"Alert zoo security too," Li said. "Get them looking. Hands off, though."

"Roger that. Hold on." More muffling. "Yeah, update. A traffic unit gave a speed warning to Shaw about an hour ago. Northbound at Chicago Avenue. No ticket issued. It was before we put the flash out. And there was a kid in the car. Looks like you're headin' in the right direction. We're right behind you."

Foster sped up, weaving around slow traffic ahead of them as Li started dialing numbers, the phone on speaker. Moore didn't answer her cell after several rings, but Zoe answered hers on the first.

"Hello?" The small tinny voice was rattled with fear.

"Zoe, this is Detective Foster and Detective Li. You remember us?"

"I need help. Aunt Char is acting weird. She said she was taking me to Mom, but she's not here, and Aunt Char won't say where she is."

Li turned up the volume on the call. "Where are you, honey?"

"We're sitting in Mom's car in the parking lot at the zoo. Aunt Char's just looking at the lagoon. Her arm is bleeding. I . . . um, I don't know what's going on."

"Can you get out of the car, Zoe?"

"I tried. She has the safety locks on. It's like she doesn't even know I'm here, though. I'm scared. Where's my mom? Is she okay?"

Foster calculated they were about six minutes out. She sped up just a little more. "She's okay. We're on our way, Zoe. Hold on."

"Okay, but—"

The line went dead. Li hurriedly called back, but there was no answer. "Son of a—"

Foster wove around a slow Kia covered in winter salt. "Almost there."

Cutting the siren and lights as she got off the Drive at Fullerton, Foster saw three squad cars at the mouth of the zoo's lot, keeping anyone from entering and anyone inside from getting out. Li rolled down the passenger window as they passed. "Anything?"

The PO in the nearest squad came alive. "Security is keeping everybody out of the lot. The car's there. Two occupants. One adult female. One tender age child. Engine's off. No one's tried to get out. We were told to just watch and monitor."

"We've got reinforcements coming," Li said. "Hold here. Nothing but badges in. We'll see if we can make first contact."

Foster eased the unmarked car into the lot, then spotted Shaw's vehicle pulled into a spot facing the frozen lagoon. The lagoon was a popular spot in summer, with kayaks and ducks and life taking advantage of the heat reliever and the lazy roll of the narrow waterway. Not so much in February, with the lagoon frozen and covered in snow and the bitter wind coming in off the lake just east of it. The spots on either side of Shaw's car were empty, which gave them some wiggle room right or left if they needed to make a charge. But Zoe was right about Moore. Foster could see through the driver's window that she was sitting there, her eyes forward, not moving, as though she were in a trance. She could see Zoe looking back at them, her eyes wide with fear.

"Any ideas?" Foster asked.

"The doors are locked, Zoe said. Technically a hostage situation. If we approach, we have no way of knowing what she's got on her. She might not want to hurt Zoe, but we can't be sure what frame of mind she's in."

It was all true. "I don't think we can wait too long, though. Zoe's scared. If she gets agitated, if Moore starts to feel pressed . . ." She didn't have to finish the sentence. Li got it.

Foster eased the car into a spot a row behind Moore, and she and Li waited for the team to file in, one unmarked car after the other. An ambulance stopped at the lot entrance, as did a fire truck, lights flashing, just in case something went horribly wrong. There were even news trucks lined up on Fullerton, reporters manning their scanners already ahead of the game. Hastrup wouldn't be far behind, Foster thought bitterly. This was turning into a circus.

Li dialed Zoe's number again, putting the call on speaker; only this time Moore answered. "Zoe and I would like to be alone, please."

"That can't happen, Charlotte," Li said. "We need you to let Zoe go, and then you step out of the car."

"Where's the other detective? The one with the notepad. Foster?"

Foster braced herself in the driver's seat. "I'm here."

"I was just telling Zoe how nice the lagoon is in summer. She wouldn't remember the swan boats, but they were so much fun, and she would have really enjoyed them. They don't have them anymore."

"You're hurt, Charlotte," Foster said calmly. "We can help you."

"It's your fault. All of it." Her words were bitter, angry. "If you'd done what I needed you to do, we wouldn't be here, would we?"

"Explain that to us, Charlotte," Foster said.

"They betrayed her, didn't they? Left her to hang when they were just as responsible. That's why they needed to pay. I did it for her! I did it for her because she wouldn't do it."

"You did it for you," Foster said. "And you were going to let her pay for it."

Moore paused. "She had everything." She glanced at Zoe. "Has. The shining girl. I wanted to know what it was like, just once." Her expression soured. "I needed you to believe it was *her*. That she was exacting her revenge. But the dimes never moved the needle. You keep digging and digging. You *never* arrested her."

"Because the dimes never fit," Foster said. "Shaw had motive, but means? Marking the killings with dimes? That wasn't her, that's *you*. All Marin cares about is Zoe."

"They were a gang of Judases. They deserved to die. I expected her to come out angry and vengeful. It would have all worked if she'd come out hating them and wanting them to suffer, but she didn't. All she wanted was Zoe. But she couldn't have her. Zoe is *mine* now."

"Aunt Char, let me out. What are you doing?"

The girl's frightened plea leaped through the phone. Foster and Li exchanged a knowing look. They both knew they were it; they were closest, had made first contact . . . they would have to save Zoe. Foster scanned the lot, counted the cars, gauged the distance between the car with Zoe in it and the frozen patch of water yards from its front bumper. If Moore decided to put the car in gear, gun the engine, careen through the snow-covered parkway, and skid into the icy water, there was nothing they could do. She turned to Li, but her partner must have read her mind. She was already radioing in for the marine unit.

"Let's talk, Charlotte. You let Zoe out of the car. You come with us, and we'll discuss everything."

"I couldn't hurt Marin, any more than I could hurt Zoe. You know that. I just needed Marin back inside." She let a moment go. "Zoe always liked the zoo. We came here together many times, didn't we,

Zoe? I wish it was summer now so we could sit by the lagoon with a picnic basket." She fell silent. "All I wanted was her to go away, so I could have this, the life I could have had."

"We can talk about all that when we get somewhere warm," Foster said. "Are you hungry? Is Zoe hungry? We could bring you both something, and then you could come with us, and we can have that talk."

"I think we're beyond talking. I've gone too far. You believed her. You kept *coming*. Why? Why couldn't you just accept what I was giving you?" Moore didn't appear to be talking to Foster anymore. "Doesn't matter. It's done. I just wanted Zoe to see the lagoon with me. One last time."

Foster's breath caught. "What do you mean by 'last time'?" There was no answer, but the line was still open. "Charlotte? Charlotte, talk to us."

The driver's door opened suddenly, and Moore jumped out and raced around to the passenger side. She pulled Zoe out, held her by her collar, and pulled her toward the lagoon.

"Oh shit!" Foster bounded out of the car, Li right with her. "Move in. Move in." Foster waved for the cops around them as she and Li ran toward the lagoon across the parkway, Zoe being pulled from behind by a determined-looking Moore.

"Stop. Charlotte," Foster called. "Don't do this. You don't want to hurt her. You said so."

"I won't. She knows I love her." Moore gave Zoe a light kiss on the back of her head, all the while pulling her along. "But she *must* see the lagoon. She'll have to picture how it would be in summer if the boats were here. One more outing for the two of us."

Zoe struggled to free herself but couldn't do it. Moore was taller, stronger, and the grip on her uninjured side was too tight. Moore dragged the girl all the way across the snowy lawn separating the lot from the lagoon, Zoe's heels creating deep gullies in the high snow. The two finally stopped at the water's edge.

"That's as far as you go, Charlotte," Li called out. "Let her go."

Foster and Li stopped, watching terrified as Moore teetered on the brink with Zoe. Cops rushed in behind them but held back, not wanting to force Moore beyond the edge. Lonergan and Symansky joined them, Kelley and Bigelow still coming, slipping along the snow, eyes wide. The uniforms held back, as did the paramedics and firefighters. They would rush in if the worst happened.

Moore glanced back at the lagoon. "Stay back. I don't want you ruining our time together."

"We're not moving," Foster said. "And we don't want you to either. Walk back this way."

Moore wasn't listening. "The lagoon isn't so nice in winter."

Moore took a step backward, closer to the ice, holding Zoe. Foster knew the ice would be thicker at the edge than in the middle. How far did Moore intend to go? Just as the thoughts ran through Foster's mind, Moore's feet left firm ground and she stepped out onto the edge of the icy lagoon. Zoe, terrified, began to cry. The fear in the girl's eyes was wild, desperate. Moore took another step back, and then another, the sound of cracking ice loud and ominous. There had been days of subzero temperatures, but a few with above-freezing numbers. The freeze would be uneven. The lagoon was a death trap.

Foster began to advance. Li grabbed her arm. "What are you doing?"

"Moving a little closer. Get marine up here."

Moore gripped Zoe tighter. "I didn't want to kill Marin, you know. I just wanted . . . she had everything. The perfect life. A beautiful baby. She ruined it. Didn't deserve it. I needed her away, and those people weren't good people anyway. Two birds. One stone." She smirked. "Or thirty dimes." Another step back. More cracking ice. "Vengeance is mine, saith the Lord." Moore chuckled. "It was also mine. Justice. I meted it out. And I won't feel sorry for it."

Foster rushed to the edge, her boots teetering on the low rocks bordering the lagoon. "Stop walking, goddamn it!" For a moment the cop fell away and she was only a mother who couldn't bear to watch a child die. "Stop."

Li turned to a cop behind her. "Get me a rescue ring. Two, if you can find them."

"Tell me Foster's not thinkin' about goin' out on that ice," Lonergan said.

"Harri, don't move another inch." It was Symansky, who then turned to Bigs. "We need to move them firefighters up here. Now."

The PO ran back with two rescue rings. Li held one. She handed the other to Kelley.

"Anybody see a gun?" he asked, scanning the ice and looking at Moore and Zoe. "Is she armed?"

"Not that we've seen," Li said.

Foster kept her eyes on Zoe. "The ice is enough."

She stared at Moore's feet as they slid and shuffled along the thin ice. Zoe was in a parka and boots. If they went in, once the coat got wet, she'd sink like a stone. Hypothermia. Drowning. Both. Foster stepped out onto the ice, arms up and out. A sign she was coming not as a threat but as an aid. Help, not harm.

"Harri, what the hell are you doing?" Li barked. "Get back here."

Foster flicked Li a look. "It's all right. I've got it. I won't go far." She turned back to Moore. "Charlotte. Listen to me. The ice isn't safe. We need you to walk back this way. Let Zoe go."

"I told you I would never hurt her. I'm like a mother to her. A better mother than Marin could ever be." She took another backward step. "I was never the shining girl. She is, and she squanders it? Just throws it away? Zoe deserves a mother who'll really be there for her. The drinking wasn't enough? The risky behavior? She had to go and commit a *crime*? What happens to Zoe? To Will? Family should *always* come first." Moore laughed. "She thought I didn't know about Valdez? I knew. She

321

told me herself in a drunken stupor way before the trial. I knew about the key and where she kept it. Of course, she doesn't remember now."

Foster only half listened to the details. She knew the others were getting every word. She was focused on Zoe. On getting her off the ice safely. "Let her go, Charlotte."

"I thought when you found the key with her prints on it, you'd do your job. But you didn't. I had to keep doing it. I was in too deep to stop, you see that, don't you? They weren't good people, anyway. They were crooks. They'd each ruined themselves, especially Meehan."

Moore wasn't using her left arm much, though her grip on Zoe with her right was holding. "Meehan shot back. You didn't expect that."

Moore stopped. "He was a thug. I should have known he'd . . ." She smiled. "I was very surprised."

Zoe no longer resisted. Foster could see she was in shock, that she had disengaged. Despite the bitter cold, Foster peeled off her gloves and clapped her hands together to get the girl's attention. She needed Zoe present and able to follow instruction. "Zoe. Hey. Look at me. Zoe!" The girl refocused. "A little longer."

"I want my mom," the girl wailed.

"We're going to take you to her real soon." Foster's eyes shifted to Charlotte. "Isn't that right?" Moore took two more steps back.

As the ice cracked, Foster could just imagine all the little fissures and spider lines popping up beneath them as the weight of three bodies pressed down on uneven layers of frozen water. She moved farther away from the edge, farther toward the middle of the lagoon.

"Harri, do not take another step," Li commanded.

"Hand me the ring."

"Are you crazy? I'm not handing you the fucking ring. Fire's right behind us."

"I'm closer. If they fall through, Zoe might be able to grab it."

"If they fall through, *you're* gonna fall through, too, and Moore will drag Zoe down with her. She won't be able to grab *anything*."

Symansky waved everybody back except for the team. "C'mon, move back, all of ya. Let's take some of the pressure off this. And get them fire guys up here. We might need a ladder, or somethin'." He turned back to see Foster take a few more tentative steps away from the bank. "Harri, get your ass back on solid ground," he ordered.

Instead, Foster peeled off her jacket, her eyes on Moore and Zoe. "She's not listening."

"Neither are you," Li shot back. "This is a dumb move. Dumb."

Foster reached for the rescue ring. "I'm getting this out there."

Li shook her head, adamant that she wasn't okay with the plan. "This is insane. I'm partnered with an insane woman."

"The ring," Foster demanded.

Li tossed it to her. "Big mistake. Huge. All of *this*." She turned to the nervous first responders around her. "See this? Crazy. *Crazy.*"

Gripping the ring, Foster walked away from the edge in only a sweater and jeans to keep her body warm. One false step, one wrong patch of ice, and she'd plunge through and freeze to death.

"Hey, find me another ring!" she heard Li shout behind her, though she was too focused on every tentative step she took to look around. "Harri, if you die out there, I swear to God, Griffin is going to kill me." Foster took another step. "Move those paramedics closer."

Foster took a bead on Moore and Zoe, the sound of cracking ice getting worse. She could feel sheets of ice shifting, bouncing beneath her. She was with Li. This was crazy. It was unwise, yet here she was. She just couldn't let Zoe get away from her. "Charlotte, you're hurting Zoe. Mothers don't hurt their children."

"Marin did, didn't she, Zoe? Selfish. She threw it all away. If she only knew how hard it was to come by for others. For me. All I'm doing is showing Zoe the lagoon. She knows I love her."

"I'm coming to get Zoe, and you're going to give her to me. That's how this ends."

Moore laughed as Foster moved forward one shaky step at a time, her eyes on her boot tops, then on Zoe, then on her boots again, listening to the moving water, the cracking, dreading every step, but knowing she had to take it. She held fast to the rescue ring, ready to toss it to Zoe if things took a turn. Another advance. "Charlotte, listen to me." She searched for the right words, not wanting to frighten Zoe any more than she was already. "If you walk back this way, come with me, we can talk all of this through over a nice cup of hot coffee. You're hurt. I can see that. There're paramedics behind me. We're five minutes from the ER. A warm bed. Doctors. We can help you."

"I killed my best friend."

Zoe's eyes widened, and her body stiffened in terror. "Mom?!"

"No. No. You did *not*. Marin's not dead." Foster's eyes held Zoe's. A promise. "She's alive. And she wants her daughter." A fresh peal of emergency sirens went up behind her. "Let's end this. Let's get Zoe home warm and safe. That's what a mother would do."

Charlotte suddenly seemed to notice the crowd lined up along the water's edge, the cops and paramedics, the cop cars and ambulances and fire trucks crammed into the lot with their lights flashing blue and red. She looked at Foster like she was just now seeing her, then at Zoe's stricken face as though she couldn't imagine how she'd gotten there.

"Charlotte? Just let her go."

"Zoe used to love coming to the zoo. We'd walk for hours watching the animals. Too bad it isn't summer now. The zoo is so magical in summer."

Foster held the ring in one arm and held out the other to Zoe. She had gotten as close to the two of them as she dared. The ice wouldn't hold their weight for much longer. If Moore didn't let her go, Zoe was going to have to try and break away. Could she do that? Foster wondered. Would she if the time came?

"She belongs with me," Charlotte said simply, as if that excused everything—three murders, the subterfuge, the betrayal. "She should have been *mine*."

Foster was no hostage negotiator. She didn't know the right things to say in a situation like this. All she could think about was Zoe and the ice. So, what should she say? What was the right thing in this moment?

"If she dies, you'll never forgive yourself. *Never*."

Charlotte's eyes held hers. Something returned. She looked at Zoe, a moment passed, and then she slowly released the grip on the girl's jacket. "No. I wouldn't."

Zoe stood there trembling, frozen with fear and cold, unaware that she was free to move, to go.

"Zoe," Foster said. "Slowly. Walk toward me. This way—"

But it was too late. At that moment, the ice beneath the girl's feet fractured, and she and Moore plunged into the lagoon. Foster watched for half a beat in horror as Zoe screamed and flailed in the frigid water as more ice broke away, the sound of the girl's distress reverberating like the wail of a thousand crows. Foster suddenly felt the ice beneath her boots start to give way, too, as cold water rapidly soaked her boot tops. She dropped to her stomach, scrambled to a firmer patch, then clocked the struggling Zoe a few feet ahead of her as she fought to stay above water. Her coat was dragging her down, as Foster had known it would.

Moore was gone. Submerged. She'd gone down without making a single sound.

Foster tossed the ring toward Zoe, then crawled after it, wrapping the rough rope around her shoulder and forearms to anchor it and pull Zoe toward her.

"Don't let go," she ordered the girl. "Kick. This way. Hurry."

"I can't," Zoe cried, her arms slapping against the deadly surface, clutching for jagged pieces of floating ice.

"You *can*. Do it. *Now*."

Zoe reached out for the ring, snagged it, then held tight as Foster started to pull, feeling the ice sheet beneath her slacken and dip. Seconds. That's how long she had before she went in too. She turned her head toward the embankment to summon help, to find that Li, Symansky, and the team had already dropped to their stomachs and had formed a human chain behind her. Racing onto the ice behind them were two firefighters in wet suits with a rescue ladder and apparatus.

The ice around Zoe fractured and floated away like giant pieces of a jigsaw puzzle. Foster strained to pull the ring, her clothes frozen stiff, her hands close to frostbitten, losing vital body heat by the millisecond. The sound of the approaching rescue boat drowned out the sound of the cracking ice, but Foster could feel the ice undulate beneath her as it finally gave way. Just as she began to drop, just as she began to go, someone grabbed her by the ankles and yanked her back onto a safer patch. She twisted around to get a look at her savior. Lonergan. And behind him there were Li, Symansky, Kelley, and Bigelow. She turned back and pulled Zoe toward her, watching as the patch of ice she'd been lying on just seconds before fell away.

"Get up," she commanded Zoe as she scrambled to her wet knees, frantically freeing the girl from the ring. "Run." Foster handed Zoe off to Lonergan and Li, and they all ran for the bank, ice popping and breaking beneath them, as the firefighters raced past them going in the opposite direction, toward the hole Moore had fallen through. One by one they made it back to solid ground, safely off the lagoon. They each fell to the snow on their backs, alive. Frozen, wet, scared, but alive. Minutes later, when they'd recovered some, Foster slid a look at Lonergan standing at the back of the ambulance where Zoe was being looked after. It had been his hands on her ankles. She had to admit she'd worried whether he would if they ever got in a situation. That worry was done. Things would be easier going forward.

Despite Foster having been given a warming blanket, her teeth still chattered in the cold. Li slid in beside her, wrapped in a blanket of her own, her clothes soaked beneath. She'd seen the look Foster had given Lonergan. Li began to hum "We Are Family."

Foster narrowed her eyes. "Sister Sledge, really?"

Li shrugged. "One big happy, Foster. All I'm saying."

# CHAPTER 47

No one could coax Zoe out of her mother's arms. Marin held her close as they lay in the hospital bed side by side. Shaw was fine, the doctors determined. A mild concussion and head laceration. She would live.

Foster, dry, changed, but nowhere near warm, stood at the foot of the bed with Li. There was still work to do. The job didn't end because your clothes got wet and you nearly died in a frozen lagoon. She plunged her cold hands into her coat pockets. Would they ever warm up? Li had acquired a wool scarf and mittens from somewhere.

"Char, is she . . ." Marin glanced down at her sleeping child.

Foster answered the question Marin had asked without really asking. "Yes. Her body was quickly recovered."

"I don't understand what happened. Why would she do this . . . all of this. It just doesn't make sense."

"You sort of pegged it," Li said. "She wanted what you had. This was the way she figured she'd get it."

Marin shook her head, tears dampening her eyes. She squeezed Zoe a little tighter, kissed her on the top of the head. "I need to go home. I want Zoe out of all this. What happens next?"

Foster shrugged. "You're free to go once the doctors clear you. We have nothing to hold you for."

"But they're still dead. Because of me."

"Because of *Moore*," Li corrected.

Shaw's face fell. "I don't think the press will make the distinction. But I'm free. So is Zoe. We can go anywhere. Start fresh. There's a whole world out there."

"True," Foster said.

There was a commotion in the hall. The door opened suddenly, and Will Barrett rushed in looking flustered. He made a beeline for the bed. "Oh my God, Marin. What? Charlotte? I can't believe it. Are you all right? Zoe?" He reached out a hand to stroke Zoe's hair, but Marin drew the child closer to her.

The room fell quiet. Marin stared up at her husband, but Foster didn't see an inkling of affection in the look.

"Zoe is fine," Shaw said. "I'll be released soon. We'll go to the condo."

Barrett turned to Foster and Li. "Could we have some privacy?"

"No," Shaw said. "They're not finished with what they have to do. Why are you here, Will?"

Confusion crossed his face. "Why? Zoe's kidnapped? You're attacked? Where else would I be?"

Foster heard the slow escape of frustrated air leave Li's lips and squashed the smirk she felt forming on hers. It was a lot of nerve, for sure. The concerned father and husband who'd thrown his wife out of their home when she needed it most? Why the interest now, she wondered. Then she got it, or thought she did. When the dust settled, Barrett wouldn't look too good. He'd cheated on his wife with her best friend. That woman ended up killing three people to cement the relationship. Marin Shaw, on the other hand, had done nothing in all this but fight for her kid. Barrett needed the cover of the marriage.

Barrett held on to the railing of the bed, looked into his wife's eyes, turned his back to them, and then lowered his voice. "I've forgiven you. You can come home where you belong. We'll start again. We'll make it right." He reached over and touched Shaw's knee. She didn't flinch or pull away. It didn't appear that she cared even that much.

Li cleared her throat, but the awkwardness in the room wasn't going anywhere. "We found a bug in your apartment. Moore was listening in. It's how she knew what you were up to and when you were in or out. I think she pushed you into the street. If that had worked, she wouldn't have needed to go any further."

"But it didn't," Shaw said, "so she killed Meehan? That's sick. I thought it was him. I was so *sure*."

"She knew about the key to Valdez's, she said, because you told her." She looked over at Zoe to check that she was still sleeping. "While you were intoxicated. Before your trial."

Shaw squeezed her eyes shut from shame and embarrassment. Foster could see it all on her face. But she also saw strength and determination and grit there too.

"Jealousy," Li said. "And it got very twisted."

Barrett cut in. "Yeah, well, if you people had caught on quicker, we wouldn't be here, would we?"

Foster ignored him and spoke directly to Shaw. "If you have any questions, we'll be happy to answer them. We'll be in touch regardless, just to see how you're getting on."

"Thank you both for saving her," Shaw said. "And me."

Barrett turned to them, exerting his maleness. "Now I'm taking my family home, if you don't mind."

Shaw smoothed Zoe's hair, then turned to Barrett. "You're taking us nowhere. You'll be served with divorce papers soon. The house is mine. Zoe is mine. We'll work out visitation, if you're even interested. But I never want to speak to you ever, *ever* again."

Barrett's face colored. "*You're* throwing *me* out?"

"I should have done it years ago, but yes, I am."

He stiffened. "I'm not going anywhere. That's *my* kid."

Shaw glared at him. "We both know it's the money you want. I'll make it plain. You're not getting it."

"You can't get rid of me that easily."

Foster and Li, almost as a unit, rose up together, planted their cop feet apart, ready position. Shaw noticed.

"I don't think that's true," Shaw said.

Li gave Barrett the cop face. "I don't think so either."

Foster shrugged. "We're all in agreement."

Barrett checked every face in the room but found no give anywhere. Fuming, he stormed out. "This isn't over."

Shaw lay back on the pillow and exhaled. "He's wrong. It *is* over."

Li grinned. "Amen, sister."

Foster smiled. "Detective Vera Li goes to church."

# CHAPTER 48

"*Another* news conference?" Symansky groused. "It's wrapped. Why's the *mayor* taking the friggin' victory lap?"

They crowded around the small television set in the office the next morning, their chairs rolled up close, watching as the mayor, the superintendent, Griffin, and top brass, all spick-and-span polished, stood before the media and declared to Chicago that the threat to city leaders had been neutralized.

"Too bad Lonergan and Foster couldn't be in on it this time." Kelley grinned. "That was fun to watch."

The team laughed. Foster stood. "Good one. But while we're all here, I did want to say something."

"Speech," Bigelow said.

"*Not* a speech. A thank-you. We saved a kid's life out on that ice. And you all saved me too." She glanced over at Lonergan, leaning back in his chair, his beefy hands crossed over his middle. "Thanks to each and every one of you for having my back . . . and my ankles." The room erupted in laughs again. "We did good." She looked over at a smiling Li. "Anyway, thanks. That's all."

Lonergan stood, approached her. The room stilled. They stood looking at each other for a moment, and then he held out his hand for a shake. "You're good police, Foster. Even if you are a girl."

Li groaned. "One step forward, and one step back."

Foster smiled. "I'll take that step, and I'll add one of my own." She took the hand offered. Foster turned to find Li grinning at her. "What?"

"We won the bet." She waved at Kelley and Symansky. "They owe us dinner. Added bonus, we showed up Tennant and Pienkowski, who, by the by, missed the lagoon while we all got wet and frozen." She grinned at Foster. "And, lest *you* forget, you have to come to my house for dinner with my family."

Foster paled. "Don't you ever forget anything?"

"Rarely."

Foster eased down into her chair, checked her plant. Li's fertilizer and new soil were working. All she needed to do now was keep it alive. Her mind flashed to Reg, then to Glynnis, and a sharp stab of guilt reasserted itself. She managed to breathe through it. "Fine. Tell me what kind of red wine to bring."

Li smiled. "Anything wet. This is going to be fun."

Fun. Foster wasn't sure she remembered what that was anymore. Four people dead on this case, and for what? Fear, ultimately. Moore's fear that life, the one she wanted, the one she thought she could commandeer, would be taken from her. And the voice. Lurking. She thought of him and of Mike and the kids, and her gut twisted. She thought of Reg, too, and would a hundred times more before the day was done. This led to a bitter thought for Terrell Willem and the forgiveness she couldn't find.

She eyed Griffin's door, unsettled by what she'd done. It was as though she had handed Glynnis off to the bosses, abdicating all responsibility to her. Griffin expected her to let it go. Glynnis wasn't dirty, and Foster needed to prove it. *She* did, not them. And she was going to protect her family, whatever it took. These were the things she knew for sure.

Foster caught Li staring at her, her eyes narrowed. "You're not letting go of it, are you?"

They both knew what they were talking about. "Can't."

Li nodded. "Then we better get ready to rock and roll."

"*Me*, not we."

Li pushed her drawer in, slung her bag over her shoulder. "I said it right the first time. I'm ride or die, Harriet Foster. Deal with it."

Moments passed before Foster finally stood. Her eyes broke away from Li's to land on a paper clip on her desk, which she didn't pick up. Instead, she neatened up the folders on her desk, and glanced around at family—Symansky, Bigelow, Kelley, Lonergan. Together they'd caught a killer and saved a kid. She turned to Li, nodded. "Then I choose ride, Vera Li."

# THE END

# ACKNOWLEDGMENTS

I didn't get here on my own. I had help. I had a village. I still do. I want to thank my supportive advocates, those people who help me live this dream. A million thanks to my wonderful agent, Evan Marshall; my brilliant editor at Thomas & Mercer, Liz Pearsons; and the eagle-eyed Clarence Haynes, my developmental editor, who elevates my words each and every time. To my wonderful team at Kaye Publicity—Dana Kaye, Julia Borcherts, Jordan Brown, Nicole Leimbach, and Eleanor Imbody—who puts my work out there and champions it far better than I ever could, thank you. Thanks, too, to Dennelle Catlett at T&M for holding it down on her end.

And to my lifelines in crime, those dedicated peace officers who serve and protect and wear the badge proudly and with honor, who take my silly cop questions with great aplomb and patience. Thank you, Detective Gregory Auguste, Chief Keith Calloway (retired), and Officer Marco Johnson (retired). Any police mistakes found herein are mine alone. They tried to school me, but sometimes I took a few liberties for a better story. Writers are funny that way.

Thanks also to my writing community, my friends, my peeps, for the fraternity and the support and the love. I return it all tenfold.

Thanks also to my family—Mom, Jennifer, the four little dudes—for their support, cheerleading, and allowances for a writer's eccentricities. And a humble thanks to family farther afield who lift me up and spread the word.

This is a wild ride, but a good ride. It is my hope to keep Detective Harriet Foster in good trouble.

To the prepublished writers out there, *keep writing*! Don't you dare stop.

# ABOUT THE AUTHOR

*Photo © 2022 Bruno Passigatti / Bauwerks Photography*

Tracy Clark is the author of the acclaimed Cass Raines Chicago Mystery series featuring Cassandra Raines, a hard-driving African American PI who works the mean streets of the Windy City dodging cops, cons, and killers. Clark received Anthony Award and Lefty Award nominations for series debut *Broken Places*, which was shortlisted for the American Library Association's RUSA Reading List and named a CrimeReads Best New PI Book of 2018, a Midwest Connections Pick, and a Library Journal Best Book of the Year. *Broken Places* has since been optioned by Sony Pictures Television.

A Chicago native, Clark roots for all Chicago sports teams equally. She's a member of Crime Writers of Color, Mystery Writers of America, and Sisters in Crime and sits on the boards of Bouchercon National and the Midwest Mystery Conference. Find her on Facebook (https://facebook.com/tclarkbooks), Twitter (@tracypc6161), Instagram (@tpclark2000), or her website (https://tracyclarkbooks.com).